I0833111

Dr. Kingston

A Novel

by:
Grace Maxwell

Cover Design: Jennilynn Wyer Designs
https://www.jennilynnwyerdesigns.com
Cover Model: Authur
Photographer: WANDER AGUIAR

Brothers Paradise: Dr. Kingston/Grace Maxwell—1st edition

One

Elise

My dad's voice booms, crooning off-key about whiskey and heartbreak over the noise of the shower. I drag a pillow over my head. So much for sleeping in on a Saturday. His voice carries down the hallway, echoing through the thin walls of my childhood bedroom. It's endearing in a way, but mostly, it's a reminder that I'm twenty-eight years old and back to living in town at my father's home. Thanks to the fire, the cottage I shared with my best friend, Tarryn, is gone.

I never say it out loud, but losing that place feels like losing the only corner of the world that belonged to me. Now, everything feels borrowed, not exactly the glamorous life I imagined.

I roll onto my back and stare at the ceiling fan, the blades unmoving because this time of year the air doesn't need circulating; it still needs heating. The room smells faintly of sandalwood and old paperbacks, the same way it did during university when I crammed for chem finals while home on weekends and taped wine tasting charts over my dresser mirror. The floorboard by the closet still squeaks. The window still fogs at the bottom right corner if you breathe on it. Time is paused here, waiting for me to catch up.

Down the hall, the shower cuts off and the pipes clank. A minute later, Dad's boots thump across the kitchen.

I can practically map his morning by sound—the kettle on, the two taps on the counter he does habitually with his ring, the rattle of the sugar tin even though he drinks it black, and finally, the scrape of a chair as he sits to work a crossword with a pencil that's always sharpened to a ruthless point.

He'll leave a thermos by the door for me without saying anything, like always. We're a symphony of routines. There's comfort in it, but also a weight. He trusts me to slide into the melody someday, when he's ready to retire from the vineyard, but what if I can't carry the tune?

I should at least be out on my own. My own place. My own rules.

Instead, I'm stuck in the house I grew up in. And every time I slip through the door after nine p.m., Dad looks up from whatever he's doing like he's been timing me. Not that I have much of a social life to keep track of, but still. It's a real crimp in my dating life. Nothing says undateable like "Come back to my place, but my dad might be watching TV in the next room."

I laugh it off with friends, but it stings. Everyone else is moving forward. I'm still proving I belong somewhere.

I'm not a kid anymore, but it feels like I've stepped backward. One million loser points for me.

Still, moving out isn't something I can tackle immediately. The fire that burned the cottage flipped everything upside down. Both Tarryn and I lost our home, our routines, and the sense of safety we'd built. But Tarryn got something unexpected from the experience. Declan Conner, her ex, was one of the first EMTs on scene after we got out. He took care of us while his team fought the fire, something rekindled between the two of them, and now they're engaged. She has him to lean on. The Paradises are rebuilding the cottage, but let's be honest, It won't be for me. That place will be Tarryn's home with Declan and, eventually, their family. I knew that the minute the flames died down and I saw the two of them together.

I'm thrilled for her, but that means I need to figure out my next move. After my upcoming work exchange is done, I'll deal with it.

Ah, the exchange. Three months in Bordeaux. The words fizz under my skin like Champagne. I want it so badly I'm afraid to hold it too tight. But chasing something bright doesn't erase the thing I'm walking toward here at home. When Trace Paradise steps aside at the end of the year, my dad will also hang up his tools as the vintner for Paradise Hill Family Estate Winery, and I'll step into his shoes. He's never said it like a decree, more with a quiet faith. He's been saving the seat and warming it for me without ever asking if I wanted to sit.

And it's not that I don't. Tarryn and I have been planning this for years. But now that it's nearly here, I'm not sure I'm ready. *What if I'm not as good as he is? What if everyone is watching and waiting for me to fail? What if I ruin the thing Dad loves most?* Being the master vintner has a lot of people depending on you to get it right, and I'm nervous.

Dad hums as he goes about his morning, off-key and happy. My throat loosens. He's not a man who worries about the what-ifs. He checks the weather and goes out to the vineyard to meet whatever the day brings. Maybe that's the job.

Dad hits a particularly loud note, and I give up on sleep. Throwing back the covers, I tug on jeans, a thick wool sweater, and fleece-lined boots—practical armor against the March cold in Paradise, British Columbia. A storm's rolling in later today, and before it hits, I need to check the drip lines at the Black Bear blocks. They're on the far side of the lake, which means at least an hour's drive on dry roads—and they won't stay dry for long.

But first, Tarryn.

Out in the kitchen, I find my thermos of coffee as expected, and as I sip from it, I wander down the road toward the Paradise Hill offices, breath puffing in the cold morning air. The sky has that heavy, leaden look, and the valley smells like wet cedar and snow waiting its turn.

Inside the office building, the lights are already on, and sure enough, Tarryn is bent over the conference table with rolls of paper spread everywhere—blueprints, elevations, paint swatches. Her brow is furrowed, one hand pushing her hair out of her face as she studies the plans for the new house. There's a cinnamon bun half-eaten beside a ruler and three sticky notes that say *ask Declan*, *fire permit*, and *don't forget outlets*.

"Morning," I say, dropping my gloves on the table.

She looks up, her whole face lighting when she sees me. "Morning. Come look at this. You're going to love where your room ended up."

My room. The words feel like a stone and a hug at the same time. I want to believe I'll always have a place with her, but it seems clear that eventually I'll be the extra piece that doesn't fit. I lean over the plans, tracing the outline of walls and windows—corner room, mountain view, a little alcove that would be a perfect reading nook if I lived there long enough to read in it. "It's beautiful, Tar. But…what does Declan think about me moving in with you two?"

She makes a face like I've just insulted her. "Please. Declan adores you. He thinks of you as family. And you're not going to be homeless on my watch."

Homeless lands with a sting. "I'll find my own place," I say softly. "Eventually. I refuse to be the weird permanent third wheel."

"You could never be a third wheel." She unrolls another sheet. "Besides, the weird aunt is a badge of honor. All the kids love the weird aunt."

"I'll bring sticky hands and drum sets to every birthday," I threaten.

"Perfect." She moves toward the coffeemaker in the corner. "Cream?"

"Just a splash." I take the mug, letting the heat burn my palms in that good way as I slide onto the chair beside her.

She takes a long sip before speaking again, eyes on the plans. "Promise me you won't take a permanent role at Château after your exchange. You're too important here."

I roll my eyes. "Oh please. You know me. Three months on the Left Bank is going to be incredible. Gravel and clay and wind off the Gironde? I'll learn more as they do all the pre-season work than I could in a year at a desk. But Black Bear Valley is in my blood. I'm not going anywhere."

She narrows her eyes like she can see my daydream anyway. And, fine, it's there—a flash of limestone cellars, midday light on rows older than my grandparents, a master vintner's hands showing me a technique my dad never needed because our climate is different. The tug of it scares me a little.

"Say the words," she insists.

"I promise," I say, grinning when she keeps staring. "I promise I'm coming home. This is home."

Her shoulders relax a fraction. "Good. Because you're not only my maid of honor, you're my right hand. I need you for all the planning."

That makes me laugh. "You've helped plan your brothers' weddings. You could do this blindfolded. By now, you know the cake vendors who won't fight us on buttercream in winter and the florist who can source ranunculus without pretending peonies are in season. But I'll be here holding your hand the whole way."

"Bless you," she says. "Declan's schedule is chaos, and the firefighters' rotation means we have to dodge half the weekends—"

"Already built a spreadsheet," I admit, pulling out my phone. "Color coded. With a tab for childcare for your future tiny humans because I'm manifesting—for your mother, of course."

"You're a menace, and I love you." She sets her mug down and turns to me, serious now. "You know how much you mean to me, right? Not just as my best friend, but to Paradise Hill. You're part of the backbone here. And you know I can't do this without you."

Her words bring a surge of emotion I didn't expect. "You're just as important to me," I say, hugging her, blueprint paper rustling under our elbows. "And I do love it here. Even when it feels like the valley is trying to push us out."

The sabotage at Paradise Hill began in earnest after her dad hinted at retiring and announced that Tarryn would take over for him. Since then, we've taken turns blaming ourselves for the fallout we can't seem to move past.

We stay in our embrace a moment, warmth between us, until I finally pull back and glance out the window. The sky's gone darker, the clouds gathering thicker and faster than forecasted, making the mountains seem closer than they are.

"I need to get on the road," I tell her. "Jerome says there's a drip around block ten at Black Bear. They blew out the lines months ago, so there shouldn't be any water left to leak. I want to check it before the storm hits."

Tarryn follows my gaze. "It looks like the storm's coming earlier than expected."

"I can make it there and back," I insist, standing and tugging on my gloves. It's not far as the crow flies—five kilometers south, maybe. Too bad I'm not a crow. "If I leave now, I'll beat the worst of it."

She doesn't look happy, but she nods. "Text me when you get there."

"Always," I promise. "And if the weird aunt comes home covered in mud, pretend to be surprised."

"Deal."

I wave goodbye and head out to the truck, the cold biting my cheeks as I climb into the driver's seat. I drop Dad's thermos into the cup holder, and the engine rumbles to life. As I steer out of the lot, I look up once more at the clouds rolling over the peaks. *I can make it there and back. No problem.*

But almost immediately, the drive is worse than I expect. Much worse.

I'm moving at the kind of crawl that leaves my shoulders knotted and my fingers white on the steering wheel. The microclimates around the lake make every mile different—the first stretch glazed in black ice that has me feathering the brakes and counting to four at every curve, then a section of sleet that slicks the pavement into a mirror, then bare asphalt for twenty blessed minutes before the temperature drops a degree and the world skates again. I'd turn around, but I'm hours in at this point, and I still have an urgent problem to address. A leak in the irrigation at this time of year means the drip system wasn't blown out correctly, and we're expecting another freeze tonight. We'll lose the sprinkler system if the water left in it turns to ice.

The radio fades in and out, the weather announcer switching from cheerful to stern mid-sentence. "Bands of precipitation…lake effect…gusts to forty along the ridge." On the far shore, the vineyards look like stitched corduroy, neat and sleeping and doomed to wake up cranky if this storm hits wrong.

I slow for the switchbacks where the rock wall leans too close, remembering Dad's voice, "*Don't be a hero, be a professional. Professionals get home.*" I text Tarryn from a pull-out.

Me: Roads are a mess. But still moving. Will check in at Black Bear.

I tuck my phone away before I see the typing bubbles appear like disapproval.

A sanding truck roars by in the opposite lane, tossing grit that pings my windshield like sleet. I unclench my jaw, sip lukewarm coffee, and keep going. Every time I think I've found my rhythm, the road changes, demanding more caution. It feels like being tested. Or warned.

By the time I finally roll down into the valley toward the Black Bear blocks, it's afternoon, and I'm exhausted in that unglamorous way that makes everything feel heavier than it is. I make a mental note to get a reservation at the little motel in downtown Black Bear. I don't think I'll make it back tonight.

I pull the truck onto the vineyard's dirt road, only to feel the tires sink. Mud. Thick, sucking mud that swallows the wheels up to the hubs. My stomach drops. There shouldn't be mud, not this time of year. The water should be off. Something's wrong.

I climb out, boots squelching as I land, and the smell hits first—wet earth and something metallic, the cold tang of water where it shouldn't be. The wind picks up, threading through bare canes and rattling the wire like a warning.

Block ten's supposed to be the problem, but as I walk the lines, it's clear this isn't isolated. It's worse. So much worse.

I kneel at the irrigation box. The lid is rimmed with ice, and when I pry it open, my fingers burn. The gauge shivers higher than I'd like, and there's a muffled hiss beneath it that shouldn't be there. I follow the sound, boot-prints filling with water as fast as I lift my feet.

As I chase it, I realize the water has spread across more than half the acreage, impacting almost a hundred acres of vines—our prized merlot and cabernet. This isn't the drip line having a bit of water left in it. This is a full-on water pipe issue. These rows represent years of choosing, pruning, and mending. Years of saying no to impatience. It's the kind of fruit you can't buy with money, only with time. Sweat pops out on my forehead. If we lose these, the damage won't just sting. It'll cripple.

Panic claws at my ribs, but I shove it down and throw myself into solving the problem. The water main gate isn't shutting. Dammit. Why now? This should have been done when they blew the lines out. Was that not done correctly?

Hands raw from cold, I twist valves that fight me, wrestle a stubborn regulator back into place, dig with numb fingers to redirect the water that keeps pooling in the low spots. Mud sucks at my boots like it wants to keep me. Twice, I have to brace on the post to yank my foot free. I curse, then apologize to no one, then curse again.

The water is running somewhere I can't see. I crawl under the trellis to check the drip line and catch a thin silver stream cutting across the row. I follow it until I reach a small waterfall, where part of the bank has crumbled away. It must be that the sprinkler system didn't get blown out right. This system is being pushed to the edge when it should be sleeping.

I pull a shovel and begin digging trenches to reroute the

water away from the vines, but I struggle to keep up with the amount of water flowing. I need to get it turned off.

The sun drops fast, shadows swallowing the rows, until I'm left with only the harsh beams of my truck headlights cutting through the dark and a head lamp to keep me from falling on my face. The light turns the mist to glitter and the mud to tar. My sweater sleeves are soaked through, my jeans heavy, and still, I work, mud streaking my hands and knees. My breath fogs out in ragged bursts, stinging in my throat.

I do the math in my head because numbers keep me from panicking. Even if I stem half the flow tonight, the ground is saturated. We'll need a pump at first light. We'll need sandbags along the bottom rows. We'll need…*help*. I hate the word. I hate needing it. But the vines don't care about my pride.

This isn't my kind of Saturday night. Most people my age are at bars or curled up with Netflix. Me? I'm knee-deep in mud, trying to save vines worth more than my entire life savings. And when I finally stop long enough to take in the reality, one thought pounds through me. *I'm not going anywhere tonight.*

The truck's stuck. The storm's rolling in. I'll need a ride into Black Bear, and I've not made a reservation yet. Dad will worry, but there's nothing I can do about it now. I'll text him once I get back in the truck, tell him I'm safe, tell him I've got it contained "for now." I'll lie just enough to let him sleep.

I stand, brushing my filthy hands on my jeans, ready to turn back toward the truck—and freeze.

The sharp, unmistakable sound of a rifle being cocked slices through the night.

Every muscle locks, and my breath stops in my throat.

I'm not alone.

Two

Kingston

The rifle feels wrong in my hands tonight. I carry it for predators—bears nosing for fallen grapes, coyotes testing the fence line—not for people. But for weeks, someone's been digging up vines across the valley, yanking out years of work like weeds. I caught headlights sweeping our rows, and I knew I needed to do something. I built a house on this land so I could keep an eye on this part of my family's vineyard.

I was taking a break from work when I noticed the truck in the vines and grabbed the rifle. There's a storm coming in, and it's the perfect time for a thief to take advantage. Shadows flicker between posts. One of them moves.

I cock the rifle. It's purely a scare tactic. I'm a doctor, and I save lives, not take them. "Come out with your hands up!"

My voice snaps the quiet in two and ricochets off the ridge.

The only answer is the low hiss of water somewhere it shouldn't be. A trickle? No, more than that. A steady stream. The sound lifts the hair on my neck. Flooding on a March night means ice by morning. Ice means death.

Boot scuff. Quick. Close.

I sight down the barrel, breath fogging. "Now!"

A figure steps into the light—small, layered up, mud climbing from boots to knees, hands lifted. A beanie under a headlamp. Dirt across the cheek like war paint.

"Don't shoot me, Kingston." The voice is sharp, familiar, and absolutely furious. "Unless you plan to take out a burst main while you're at it."

For a second, my brain refuses to catch up. My finger freezes near the trigger guard, my breath locked in my chest. Of all the people I expected in the rows, Elise Anderson wasn't one of them. Shame burns through the adrenaline.*What the hell am I doing aiming a rifle at her?*

I drop the muzzle so fast my shoulder twinges. "Elise?"

She yanks off her headlamp and squints into my lights. "Yes. And if you've got another order, make it 'Hand me that wrench.' I'm losing block ten."

The relief hits first—*she's not a thief*—but a different kind of panic follows. "What the hell are you doing out here alone?"

"Trying to keep half your merlot and cabernet from drowning and freezing solid before sunrise." She jerks a thumb over her shoulder. "Your main is jammed open. I can't shut the gate. The water's running blind, and the truck got mired. I was told there was a problem in block ten, but it looks like this is covering close to twenty blocks."

I push past her, the rifle bumping my thigh, and listen. She's right. The water's not just running, it's roaring low, a steady press through soil. I angle my light down a row. The ground gleams dark around the trunks, a slick that shouldn't be there this time of year.

"Pump house," I say, already moving. "Now."

Elise keeps pace, her breath huffing beside me. "If we don't relieve pressure and shut off the flow, this whole block turns into a skating rink when the temperature drops."

"This close to spring, we won't survive a freeze," I murmur. "The ground will be too hard for new growth and roots."

"Which is why I didn't wait for the night crew," she fires back. "Or for you to stop aiming guns at me."

Point taken. "I thought you were the one digging vines."

"Trust me," she pants, boots slapping frozen mud, "if I was stealing your vines, I wouldn't wear a headlamp."

The pump house squats at the edge of the block, a metal box with an attitude. I swing the door open. The control panel flickers—then dies—then flickers back. *Not right.* I kneel, pull open the manual valve cover, and swear. The gate wheel is jammed, metal teeth chewed.

Elise shines her headlamp for me. Her hands are raw through ripped gloves, knuckles nicked. She's been out there a while. "Someone wedged it?"

"Or worse." I grab the big wrench off the wall. "Hold the light steady."

She does, bracing one shoulder against the frame as I lean into the wheel. It groans. Doesn't give.

"It's seized," I grit out. "Or blocked."

Elise angles closer, lamp steady. I smell damp wool and cold air and the barest hint of citrus shampoo under mud. *Why the hell does that come through now?* It's disarming how the smallest details sneak past my guard. I've spent years building walls, and one whiff of citrus shampoo makes me wonder if I trust them to hold.

"Again," she says.

I put my back into it. The wheel moves a quarter turn. The pipes thump. Pressure shifts. With another shove, it moves another notch. The water noise eases a fraction outside.

"Keep going," Elise says like she's calling a play. "You've got it."

"Don't coach me on my own valves."

"Then move faster."

I push, breath burning, and the wheel finally spins free.

Somewhere down the line, a clamp rattles and settles. The outside roar drains to a good, solid hush.

We both stand there, listening, like we don't trust it. Then we step out. The flood is still there, but the shine on the soil isn't growing. The water finds the little trenches Elise must have cut and slithers away from the trunks.

"You did those by hand?" I ask, following the faint channels snaking between rows.

"With a shovel and a lot of swearing," she says. "The truck's buried to the axles in mud, but the headlights helped."

I turn toward the row road. Her pickup sits cocked at a bad angle, deep in muck that shouldn't exist in this cold unless something warmed the ground—like running water.

"You shouldn't be out here alone," I say again, softer.

She tips me a look. The beanie shadows her eyes, but I still catch the spark. "I didn't think you were in town. If I'd called, would you have answered?"

"Yes."

She nods once, accepts it, and points back at the pump house. "The panel's not just glitching," she notes. "This doesn't make any sense. It has to have been messed with."

Cold crawls up my spine. I return to crouch by the control box and pop the lower cover. Inside, the timer wires are neat, except for one that's been cut and stripped, then twisted back together sloppy. There's a thin wedge of metal stuffed behind the gate wheel teeth.

"Sabotage," I say. The word tastes bitter. Somebody isn't just careless. They're targeting us. And if they can get to Paradise Hill land, which clearly they can, then every block is at risk.

Elise nods. "That's my read. This is the first time it's come to this side of the property. Tarryn is going to be upset."

I look at her. Mud to mid-thigh. Hands shaking from cold, not fear. My jacket would swallow her, and for some reason, that image comes into sharp focus.

"Move," I say. "You're freezing."

"I'm working."

"Not an either-or." I shrug out of my coat and drape it over her shoulders before she can argue. She opens her mouth anyway, then closes it when the heat hits. The collar swallows her chin. She looks smaller, but not fragile. Just stubborn and capable and all too willing to bleed for our land.

"Thanks," she says, muffled.

"Come on." I shoulder the rifle and gesture toward her truck. "I'm putting a watch on this block until dawn."

"We need sandbags," she says, back to business. "There's a pallet by the lower shed."

"I'll grab them." I hesitate. "You okay?"

She gives me a look that says *don't be ridiculous* and *yes, but also you're not wrong to ask.* "I wish you'd recognized me before you tried to scare me out of my skin."

"I'm not used to catching friends in the rows after dark," I say. "I'm used to catching trouble."

Her mouth twitches. "To be fair, I can be trouble."

I don't smile. But it's close. "Let's go."

We jog to the lower shed, our lights bouncing. A coyote yips way off on the ridge, and another answers. The night feels thinner now that the water is quiet. Elise helps me muscle the sandbags into the bed of my truck. The sleet falls from the sky. We build a lip around the worst pooling. It's ugly but effective. The water runs off toward the ditch instead of hugging the trunks.

Fifteen minutes later, the crisis is contained. My fingers are numb. Hers have gone from red to pale under the ripped gloves. I load the spent shovel. We stand there, steam rising from our clothes in the headlights' heat, breathing like we just ran a race we didn't train for.

"Whoever did that to the valve knew exactly what to hit," she says, watching the trench carry the last of the overflow. "Timer wire. Gate teeth."

"The thief rumors," I say. "All those vines pulled up in the valley—maybe not just theft. Maybe a campaign."

"Against the valley or against Paradise Hill?" she asks, and the way she says Paradise Hill carries both meanings—the place and my family.

"Don't know yet." I scan the ground. The mud is a mess, but there are prints besides ours—wider stride, deeper heel. Not work-boot treads I recognize. I take a picture. "But whoever it was has been here recently."

She nods. "The water was already running when I arrived."

"You came alone," I say.

"You were alone too," she counters.

"I live here."

"You pointed that rifle at me."

"Because I care about the land."

Her chin lifts. "So do I."

We stare each other down for a beat, breath fogging between us. Then she shifts, practical nature winning over pride. "We should flag the bad rows for the morning crews and call Tarryn. And Trace. They'll want to know."

"They'll hear it from me." I pull out my phone, snap a few shots of the panel, the wedge. "And from you. You're staying while I make the calls."

"I'm not leaving until I'm sure the flow is staying off," she says. "And my truck still needs rescuing."

"I'll have it pulled as soon as I can and towed to the garage here in Black Bear," I say. "No sense in trying tonight. You can't go anywhere." I glance toward the black line of the lake. "Come into the house. Warm up. Eat something. Let's see what happens with this storm, and hopefully, it snows before the ground can freeze. That will protect the vines. At dawn we can go back to work."

Her headlamp throws a halo when she looks at me. "You don't have to play host, Kingston."

"It's not hospitality. It's logistics."

"And you don't have to take care of me."

"Maybe not," I say. "But I'm taking care of the vines, and you're part of the solution."

She studies me for a second, the edge sliding off her face. "Logistics, then."

"Good." I point at her legs. "Those pants are a lost cause."

"I know." She shakes one foot, and mud cracks and flakes. "I'll bill you."

"Send it to accounts payable."

"Do I get interest on the trauma?"

"You pointed me to a seized gate and told me to push harder. We're even."

That gets a real smile—quick, surprised, almost private. It does something to my insides I don't have time to name.

I call Dad, then Tarryn, and I keep it crisp—valve tampered with, flow now shut off, sandbags, the mud, and the plan. We agree on a dawn sweep and a locksmith for the gate, plus a camera install by noon—weather permitting. When I hang up, Elise is marking trunks with flagging tape, moving fast, efficient, like she's been doing this since she could walk.

"Leave some for morning," I tell her. "You can barely feel your hands."

"They'll warm up." She flexes her fingers and winces. "Eventually."

I step closer and catch her wrists gently, turning her palms up. The cuts are shallow but raw. "We should clean these out. You won't be able to hold a pruner next week if they get infected."

"You planning to add a tetanus lecture to your logistics memo, doctor?"

The corner of my mouth pulls. "I might."

She swallows. I let go. For a second, heat from my coat trapped around her neck fogs in the beam between us.

"Okay," she says finally. "Let's get inside. I'll call a tow truck and a rideshare."

We kill the truck lights and lock the pump house. The night swallows us, full of distant water and the faint tick of cooling metal. Above, the sleet has stopped and the clouds have lightened. The bulk of the storm's still yet to come, though. This is but a reprieve.

At the edge of the block, I look back. The vines stand in rows like ribs, lean and sleeping, and I swear they breathe easier now that the water's down.

"You really thought I was stealing vines?" she asks as we walk up the hill to my home.

"I thought someone was," I answer. "They have before. But then I saw you. I still have a lecture about you being alone in the dark."

She exhales, a sound that might be a laugh if she wasn't so tired. "Next time, lead with the lecture before you point a gun at someone."

"Next time," I say as I open the back door of my house, "call me before you fight a flood alone."

She gives me a look.

"If we're lucky, tomorrow's storm will drop snow before it freezes." I look away as warmth and the faint smell of cedar greet us as we enter the mudroom. "Try not to drip everywhere. Simone will have my head. She's likely in her apartment for the night, but she'll start the morning angry if there's a mess. Anyway, you won't get anyone out here until this storm passes."

When I look over again, there's a stubborn glint in her eyes. "Then I'll need a ride into Black Bear. There's a motel off Main. I'll get a room."

I shake my head. "You don't need a motel."

Her brows lift. "What do you suggest?"

"Here. I've got a guest room, actually three you can take your pick from."

She blinks like I've just suggested she move in for the season. "That's not— Kingston, I can't. It's—"

"It's late, and you have to be back at dawn. Your truck's stuck, and the temperature's dropping fast." I keep my voice even, firm. "You're not walking into Black Bear in this weather, and no motel's worth freezing over. You'll take a guest room."

She sits up straighter. "I'll be fine."

"There's nowhere else for you to go tonight, Elise. The guest room's waiting. That's it."

Her lips press together, the fight still there. She huffs out a breath and mutters, "Fine. Guest room. Just tonight." Her voice is clipped, but the way she pulls my coat tighter says she's colder than her pride will admit. I bite back the urge to tell her she'll thank me in the morning.

"Good." I sit down on the bench and untie my boots, placing them neatly in their spot.

She slips off her boots as well, and I move on to strip all the way to my boxer shorts. She can't look at me, and she makes no move to do anything about her ruined clothes. I leave my wet clothes in a pile on the tile floor.

"Bathroom's down the hall, second door on the right," I tell her. "Guest rooms are just past that. Get cleaned up. I'll find you something dry to wear."

She nods once and heads down the hall. After a moment, I hear her wet sweater hit the floor, followed by the rush of water as the shower kicks on.

I drag a hand down my face, sighing. *This is fine. It's the only option.*

I head down the hallway myself, and in the dresser in the guest room I pull out a T-shirt and an old pair of sweats. They'll swallow her whole, but at least they're warm and dry. I fold them over the bed, glancing toward the closed bathroom door, steam already leaking under the crack.

I shouldn't picture her in there, mud sluicing down the drain, her hair loose instead of tucked under a beanie. But the image comes anyway, sharp and unwelcome. I scrub a hand down my face. I don't even know where these thoughts are coming from. *I've shut the door on caring for women, and I don't plan on opening it again.*

I can't believe I asked her to stay. But what choice did I have? The storm is coming. Her truck is stuck. The valley's under threat. And whether I like it or not, Elise Anderson is under my roof.

Three

Elise

Steam clings to my skin as I step out of the bathroom and into the guest room. The bed is neatly made, a folded bundle placed at the foot like a hotel turn-down. A giant T-shirt and an even larger pair of sweatpants—Kingston must've slipped them in while I was showering.

I tug on the shirt—it could be a dress—and roll the waistband of the pants again and again until it's bunched thick like an inflatable inner tube. I catch my reflection in the mirror and snort. If he doesn't laugh when he sees me, I'll know he's not paying attention.

The fabric smells faintly of him—cedar, citrus, and something darker I can't place. It's ridiculous how quickly that smell makes me aware of every inch of skin underneath his clothes. I'm supposed to be worrying about my truck, not have Kingston Paradise's laundry giving me goose bumps.

I almost convince myself to stay in the guest room and starve, but my stomach has other ideas. Besides, hiding feels childish. If I'm going to wait out this snowstorm, I might as well face the man who owns the house.

The scent of garlic and herbs drifts down the hallway, my stomach growling so loud it echoes in the quiet. A draft sneaks under the door, carrying the distant rattle of the storm outside, which is now making its arrival known. I climb the stairs carefully, the too-long sweatpants dragging like a mop.

Kingston is at the counter, sleeves shoved up, reheating a dish in the microwave. His hair is still a little mussed, and the sight of him here—big, capable, calm—does something odd to my pulse. The windows behind him are dark, filled with whirling snowflakes illuminated by the kitchen lights. It feels like the house is an island in the storm.

"Sorry about the drop-in," I say, tugging at the hem of the shirt. "I promise I don't make a habit of showing up half-drowned and uninvited."

His eyes flick down to the clothes hanging off me, but his expression barely shifts. He's always controlled. "And I'm sorry you're stuck here. If I'd been home earlier, I would've caught the water running and dealt with it."

"Where were you this week?" I ask, mostly just to fill the silence.

"London." He says this like someone else would say *Paradise*. "Work. Surgeries. Meetings. I flew back early this morning and slept most of the day."

His casual nature makes me blink. *London*. While I was doing prep work for the spring growth, he was… I don't know, changing lives, building empires. Kingston has developed a new type of replacement joint, and he often does the surgery to show other doctors how they can be used. We live in two different universes, and right now, they're colliding in his kitchen.

"So jet-lagged billionaire doctor saves runaway truck girl." I give a wobbly smile. "That's not intimidating at all."

The corner of his mouth twitches, and it feels like a small victory.

He plates the food—Tuscan chicken, creamy and fragrant—and sets one serving in front of me. Steam curls upward, carrying the smell of garlic, tomatoes, and cream. My stomach clenches with hunger, but my chest feels strange—too full, too aware of him.

"Truck girl might be here a while," he notes. "I'm not sure when the storm will make freeing her vehicle possible."

"Really?" My voice pitches embarrassingly high. "You're joking, right?"

He shakes his head.

I groan. "Tarryn is going to kill me."

The silence stretches between us as we eat, broken only by the whistle of wind against the glass. For a flicker of a second, it feels like we're a couple sharing a late dinner after a long day, and that thought jolts me straight to my phone. I need to check in before anyone worries.

My phone is still in my bag. I dig it out and quickly text both Tarryn and Dad.

Me: Staying at Kingston's. Truck stuck, but I'm safe, and the problem is managed for now.

Tarryn's reply comes fast.

Tarryn: Glad he was home. Don't worry about the truck. We'll get it out later.

Dad's message is slower but steadier.

Dad: Good you're with Kingston. Family taking care of you makes me feel better.

Family. He trusts Kingston without question. I want to. I think I do. But he's still Kingston Paradise, the grown-up version of the boy who thought his sister and I were a nuisance. Now, he's a self-made billionaire, larger than life, and a little intimidating in the way only people who never seem to stumble can be.

The first bite of chicken melts in my mouth, and I almost moan. It's worlds better than the reheated sandwiches I usually wolf down after a twelve-hour day. "Okay, your chef is a genius."

He shrugs. "Simone."

I've known Simone my whole life. Her brother was in my year at school, and she's a few years older.

His voice goes flat. "Cara picked her and everything in this house. At least, Simone stayed with me when Cara left."

The words hang in the air, and I remember now that Kingston has stumbled a bit. His marriage to Cara ended with her choosing his best friend. He's been different ever since, but right now, he doesn't blink, doesn't flinch, just carries on with his meal like he hasn't detonated a landmine between us. I stab at my chicken, pretending to focus, but the truth is I don't have any idea how to respond. I know that story, but I certainly never envisioned myself talking to him about it. Should I say I'm sorry, or just sit in the silence with him?

"They live at the north end of the lake up in Vernon now," he adds after a moment. "They have a small winery." His face gives nothing away, but I can feel the steel under his words. It's like he's locked that part of his life in a vault and welded the door shut.

I just keep chewing. I want to ask if he's okay, but I can't quite get there.

"So," he says, tilting his head. "Master vintner. You ready for your dad to retire?"

"Yes." I nod, slightly bewildered that we've now moved on but thankful for the new topic. I want him to see me as more than Tarryn's sidekick. "My red blend won again at the International Wine Festival earlier this month. And…I've been invited to Château for a three-month work exchange. I leave next week."

That gets his full attention. Fork clatters against porcelain. "Exchange? Or are they trying to recruit you?"

I shrug, even though my stomach flips. "Maybe both.

Sebastian Bernard thinks he's God's gift, but I'm not going for him. I want to learn from their process, see their operation. Château is on the Left Bank. Legendary."

If Kingston notices the crack in my voice, he doesn't show it. And I don't say the other part, that I'm terrified. Terrified of being exposed as not good enough, of standing in one of the most famous vineyards in the world and hearing the whisper in my head, *You don't belong here.*

I also worry that the assistant vintner who's coming over to step in here while I'm gone could be better than me, and everyone might like him more. I should be proud, even thrilled, at this opportunity, and I am, but reality still gnaws at me. Leaving means putting more pressure on Tarryn, and I have to admit that I might be running from the hardest thing of all—proving I can lead on my own soil instead of someone else's.

"Tarryn will be lost without you," Kingston notes.

I shake my head. "She won't. She's brilliant. She has the vision, and Trinity, Sadie, Ginny—they're the soldiers making it happen. I just keep things moving. Plus, they're sending an assistant vintner over to help out here as part of the exchange."

He leans back, studying me. "Strange. None of us brothers wanted the vineyard. We followed Mom into medicine. And now, they've all partnered with women who are moving the business farther along than we ever imagined."

I laugh. "Maybe that's the secret."

For a second, our eyes lock, and warmth flows through me. He's close enough that I notice the faint shadows under his eyes, the tired crease at the corner of his mouth, vulnerable details that make him seem more human. Then he scoffs, though he doesn't elaborate.

I look away, busying myself with chasing sauce around my plate. Dangerous territory.

When we finish, I stack the dishes in the sink, rinsing them as the snowflakes swirl outside the windows. The kitchen is too pristine, too curated, like a life someone else designed and abandoned. I guess that's what he said it was. I wonder if Kingston ever feels like a guest in his own home.

When I finally turn, he's half-asleep at the counter, and something inside me softens. The great Kingston Paradise, undone by jetlag. I nudge him and gesture toward the hall. "Go. Bed. Doctor's orders."

He gives me a half-smile, almost boyish in its exhaustion, and disappears into his room.

The click of his bedroom door echoes in the stillness. I stand here for a moment, caught between feeling like an intruder and...something else. Something I don't want to name. I finish cleaning up and retreat to the guest room while the storm swallows the world whole.

The wind buffets the windows, wet, heavy, snow thickening by the minute. But inside, it's warm, still, almost too quiet.

I pull back the curtain. Outside, snow piles higher and higher, and it may be just what we need to avoid losing the blocks of vines. It's like a giant, insulating blanket. And my truck is buried somewhere under it, frozen in place, just like me.

I press my hand to the cold glass. I don't know when I'll get home.

But I'm also not sure being here is so bad.

Four

Kingston

My eyes snap open at three thirty a.m., and I know right away that I'm not going back to sleep. My body clock is messed up. London time lingers in my veins, pulling me toward action while the rest of this valley sleeps.

I shove back the duvet and swing my legs to the floor. The house is silent. No faint hum of traffic, no voices on the street, no city energy bleeding through the walls like in London or Vancouver. Just the storm. And this is what I love.

I pad to the window and curse under my breath. The helipad is buried under a thick white quilt, its clean lines erased, the landing light barely visible. Clearing it will take half the day. No quick escapes.

Big Bear Valley doesn't get much snow for the most part. A flurry here and there, a dusting that melts by noon. But once or twice each winter, we get hit with a storm that buries everything. This is that storm, the kind that shuts down the roads, bends fences, and makes the world feel smaller, quieter.

This means Elise isn't going anywhere. No chance we can dig the truck out today. I doubt the plows make it up here before afternoon. She's stuck in this house with me.

I rub a hand over my jaw. Tonight is family dinner. My mother will insist I be there. I've skipped too many lately with half-hearted excuses, and she sees through all of them. For her, Sunday dinner is tradition, obligation, ritual. For me, lately, it feels like punishment.

Because I'm the odd man out.

Greyson has Trinity and Theo. Beckett has Sadie and a baby on the way. Ryker has Ginny. Even Tarryn has Declan. The table is loud with laughter, crowded with private smiles and inside jokes, couples leaning close. And me? I'm sitting there like an extra chair pulled up to the side, empty in every way that counts. Because that's what I've chosen. That's what protects me, makes sure no one can ever hurt me like Cara did again.

I think about Hope in Vancouver—beautiful, ambitious, sharp as glass. She's been my lawyer for a few years now, and somewhere along the way, we blurred the lines. For months, we circled each other, and then started connecting occasionally, but it's always been more convenience than anything else. She's made it clear small-town life isn't for her, and I've never thought we were heading anywhere. My business trip to London only reinforced that, as I hardly gave her a second thought, and she didn't reach out either. We're not building a future, just sharing the benefits of something that works right now.

But then, inexplicably, another woman comes to mind.

Elise.

She was swimming in my clothes last night—my T-shirt swallowing her, my sweatpants rolled at the waist until she looked ridiculous. And still, she pulled it off. More than pulled it off. That image has been burned into my brain ever since—her small frame lost in my things, hair damp from the shower, face soft and unguarded. She didn't look like a guest. She looked like she belonged.

But that can't possibly be right.

It's just that I know her. She's practically family. Tarryn's best friend. The kid who used to chase us across the vineyard rows, demanding to play. I can still hear her laughter from those summers, shrill and determined.

That was a long time ago, I remind myself. I was someone different then. I drag myself downstairs to the gym, hoping sweat will burn these strange thoughts out of me. I push through ten kilometers on the treadmill, every stride pounding out frustration, and then punish myself on the stair climber until my legs are on fire. By the end, sweat soaks my shirt, my chest heaves, and my muscles tremble. And still, the restlessness lingers.

A shower doesn't fix it either. The storm is still lingering when I come out, snow weighing on the house, the sky mostly dark. I fill the percolator and let the slow hiss and gurgle ground me. My father has always made coffee this way, long before single-serve machines and pods. He'd let me sip the bitter dregs, warning me not to tell my mother.

When the coffee is ready, I pour a mug and open my laptop at the long farm table in the kitchen. The inbox is worse than I expected, bloated with overnight emails. Half of them are board questions, updates, and issues that should've been handled without me. Renew Motion, the medical device company I founded to produce less-invasive knee replacements, is supposed to run itself while I'm gone. Apparently, no one got the memo. I have a great team, but sometimes, they don't want to make decisions without my buy-in.

I'm so deep in irritation that I don't hear Elise until she speaks.

"I smell coffee."

I look up, and Elise stands in the doorway, her hair a wild halo, cheeks pink from sleep. She's still drowning in my clothes, bare feet curling against the cold tile. She looks...cute. I wave toward the pot. "Help yourself."

She pads over, pours a mug, and takes a sip. Her eyes

widen. "I think this is the best coffee I've ever had."

A smile tugs at my mouth before I can stop it. "Kopi Luwak. Beans go through a civet before they're roasted. The percolator helps, but the beans make the difference."

"What's a civet?"

"It's a mammal in South America."

Her nose wrinkles. "You're telling me I'm drinking coffee some animal has pooped out?"

I nod.

She stares at the mug, and then takes another slow sip. "Well, whatever it is, don't say anything else and ruin it for me. I don't want to think about why it's perfect."

The corner of my mouth lifts again. *What is going on with me?* This storm has shifted more than snow.

She looks out the window. "I take it no one came in at first light?"

"Nope, but the rain, then sleet, and now, snow may protect the vines since they haven't budded yet." I close the laptop and head for the fridge. "You hungry?"

She grins. "You're going to make me breakfast?"

"What's that supposed to mean?"

Her arms fold, lips twitching. "Growing up, you always made me cook for you. Sure, you're eleven years older, but you treated me like your personal chef. Don't pretend you don't remember."

I stop with the eggs in hand, frowning. "I never did that."

"Oh, yes, you did. You'd sit back and issue commands. And the one time I refused? You bullied me until I cried. Then I made you scrambled eggs."

I blink, stunned. "I have zero memory of that."

"Convenient."

"God." I shake my head. "I was an ass. I'm sorry."

She shrugs, but her eyes sparkle.

"I'm surprised you didn't spit in them," I say.

Her smile turns sly. "Who says I didn't?"

A laugh rumbles up, unexpected. "All right. Watch this time. I'll prove I can do better. And I promise not to do anything to the eggs."

Her brows rise. "This I have to see."

I cook a few pieces of bacon, whisk the eggs with cream, and fold in green onion and cheese. And after the bacon is crisp, I pour the eggs into the bacon grease. The skillet hisses. The smell fills the kitchen, rich and warm. When I set the plate in front of her, she takes one bite, closes her eyes, and groans.

"Okay, fine. You win. These are the best eggs I've ever had."

Grinning, I dig into my plate. "Redemption at last."

We eat in companionable silence, snow hurling itself against the window.

Finally, she sets her fork down. "I should see about digging out the truck."

"Don't bother." I sip my coffee. "You're not driving out of here today regardless. I'll fly home in my helicopter for family dinner tonight and take you with me."

Her head tilts.

"You can pack a bag," I tell her. "And we'll come back after. That way you're here tomorrow, ready to get back to the vines and deal with the truck."

Her lips part, surprise flashing across her face. "You're sure?"

I nod. "My mother will insist that I show up," I say dryly. "So this just makes sense."

She studies me, and then nods. "All right. How long do you plan on staying?"

"I'll leave whenever dinner's over. Won't be late."

"Okay, let me know, and I'll be waiting by the helicopter pad."

I narrow my eyes. "Why aren't you coming to dinner?"

Her expression shifts, shutters. She lifts her mug, stares into the coffee. "My dad and I—we only come when we're invited. Max and Zach show up, and we learned a long time ago to stay out of it."

I don't like that at all. Elise and her father should be at the table. They're as much a part of this valley as any of us. I lean back, jaw tight. If Elise declines to join us tonight, I'll hear about it from my mother. And if Zach has the gall to show his face? I'll lose it. My brothers will have to hold me back, because after what he did to the Dempsey vineyard, Tarryn's cottage, and possibly the sabotage here, I can't sit across the table from him. And that's only the things we know about.

Zach disappeared nearly six months ago. My gut tells me he's behind more than we realize. A lot more. And Max has been all over the place lately, but considering we watched Zach try to poison the water well on Dempsey property, I figure Max is keeping his head down because he's embarrassed. Can't say I really miss either of them.

"I need to check the vines. What time were you thinking of going?" Elise pours herself another cup of coffee.

"It's going to take some work to get the helicopter out, so that's my first order of business. We don't need to be there until maybe four, and it's a quick trip."

She smiles and nods. "Just let me know. Do you know where my clothes are?"

"I'm sure Simone took care of them. She acts as my house manager too."

"Great. Thank you."

I watch her leave, still feeling a strange wave of nostalgia and warmth and…something else. She's not the nuisance she once was. Not that it should matter to me in the least.

Five

Elise

When I slip back into the guest room, my clothes are clean—folded, even—on the chair by the window. I stop and stare like the denim might explain itself. I've only been here overnight. How did Simone get even my sweater washed, dried, and folded in the span of a few hours?

I bring the sweater to my face. It smells faintly of some expensive detergent I don't recognize—clean, almost citrusy. A little piece of this house clings to the fibers. A little piece of Kingston's world wraps around me as I dress.

Boots. Coat. Gloves. Hat. Back downstairs, I layer up until I feel like a walking duvet and step outside into air so cold it steals my breath. The storm faded away at some point this morning, and the sun is finally shining. But as I walk out to the vines, the snow is knee deep, heavy and wet, clinging to my boots like it wants to keep me here. The vines rise in quiet rows as I approach, cloaked in snow, black ribs against a white sky, their fragile arms not yet sprouted. I brush snow from a spur, run my thumb along the wood, and listen the way my dad taught me, noticing how sound feels through my skin. Some of these may not make it. Some can be coaxed back. The blanket of snow might have bought them a chance. Water's cruel, but it can be merciful too. Hope is stubborn like that. So am I.

The truck looks worse in daylight—three tires swallowed to the rims in frozen mud. I dig around them anyway, breath puffing in angry little clouds. The shovel's handle burns through my gloves, and the metal clinks against rock. I scrape, pry, curse under my breath. After ten solid minutes, I've made exactly the kind of progress that makes me want to throw the shovel like a spear.

"Great," I mutter, leaning on the handle. "You win." The truck ignores me, smug in its pit. There's a reason Kingston told me not to bother today.

I force myself to look somewhere, anywhere else. When I turn, the lake does what it always does and hushes me. It's a sheet of glass, steel, and pearl under a sky the color of pewter, the banks softened by a frosting of snow. A long-ago memory flickers—skates biting into ice on the pond by the main house. Kingston and Tarryn racing, me wobbling after them, cheeks burning, breath hot inside my scarf. Back then, the world was simple. Vines and math homework. Sunday dinners with dad and harvests. No exchange programs, no leaving, no burgeoning career, no wondering whether I belong to land or people or neither.

Movement catches my eye, a dark figure bent and repetitive against a drift. *Kingston.* He's shoveling like he's in a contest he refuses to lose.

Curiosity, or maybe some stubborn desire to be useful, drags me toward him. Every step is a negotiation with the snow. By the time I reach the clearing, my thighs burn and my lungs sting.

"Need help?" I call, voice swallowed by the quiet, my

words coming out in visible puffs.

He doesn't stop, just straightens enough to lean on the shovel. "If I don't clear this, we don't fly."

My gaze skates across white nothing. "Clear…what? You're shoveling a pad of concrete?"

"Doors," he says, stamping his boot on the packed surface. "The helicopter platform sits below ground. Doors open inward. If I don't get this snow off, all of it drops into the bay the second I release the locks."

Ah. Not a magical billionaire dome after all. Just two giant steel doors pretending to be ground.

"Wouldn't it be easier if the platform was heated?" I ask. Teasing him is a reflex I've had longer than my driver's license.

His mouth twitches like he wants to smile but refuses. "Already on the punch list." He thumbs the starter on a snowblower.

It coughs, growls, and dies the saddest death I've ever heard a machine die. "Too wet," I say.

"Too heavy," he agrees, jaw ticking. "And I didn't get the front blade swapped after the last storm."

My eyes find a wide push broom leaning against the equipment shed, bristles splayed from honest years of work. "Well, if your toy won't do the job…" I grab the broom, set my feet, and bulldoze a swath of snow off the seam where the doors meet.

He looks deeply unimpressed. "That's pointless."

"Try the snow blower where I just cleared," I say, breathless but delighted by my own pettiness.

He humors me. The blower bites. The snow breaks clean. His brows lift a millimeter, which for Kingston is the emotional equivalent of confetti and a marching band. "Hmm…" he says.

"Translation: you were wrong," I inform him.

"It helped," he counters, which is as close to a capitulation as I'll ever get.

We fall into an easy, word-sparring rhythm—me pushing broad lanes, him shaving the stubborn edges. The work is monotonous and brutal, and I measure time by the ache that creeps into my forearms, the damp that seeps through the knees of my jeans, and the way my scarf goes from dry wool to a chilled, damp rope pressed against my neck. Every so often our gloves bump on a handle exchange, and there's a jolt that isn't static electricity. I ignore it. Or I try to.

"You enjoy being right way too much," he says eventually, which makes something bright unfurl under my ribs.

"Someone has to keep you humble."

"Medical conferences usually do the trick," he says dryly.

"So you're saying I'm as effective as a ballroom full of orthopedic surgeons?" I ask, pushing another heavy drift. My boots slip, and he steadies me with a hand at my elbow. Heat explodes across my skin under the insulation, which is ridiculous in this refrigerator of a morning.

"You're louder," he says.

"I'm not loud," I protest, even though I absolutely am when the situation calls for it.

He glances up, and there's a flash of amusement—Kingston unguarded, boyish for a heartbeat. I look away so fast my neck twinges.

We work until the world narrows to *scrape, sweep, pant, repeat*. When the last of the heavy snow has finally been driven away and the black seam of the doors lies clear like a precise incision, I straighten and groan, pressing a palm to my lower back.

"Okay," I gasp. "That was…not glamorous."

"Effective, though," he says.

He taps something into a recessed keypad housed in a stainless box that probably cost more than that truck I've buried in the mud. Locks thud. Metal groans. Somewhere below us, hydraulics whir to life, a steady, hungry sound that reverberates through my boots. The twin doors split down the center and fold inward, swallowing their own weight like slow jaws. Beneath, the platform rises—first a sliver of dark, then a widening circle, then sleek carbon fiber and glass and the knife-clean lines of a machine that looks like it should not be real.

The Sikorsky S-76D helicopter lifts into the morning like a

secret surfacing. It's bone-dry, rotors tied down with neat red straps, paint gleaming, windows reflecting sky and me—pink-cheeked, hair plastered to my forehead, ridiculous.

"There," Kingston says as he keys in a short series on a second panel. The platform locks with a reassuring clunk. "She's ready."

"That is so amazing. You hide your helicopter."

"This way," he says, "no one messes with her. I still need to do all the regular checks, but I was in her yesterday coming from the airport in Paradise." He concludes with a look that is ninety-percent deadpan and ten-percent warning.

I laugh and immediately regret it when the cold stabs my exposed teeth.

We slog back toward the house, leaving deep proof of our work in the snow. I can feel every muscle from hip to ankle registering a formal complaint. My jeans are again soaked through, my coat heavy with wetness, and my gloves iced into claws. The mudroom door swings open before I can touch the handle, and warmth rolls out in a blessed wave.

"Stop right there," Simone says, blocking the threshold with an arm that could halt a stampede. She evaluates both of us in one sweep, eyes sharp. "Absolutely not. You're not dripping on my floor."

"Your floor?" Kingston says, but it's soft around the edges, no real heat.

"Mine," she says. "By virtue of caring about it. Boots off. Coats on hooks. You—" She flicks a glance at me. "—come with me. I've got something that'll fit you better than whatever you wore last night."

"Simone," I manage through chattering teeth. "You're a saint."

She snorts. "I'm a house manager who hates puddles. Move."

Kingston disappears deeper into the house without waiting to be dismissed, though he does remove his shoes. *Typical*. Simone rolls her eyes at his retreating back, then slides a large boot tray under my feet and waits the way only someone with older-sister energy can—hand on hip, eyebrow up, patient and terrifying.

Once I've shed enough water to irrigate a small field, she shepherds me down the hall to a bright room, rummages in a closet, and emerges with black leggings and an oversized slate sweatshirt.

"They'll be a little big," she says, "but closer than that man's castoffs." She pushes them into my arms. "Shower, warm up, and meet me in the kitchen. I'll make hot chocolate for both of you."

Hot chocolate. My bones sing at the very phrase. "You're serious?"

"I don't joke about chocolate," she says, already turning away. "And Elise? Great to see you on this side of the lake."

Something tender loosens in my heart. "You too."

In the bathroom, I peel off wet layers that slap the tile like fish. I turn the water hotter than any dermatologist would approve, step into the hiss and steam, and stand there until the sting softens into a slow, encompassing heat. Sensation creeps back into my fingers in painful pins and needles. I brace my hands against the tiles and bow my head, letting the water drum between my shoulder blades.

Of course, this is when my brain fires up a reel I don't approve of—Kingston beside me on the pad, jaw shadowed with stubble, moving with that economical precision he gets when he's focused. The flash of humor he tried to swallow. The feel of his hand around my elbow, steadying me. The way we worked—synchronized without having to talk about it, like we'd done this a hundred times, and maybe we have, in different costumes. Sprinkler lines. Fence posts. Teenagers trying to move a fallen pine because waiting for adults was unbearable.

Stop it, I tell myself. He's practically your brother. You grew up together. He made you cry, and he was a bully about who did chores. My mouth quirks, remembering the story I told him last night, the way his face fell, real remorse cracking through his certainty. He is carved from this land in a way I understand down to the marrow. But he's also damaged, closed, uninterested in seeing me clearly.

Our common history is not at all the same thing as being made for each other.

Simone's leggings slide on with a soft whisper, and the sweatshirt is heavy enough to be called a hug. I towel-twist my hair, rub warmth into my calves, and catch my reflection. Pinker cheeks. Softer eyes. I look…like me. Maybe even a me that slept well, finally.

The kitchen is warm and smells like buttered toast and chocolate and cinnamon, like holidays and childhood and good decisions. Simone stands at the stove, whisk in hand, cocoa already at that perfect edge of steaming but not scalding. She pours it into two mugs, white porcelain with a clean blue rim, then shakes a dusting of cocoa over the tiniest cloud of whipped cream and slides one across the island toward me.

"There," she says. "Prescription strength."

I wrap both hands around the ceramic and nearly whimper. The heat seeps into my fingers and up my wrists to the sore places. The first sip is ridiculous. Silky. Deep. Not too sweet, with something like vanilla at the end.

"Oh," I say, eyes closing. "That is…unfair."

"I know," she says. "It's the good cocoa." She leans her elbows on the counter across from me, chin in hand, studying me over her own mug. "So. Tell me everything. I hear you're running off on an exchange. Tarryn's still trying to decide whether to chain you to a barrel or bless the plane."

I laugh, surprised. "That tracks. But it's not forever. Just a few months. Maybe a season if it's a good fit. The truth is…aside from four years in Vancouver for school, I've only ever known Paradise Hill. I know my vines the way some people know a favorite hymn. I want… I don't know…more ways to listen."

"More ways to listen," Simone repeats, as if tasting the words. "I like that."

I shrug, embarrassed by how earnest I sound. "Tarryn and I met the red wine vintner and owner of Chateau at the International Wine Festival. They liked the wine I designed, and they were kind enough to offer the exchange. They do things differently over there—new clones, different pruning philosophies, fermentation tweaks I've only read about. Maybe I'll come home with better hands."

"You already have good hands," she says plainly.

Warmth blooms within me, unexpected and big.

"And the guy?" she adds because, of course, she does. Her grin turns sly. "What about the guy coming in your place? Tarryn is convinced half the valley will camp at your crush pad to watch him breathe."

"I've never met him."

"Hmmm… What about the master vintner? Is he a hot French guy?"

"I won't be working with the master vintner. The exchange will have me shadowing the vintner for some of the reds, and he's Italian."

"I hear Italians are incredible lovers. Not that I would know."

I cough on a mouthful of cocoa, which is a tragic waste. "I don't know either, but he was a good kisser."

"You don't say…" A sly smile stretches her mouth.

"He's very competent," I try, feeling my cheeks heat as I try to steer us back to business. "He—he seemed interested in what we're doing. And in me. Professionally. Maybe…more."

"Ah," Simone says, seeming delighted. "So he's not just smart. We love a brain, but when they have eyes, they're more fun."

"Simone."

"What?" Her eyes widen. "I'm rooting for your happiness in any form it wishes to present."

I scrape my spoon across the rim of my mug to avoid answering. "How's your brother?" I ask, deflecting. "Last I heard he was leaving for. Was it Laos?"

"Guatemala," she says. "He's building houses with a team. Sends pictures that make my heart stop. We were not built for the same level of chaos. He comes home every few months, eats everything not nailed down, tells me I need to travel more, and then leaves again with my good sunscreen."

"That sounds right," I say, smiling. "I remember him from school, and he never did sit still. I'm glad he found a way to make that a calling."

She lifts a shoulder. "We're all just trying to find the thing that quiets the noise in our heads. For me, it's a well-run house and a clean boot tray. For him, it's a muddy build site and a sunset. For you..." She gestures at me with her mug. "I suspect it's a row of vines you nursed through a bad week and the exact moment a ferment tips from worry to promise."

Something in me opens, like she's seen me clearly, perhaps more clearly than I've seen myself. "Yes," I whisper.

"And Kingston?" she asks lightly, as if she isn't dropping a pebble into a still pond to watch the ripples. "What quiets his head?"

"Work," I say. "Building things that last. Fixing what's broken." I hesitate, and then add, "Family. Whether he admits it or not."

Simone's mouth tilts. "He would die of mortification before he said that out loud."

"He would," I agree, and we both laugh.

She taps her nail against her mug. "When I worked at the vineyard when we were kids, you two were funny," she says. "Oil and water unless there was a job to do. Then you were...a well-oiled machine." She winks. "Pun intended."

I can't help smiling. A memory surfaces of building a booth for a lemonade stand out of scrap wood and cinderblocks—Kingston bossing, me arguing, Tarryn rolling her eyes and making the lemonade so strong the first sip kicked like whiskey.

There's a sound behind us, and Kingston strides into the kitchen with damp hair, a gray sweater, and that unavoidable gravity he carries. He looks clean in a way that makes clean dangerous. He smells faintly of cedar and soap. My brain notes all of this with scientific detachment. My body doesn't.

He takes us both in—Simone perched like a benevolent cat, me clutching a mug like it's a life preserver—and one corner of his mouth tucks, like he's trying not to be charmed and failing a little.

"I talked to my mom," he says, all business. "She wants you to come for dinner. That's in a few hours, so we should get there so we have time to do other things. I heard on the radio that the road's closed. We can check it out on our way."

"Okay then," I say, pushing away from the island. If I stay in that chair any longer, I'm going to start thinking about the way that sweater fits his shoulders like it grew there. "I'll go grab my boots."

"Leave the truck keys," Simone says. "Maybe my uncle's boys will come tow it out. They owe me."

"Simone, you're—"

"Not a saint," she says. "Just very persuasive and in possession of embarrassing photos from my cousin's wedding." Her eyes sparkle. "Go. I'll send you with muffins. If your mother is cooking, you'll need backup sugar."

"She bakes just fine," Kingston says, appearing injured.

"She burns toast," Simone says.

"She doesn't."

"I ate it," Simone says flatly. "It was carbon with butter."

I can't help it. I laugh out loud, and Kingston slides me a look that is part warning, part helpless amusement. Vicky loves big family dinners, but she mostly orders in. Her house runs on a pecking order and a certain quality of love you can trip over if you aren't watching your feet.

I duck back to the mud room to tug on boots and grab my coat. My muscles are already beginning to tighten, the post-adrenaline tremble a reminder that I will pay for this morning's exertion with a chorus of aches tomorrow. *Worth it.* The helipad is clear. The vines are checked. The truck has a plan. There's a line in the day I can step over and call it progress.

Kingston joins me in zipping on a jacket, his whole attention bent to the motion, the usual way he gives himself to tasks. "Ready?" he asks when he's finished.

"As I'll ever be," I say. "Full disclosure, I've never flown in a helicopter. If you pull any stunts, I might never forgive you."

"No promises," he says, and the smile he doesn't quite

unleash is infuriating and fantastic.

We step out into the cold again, the air bright. Our footprints from earlier have softened at the edges, but the pad still gleams dark and clean as we approach, its doors locked open, the platform flush with ground, the machine sitting patient and precise like a hawk at rest.

Kingston moves with an easy certainty around his bird. He's done this a thousand times—checks a tie-down, runs a gloved hand along a seal, taps a gauge through the glass like he can communicate via osmosis.

"Come on," he says, opening the door and offering a hand I pretend I don't need but absolutely take because my pride doesn't want to test gravity today.

The step up isn't high, but my muscles voice their dissent anyway, and the heat of his palm leaks through my glove and skin into some place I won't name.

Once inside, the world shifts. Sound is different in here, padded and close. Leather and resin and a faint, clean note of machine fill my nose. I settle into a seat that hugs without apology and fumble with the four-point harness until Kingston reaches across and snaps the last latch. His sleeve brushes my arm, and I hold very still.

He hands me a headset. "Put this on," he says. "It'll keep the noise from eating your brain. And we'll be able to talk to one another."

"Tragic," I say.

"You love it," he says, deadpan, and for a second, it's exactly like being fourteen again, except absolutely nothing is the same.

I fit the headset over my hat. The muffs seal around my ears with a gentle, authoritative pressure. My own breath suddenly sounds intimate, like I've been moved to the inside of my body. Kingston slips on his headset and flips a row of switches. Systems come alive in a polite cascade—lights that blink, a soft whir beneath us, the rotor above beginning to turn slowly and then faster until the blades blur to a pale halo that makes the world look like it's trembling.

"Last chance to bail," his voice says in my ears, warm and richer through the headset. "We can just stay here and have dinner and roast marshmallows."

"If I say yes, will I still get Simone's muffins?" I ask.

"Nope. For that you have to fly, but if we crash, I'm sure she'll bring them to your hospital bed," he says with a smile.

"Up we go," I say, trying for brave but feeling somewhere near reckless.

Six

Kingston

The helicopter rises steadily, the rotors beating against the cold March air. Elise sits beside me, her braid tucked into her coat, loose wisps flying in the draft. The storm has cleared, but the valley below is still buried in white. Normally, I'd cross the lake in a straight shot, quick and efficient. Today I let the speed bleed off, following the shoreline instead. I tell myself it's so I can check the roads—see if the plows are keeping up, gauge whether people can get in or out of the valley. But strangely, I think it's also because I want to prolong this time that's just me and her.

The roads wind below us, partially visible like black scars against the snow. Headlights creep in long, frustrated lines. At one curve near the cliffs, the heavy snow has caused an avalanche, and the road is completely closed. That will take some time to clear. From up here, everything looks fragile—tiny vehicles against the immensity of the mountains.

"Roads aren't great yet," I murmur into the headset.

Elise presses her forehead close to the glass, eyes wide. "I've lived here twenty-eight years, and I've never seen it like this. It's like a whole other world."

Her voice is soft, full of awe. She's wonderstruck by a place that's been her backyard all her life.

I smirk. "You sound like a tourist."

"Maybe I should've been one all along." She doesn't look at me, only out, as if trying to memorize every snow-dusted ridge and frozen field.

For a few minutes, it's just the two of us and the hum of the rotors. When we crest over Paradise Hill, I bank wide, giving us a clear view of the winery buildings. The blackened skeleton of what used to be her and Tarryn's cottage scars the snow. Elise goes very still.

Her hands knot together in her lap. Her breath fogs the window in front of her. "It looks worse from up here, like the earth swallowed my whole life." Her shoulders have gone rigid. "I keep telling myself it was only things," she adds, voice trembling. "But they weren't just things. They were pieces of her—my mom's journals, the quilt she made me when I was young, a box of birthday cards she saved. Gone. And I'm twenty-eight years old, living with my dad, with nothing to show for her but—" She lifts her hand to the chain at her neck. The gold locket catches the last of the sun. "This. A locket with a baby picture of me. That's it. I wear it every day. And sometimes, it feels pathetic, like I can't grow up enough to let go. Like if I had moved out of Paradise and made a life of my own, I wouldn't feel so stuck."

Emotion rises in my throat. I remember not even being in high school when we stood at her mother's funeral—Elise in a little black dress, holding her father's hand like, if she let go, she'd disappear too.

"You still have her in you," I say, my voice thick. "I remember your mom."

Her gaze moves to me, wet and searching.

"She made my birthday cake every year," I tell her. "Not

just cakes—masterpieces. For my thirteenth birthday, when I was all hockey all the time, she made me an edible jersey. My number across the back, two gingerbread hockey sticks, and a puck. The puck was chocolate cake filled with cream, dipped in chocolate so it looked like a real puck. Nobody wanted to cut it."

Elise's lips curve. "I remember that cake. I was little, but I remember sitting in the kitchen while she worked on it. She loved making cakes. Said it was the one way she could give people something lasting, even if it was gone the next day."

I nod. "She wouldn't even let my mom pay her."

Elise gives a shaky laugh. "She wouldn't. My favorite was the last cake she ever made—for your mom. Pink, covered in flowers. She was exhausted by the cancer treatments, so I got to help pipe the petals. My hands cramped so bad, but she said I was a natural. We laughed all day." Her voice catches, and she looks back down at the ruined house. "That's the last time I remember her really happy."

I don't know what to say. What is it like to carry grief like that? Grief that still hasn't dulled. Actually, I suppose I do have some sense. Even now, Cara's betrayal can take my breath away at the odd moment.

Finally, I lower us toward the helipad at Paradise Hill, the vineyard buildings rising up around us. Elise stays quiet, staring at the scarred land.

Then the skids hit the ground, the blades slowing, the engine winding down. Her father is already waiting, a hand lifted against the snow blowing around as we land.

Elise unbuckles and waves. "I'll just pack a few things," she says, her voice clipped, all business now.

"Don't forget dinner," I remind her.

She nods. "I'll be back. Promise."

She hops down and crosses the snow toward her father, shoulders squared, her braid swinging.

I sit in the cockpit a moment longer, watching her go. She's grieving, weighed down by the fire, by what she's lost, by the life she feels stuck in at twenty-eight, still under her father's roof. And yet even in that grief, she shines. Her resilience. Her refusal to fall apart in front of her dad. The way she found a smile remembering frosting flowers with her mom.

The pull I feel toward her is undeniable, rooted in years of shared memories and in the strength she doesn't even realize she carries. *Why am I thinking about all this?* This does not at all match my pattern. I keep women at arm's length. Even the beautiful ones—especially the beautiful ones. But Elise is different. I knew her before I became the person I am now, and somehow, she keeps getting past my guardrails.

When I finally make my way inside the house, the warmth of the kitchen hits me like a wave—garlic, bread, something sweet baking. It's the same smell I grew up with. Tarryn is beside Mom, her sleeves rolled up, chopping a big pile of vegetables for salad.

"Need a hand?" I ask.

"Not from you," Tarryn says without looking up.

Mom grins, brushes past me with a spoon, and pats my back.

I take off my coat and shoes, get myself a glass of water, and lean against the counter, casual. "I overheard Elise earlier, talking with Simone. That guy in France offering her the exchange? He wants to get into her pants." I aim to make it sound protective, a brother looking out for her best friend, though once again, I'm not sure why I'm giving it a second thought.

Tarryn looks up now, one eyebrow raised. "Why exactly are you worried about Elise's pants?"

An excellent question. "I'm not. I'm worried about her," I insist. "The guy's slimy."

Her gaze sharpens, and I know she sees straight through me. "First of all, Elise is an adult. You don't get to decide what she does. Second, yes, he's into her. And I love that for her. She deserves to have someone to look at her that way." She stabs the knife into the cutting board for emphasis. "Third, she's my maid of honor. Which means she's not running off to France without coming back here to help me plan this wedding."

Mom drifts by again, touching my shoulder with a knowing softness. "Sometimes, people need to leave Paradise before they realize what matters most."

I don't have a response to that, so I stay quiet.

After a minute, Mom and Tarryn start talking wedding plans, and they still won't let me help, so I go in search of my brothers.

I find Ryker in the barn. The space smells of gasoline and oil, but the concrete floor includes a half-court Dad poured when we were kids. This is where we fell in love with the game. A single light dangles overhead, shadows swinging as Ryker dribbles.

"First to eleven," he calls.

"Loser buys beers for the week," Beckett adds as he walks in.

"Good thing I don't lose," I mutter, tugging on the old Toronto T-shirt I keep here.

Ryker smirks. "Cocky for a guy who's out of practice."

"Somebody's got to make the money to keep you two in sneakers," I shoot back.

The ball thumps and laughter echoes. For a while, we're kids again. Beckett trash-talks, Ryker showboats, and I find myself leaning into the rhythm. My muscles burn, and my lungs ache, but it feels good, real.

Beckett wipes his forehead. "Mom always said this court saved us from killing each other."

"She wasn't wrong." I grunt after blocking his shot.

Ryker checks the ball to me. "So. Elise. Why was she in your helicopter?"

I give them the short version—sabotage, the water main, the storm. Their laughter dies, replaced by grim faces.

"That bad?" Beckett asks.

"She's optimistic because the wet snow blanketed the vines, insulating them," I say. "But if she hadn't been there, we could've lost half the southeast vineyard."

Ryker scowls. "Zach."

Maybe. But I don't say that out loud.

We play on, though the energy has shifted. I can't stop thinking about Elise now—her braid swinging as she walked away, shoulders squared against the weight of her grief. And about how she belongs here at Paradise Hill, even if she doesn't fully believe it yet.

By the time Beckett's phone buzzes, we're all dripping sweat and grinning like idiots. He holds it up. "Twenty bucks says dinner's ready."

We laugh, shoulders bumping as we head back to the house. My legs ache and my shirt sticks, but I feel grounded. I want that feeling for Elise too. And for some reason, I want her to find it here, not in France.

Seven

Elise

Sunday dinners at the Paradise home are legendary, though as I told Kingston, Dad and I only come when invited. Thanks to Kingston, tonight, that's the case. The house glows against the winter dark, golden light spilling through tall windows, laughter carrying even through the heavy front door. My father straightens his coat like we're about to walk into a board meeting, and my heart pounds as well.

When Tarryn meets us as the door, I can tell lasagna is on the menu tonight. It's one of my favorites, and Vicky orders in from Nonna's. Their garlic knots are to die for, and it usually means tiramisu for dessert. Tarryn whisks our coats away, and in seconds, we're swept into the dining room, where the noise is already deafening.

Vicky's voice floats above it, warm and commanding, like the matriarch she is. Trace sits at the head of the table, stoic but with a dry glint of amusement in his eyes.

And then there are the kids—no, they're adults now, each with their partners. Greyson and Trinity beam over baby Theo, who's being passed around like a football. He just had his first birthday. Beckett and Sadie, who is finally showing her pregnancy whisper to each other, heads too close together for polite company. Ryker has Ginny draped against his side, smirking like they've got some inside joke no one else is privy to. And Tarryn practically glows with Declan at her side. Kingston, who looks like he stepped out of some glossy magazine spread, is also the odd man out. I can't help but notice that. He sits at the far end of the table.

For a moment, I imagine what it would be like if I truly belonged here, if I had a permanent place in this loud, loving chaos. The Paradises are a family who bickers and teases but always shows up. I feel a twinge of longing as I compare this to the quiet dinners I share with Dad, just the two of us—polite conversation and lengthy silences.

Vicky clasps her hands together, eyes shining. "All of my children, and their partners, and my sweet baby grandson. My heart could burst." Her voice catches, and the whole room hushes. "But don't think for one second I'm satisfied. There's still plenty of room for more grandchildren. And I expect each of you to deliver. Beckett, you and Sadie just keep doing what you're doing."

The room breaks into laughter, groans, and mock protests. Kingston mutters something about being too old to be threatened by his mother's matchmaking schemes. Beckett rolls his eyes and passes Sadie a basket of garlic knots like he's shielding her from the line of fire.

Then baby Theo squeals, and someone drops a spoon with a clatter. Ginny shrieks that Ryker stole the salad right out of her hand. Beckett and Ryker argue across the table about which vintage should have been opened—2015 or 2018—as if the fate of the universe depends on it. Greyson tries to swipe a roll off Trace's plate and nearly loses his hand. Trinity and Sadie loudly insist that their babies—current and future—will be the most spoiled of all the cousins, and Trace mutters that spoiled children aren't anything to brag about.

It's ridiculous, messy, and loud. A family in full swing. For a moment, I let myself smile at the pure beauty of it.

Then Kingston clears his throat. "Since everyone is here…"

The room stills, though Ryker keeps one arm draped around Ginny like he's bracing for impact. Kingston's gaze sweeps the table, his usual easy control edged with tension. "I need to let you know that the Black Bear vines were sabotaged. Elise and I have confirmed it. And I think someone should be staying at the property on that side to keep watch."

"Living there?" I ask aloud.

Kingston's eyes meet mine. "Well, I suppose so. I'm not there all the time. The vines are exposed." He thinks a moment. "You know them better than anyone. In fact, I can't think of anyone more capable than you." He says this like it makes perfect sense.

Tarryn jumps in before I can answer. "Hold on. Elise's work is all over the estate, not only Black Bear. You can't just move her like she's another piece on the board. And she's also getting ready for her exchange."

I'm still processing what she's said when Dad clears his throat. My stomach knots.

"Kingston has a point," he says. "I'm still working full-time. Black Bear's always been neglected. If Elise took it on when she returns, it would be a chance to show what she can do with her newfound knowledge, though we all know she's more than capable already."

I blink at him, the weight of his support hitting at the wrong angle. "So you agree?"

His brows rise, but he doesn't flinch. "You'd do better than I ever managed to. That's the truth."

A murmur runs the length of the table, all eyes on me. Waiting. Measuring.

I set my fork on the plate. "Thank you for the vote of confidence. Truly. But I'll remind you all, I leave Thursday for

Bordeaux." I glance from my father to Kingston. "France, in case anyone forgot."

Silence stretches.

"I can focus on Black Bear for these few days before I go," I add. "Check the vines as the snow melts. Beyond that...I'll need some time before I can decide what I want."

No one argues when I excuse myself.

The hallway swallows the sounds of silverware and voices, leaving me in the hush of my own thoughts. I force myself to take a deep breath, and behind me, the muffled voices grow clearer.

"She'll come around," Kingston says, calmly.

"She shouldn't have to 'come around,'" Tarryn snaps. "She's not your employee. You don't just get to decide."

"She's practically family," Beckett argues.

Ryker laughs. "Family or not, it's about time someone stepped up at Black Bear. That land's been trouble since the beginning."

I keep walking, jaw tight, until the side entrance to the kitchen comes into view. I turn in, not sure where else to go, and the smell of lasagna lingers. I grip the counter near the sink, steadying the rush of my thoughts.

Dad slips in behind me, closing the door softly. "Elise—"

I turn to him. "You couldn't back me up in there?"

His mouth tightens. "It's not about sides. You've proven yourself everywhere else on the estate. Black Bear needs you. They see it. I see it."

"That's not the point," I say quietly. "You could've reminded them it's my decision."

"I know." His voice is low, firm. "But sometimes having your back means nudging you toward the places you don't want to go."

I hold his gaze, unwilling to argue further, unwilling to break.

The door creaks again, and Tarryn slips in, her eyes full of apology. "Elise." She hugs me before I can protest. "I didn't know Kingston was going to bring it up like that. He should've asked, not announced."

I let out a breath against her shoulder, and then pull back. "I felt cornered."

"You were," she says bluntly. "But if he suggested it, it's because he trusts you. He doesn't trust anyone else to live in that house."

For some reason that feels good, though I only manage a small smile. "Maybe. Still felt like an ambush."

Tarryn squeezes my hand. "He bulldozes, but he means well. And Mom will still invite you to Sunday dinner no matter what you decide. Trust me. You're part of this family, whether you like it or not."

Kingston

I didn't mean it to come out like that at dinner. I know it sounded like I was volunteering Elise to move into my house. Like it had to be her. Truth is, I just want someone keeping an eye on the Black Bear vines. Someone I trust.

But I do like the idea of it being her. At least for a few days, until she's gone.

Now, she climbs back into the helicopter, jaw tight, shoulders stiff. I hand her the headset. She shakes her head and refuses, lips pressed together, stubborn as ever.

Fine.

I slip on my headset and lift us into the air. Once again, rather than cutting across the lake, I bank wide, following the road. I want to see the progress they've made on plowing where the avalanche slides covered the road, but there isn't much change. The commute from Black Bear to Paradise right now is probably a three-hour drive, if they can get through at all.

Thirty minutes later, the skids kiss the pad with a solid thump at my house, the chopper shuddering around us before settling. My pulse hammers at the way Elise sat stiff beside me the whole trip. She seems to have no desire to communicate with me.

I cut the engine, the rotors slowing overhead, the rush of wind whipping her hair across her cheek. For a second, I don't move. Neither does she, though the cockpit feels too small, too close, the hum of silence louder than the blades.

Before she can unbuckle, I reach across and rest my hand on her leg. My fingers curl lightly against the denim, not enough to hold her there, but enough to make her pause. Heat from her body seeps into my palm, sharp and distracting.

"I'm sorry," I say. "I didn't mean it had to be you. Just…someone. I'm not here enough. But in the meantime, if you need a ride back to the vineyard before this snow clears up, I can fly you. I'll take you. Anytime. And you're also welcome to use my car to get around if you need it."

Her gaze finds mine, startled at first. Then her shoulders lose some of the tightness she wears like armor. "Thanks," she says quietly. "Maybe at lunch tomorrow? You could drop me at Paradise Hill, and I'll figure it out from there. Or…get a new truck if the roads open."

I clear my throat, pulling my hand back, though inexplicably, I'd really like to leave it there. "Easy. Whatever you need."

She pushes open her door, cold air blasting in, carrying the sharp tang of fuel and snow. I climb out with her, boots crunching against the snow that's blown across the pad. For a moment, I just watch her, hair whipping in the wind, cheeks pink from the cold, the line of her jaw set.

I grab her bag from the back before she can, slinging it over my shoulder.

She tilts her head. "Show off," she mutters, but her voice isn't as sharp as before.

When the blades finally spin to a stop, Kevin steps out

from the edge of the pad.

"Elise, this is Kevin Nishida. He's my pilot and mechanic for the helicopter. You might see him around." I turn to Kevin. "Elise is from Paradise Hill, and she'll be here for a few days to deal with the grapes."

Kevin dips his head. "Sorry about not being here earlier. I got stuck up in Appleton at my girlfriend's."

I hold up my hand. "No worries. That storm was a monster. Anyway, Elise will need to get up to Paradise Hill most days. If I can't take her, I'll have you take her."

He nods. "Just let me know. Simone can always get a hold of me."

"Thank you," Elise says.

Kevin nods and moves toward the helo with easy familiarity, crossing to check the latches and begin the shutdown I've left for him to do. With steady hands, he straps the bird in place and will lower it into the below-ground garage. There he'll make sure it's fueled, polished, and ready for the next flight.

Elise and I start across the yard, our footsteps crunching in the snow on the concrete path. It glitters under the security lights, flakes catching moonlight like glass.

I point toward the shed built against the side of the pad, the metal stairs inside leading down. "Maintenance access," I explain. We watch Kevin click a button. He and the helicopter lower and the doors close. It's ready to go to bed.

"How does Kevin get out of there?" she asks.

"He has a huge garage down there to play around in, which opens up to the basement in the house. He and Simone have their own apartments."

She follows my gesture, then quirks a brow. "Do you ever think you've got too much money?"

I shrug, adjusting her bag on my shoulder. "Not really. I like what I can do with it."

She studies me, silent.

"I provide school supplies for every kid in the valley," I add because for some reason I want her to know. "And computers for the ones who can't afford them."

Her head snaps toward me. "You do?"

I nod. "We fund hockey too. But school—that's the real gift. That's how you change things."

She blinks at me, and her face softens. The anger's gone, replaced by something that makes my chest tighten. "That's…incredible, Kingston."

The way she says my name—quiet, earnest—burns straight through me. Suddenly, I don't care about money or vines or even the damn helicopter. I just care that she's looking at me like that.

"Should we have a drink upstairs?" I ask, wanting to spin this moment into…something.

She hesitates only a second before nodding.

We walk into the main house and change our shoes before she follows me into the living room. It opens up around us, floor-to-ceiling glass walls framing the valley. The fireplace glows in the center, flames rising from stone. Outside, moonlight skims the snow, throwing the world into silver.

"Wow," she whispers.

I set her bag by the stairs and cross to the bar, reaching for two glasses. "Whiskey? Or wine?"

She eyes the bottles, then me. "Whiskey. Neat."

Of course. Stubborn to the bone. I pour two fingers into each glass and hand her one, my knuckles brushing hers. A spark jumps at the contact, and her breath stutters just enough that I catch it.

She walks toward the window, glass in her hand. I follow, standing just behind her. The citrus of her shampoo mixes with the smokiness of the whiskey between us. She takes a sip, throat working as she swallows, and I have to look away before I stare too long at the line of her neck.

The stars are sharp tonight, scattered across the black sky like diamonds flung by a careless hand. "You know the constellations?" I ask, moving closer. My chest almost touches her back.

She shakes her head. "Not really."

I lift my hand, pointing. "That's Orion. See the belt? And

over there—Cassiopeia."

Her head tilts back, hair grazing my jaw. She turns slowly, and suddenly, she's facing me, her lips parted. Her breath mingles with mine, whiskey and warmth, and the world outside fades.

What am I doing? This is an entirely unfamiliar place for me. My heart pounds so hard I feel it in my throat. I lean down, just a fraction, every muscle tight. Her hand twitches like she might reach for me.

And then her phone explodes with "Urgent" by Foreigner.

We both jolt, and she curses, fumbling it out of her pocket. "Tarryn."

I drag in a breath, forcing a laugh. "You gave my sister that ringtone? Figures."

She's already answering, voice tense. "Hey, Tarryn."

I stand frozen as she slips down the hall, her footsteps fading.

The fire snaps. My mind reels with what almost happened. *What did almost happen?* Maybe nothing. But I can't stop seeing that look in her eyes. Can't stop feeling the ghost of her breath against my lips. And the strangest part of all, I was open to it, even though it was her, not some woman I'd found for that singular purpose.

I pace the room, glass in hand, the whiskey sloshing against the rim. I throw it back in one swallow, the burn doing nothing to quiet the restlessness in me. The bottle clinks as I pour another.

I can't stand the idea of Elise leaving, being with some smarmy Italian, though maybe that's the best thing for me. Clearly, I need some space to straighten out my head. She has to take this journey, but I hate that I'll spend it hoping she comes back.

Nine

Elise

Four days.

That's all I have left before I fly to France, and instead of feeling excited, I'm standing in Kingston's guest bathroom staring at my reflection like a fool.

The mirror has fogged faintly from the shower I just finished, blurring the edges of my face. I swipe a hand across the glass, revealing flushed cheeks and wide, restless eyes. I still feel the ghost of Kingston's hand on my leg from last night, warm through my jeans, steadying me as the helicopter landed.

God, what was I thinking?

My toothbrush hangs uselessly in my hand. My lips tingle, as if they almost remember what it would have been like, how close I came to leaning in, to closing the space between us. If Tarryn hadn't called at that moment… I don't let myself finish the thought.

After Kingston told me what he does for the next generation of Paradise—without any accolades or announcement—I saw him differently. My stomach knots. He's not the same person I grew up with.

Because Kingston Paradise doesn't look at me the way he did last night. He never has. He's too controlled, too busy, too…him. But his eyes were different, and I was leaning in to kiss him. That would've been a mistake.

A beautiful, dangerous mistake that I'd replay for the rest of my life.

I force a shaky laugh, pressing my palms to the cool counter. *What is going on with me?* I'm clearly freaking out. Having some kind of existential crisis before my trip. The bathroom smells of cedar and whatever crisp soap Kingston uses. Everything about this house feels like him—quiet, deliberate, immovable.

I set the toothbrush down and push away from the counter. The only thing I can do is bury myself in work. With that in mind, I find my focus, and I'm ready when Simone taps lightly on the doorframe.

"Hey. My cousin and his tow truck just pulled your truck to their shop," she tells me. "I can take you in to Black Bear."

"Oh! Great. I'll be right there."

She nods and returns downstairs as I rush to dress and follow her out.

The air today is crisp and damp with the scent of thawing snow as Simone drives me into town. Black Bear is smaller than Paradise, but in the summer, it bursts with energy, the lakes brimming with boats, the sandy beaches packed, and the vineyards rolling right down to the water's edge.

"I want to go to France one day," Simone says wistfully.

"I've never been," I tell her. "I'm so excited. And not just because of the wine, but because of the history."

She nods as she pulls up and parks at her cousin's shop.

The truck sits in the garage like a stubborn old friend, mud still caked thick along the tires and wheel wells.

One of the mechanics straightens from where he's been

crouched beneath the chassis as we approach, wiping his hands on a rag. "You're not getting this one back on the road."

I blink, trying to reconcile that with the perfectly straight hood, the uncracked windshield, and the body that still shines between the streaks of dried muck. "It doesn't look that bad."

"Looks deceive," he says firmly. He crouches again, shining a flashlight beneath. "That mud seeped into every seam and bearing. You'll never get it all out, and you'd pay double what it's worth trying. Better to strip it for parts."

I kneel, the concrete floor leaching cold through my jeans. My gloved fingers brush the mud crusted along the wheel, flakes breaking away damp and sour against my skin. "But it still runs."

He shakes his head. "Not for long."

My heart sinks. Another thing broken. Another reminder that nothing here comes without a fight. I stand, brushing my palms on my thighs.

Simone leans against the shop's front desk, one brow arched like she's been waiting for me to catch up. "You getting sentimental over a hunk of metal?" she asks. "One phone call, Elise. You'll have a new truck tomorrow. Paradise Hill will replace it without blinking."

I glare, my throat tight. "I'm the one who drove it into the mud. It's just…one more thing I have to fix."

Her gaze softens. "Then fight smarter, not harder. You didn't drive it into the mud on purpose. You were solving a problem, and it wasn't supposed to be that wet. Let Tarryn know. I doubt she'll be upset at you."

I exhale, the cold air of the garage carrying away what little warmth I have left. She makes it sound so simple, and maybe it is. But it feels like another burden piled on top of everything else.

By noon, Kingston has flown me back to Paradise Hill, and I'm at work. Thin sunlight pushes through the clouds, glinting off patches of meltwater that snake between the rows. The ground squelches under my boots as I trail my fingers along a cane, bark rough against my glove, brittle enough that it snaps under my thumb with a dry pop. Spring feels impossibly far away.

"Testing their strength?" Tarryn's voice carries across the row. She trudges toward me, cheeks pink from the cold, knit hat tugged low. Her breath fogs in white puffs.

"Just wondering how many we'll lose," I say, tugging gently at another cane.

She steps up beside me, studies the vine, then snaps a cane clean with a practiced twist. The sound is sharp, final. "Any that don't bud like they should—" She tosses the piece into the mud. "—we'll yank and replace."

"Let's hope it's not two hundred," I mutter.

"Already called the nursery. If we need grafts, they're ready."

We walk together, footsteps punctuated by the squeak of mud and the drip of meltwater from the wires.

"Every time I think we're steady, something else crashes down," I admit.

"I feel the same." She casts me a look. "We're always one frost, one storm, one broken tractor away from humiliation."

I huff a laugh. "Inspiring."

"Think of it as job security." She bumps my shoulder. "You'll never get bored here."

I glance at her, but she's already crouched over a vine, absorbed in her work.

We've gone a few more rows when she says, "Crew wants to throw you a send-off Wednesday night. Barbecue in the barn."

I stop. "For me?"

"Don't act surprised." She grins. "You're part of the family. They want to celebrate you before you run off to France. They're already arguing over food. Someone even suggested roasting a pig."

I blink at her, stunned. "They want to do all that…for me?"

"Of course." She shrugs. "You're out here every day, and you stand beside them year round, not afraid of doing whatever needs to be done. They see you as one of them."

I grew up on Paradise Hill, running through the vines with Tarryn, my best friend since I could walk. We've always planned to take over together once our fathers stepped aside. Now, I'm leaving for three months on this exchange, and suddenly, I'm not sure I want to go.

My throat prickles. "That's…really kind."

"They don't want you to go," she says softly. "None of us does, not really, though I understand a necessary step. But the barbecue is their way of saying that out loud, and hopefully, it convinces you to return."

"I don't know what to say."

"Say you'll come." She nudges me with a grin. "And maybe say you'll come back from France too."

I try to laugh, but it comes out thin. "I'll be there."

"I'm counting on it." She smirks, and then lets it drop when she sees me struggling not to cry. "Any word about the truck?" she asks after a moment.

"Simone's cousin thinks our best bet is to sell off the parts, as all the seals are full of mud. I'm so sorry."

But just as Simone predicted, Tarryn nods and waves that away. "Then that's what we'll do. It was likely about time to replace that one anyway. You need a reliable vehicle when you're out on these roads."

I resist the urge to gush my thanks and simply nod in return. The personal and professional are all mixed together for me right now.

We continue our work as the afternoon passes, and fortunately, the majority of the vines on this side of the lake seem poised to make their usual spring return.

As the sun begins to sink lower, the faint thrum of rotor blades rises, steady and rhythmic in the distance. My heart matches the beat, quick and uneven. After a minute, wind sweeps across the vineyard as the helicopter crests the tree line, whipping my braid loose and stinging my cheeks.

Tarryn lifts her hand against the glare of the sun. "Private chauffeur. Not bad."

I force a laugh. "It's practical."

She shoots me a sly look. "Have you been lonely out at Kingston's place?"

I shake my head. “Kingston’s been great. And Simone’s making mushroom risotto tonight, my favorite. He said he’d be done with his work in time to eat with us.”

Tarryn’s brows rise. “He usually eats at his desk and crashes. You’re making him sit at the table?”

Heat crawls up my neck. “Guess so.”

“See you tomorrow,” she calls, grinning as she steps back from the spray of snowmelt.

The helicopter lowers, blades whipping grit and water into the air, the ground trembling beneath my boots. I wave goodbye as Kingston steps down, tall and sure, his coat snapping in the gust, late sun gilding the sharp lines of his face.

The blades slow, the air settles, but nothing inside me steadies.

Ten

Kingston

The rotors build as we prepare to take off from my place on Wednesday at noon. The helicopter rises, and Elise and I skim out over the lake. In the last few days, the whole valley has changed, patches of green now pushing through the white. The road that was buried earlier this week now shows like a scar, cleared to a single lane. By tomorrow, two lanes will be open. The thaw is a reminder that seasons change whether we want them to or not.

Elise leans forward, her face soft. "I'm going to miss this," she says. "The valley, the air, the vines…" She turns to me, earnest. "This is the only life I want, you know? It feeds me in a way nothing else does."

My hand clamps on the collective until my knuckles ache. That's my truth too, the one I never say because it sounds like sentimentality when it's actually the only thing that keeps me sane. This land feeds me. Grounds me. Hearing Elise say it—without apology—strips me bare.

For a second, breathing is difficult. We've built lives that look nothing alike, yet here she is, articulating the thing that tethers me to this valley. In that way, we are the same. Perhaps this is why she seems to confuse my defenses in a way no one else has.

I clear my throat. "Yeah. I get that."

What I really want to say is, *You get me.*

We arrive at Paradise Hill, and the helicopter blades wind down. I ease us into place, the familiar vibration settling into my bones before I cut the engine. For the past few days, I've flown Elise over around lunch and back every night. She's given me a reason to leave my home office at a reasonable time and have an actual dinner with pleasant conversation. The rhythm of it has become…comfortable. Too comfortable.

And this will be her last night before she goes.

I tug off my headset, and she's already unbuckling, hair whipping in the last lazy swirls of wind. She laughs as she tames it with both hands, and the sound twists my heart. For a moment, I feel entirely untethered. None of this makes any sense. It's not what I want, not what feels safe.

"Thanks for being my chauffeur," she says.

"Guess this makes me officially out of a job."

"You'll survive."

I've liked having her under my roof. Her soft footsteps in the hall at night. The way she sings in the kitchen when she thinks I'm upstairs. The place already feels empty, and she hasn't even left for France yet. But that's just my confusion. Her departure gives me a chance to reset.

"You're staying with your dad tonight?" Despite myself, I reach over to unclip her harness before she can do it. My fingers brush the back of her hand, and she stills for a heartbeat, then pulls away gently.

"Yeah. One more night at home before…" She looks past me, out over the vineyard like she's trying to memorize it. "Tomorrow morning I fly to Vancouver. Then direct to Paris."

"And then the train to Bordeaux." I grimace. "That's brutal."

She shrugs bravely. "Part of the adventure."

She didn't have to make it that hard. She could've asked me to fly her. We could've taken my plane and skipped the layovers and the shuffle. Thirty-six hours of travel versus a smooth glide over the Atlantic. But she didn't ask. And I didn't volunteer. That would involve me even more deeply in this process, and I might have admitted I don't want her to go.

"You'll be jetlagged for days," I mutter.

"Probably." She smiles. "But I have the weekend to adjust. I don't start until Monday morning, so I'll deal."

There's that smile again. I want to bottle it.

I sigh as I lift her bags out of the storage compartment. When I help her out of her seat, my hand lingers at her elbow until I make myself let go.

Mitch comes out to meet us, his hat shoved back, smiling the way fathers smile when their kids come home.

"You got a few packages," he says, hauling her bags into the back of his SUV. "Amazon guy thinks we're running a warehouse."

Elise laughs, tucking hair behind her ear. "I needed a few things for the trip. After the fire…I don't have much."

"You staying for the dinner, Kingston?" her dad asks.

I glance at Elise. Her eyes are bright, waiting. "Yeah," I agree. "I'll stay."

"I'll run her home real quick," her dad says. "Then we'll see you at the barn."

They head off, and I walk into the main house and look for my mom.

I follow the clatter of pans to the kitchen. Mom looks up as I enter, her eyes lighting the way they always do when she sees me.

"Kingston." She wipes her hands on a towel and pulls me into a hug. "How are you? How did it go with Elise staying at your place?"

"Simone liked it," I say. "Having Elise around gave her

more to do."

"And for you?"

"I felt like I was here all the time." I already wish I hadn't come in here. This isn't a conversation I want to have. The ferrying, the meals, the late-night talks—days blurred. I didn't mind.

"That isn't what I asked," Mom says softly.

I rake a hand through my hair. "What worries me is this lothario she's running off to France to work with. I don't trust him. He's probably only interested in—" I clamp my jaw closed.

Her lips twitch. "And why does that bother you so much?"

"It just does," I snap. "Call it instinct."

Her gaze sharpens. "You're not worried about France. You're worried about losing her."

Her words are a dare. "She's important to Tarryn," I explain. "And the business. I want her to come back."

"And to you."

"Yes." It bursts out, and I grit my teeth. She's cornered me, and we both know it. How can my mother see things I don't even understand about myself?

Her eyes soften. "That's exactly how it was for me and your father."

"What?"

"I told him I had a job on Vancouver Island when my residency ended. Leaving was awful. But I did. And then, he wrote to me. Every day."

"Dad?" I blink. "He's never been a share-your-feelings type."

"Not with words spoken," she says, smiling. "But on paper, he poured himself out. I still have the letters tucked away. Our whole courtship was ink and envelopes."

Envy stabs inside me. My father—stoic, steady—found a way to put his heart somewhere it could be kept. I've never been good at saying what I feel or even knowing what I feel, in some cases. And the times I've tried haven't ended well. Sometimes, there's not even a point in putting yourself out there.

"One day," my mother goes on, "he asked if he moved to

the island, would I date him. I never expected it. He'd always been in love with his legacy here. So when he said he'd give it up, I knew he was serious."

She sets a plate down, eyes warm. "We lived there for eighteen months. When my contract ended, we came home and got married. You arrived ten months later. I've never regretted it. Not for a minute."

Her words leave me with a picture I can't shake—my father at a desk, lamplight on paper, writing truths he couldn't convey any other way.

Tarryn strides in like a storm, ponytail swinging. No hello. Just the hit. "Someone got in last night and messed with the cultivators and aerators."

"Zach?" I straighten.

"I don't know." She pulls out her phone. "Here. Look."

The footage is grainy, but a figure moves through the rows. The sodium lamps wash everything dull, but it's clear enough that I can see the man bend, finger the cultivators, and crouch at the aerators like he knows which levers matter.

My stomach knots. Seeing someone among the vines is worse than hearing boots on gravel. Elise's words echo, "*This land feeds me*." It feeds me too. And right now, someone's poisoning it in the dark.

Beckett and Ryker step in, their easy mood evaporating when they see our faces. Beckett takes the phone, and Ryker leans over his shoulder.

"Too tall," Ryker says after a beat. "Zach's lanky. This guy's got twenty pounds on him."

"But the way he moves," Tarryn argues. "That little hesitation before he touches anything. That's Zach. Or someone coached by him."

"Or someone setting him up," Beckett counters. "It's grainy. Could be anyone."

I squint. A flicker at the man's wrist catches the light—metal. Not farm gear. A watch. No one on the crew wears jewelry in the fields. Too dangerous. But he goes right to the engine. You have to know the cultivator to get it open so quickly.

"He knows what he's doing," I say. "That's not random. It's targeted."

Tarryn exhales, sharp. "So which is worse—Zach doing it, or Zach helping someone else?"

"Or the Dempseys," I add bitterly. Zach killed their prized vines too, and this may be retaliation.

We have a multigenerational feud going with the Dempsey family, who own a neighboring vineyard. We hoped that Ryker marrying a Dempsey would calm them down, except that Zach poisoned their award-winning crop of grapes last year and then ran off.

Ryker's jaw ticks. "Wouldn't surprise me. Evelyn never forgives, never forgets."

"This isn't about bruised egos anymore. If those machines go down, we lose weeks of soil prep," Beckett says, rubbing his neck.

Weeks. Lost vines. My rage sparks, low and hot.

"I'll talk to Ginny," Ryker says, already moving. "Have her reach out to her sisters. See if Evelyn's behind it."

"Be careful," Tarryn warns.

Ryker smirks without humor. "If the Dempseys want a fight, they'll get one."

"Come on," Tarryn says finally. "Everyone's waiting. Tonight is about Elise. We'll pick this up after dinner."

We step out onto the patio. As I look toward the barn, smoke from the grill curls into the cooling evening. Strings of lights cast warm pools across the lawn. Voices overlap, laughter bright against the knot in my chest.

Elise and her father have returned, and she now flushes under all the attention. Tarryn tucks her into a hug. "You didn't have to do this," Elise says, hands up, trying to wave it away. "Really. I'll be back. I promise." Her eyes shine a little too bright.

"And if you have to bring Sebastian with you, that's okay," Tarryn teases.

Laughter ripples. Elise groans into her hands. "Please stop."

I don't laugh. The name lands like gravel in my throat.

Sebastian—Italian accent, probably a perfect jaw, all hands and charm. I force a smile anyway.

Throughout the meal I watch her, the way she leans in when my mom speaks, the quick crinkle of her nose when she laughs, the way her fingers keep circling the stem of her glass, as if she needs something solid to hold. She fits here. She belongs here. The thought of her gone for even three months feels wrong, like cutting a piece out of the vineyard itself.

When the platters are picked over and the moon is climbing, I help her gather chairs because, of course, she's helping to clean up. Away from the chatter, it's just the scrape of metal on stone and her boots whispering beside me. Firelight softens the edges of everything.

She sets a chair down and faces me, her cheeks flushed from heat and her hair loose on her shoulders. "I'll miss you, Kingston."

I have no choice but to respond with truth. "I'll miss you too."

Her gaze flicks away, then back. "When I get back, I might…want to stay down at Black Bear a few nights a week to work on your vines."

Hope surges, reckless. Before I can think, I step close, and my hand slides to her cheek. She inhales, breath warm against my mouth, and I kiss her.

It starts tentative and slow. The second she leans in, it changes, slow and hot, like we've been circling this and finally collided. Her fingers fist in my shirt and every nerve wakes up. A small sound in her throat undoes me. My senses fill with the smoke on her sweater, the taste of wine and something purely Elise. My pulse pounds in my ears as the world drops away.

Then come voices. Too close. My brothers' laughter.

We break apart, breathless. She stumbles a step, lips swollen, eyes wide with shock and want.

Boots scrape stone outside the shed, and I shove the last chairs in, forcing my hands to steady. My chest heaves as I lean close enough that only she can hear. "I can't wait for you to get back." I don't know what those words mean, but in this moment,

I know they are true.

Her eyes meet mine, dazed and burning. She nods once, tiny but certain.

I step out to meet my brothers, the night air hitting skin that now feels branded. My mother's story flickers in my thoughts. Ink and envelopes may be too old school, but email might work. And truth written down because speaking failed may be a solution. Maybe that's the way to untangle my thoughts, understand them myself.

I've never been a writer. But maybe it's time I learn.

Eleven

Elise

The train rocks gently beneath me, a steady rhythm that should be comforting but only makes me feel more untethered. Thirty-three hours. That's how long it's been since I left Paradise, and still, I feel like I haven't landed anywhere—not in San Francisco, not here in France, and definitely not in my own head. My body is present, in a plush red seat with countryside blurring past the window, but my mind is still back in Black Bear Valley.

I pull out my phone and hit Sebastian's number before I can talk myself out of it.

He answers on the second ring. "Elise," he says warmly. "You made it."

"I did." I force brightness into my tone. "I landed this morning and just got on the train. Three hours to Bordeaux."

"Perfect. I will pick you up at the station." His voice dips lower, a smile in every syllable. "And tonight, I'll take you somewhere unforgettable."

My throat tightens. "I'm looking forward to it," I say because that's what he wants to hear.

When the call ends, I stare at the darkened screen. *Am I looking forward to it?* To him? I don't know. Every time I close my eyes, all I see is Kingston leaning toward me, the taste of him, the spark that made me see actual stars. I've been kissed before, but never like that, never in a way that made me question every plan I thought I'd made.

I set my phone down, breathing through the knot in my chest. The train rattles, people chatter softly around me in French, and the scent of roasted coffee drifts down the aisle. It's just normal life, but my world feels cracked open.

I log on to the train's spotty Wi-Fi, more out of habit than anything, and open my inbox. My heart trips over itself at the sight of his name. *Kingston Paradise.* My palms are instantly damp, and for a long moment, I can't bring myself to click it open.

A man clears his throat beside me, and I look up into the face of the train inspector. "Billet, mademoiselle?"

"Oh—yes." I fumble, handing over my ticket.

He scans it, and then lingers with a curious smile. "First time to Bordeaux?"

"Yes," I say, forcing a polite smile.

"And what brings you?" His accent makes the words smooth and easy.

"A job," I answer. "Just for a few months."

"Ah, you will love it," he says, eyes bright. "Wine, sunshine, long evenings—it's… How do you say? Perfect for romance."

I laugh lightly, though my pulse flutters. "I'll take your word for it."

He tips his hat, a twinkle in his eyes. "Bienvenue. Enjoy France."

When he moves on, I sink deeper into my seat. *Romance.* If only he knew.

My gaze falls back to the unopened email. I can't avoid it

forever. With trembling fingers, I tap it open.

> *Elise,*
> *I haven't been able to stop thinking about last night. That kiss. It's part of me now.*
>
> *The house feels different without you. Quieter, emptier. I didn't expect that. You once asked why my company is in Vancouver when I insist on living here in Black Bear. I couldn't answer then, but I can now. This valley is more than home. It steadies me, feeds me in ways nothing else can. When you told me it feeds your soul, I realized you understood me better than anyone else has.*
>
> *My mother told me recently that after her residency here in Paradise, while she worked on Vancouver Island, my father wrote her letters. She said that was how she held him close across the distance. I'd like to do the same with you if you'll let me.*
>
> *So this is my first. Just so you know, you are already missed.*
> *–K*

The train tilts around a bend, but it's not the motion that makes my stomach drop. It's him, the way he's put himself on the page, vulnerable in a way I've never known him before.

I press a hand to my lips, that kiss still alive there, and hit reply.

> *Hi,*
> *I made it safely to France. The flight was long, and I don't think I slept at all—at least partially because I couldn't stop replaying last night in my head. You kissed me, and every time I closed my eyes, I was right back there with you.*
>
> *Somewhere over the Atlantic, I caught myself smiling*

like a fool, and the flight attendant asked if I wanted wine. I almost said no – because nothing could distract me from the thought of you.

So yes, Kingston. I felt the stars too.

Write me. Please. I want to hear from you.
– E

After I hit send, I sit back, my heart caught between two worlds – Bordeaux waiting ahead but Paradise refusing to let me go. Out the window, the fields roll by in soft greens and browns, stitched with stone walls and dotted with villages where church spires rise above weathered rooftops.

Beside me, a woman who boarded with me in Paris sets down her book and turns toward me with a friendly smile. She looks about my age, maybe a little older, with shoulder-length chestnut hair and kind, curious eyes. "I'm Claire. Claire Logan," she says in North American-accented English.

I smile, relieved to hear English after hours of stumbling through half-remembered French. "Elise Anderson."

"Are you visiting?" she asks.

"Sort of." I link my hands in my lap. "I'm going to Bordeaux for a job exchange. I work at Paradise Hill Winery in Canada, but I'll be a vintner here for a few months."

"You're so young." Her brows lift, impressed. "The wine industry runs Bordeaux."

"It's a lot of hard work," I admit. "But I love it. My father's been the master vintner at Paradise Hill for more than forty years, so I grew up in the vines. It feels strange to be leaving them behind for a while."

She nods. "I know that feeling. I work in Bordeaux, but I've just come back from visiting my family in Massachusetts. The vineyards there are…different, but still, there's something about home, isn't there?"

"Yes," I agree, my throat tightening. *Home. Paradise. Kingston.*

Claire leans in, lowering her voice. "It can be overwhelming when you first arrive, but it helps to have someone who knows the place. We should be friends. I'll make sure you don't just work but also enjoy Bordeaux."

I like that idea very much, and we fall into easy conversation. She asks about harvests and soil types, and I ask her about Bordeaux, about the lifestyle, about the rhythms of living in wine country here compared to back home. She tells me about her favorite cafés tucked down cobbled streets, the farmers' market that smells like lavender and warm bread, the festivals in late summer when the grapes swell heavy on the vine. I listen, enchanted, scribbling mental notes.

By the time the train begins to slow, the sky outside is washed in honey-colored light. My nerves buzz with anticipation and something like dread, Sebastian waiting on one side, Kingston's words still echoing on the other.

Claire gathers her things, then fishes in her purse and pulls out a sleek, white card. She presses it into my hand. "If you want a break sometime—or just someone to explore with—call me."

I glance down, and my eyes widen at the bold black lettering. *Château*. My heart skips. "This is where I'm going."

Her smile brightens. "Really? Then we must meet for lunch at the very least. We'll be neighbors, in a sense."

The train glides into Bordeaux, the brakes squealing softly. I clutch her card, grateful for this unexpected kindness. I came here expecting to feel lost, untethered. Instead, I already have a connection, someone who might make this place feel less foreign. As the doors slide open and the crowd surges forward, I tuck the card safely into my bag.

The platform is crowded when I step off the train, people rushing in every direction with rolling suitcases. I spot Sebastian immediately—tall and impeccably dressed in dark jeans, a field jacket, and a very French scarf wrapped around his neck. He stands with a confidence that draws eyes without him even trying.

He strides forward and greets me with three quick kisses,

brushing each cheek before leaning in once more. It's warm but seems more familiar than a boss should be. I stiffen, unsure how to respond as I force a smile. Inside, unease twists through me.

The spark I entertained between us when we met is gone now—at least for me—and I realize it never should have been there in the first place. Sebastian was a welcome distraction, but that's not what I need now. Not what I want. I came here because I admired his talent and thought this opportunity would push me forward. But standing in front of him now, I realize that may not be clear to him. Suddenly, I feel the weight of expectation instead of excitement. His charm feels rehearsed, too smooth, and I wonder if I've stepped into something I can't quite control. I want to respect him as a mentor, but I hope I haven't started this exchange on unstable footing.

"It's good to see you, Elise," he says. "I've been looking forward to this."

"Me too," I manage.

Out of the corner of my eye, I catch Claire stepping onto the platform, and relief floods me. Sebastian turns, his face breaking into an equally warm smile for her. "Claire!" He greets her the same way—three quick kisses, his hand resting briefly on her arm. "Back from the States, yes?"

"Yes." She laughs. "And apparently, I've made a friend on the way. Elise and I shared the ride down."

Sebastian's brows lift, clearly pleased. "Excellent." He turns to me. "Then you've had the best possible welcome to Bordeaux. Claire is one of our most talented colleagues. You're in very good hands." He gestures toward the exit. "Come, I'll drive you both to the vineyard. You must be exhausted."

We pile into his sleek black car, the leather seat cool against my skin. Claire slips easily into conversation with him, the two of them catching up in rapid French, and I let the rhythm of their voices wash over me. I speak French, but as tired as I am, I struggle to keep up. My eyes close as we head toward the open countryside and my adventure.

Twelve

Elise

A little while later, Sebastian's car glides through narrow streets, French jazz soft on the radio. The city quickly falls away, replaced by open countryside. Bare winter vines stretch in endless, perfect rows across pale, gravelly soil.

"Look," Sebastian says, gesturing grandly with one hand. "Straight as soldiers. Discipline. Order. This is Bordeaux."

I lean toward the glass, studying the lines. He's right. They're not wild and unruly like the vines back home in Paradise. My vines cling to slopes, bending with the terrain, stubborn against the weather.

Tell Tarryn this, I remind myself. She'll laugh and say they look like recruits in formation. But she'll understand.

From the back, Claire murmurs, "It's beautiful. Like a woven cloth."

"Yes, ma chère, yes!" Sebastian beams at her through the rearview mirror. "Each row a stitch. A masterpiece." Then his eyes return to me, his smile sharpening. "But beauty is wasted if there's no one to enjoy it with. Non?"

I press my lips together, refusing to give him the laugh he wants. "The soil looks different," I say instead, keeping my tone neutral. "Lighter."

He leans across the console, as if my observation is intimate. "Ah, you notice. Gravel, limestone, clay. The cabernet thrives, gives power, backbone. The tannins live forever."

I focus on the scatter of white stones flashing in the sun. Home soil is darker, volcanic-rich, streaked with basalt. That's why our merlot ripens so lush, why our pinot holds such delicate layers. Another note for Tarryn is the sparkle in the dirt, almost like shards of glass.

Sebastian glances at me again, grin tilting. "Don't look so serious, Elise. You are here to work, yes, but also to live. You will charm the vines as easily as you charm me."

Claire laughs softly from the back, and I'm grateful for her presence, proof I'm not imagining the weight in his voice. I force a small smile, nothing more. "I didn't come here to charm anyone."

"Ah, but you can't help it," he says, clearly amused at my resistance. "It's natural."

I stare out the window, ignoring him. Excitement buzzes in my veins anyway. The chance to learn here, in this soil, under this sky, is too big to be diminished by his theatrics.

He points ahead. "Margaux, elegant, refined. And there—Lafite, Latour, St-Julien. You know the names, oui?"

"Of course," I murmur. *Who doesn't?* They're legends, wines locked in cellars, poured only on anniversaries, whispered about with reverence.

Kingston would scoff at the admiration, I think. But he would want to know what it feels like to stand here, to see them in person.

The road curves, and Château comes into view—turrets rising from golden stone, a line of cypress trees guiding the way.

The sunset paints the walls with a glow so rich it looks unreal, like something lifted from a painting. I draw in a breath. *This is it.* For the next three months, this is where I'll live, work, and learn.

Everything here feels older, steadier, as if time itself has been flowing through the soil for centuries.

Sebastian sighs dramatically, slowing the car. "Voilà. Home."

Not home, I think automatically. Not mine.

We stop in front of a tall, narrow stone building that sits in Château's shadow. It's practical, not grand—shutters weathered by rain, bicycles leaning against walls, laundry strung from windows. I'd imagined a romantic apartment with wrought-iron balconies and a view of the vines. Instead, this looks…temporary. Like a place you pass through, not settle into. *But that's what I want, isn't it?*

He parks, and we walk in. I'm pulling my luggage behind me.

Claire nudges her bag higher on her hip. "I'm just downstairs, first floor close to the women's restroom," she says. "You'll see. It's a bit like a college dorm."

College dorm? My heart sinks as she waves and heads off.

Inside, the stairwell smells of stone dust and lingering wine. My suitcase bumps against each step as I drag it upward, following Sebastian. By the third floor, my arms ache.

On the landing, a cluster of vineyard hands leans against the banister, their voices a jumble of languages—Spanish, German, and Portuguese. A man with a sun-browned face smokes a cigarette, the sharp scent curling into the stairwell. A woman holds a baguette under one arm, her boots still caked in vineyard mud. They look relaxed, like they belong here in a way I don't.

They pause when I appear, their gazes sweeping over my suitcase and wrinkled travel clothes.

"First day?" a tall man asks, his grin easy, teeth flashing white against his tanned skin.

"Yeah," I manage, shifting the suitcase higher. "Elise. I'm

Canadian. I'll be here three months. Job exchange."

"Ah, Jérôme Pelletier went to Canada," I hear someone say. "He's not coming back."

The woman with the baguette smirks. "You won't be climbing the stairs for long. Not with Sebastian circling."

He grins like a cat that's caught a canary.

Ugh. I need to make my intentions clear. I smile, keeping my voice calm. "Well, he can circle all he wants. I'm here to learn, not to be chased."

Laughter breaks out, a knowing chorus. Heat crawls up my neck, and my stomach twists.

The smoker flicks ash into a tin and shrugs. "I said three months too. Been five years."

More laughter. A younger guy with freckles raises his bottle of beer in mock salute. "Bienvenue à Bordeaux, Canada."

I smile weakly, dragging my bag past them, their voices echoing after me.

"We go up," Sebastian says. He starts up the stairs again, leaving me to wrestle my bag.

Maybe telling everyone there was no chance for anything between us was not my best move. I draw in a steadying breath, nod, and push myself up the next flight of stairs, lungs burning, sweat sliding down my face.

On the next floor, Sebastian opens a door with a flourish, grinning. "Your home while you are with us. Comfortable, oui? I will return at seven to take you to the welcome dinner." His grin lingers, as if the words carry more meaning than the invitation alone.

I nod, with a polite smile. "I'll be ready."

He closes the door behind him and is gone. The room is small—bare walls, a narrow bed, a desk with a lamp. Stark. Clean. And no bathroom, though I'm sure it's down the hall.

I let the suitcase fall with a thud and sit on the bed. The thin mattress dips beneath me, springs squeaking. This isn't the fantasy I imagined on the flight over. There's no charm, no glamour. Just a plain room five flights up and a borrowed life that I worry may not fit me at all.

My eyelids burn. I mean to unpack, to wander the halls, to find the bathroom. But instead, the weight of travel and jetlag pull me under. Shoes still on, jacket still zipped, exhaustion swallows me whole.

I don't even close the curtains before my eyes are too heavy to open again.

A sharp banging rattles my door, and I jolt awake, disoriented. *Where am I?* Oh—right. Château. I fumble for my phone. Nearly seven twenty. I'm late.

I swing open the door, and Sebastian looks me over. "You're going in your travel clothes?"

I look down. I'm still in the same rumpled outfit. "No. Sorry. I meant to change, but I sat down and must've fallen asleep." Truth is, I'd rather crawl back into bed than face dinner.

He shakes his head. "You made me climb these stairs again. We need to go."

"I just need a bathroom, and I'll change quickly."

"The bathroom's on the first floor."

I blink at him. "The building only has one?"

"No. But the femme toilet is on the first floor."

Not worth arguing. I grab a sweater dress and boots and hurry downstairs to get ready. I won't be as fresh as I'd like, but that doesn't matter. I'm here to learn from Sebastian, and that starts tonight at dinner.

Just a few minutes later, the car slips out of Château's gates and onto a narrow country road, headlights bouncing off stone walls and rows of vines that stretch into the dusk. The village is like a postcard—shuttered windows, wrought-iron balconies, cobblestones slick in the evening air. A bistro on the corner glows golden, its terrace crowded with small tables and locals bent over glasses of wine.

Sebastian pulls to a stop and slides out of the car with his usual flourish, opening my door, as if we're stepping onto a red carpet. "Quaint, non? This is real Bordeaux, not the tourist version."

Inside, the air is warm with garlic and butter. Wooden beams crisscross the low ceiling, and the tables are pressed together, covered in simple white cloths. He guides me to one near the window, orders without even glancing at the menu, and leans back in his chair, as if he owns the place.

"You will see," he says, swirling the glass of deep garnet wine the server sets down. "In a few weeks, this town will be overrun. Tourists everywhere, clumsy and loud. Like they own the vineyards." He says this like a curse, and I can't help but think of how many wineries back home survive on visitors like that.

"Isn't it good for business?" I ask, tearing off a piece of bread.

"Perhaps," he says with a smile. "But I prefer it like this. Quiet. Intimate."

The word lingers, and I busy myself with my glass of wine. It's smooth, like silk across my tongue. My stomach growls, reminding me I haven't eaten properly since the flight. The warmth of the wine spreads fast, heavy in my limbs. Close behind it, exhaustion claws at me, and it takes effort to sit up straight.

Sebastian watches me over the rim of his glass. "You should know something about me," he says. "I was not supposed to be a vintner."

"Oh?" I tilt my head, stifling a yawn.

He leans forward, elbows on the table, the low light carving sharp lines across his face. "My family has a vineyard in Italy. But I am the youngest of ten children. Ten! There was never going to be a place for me. The land, the cellar, the decisions—they belonged to my older brothers. Always."

I imagine him as a boy in the vines, watching his siblings step into roles he could never have. I'm almost sympathetic, except the way he says it—half bitter, half boastful—makes me wonder if he believes it or if it's part of the tale he's woven for himself.

"So," he continues, "I left. I went to South Africa and took a job with a vineyard there. They thought I was only a worker, but I showed them, eh? We created wines that won medals. People began to talk."

My dinner is placed before me. It's steak with a red wine sauce. The server tells me it's Entrecôte à la Bordelaise. One bite, and it melts on my tongue.

Sebastian is animated, gesturing with his hands, but I'm sinking into my chair. The warmth of the food—my steak is flanked by rich potatoes cooked in duck fat with garlic and parsley—makes my eyelids feel even heavier. I nod at the right times, though some of his words run together.

Still, I catch the gleam in his eyes as he sits back. "I wanted to be closer to my mother," he concludes. "She isn't well. So I came back to Europe."

I nod, though something in the way he says this feels rehearsed. His tone doesn't soften when he mentions his mother. His eyes don't flicker with worry. Instead, he drinks. It feels like a story he's polished before.

Sebastian continues talking, louder now, his hands sweeping wide, as if he's the star of a stage. He's charming, yes, but a little boorish. And I'm too tired to sift through and find what's real.

I think back to London, to the night we met last month at the International Wine Competition. We sat in a noisy bar and argued about wine culture and identity. The chemistry was there, strong enough to feel like a current under the table, but we didn't really act on it. We talked for hours, and he kissed me at the end of the night, but that was as far as I let it go. I remember feeling exhilarated by the conversation, not the man.

Now, with him flirting across the table and spinning stories that don't always add up, I can't tell if I'm seeing him differently because I'm tired or because of the vineyard hand's insinuation earlier, the comment about me not climbing stairs for long. Or maybe things shifted enough back in Paradise with Kingston to change the lens I'm using to view this experience.

Either way, the food is good, the wine is better, and I decide I don't need to solve Sebastian tonight. Regardless of what else he thinks may be on the table, I was invited here to learn, to see how Sebastian works, how he shapes the wine, what I can take home and use in my own vineyard. That's what matters. The rest is noise, no matter what he wants.

By the time we drive back through the vineyard gates, Château glows like a lantern against the dark. The main building is alive with noise, laughter spilling from the open doors, music pulsing faintly into the night.

Sebastian leads me there, rather than back to my room, and as we step inside, the foyer is packed. Glasses of wine glint in every hand, and the air smells of oak barrels and perfume. It's a full-blown party, bigger than anything I expected.

Across the room, Claire catches my eye. She lifts her glass in a salute, her smile quick and knowing. I smile back, grateful to see a familiar face in the crush of strangers.

Sebastian leans close, his voice low. "Would you like to see my apartment?" His grin makes the invitation clear. It's not at all about architecture.

I steady my shoulders, giving him the polite smile I've practiced since I arrived. "Thank you, but no. I think I'll take a shower and sleep all day tomorrow so I'm ready for work Monday morning."

His brows lift for a fraction of a second before he masks his expression with another smooth smile. "Ah. Very disciplined."

I nod, already edging away. "Bonne nuit, Sebastian. Thank you for dinner."

I slip toward the stairs, clutching the railing as I go down, letting the thrum of music fade behind me as the door closes. Tomorrow is for rest. Monday, for work. And no matter what Sebastian thinks, I'm here to work beside him, not fall into his orbit.

Thirteen

Kingston

I can't stop smiling at my phone. Elise wrote me back. Not only did she make it to France safely, but she admitted she's also been thinking about our kiss. She felt it too.

Now, I just need to determine what that means.

I set the phone down on the bench press beside me. My Saturday evenings are predictable—workout, protein shake, and maybe a late-night run if the weather's decent. Simone is off, so it's mostly just me and the silence. Tonight is no different until Greyson's name lights up my phone.

Greyson: Hall pass. Anyone free?

I wipe the sweat from my forehead with a towel, grinning. Leave it to my brother to turn fatherhood into a tactical operation, sneaking out like he's breaking curfew.

Me: Depends. What do you have in mind?

A bubble pops up almost instantly.

Greyson: As long as there's no baby duty, I'm good for anything.

I laugh. I can picture him, already halfway out the door.

Me: Meet at Mom and Dad's? We could hit Mikey's. Grab a drink. Play pool.

Greyson: Perfect. Seven?

I send him a thumbs-up and rack my weights, still buzzing with energy that has nothing to do with the workout. Elise's email is swirling within me, and a beer and a couple of rounds of pool with Greyson is exactly the kind of distraction I need, so I don't spend the evening analyzing and agonizing.

After a quick shower, I change into jeans and a button-down, rolling up the sleeves. I lace my boots and climb into the helicopter, lifting off toward my parents' place. The restless edge in me hasn't gone anywhere.

Greyson's waiting out front when I land, leaning against his brand-new Mercedes SUV. It gleams under the porch lights, the kind of car you buy when you've traded bachelor freedom for midnight feedings.

I spot the car seat strapped in the back and can't help grinning. "You've gone full dad," I call as I walk up. "A dad car, Grey. Next thing, you'll be wearing cargo shorts."

He smirks. "Don't knock it till you've tried it. And hey, you can join me in wedded bliss whenever you want."

"With whom?" I laugh, shaking my head. "Tried that with Cara, remember? Look how well it turned out. She left me for my best friend."

His eyes darken, just for a second. "He wasn't your best friend if he'd act on his feelings for your wife."

I shake my head. The truth of it still stings, five years later. But I'm not ready to crack that scar open tonight, especially since Elise has thrown my whole defense mechanism into shambles.

We climb in and make the short drive into town. Mikey's is buzzing when we walk through the doors—warm lights, music in the background, Shoreline Brewery's latest seasonal blend pouring from the taps. Half the crowd is people we grew up with, and we shake hands, clap backs, and trade a few stories before finally making it to the bar.

Two pints later, we're in the back room, settling in at our usual pool table. The clack of the balls echoes against the wood-paneled walls, muffled by the conversation bleeding in from the main bar.

Greyson racks the balls with deliberate precision, like he's setting up a surgical tray. I lean on my cue, watching the triangle fill.

"You've really gone soft," I say as he lines up the break. The cue ball smacks, scattering solids and stripes in all directions. He sinks one, then scratches, and I grin. "Completely settled."

He straightens and gives me that calm little smile he's worn ever since meeting Trinity. "Settled and happy. There's a difference. And I hope you find it too." He leans on the table, casual, easy. "Trinity and I are already talking about taking the baby to Tokyo Disney when he's old enough to enjoy it. Can you believe that? Me, standing in line for rides with a toddler."

I blink at him. "Tokyo Disney? Since when did your vacations stop involving cocktails on the beach and whatever nightclub stayed open latest?"

Greyson laughs, the sound warm. "Those trips were fun. But this—this is better. It feels like building something instead of chasing something."

I chalk my cue slowly, the dust clouding my fingers. He's right. He seems happier than I've ever seen him. Part of me envies that ease. The other part tightens, the old scar throbbing where Cara cut me open. Her betrayal still burns, years later. I can taste the bitterness of it. So when Greyson talks about happiness, about building a life, all I think is how easily it can crumble. And how do you ever know for sure? How do you take that risk?

"What about that lawyer in Vancouver? Thought you were serious about her." Greyson bends low over the table, cue sliding through his hand. He doesn't rush.

"Naw. It's casual. We're both focused on our jobs. Plus, she doesn't want to live outside the Vancouver area."

He hits, misses by an inch.

"I always feel anxious there," I continue. "It's not for me. So there's no future with her." I circle the table, fingers skimming the cool edge.

"If you loved her, you'd move." Greyson repeats back to me what I told him when Trinity returned to Vancouver.

"I suppose that's true," I agree as I line up, exhale, and sink another stripe. The ball rolls true, crisp against the back of the pocket. "And I never said I did."

Grey found the person worth bending for. I thought I was done with that. Though if I'm honest, I don't feel quite as certain as I once did.

That thought startles me. For years, I've told myself love is a slow collapse, something you survive, not something you seek. But when I think about Elise, I feel different.

"What about you?" he asks. "What are you doing to meet women?"

I laugh once. "Look around, Grey. I'm in a closed room playing pool with my *married* brother. I'm clearly just waiting to see who I meet."

He laughs, shaking his head. "It's not like someone's going to show up on your doorstep."

Elise did, my mind counters immediately. Snowstorm, vines, everything. She's been part of our family forever. And she's not just my little sister's friend anymore.

I roll the cue ball in my palm, gripping it before I set it down. I bend low, aim, and drive the eight into the corner. The sharp crack reverberates through the room, leaving silence in its wake.

"Guess I'll wait and see," I tell him, not willing to divulge any more.

Greyson claps me on the shoulder. "You always were stubborn."

We finish the game, order one more round, and then step out into the cool night. The neon glow of Mikey's spills across the pavement, laughter and music following us out. Greyson drives me back to Paradise Hill and my helicopter. I watch him drive off to his family, and a hollowness settles in my chest. I had that once—or thought I did. Cara proved me wrong, proved how fast a promise can turn to ashes.

I fire up the engine, the blades chopping the night sky. Despite my fears, and my vow never to hurt that way again, Elise's email rings through me like a secret song. She hasn't stopped thinking about that kiss. Neither have I.

As I rise into the sky and head for home, I let myself wonder what that means.

Fourteen

Elise

In the morning, Sebastian greets me with the kind of warmth that could make anyone feel special. His smile is easy, his voice rich and rolling with an Italian lilt that makes even the word *fermentation* sound elegant.

"Elise, ma chère, today you see what true winemaking looks like," he says, offering me his arm like we're about to stroll into a ballroom rather than a cellar.

I don't take it, but I smile politely. "I'm looking forward to learning."

"Learning, yes. But first, seeing."

I fall into step behind him, and he spends the morning guiding me through the sprawling Château, weaving stories of generations who cultivated the land, perfected the blends, and built a reputation the world envies. His gestures are wide, dramatic, and more than once his shoulder brushes mine as we walk the narrow paths between towering tanks and endless rows of barrels.

He pushes open a heavy oak door and ushers me inside. The air is instantly cooler, damp stone breathing against my skin. Rows of barrels stretch into the shadows, their curved bodies glowing faintly under soft amber lights. The scent is rich and layered—vanilla, spice, toasted wood, and the faint tang of fermenting fruit.

"Our barrels," Sebastian says proudly, trailing his hand across the smooth surface of one. "French oak, of course. Some toasted light, others medium, each giving the wine a different whisper. We replace them every two years."

I follow the sweep of his arm. There must be thousands. At Paradise Hill, we're proud of the three thousand oak barrels and two thousand stainless steel barrels we use each year. This room alone could hold ten times that. Kingston would probably run his palm across one of these barrels too, but with reverence, not the showmanship Sebastian wears like a second skin.

"Do you allow them to rest for long?" I ask, trying to sound knowledgeable.

He nods, pleased. "Two years, sometimes three. It depends on the harvest, the blend. You will learn to taste the difference." His smile lingers on me a beat too long, and I bite my tongue so as not to remind him that I, too, grew up in a winery and have been tasting wine since I could walk.

As we exit, one of the younger women on staff passes by, clipboard in hand. Sebastian greets her with three cheek kisses, his hand covering hers as he questions where she disappeared to last night. She laughs, ducking her head, cheeks flushing bright pink before hurrying away.

The exchange is harmless enough on the surface, but the way she glowed under his attention sticks with me. I'm glad I see more clearly now this game Sebastian plays with women.

The next space hits me like a wall. The heat and noise are immediate—the hiss of steam, the metallic clank of valves, the low rumble of pumps pushing juice from one place to another. Stainless steel tanks rise around me, so high they disappear into the rafters. I crane my neck, dizzy with their sheer size.

Sebastian watches me, amused. "You look like Alice in Wonderland," he says with a laugh. "Everything too big, too strange."

"Not strange," I manage, raising my clipboard higher against my chest. "Just…different."

Paradise Hill's tanks are squat and humble, lined neatly in a single row. Here, they loom like skyscrapers, dwarfing everything else.

He steps closer, pointing to a valve at chest height. "This tank alone holds more than your entire harvest back home, non?" His grin is teasing, not cruel, but it still makes me bristle.

"Size isn't everything," I reply lightly.

He laughs again, seeming delighted, and the sound echoes off the steel.

We continue on until the corridor opens into a room alive with clattering machinery. The air smells of cardboard and fresh cork, the sharp tang of sanitizer biting my nose. Glass bottles stream down a conveyor, their clinking creating a kind of music—fast, relentless, mechanical. Workers in hairnets and gloves hover along the line, catching errors, sealing boxes.

I pause, stunned. "You bottle here? At this scale?"

"But of course." Sebastian leans in, lowering his voice. "It's not romantic, I know. But necessary. Wine is art, yes, but also business. If you wish to survive, you must understand both."

His words give me a bit of a jolt. Business has never been the heart of Paradise Hill. It's family, tradition, soil. Here, watching wine packaged and boxed like any other commodity, I feel that difference more than ever.

I nod slowly, committing the sight to memory. If nothing else, it's a point of reference.

We step back outside, and I gulp in the fresh air, grateful for the break from the clatter and steam. The sun stretches long across the rows of vines, each one perfectly manicured, their leaves shivering in the light breeze.

At noon, Sebastian leads me to the staff cafeteria. It isn't glamorous, but it's full—long wooden tables crowded with workers in coveralls, boots kicked off at the door, laughter echoing against the stone walls. I look over at the wall for today's menu.

Entrée: Country pâté with cornichons and baguette
Plat Principal: Boeuf bourguignon avec pommes vapeur
Accompagnement: Haricots verts
Fromage: Comté, Theome de Savoie, and chèvre
Dessert: Tarte aux pommes maison
Vin du Jour: Bordeaux rouge (2019)

I blink at the menu. "How can you eat all of this and work in the afternoon?"

He shrugs. "We eat slowly, and sometimes we take a nap. Our midday break is three hours."

I look at the clock. "Three hours?"

"Of course," Sebastian says with a grin. "This is France, ma chère. The vines don't hurry, and neither do we."

Back home, lunch is a sandwich at your desk or maybe a stolen half-hour in the shade. Here, workers settle in like it's a sacred ritual, wine glasses filled from a jug at the center of the table. Kingston would shake his head at the indulgence and probably tease me for falling into it so quickly.

I pick up a tray and follow Sebastian down the line.

He carries his tray like a king, greeting everyone he passes. I trail behind and take a spot near the middle of a long table, wedged between two vineyard hands. Conversation ripples around me in rapid French, and I catch only pieces—vendange, harvest, famille.

One of the men, gray-haired and smiling, nods toward me. "Alors, la Canadienne."

I straighten, remembering my grandmother's lessons, and answer in French. "Oui, je suis Canadienne. Je viens de Colombie-Britannique."

For a second, they all stare. Then laughter bursts out around me.

"Ah, l'accent!" one of them says, dragging out the

syllables in mock imitation. Another claps me on the back, grinning.

Heat floods my cheeks. My accent—French Canadian, not Parisian—must sound clumsy to their ears.

Sebastian only smiles, sipping his wine. "They laugh, but they are pleased you try. Don't stop."

I force a smile and continue, stumbling over my verbs but determined. Every correction, every chuckle stings, but I push through, answering again and again, refusing to switch back to English. By the time the woman beside me gently corrects my phrasing, I can feel the knot of embarrassment loosening.

Once I've finished my lunch and mopped up the sauce with bread, I feel strangely lighter, like I've passed some unspoken test.

Across the table, Sebastian leans close to a younger staffer, saying something low in her ear. She laughs, brushing her hair over her shoulder, and he moves on like it was nothing.

I chew my bread, unsettled. *Is it the culture? Is it him?*

And then, not five minutes later, I catch him talking with one of the older male vineyard workers. There's no smile, no teasing, no touch—just a quick, businesslike exchange about deliveries. It's all clipped words and brisk nods.

That unsettles me too. Maybe it isn't a game. Maybe it's just me, seeing things that aren't there.

Sebastian rises, brushing crumbs from his scarf. "Come, Elise," he says, gathering his tray. "The vines don't hurry, but the cellar waits for no one. It's time you begin."

The rest of the staff lingers over their wine, but I follow him out, still chewing on my doubts.

The cellar smells like damp stone, sour must, and sweat. Sebastian points out the water spigots and explains that I'm to spend my afternoon cleaning. I'm startled because this is work usually done by a vineyard hand. But I don't complain.

By the time Sebastian finishes his instructions and disappears with his glass in hand, I'm already dripping with sweat, the coarse rag rough against my palms as I scrub sticky residue off the concrete floor. Every inch of my skin feels clingy—

under my boots, tugging at my shirt, matting my hair against my neck.

The hose slithers across the floor like it has a mind of its own. It's thicker and heavier than I expected, the rubber ridges digging into my hands until my skin feels raw. I drag it from vat to vat, water sputtering as I spray, but the weight pulls back, straining against me.

When I yank too hard, the nozzle jerks loose, and a jet of water blasts upward. Cold spray catches me full in the chest, soaking through my shirt. I let out a strangled yelp and stumble backward, my heel sliding across a slick patch. For a terrifying second, my arms pinwheel, but I manage to catch myself against a barrel, heart hammering.

Across the room, a couple of workers laugh, muttering something in French too quickly for me to catch. Their voices echo, and my cheeks burn hot. Anger flashes in my chest. I didn't come here for this. I came to learn. But swallowing my emotions, I grip the hose tighter and bend back to work.

My shoulders scream with each tug, the ache running down my spine. My hands are already tender, the skin now reddening where the rubber has rubbed them raw.

A shadow falls over me. One of the older workers—broad shoulders, sweat-darkened shirt—steps in, steadying the hose with one hand while I fight with the coupling. His English is thick but kind. "Everyone starts here," he says. "Even him." He jerks his chin toward Sebastian, who I just catch a glimpse of as he disappears down another aisle.

I let out a shaky laugh. "Good to know. But I'm only here for a short time, and I'm here to learn."

The man shrugs, offering a quick nod before moving on.

His words are meant as comfort, but they don't change my plight. Three months. That's all I have here. And if I spend them doing the work of a cellar hand, I'm not going to learn anything about vintages or blends or how a place like this builds its reputation.

Still, I plant my boots, coil the hose again, and force myself through another stretch of floor. Every pass of the spray feels like both punishment and promise. If this is how he wants to test me, fine. But I won't let this be the only thing I take away from France.

When I finally stumble back to my room that evening, every muscle screams. My clothes are damp with sweat and the lingering chill of the hose incident. I peel them off piece by piece, dropping them in a pile by the door, and stand for a moment in my sleep pants and T-shirt, staring at the plain white walls.

This morning, I walked through the barrel rooms with my chest full of wonder, marveling at the scale of it all. Now, my body aches, my palms are rubbed raw, and the only thing I've learned is how hard it is to keep a hose steady.

I sink onto the narrow bed, pulling my laptop from the nightstand. My fingers hover over the keyboard, and after a long moment, I type the first words that come to mind.

You wouldn't believe the size of this place…

I pause, staring at the line. I imagine Kingston reading it, picturing me here, covered in grime and doubt. My throat tightens. If I send what I'm really feeling, I'll be admitting that I'm in over my head.

Slowly, I type the words. The screen looks wounded as I edit and reedit through my confession.

It feels good to have it written down, but maybe that's enough. I change my mind. *No.* Kingston doesn't need to know how small I feel here. Not yet.

I close the laptop, slide it into the drawer, and switch off the lamp. My body aches, but beneath it, a spark refuses to go out.

Maybe today was just part of joining the team. Or maybe it was something else. Sebastian can underestimate me all he wants. I'll find my own way.

Kingston

Before I go to my parents' house for Sunday dinner, I sit at my desk with a mug of cold coffee and type out a letter to Elise.

Subject: For your second week

Elise,
Hello from Black Bear. You wrote that you barely have a spare minute these days, so I can only imagine the pace they're keeping for you. Still, I have no doubt you'll find your rhythm. You've always had a way of absorbing more than anyone expects, even when you're stretched thin.

You asked what I've been working on. Most of my time

has been tied up with Renew Motion. We've got a new joint we're refining, and we believe we're close to something special. It feels good to sink into the work—clean, straightforward, nothing like the politics of wine. I try not to get tangled in vineyard business anymore, but Sunday dinners have a way of pulling me back in.

That said, I've been keeping a closer eye on my land. After the water main was set to run during the snowstorm, I realized being "too busy" isn't an excuse. I check things myself now. Slower, yes, but safer. You don't have to worry about the vines while you're away.

Your stand-in made quite the impression while I was in Calgary. I came home to find out he'd thrown a party big enough to make Simone call the police. She's still fuming and keeps asking when you're coming back to restore order. I told her not soon enough.

For now, though, I like imagining you in those vast French cellars, studying their techniques, storing away every detail. It reminds me that what we're both working toward—here and there—will matter when you come home.

The house still feels different without you. Quieter. And there's a chair at Sunday dinner that should be yours.

Write me when you can, and tell me about the people you're working alongside. I want to know the names and faces that make up your days.

Always,
Kingston

I hit send, shut down the laptop, and pull on my jacket. Dinner isn't for another hour, but as I told Elise, these days I like to walk the vineyard before I go. The air is sharp with evening chill, the rows long and bare, still waiting for spring to wake them. I pass the spot where Elise's truck got stuck during the storm. The rut it left behind remains, ugly and deep. I make a note to have it filled before it causes trouble.

At the helicopter pad, I run my checks—rotor, fuel, gauges. The blades roar to life, and soon, I'm rising over the rows, banking out across the lake. From up here, the valley looks endless—vineyards stitched to the hillsides, the lower lake stretched long and silver. It's sixty-five kilometers end to end, though barely ten wide. Driving around takes over an hour. Flying? Just under eight minutes when you're not meandering.

I set down on the strip beside the main house, and Dad's already crossing the lawn, hands shoved in his coat pockets.

"Today was a record," he calls as the blades spin down. "Seven minutes, fifty seconds."

"Beats cursing through traffic," I say, climbing out.

He grins. "Your mother prefers this too, though she'll never admit it."

We fall into step as we move toward the house, gravel crunching. The windows glow with light, silhouettes moving inside. I glance at him. "What about you two? End of the year's coming fast. What happens after retirement?"

Dad makes a face. "Your mother wants to go on one of those cruises. Europe, then Asia. A floating hotel with three thousand strangers. Not my idea of fun."

"But you'll go?"

"She's earned it. Forty years of putting up with this place? She gets what she wants."

I nod but veer toward the barn. "I'll meet you inside."

The old building smells of hay and oil. Tarryn's office is tucked into one corner, its walls plastered with maps, notes, and security printouts. She's bent over her laptop when I step in.

"Don't you ever take Sundays off?" I ask.

"Not when someone's cutting corners," she says without looking up.

I lean against the doorframe. "How's Elise doing?"

That gets her attention. She brushes hair from her face.

"Busy, tired, but positive—always is. She admits she's stuck with more grunt work than time with Sebastian, but she still calls it a learning opportunity. That's Elise for you."

I keep my expression neutral. I'm not ready to tell her that Elise writes to me or how I wait for her name in my inbox. "How is the guy who's here in her place?"

"That's a better question for Mitch, but from what I understand, Jérôme isn't good for much more than hand work."

"He's used to a bigger operation and more targeted duties," I surmise.

Tarryn shrugs. "Look at this," she says, swiveling the laptop toward me.

The infrared footage shows a figure crouched near a tractor, hands glowing against the machinery.

"What am I looking at?"

"Brake lines," she says, her voice tight. "He cut them. If one of the guys had taken it out on the hill, it could've been catastrophic."

Papers are scattered across her desk, half-drunk coffee cooling beside her. She's restless, wound tight.

My jaw hardens as I study the shadowy figure. "That's not Zach."

"No," she agrees. "Not his build, not his gait. But whoever it is, they knew exactly what they were doing."

"Have you told Mom and Dad?" I ask.

She sighs. "They've seen the footage, but without proof of who's behind it, there's not much we can do. They still want to keep it quiet."

I understand that, but the idea of brake lines cut clean through sends a zing of fear through my blood. The string of sabotage has been unending, and eventually, someone is going to get hurt. I need to help her figure this out.

Dad's voice carries across the yard, calling us in.

I rest a hand on her chair. "We'll find out who's behind this. But you're right. It's not Zach."

Her jaw sets, and she nods.

Together, we cross the yard and step into the glow of the

dining room. The table can seat twenty-four, but tonight, it's just Mom and Dad, me, Tarryn, Greyson, Trinity, and Theo in a highchair. More empty chairs than full ones, but Mom has food like an army's on its way. Theo pounds his spoon on the highchair, shrieking with glee. A second later, he slaps both hands into his mashed potatoes. A glob sails across the table and lands squarely on my sleeve.

The group erupts in laughter.

"Well," I say, dabbing at the mess, "guess I'm officially Theo-approved."

Greyson grins. "Badge of honor."

"Better aim than Beckett's jump shot," I add.

"Hey," Tarryn cuts in, smirking. "Don't insult Beckett when he's not here."

"Doesn't stop me when he is," I counter, earning another round of laughter.

Theo squeals again, reaching for his father with a potato-smeared hand.

"My son's out to get me." Greyson says, leaning back.

"Payback for those three-a.m. diapers you sleep through," Trinity teases.

Dad shakes his head, smiling. "Reminds me of when you lot were kids. Food fights every other Sunday."

"They were better behaved than that," Mom says primly, but her lips twitch. "Except Kingston. He was the ringleader."

"Allegedly," I say, raising my hands.

"You once fed mashed peas to the dog," Tarryn adds.

"And succeeded," I remind her, earning more laughter.

Theo smears more potatoes across his tray. Trinity's giggling so hard she has to wipe her eyes. Dad jumps in with a story about me climbing the trellis when I was four, getting stuck halfway up, and yelling at the top of my lungs until he pulled me down. My ears burn, but I can't help smiling.

For a moment, as the table ripples with warmth, I think of Elise. It surprises me, but I can't deny it. She's on my mind in a way no woman has been for many years. She would tease me mercilessly about the potatoes on my shirt, join in with this laughter, and maybe even steal the spoon from Theo to join his chaos. The thought of her laugh stirs something in my gut.

But then Greyson clears his throat, his tone quieter now. "If we could talk business for a moment, there's the matter of ongoing sabotage around here. Tarryn and I went through the security tapes again. Whoever cut those brake lines was not Zach."

The laughter dies.

Mom frowns. "Not Zach? Are you certain?"

"Positive," Greyson says. "And the same man was caught on tape yesterday, tampering with the fermentation tanks."

Dad swears under his breath. "So someone's targeting us. But if not Zach…"

"It's not Max," I cut in. "And the Dempseys wouldn't risk something so sloppy."

"Then who?" Tarryn asks. "Could it be someone we've hired?"

Trinity hesitates, glancing at Greyson before speaking. "I'm not sure we should be so quick to dismiss the Dempseys. Franklin's son, Dylan, he's been around, asking questions. He's got the same edge his father had."

I picture Dylan the last time I saw him, leaning against the wall at Mikey's, restless, jaw tight like he was itching for a fight.

Dad shakes his head. "That boy's trouble. But accusing him without proof would light this valley on fire."

"I'll get proof," I say. "We have a private investigator at Renew, and I'm going to reach out to him. Whoever's behind this, he'll find them. And we'll stop them."

Theo drops his spoon again with a clatter, the sound echoing in the silence. Tarryn meets my eyes across the table, gratitude and fear mixing in her look. Mom lays her hand over mine. "Hire the private investigator, but you've got a lot on your plate. Let Tarryn do this."

I squeeze her hand, but I don't answer. She's right. I don't want to take over for Tarryn. She's more than capable. I just have the money to finance this, and I haven't seen all the P&L statements to know how flush the vineyard is these days.

Dinner carries on, but I barely taste a thing. When the plates are cleared and Mom shoos everyone toward the living room for dessert, Dad catches my shoulder. He steers me out to the porch, away from the others, under the silver moon.

"You can't let this sabotage take over your own work," he says. "You've got your company, and Tarryn and I will figure this thing out."

I stare out at the rows, jaw tight. "I have more money than my grandchildren's grandchildren will ever be able to spend. Let me get you some professionals. I want to protect us."

"Protect us, yes," he says. "But don't lose yourself in the fight. This place needs you whole."

I nod as he steps back inside. I don't tell him what churns inside me, that the vineyard weighs on me, that being the oldest means I've always carried the responsibility, despite walking away. That I can still see Tarryn's cottage burning and all the sabotage we've endured in the last three years.

A vibration in my pocket seizes my attention. I pull out my phone and see an alert glowing on the screen—Elise. An email, waiting. I don't open it, not yet. I just hold the phone in my hand, her presence somehow steadying me for a breath, reminding me of all the reasons to fight for land and legacy.

I look out at the silver rows stretching into the dark and make my vow all over again.

Sixteen

Elise

I wake to the ping of an email. I'm working through my second week here at Château, and for a split second, I worry it's something from Sebastian or one of the vineyard staff, another list, another reminder of something I'm not doing right. But when I see Kingston's name, my whole body loosens. He's done just as he promised and emailed me every day.

I sit up in bed, tug the duvet tighter around me, and click it open. Just a few lines, but they're enough to warm me more than the weak sun spilling through the shutters. He thought of me. He misses me.

God, it makes this Monday morning feel like it could actually be good.

I want to write him back immediately, pour out all the ways I miss him, how the dorm is isolating despite the community living, how the staff still glance at me like I'm a visitor who doesn't belong. But if I tell him the truth—how lonely I am, how much I regret agreeing to this exchange—I know exactly what he'll say, *Come home.* And the last thing I want is an excuse to quit before I've even tried to stick it out.

So I keep it light. A thank you. A comment about how

beautiful the vines looked in the mist last night. Something safe. Something that won't make him worry.

When I close my laptop, the silence of my little room presses in. I haven't made a single real friend here, not the way I thought I would. The work is grueling, and I'm the only woman working in the vines. Claire is the closest to a possible companion, but I don't see her much during the day, and in the evenings, I'm still too exhausted for much socializing. The thought of another lunch alone at the community tables in the dining hall makes my stomach sink.

I pull on jeans and a T-shirt, shove my hair into a messy knot, and step into the hall. After I hit the restroom downstairs, I knock on Claire's door.

She answers with a smile, cardigan hanging off one shoulder, a notebook tucked under her arm. "Hey, Elise."

"I was wondering..." My voice comes out softer than I mean it to. "Would you like to have lunch together today?"

Her eyes brighten. "I'd love that. I usually just eat in my room and then go for a walk, but it'll be nice to have company. We can eat in the cafeteria and walk together after if you want."

Relief floods me. "That sounds perfect."

She grins. "Then it's a date."

I wave goodbye and find myself smiling as I head out toward the vineyard. Maybe today won't feel quite so lonely after all.

By the time I step onto the gravel, the hum of activity has already begun—tractors rumbling down rows, hoses snaking across the ground, the smell of earth in the air. Workers call to one another in quick French, voices carried on the crisp morning breeze.

I tug on gloves and grab a hose, water beading down my arm before I've even started watering. The ground is soft from last night's rain, the smell of smoke in the air from yesterday's cut canes that are now being burned. My shoulders ache within minutes of lifting and dragging. Sweat prickles down my spine, stinging where my shirt clings damp to my skin.

The sun climbs in the sky, but it isn't long before I'm back to cleaning in the cellars. That's an unending job. You start at one end and clean to the other, and it takes all day. Then the next day, you start over.

When the bell clangs faintly across the grounds, I peel off my gloves and wipe sweat from my brow. My stomach growls, and for once, I don't dread the cafeteria. Claire will be waiting.

Sure enough, she's at a window table with two bowls of bouillabaisse steaming in front of her, the broth rich with saffron, and a basket of crusty bread nearby.

"This looks amazing," I say, sliding into the seat across from her.

"It's my favorite," she admits, tearing a piece of bread. "They only make it once a week."

The food is warm and comforting, but it's the conversation that sustains me. She leans in when I tell her I grew up on a vineyard, eyes wide with curiosity.

"That's incredible," she says. "And now you're here doing this exchange?"

"Yeah. But home is nothing like this place. Our vineyard is a fraction of the size of Château."

Claire tilts her head. "Still, that's more than most people start with."

"How about you?" I ask. "How did you end up here?"

Her grin turns sheepish. "I followed a man. I thought moving to France was romantic. The man didn't last, but I got a job here in marketing. My work visa's up in a few months, though, and I've decided not to renew."

"What will you do?"

She shrugs. "No idea. I'll figure it out. I'm hoping having worked for three years at Château will help." Then she laughs, but it sounds thinner this time. "Honestly, I should've pushed harder when I first arrived. I kept my head down, afraid of making mistakes, and I got stuck with every awful job no one else wanted. It took me forever to climb out of that hole."

Her honesty softens something inside me. "That must have been hard."

"It was," she admits. "Which is why I'm telling you—you

have to be direct here. Otherwise, you'll waste months, the way I did."

As I nod, an idea stirs. "I have a friend back home who oversees marketing for a wine growers' consortium. If you'd be interested, I could connect you."

Claire's eyes light up, her earlier vulnerability flickering into hope. "Really? That would be amazing."

We finish lunch and wander outside. She shows me her favorite walking path, vines stretching along either side. Sunlight filters through leaves, flickering over her hair, and a warm breeze carries the sweet tang of ripening grapes.

"Are you dating anyone back home?" she asks, pulling me out of my thoughts.

I hesitate. "I'm…not sure. There's Kingston. He tormented me growing up and always treated me like a little sister. But lately we've grown closer, and something seemed to shift just before I left." My cheeks warm. Before she can press for more, I add, "What about you?"

She laughs, kicking a stone down the path. "Plenty of men here. Many more than women. When I need an itch scratched, there's always someone. But no one's here for long. So there's nothing serious."

Her ease makes me envy her, just a little.

As we loop back toward Château, Claire asks, "Why are you doing hand work here?"

"Because that's what Sebastian gives me."

She snorts. "Then it's time you tell Sebbie you want more. If you don't, he'll keep you at the bottom rung until you leave."

"Be direct? I thought I was paying my dues. I assume he understands why I'm actually here."

She shrugs. "Absolutely you need to be direct. Otherwise, you'll waste three months scrubbing floors."

I laugh weakly, nerves twisting. "I have my daily check-in with him after lunch. Usually, he just sends me back to the cellars. Maybe today I can change that."

"Good. Tell him."

I nod, and her confidence carries me into the cellar when I

return to work, though Sebastian is running late. The longer I wait, the tighter my stomach knots. I wander between the gleaming vats, running my hands along the cool steel, rehearsing what I might say. Then the digital readouts catch my attention—sugar content, pH, blends I've never considered.

I snap a photo and text Tarryn.

Me: Ever tried this combo?

Her reply pings back.

Tarryn: I could with Declan's help. He says it's tricky but worth a try.

We volley a couple more messages until she drops news so big I almost fumble my phone.

Tarryn: Appleton Vineyard just sold to the new hospital administrator. He doesn't want to farm it. We can rent the land.

I do the math quickly and type out my findings. Forty acres. That's a hundred tons of grapes. Seven thousand more cases of wine.

Her reply is a string of exclamation points. My heart swells. We're celebrating together, even an ocean apart.

The scuffing of his boots lifts my attention, and Sebastian strides up, perfectly pressed, perfectly late.

"Sorry," he says, adjusting his cufflinks and gesturing toward his office. "Shall we begin?"

I slip my phone into my pocket, Claire's words echoing in my head. *"Be direct."*

"Actually," I say as I follow. "I need to talk about my role here."

He pauses mid-step, one brow arched. "Your role?" His tone is light, almost amused, but there's an edge beneath it.

"Yes." I fold my hands in front of me as I sit. "I came here for an assistant vintner exchange. To learn how you run things, to understand decisions about fermentation, blending, production. So far, all I've been doing is pulling hoses and scrubbing."

Sebastian exhales softly, like I've offered a well-worn complaint. "Everyone starts with the basics, Elise. You can't expect to understand wine without getting your hands dirty."

Heat climbs my neck, but I hold steady. "I grew up on a vineyard. I know the basics. I didn't travel all this way just to repeat work I mastered when I was twelve."

His gaze sharpens, a hint of challenge there. "Mastered? That's a strong word. Even the best vintners return to the floor from time to time."

"I know that," I say quickly, my voice tightening. "But I'm here for a short time. If all I do is grunt work, this exchange is wasted. I want to contribute like your assistant vintner would, or else I'll be better off back in Paradise, working side by side with my father and the Paradise family."

For a long moment, he studies me. It seems his silence is deliberate, drawing out every second, as if he's measuring whether I'll squirm.

Finally, he stands and circles back out to one of the vats, trailing his hand along the steel. "If you want to convince me you deserve more, tell me this." He nods at the digital readout. "What do you make of that blend?"

My heart stutters, but I step closer. The numbers I looked at earlier flash back in my mind. "It's unusual," I tell him. "Not typical for Bordeaux. But handled carefully, it could add depth. The trick would be balancing tannins. Otherwise, it overpowers."

A flicker of something—approval? amusement?—crosses his face before he smoothes it away. "Not a terrible answer."

I lift my chin, refusing to shrink. "Then let me prove I can do more."

He lets out a short laugh, shaking his head. "You're bolder than I expected." He sticks his hands in his pockets and looks at me. "Very well. Tomorrow, you'll shadow me during fermentation checks. We'll see if your knowledge matches your confidence."

Relief sweeps through me so quickly I almost sag in place. "Thank you."

His smile is faint, razor-sharp. "Don't thank me yet. You may regret asking for more."

With a nod, he turns on his heel and disappears back into his office. I still spend the rest of the afternoon cleaning in the cellar, but it feels different now. By the time I climb back up to my room, exhaustion weighs heavy, but there's a flicker of pride burning beneath it. I've carved out a chance at what I came for.

I flip open my laptop and type.

Kingston,
You won't believe it. Today I pushed back. Sebastian had me doing nothing but grunt work, and I told him if that was all I was here for, I'd rather go home. There aren't many women here working in the vines, and I was terrified, but he actually listened. Tomorrow, I get to shadow him during fermentation checks. It's a small victory, but a victory all the same.

And I made a friend. Her name's Claire, and she's the first person who's made me feel like I might have a place here. We had lunch and walked the vineyards on our break. It made the day better than I expected.

I scroll up to reread his earlier note about Renew Motion—the new joint venture, the travel it will demand.

I hope your upcoming travel doesn't steal you away too much. Selfishly, I like knowing you're close to Black Bear, even when I'm far away.

XOXO,
E

I hit send and collapse against the pillows, a small,

satisfied smile tugging at my lips. Today was a good day.

Seventeen

Kingston

Zach didn't set the fire at Tarryn's cottage. He didn't tinker with the tractor. We've already ruled that out, yet his absence weighs heavier by the day. If he's not guilty, then where the hell is he? And for that matter, where the hell is Max? He's checked out, offering nothing and avoiding everyone since Zach left. Whatever he's hiding, it's pulling him away from the family.

That's what gnaws at me—the silence. It isn't just a cousin skipping town. It feels deliberate. Like Zach knows something. Or worse, like someone made sure he couldn't come back.

Last night at family dinner, my siblings asked if Cal, the investigator, had found anything on him. But I haven't heard from him. Not yet. It's been nearly six months since Zach disappeared, and the longer this drags on, the more we swing between clinging to hope that he's safe and fearing we're blind to something darker.

It's Monday morning, so I decide to start the week with a call to check in with Cal. After I hang up, I'm more concerned than ever. This news needs to be discussed in person. Neither Ryker nor Beckett works on Mondays, though I don't know about Greyson. I send a text to my siblings.

Me: I spoke to Cal. Can we meet at the house around lunchtime?

Tarryn: You found something?

Beckett: I'll be there.

Ryker: Yes! Save me from the wedding planning.

I try to go back to work, but my thoughts keep circling. I won't be able to focus on anything else until this is out in the open. Soon, I'm counting the moments until I can head out to the helicopter.

When I land across the lake at the estate, everyone's already gathered in Mom's kitchen. Tarryn's at the counter, pouring hot water over tea leaves. Ryker slouches at the table, arms folded, eyes shadowed from lack of sleep. Beckett stands near the window, jaw set in that surgeon's way, always dissecting, always calculating.

"I checked in with Cal this morning," I say without preamble. "He found a new order—another fifty-gallon tank of vinegar, billed to Zach. It was delivered last week to a warehouse south of Black Bear."

The room goes still.

Ryker bolts upright. "That's impossible. You said last night that Zach hasn't touched his accounts since he ran."

"Exactly," I answer. "But now he has. Which means he's still moving pieces from the shadows or someone's using his name."

Beckett cuts in. "And whichever it is, the optics are

catastrophic. Everyone already knows block fourteen was poisoned. Evelyn made sure of that when she went to the papers after Zach tainted our shared water source. We're bleeding money just to fix that mess with the Dempseys, and now, this surfaces?"

Ryker slams his palm on the table. "Don't twist it, Beckett. We caught him once. He bolted. But since then? The fires, the tractor, the broken lines—that's not him. He doesn't have the reach. Someone else is pulling strings."

"Then why are orders still showing up under his name?" Beckett fires back. "That doesn't clear him. It makes him complicit—or careless. Either way, it stains us."

Ryker rounds on him. "Don't write him off like he's some career criminal. He grew up with us. He's family."

Tarryn shakes her head. "But he's been angry since Dad named me heir. You know that as well as I do."

"Angry, yes," Ryker says. "But not stupid. Zach's not leading this. He's being used."

"He sabotaged block fourteen with vinegar," Beckett cuts in. "He was caught red-handed. That wasn't Max, and that wasn't some faceless outsider. That was Zach."

"One act doesn't make him the mastermind behind every single thing that's happened since," Ryker counters. "Don't lay all of this at his feet just because it's easy."

"I'm doing it because it fits," Beckett snaps.

"Or because it's convenient," I point out. "Listen to yourselves. We already know Zach poisoned block fourteen. That's fact. But Cal turning up a new order in his name tells me two things. He's either still in play, or someone's using him as cover. And that should scare us more than what he's already done."

Tarryn sets the teapot down too hard, liquid sloshing over the rim. "This isn't about who yells loudest. Dad's watching every move I make, deciding if I can really take over. One slip, one sign I can't handle this, and he'll clamp down tighter. He'll never step back."

Her voice falters just for a breath before she stiffens again.

"I can't afford another fire, another broken piece of machinery, the loss of any more vines, or another question mark. If this trail leads back to Zach—or to someone framing him—it reflects on all of us. We have to figure this out."

"It already reflects on us," Beckett says grimly. "Distributors are whispering. Evelyn's circling like a hawk. If she smells blood in the water, she won't stop at compensation. She'll gut us."

Ryker paces now, restless energy radiating off him. "And maybe that's the whole game. Someone's pushing us to tear each other apart. And congratulations, Kingston, you're helping them."

The words land like a blow. His eyes burn with betrayal, like I've crossed a line somehow by providing information. "I'm not helping anyone," I bite back. "Other than trying to help us. I'm making sure we're not blindsided again. We can't sit here hoping Zach comes back with an apology tied up in a bow. We need to find him. The sabotage isn't stopping. We either face it, or it destroys us."

Ryker scoffs. "No, you're ready to sell him out. That's what this is. You go ahead, play detective with your PI. But don't ask me to stand here while you burn the family from the inside out. That's what Evelyn did to the Dempseys. I thought we were better than that."

He storms out, the screen door slamming so hard the frame rattles.

For a moment, my chest tightens. My mind searches for something solid and lands on Elise. Even as that confuses me, I know she would tell me I'm doing the right thing. Or maybe she'd see through my bravado and remind me how much hanging everything on Zach costs. But whether he's pulling the strings or just a pawn, we can't deny he's been involved.

Beckett doesn't move from the window. His voice is quiet, cutting. "Kingston, if you're wrong about Zach, you'll do more damage than any saboteur ever could."

Then he leaves too.

Doubt sizzles through me. Maybe I just chose suspicion

over loyalty, control over trust. Zach is family. He's been beside us through more than most. If I'm wrong, if he's branded with guilt he doesn't deserve, I'll carry that stain.

But what's worse—risking that stain or letting us stumble blind into whatever garbage Zach might be caught up in? I shove the guilt aside, bury it under resolve. Better to be the one they blame now than the one who failed them later.

The silence is thick, suffocating. Only Tarryn remains, her shoulders rigid as she stares at the cooling teapot.

"Don't make me the bad guy," I say.

She exhales, steady but tired. "You think I don't get it? I knew you'd take the step I can't. But if Dad sees me leaning on you, he'll think I'm not ready."

"You're ready," I tell her. "This isn't about you failing. It's about doing whatever it takes to protect all of us. I'm convinced Zach isn't in this alone. We need to find out."

Her throat works as she swallows with the faintest of nods. She doesn't thank me. She doesn't need to.

I leave her in the kitchen and step outside.

A breeze stirs the vines, leaves rattling against each other like whispered judgments, reminding me how easy it looks out here—tidy, predictable, controlled.

In truth, though, we're anything but.

The facts about Zach, whatever they are, won't stay buried forever. If he's guilty, we'll face it. If he's innocent, we'll clear him. Either way, we have to figure this out.

Eighteen

Elise

It's been nearly a week since I started following Sebastian around, and that's long enough to learn that *assistant vintner* is just another way of saying *do whatever he doesn't want to bother with.* Some days, it's endless grunt work—hoses, floors, hauling buckets until my arms feel like they might fall off. Other days, it's shadowing him while he turns on that polished charm for management and the one investor who stopped by, all smiles and cheek kisses, like he's running for office instead of making good wine.

I don't love it. I didn't cross an ocean to be someone's glorified errand girl. I came here to sharpen what I know. And yet here I am, clipboard in hand, checking off chores that feel more like busywork than real experience.

And Sebastian doesn't make things any easier. He tries to sweeten the load with his constant flirting—leaning too close when he explains a process, brushing against my shoulder as though by accident, throwing compliments about my "Canadian smile" like spare change. He wants me to laugh, to soften, maybe to step into the space he keeps leaving open. But I haven't. Not once. Each time, I shift back. I offer a polite smile, nothing more. It's one of the few things I feel proud of here, that I'm keeping my boundaries intact, making my intentions clear, even when he seems amused by that.

This morning, he hands me a clipboard with a neat column of tasks written in his looping hand. "Nothing difficult," he says, tilting his head just so, his usual smile tugging at his mouth. "You can handle it, non?"

I skim the list. Check the press to make sure yesterday's washdown dried properly, record yeast activity in one of the fermenting tanks, take barrel readings in storage. I nod.

The press is first. It still smells faintly of wet iron and soap, sharp in the cool air. I run my fingers along the inside, damp streaks visible on my skin, but the grates are clean. No leftover skins, no pulp caught in the ridges. I check the dials, finding the pressure gauge steady. I jot it all down. One task done.

The fermenting tank takes longer. Foam bubbles lazily beneath the glass port, rising and popping in thick, sticky bursts. The yeast smells alive—sweet, tangy, a little like rising bread. I crouch, thermometer in hand, waiting for the numbers to settle. When they land exactly in the range Sebastian drilled into me earlier this week, I let out a breath. One more box ticked. One more thing I didn't mess up.

By the time I make my way to the barrel room, my arm aches from carrying the clipboard everywhere, like a schoolgirl clutching homework. The air is cooler here, damp, the rows of barrels stretching into shadows. This last task should be simple—temperature, humidity, note anything unusual. *"Routine,"* Sebastian said, though the way his mouth curved around the word made it feel like a test.

I kneel by the first barrel, slip the thermometer probe into its slot, and jot the reading. Nothing unusual. The next two are the same. I fall into a rhythm—check, record, move on—until a sharp tang cuts through the usual oak-and-wine scent.

Vinegar.

I pause, nose wrinkling, and step closer to a barrel farther down the row. Dark liquid glistens at its seam, slipping down the side in thin rivulets. My stomach lurches. That's not condensation.

I crouch, pressing my fingers near the leak. They come away stained deep red. Wine. There's a gash in the top. The wood has split.

Before I can move, the trickle thickens, now streaming across the stone toward the drain. My throat tightens. I glance along the row. I can see three more barrels marked with the same clean, unnatural gash.

"Vite!" A voice barks behind me. Two cellar hands rush past, dropping cloths to the floor. One slaps his palm against the seam of a barrel, the other swings a vat beneath the leak. Their movements are fast, coordinated. No one shouts in confusion. No one hesitates.

Instinct jolts me forward. I grab a rag from the stack near the door and drop to my knees beside a barrel, pressing it against the leak. The wine seeps through instantly, soaking my palm, and before I can adjust, a man yanks the rag from my hand.

"Non!" he snaps, shaking his head. He motions me back, the urgency in his voice clear, even if I don't catch the words.

Heat rises to my face. I stumble backward, clutching my clipboard to my chest as more men flood in. Their words are sharp. They spread resin paste over the cuts and chalk slashes across the heads of the ruined barrels. Buckets collect what can still be saved.

I press myself against the wall, watching. Useless. Out of place.

Back home, this kind of damage would stop everything. People would rage, panic, call family meetings and perhaps file police reports. Here, it seems to be another Monday, a problem to be patched before lunch. Their casual efficiency in this situation unsettles me more than the sabotage itself. They've done this before. They're used to it.

The pen trembles in my hand as I scrawl a shaky note across the page. "Barrels fourteen through twenty-seven compromised. Gashes deliberate." The ink blots as my grip falters.

I press my palm to the cool stone wall, grounding myself as workers mop the floor, red stains disappearing down the drain.

Sabotage isn't just a Paradise curse. It's everywhere.

And if Tarryn sent me here to learn, I have.

By the time the last bucket is hauled away, the air is thick with the sour tang of spoiled wine and resin. I've done the math in my head, and that's nearly three hundred and twenty-five cases of wine destroyed overnight. My notes are smudged where my pen slipped, but I finish the readings anyway and make myself walk to Sebastian's office.

He's at his desk, glasses sliding low on his nose, scribbling something in a ledger. He doesn't look up when I knock.

"The barrel room," I say, holding out the clipboard. My voice shakes despite my effort to steady it. "Thirteen barrels were cut. I marked everything down."

He finally lifts his gaze, takes the clipboard, and flips through my notes. One brow arches when he sees the word *deliberate*.

"Mmm…" He sets the board aside. "So you saw."

"That's all you're going to say?" My pulse kicks. "Those barrels are ruined. That's—what? Nearly three thousand liters gone?"

He shrugs, leans back in his chair. "It happens."

I blink. "It happens?"

"Yes." His tone sharpens. "You patch what you can, you mark what you can't, and you move on. If you lose sleep over every cut barrel, you won't last a season here."

My stomach twists. "But this was deliberate. Doesn't it—" I swallow. "Doesn't it bother you?"

A thin smile ghosts across his face, but there's no warmth in it. "Of course, it bothers me. But bothering doesn't stop it, does it? Welcome to winemaking, mademoiselle. It's like Voldemort said to Harry, *Wine attracts envy, envy breeds spite, and spite spills easy.*"

Harry Potter wasn't in the wine business, but I get where he's going. I bite the inside of my cheek, shaking my head. "At Paradise Hill, they'd never accept this. They'd fight until they found out who did it."

His eyes flicker with impatience before he lets out a humorless chuckle. "And in the meantime, the vines still need pruning, the tanks still need monitoring, and the wine still needs making. You see the problem?" He leans forward, tapping the list still clipped to the board. "You finished the press and the fermentation readings?"

I nod stiffly.

"Good. Tomorrow, we'll start on the south block, checking vines for mildew and beginning the spring trimming. I want to see what you know. This—what happened today—you'll forget it. We don't waste energy on what we can't recover."

My throat burns with words I don't dare say. I do not understand his thinking at all. Instead, I nod again. "All right."

His smile is back. "Bon. Then we understand each other."

We absolutely do not. And I've been dismissed, again.

After a long dinner with everyone in the cafeteria, I climb the stairs to my room. Exhaustion makes my limbs heavy, but I'm not ready to sleep. I peel off my boots and sit on the edge of the bed, staring at the ink still smudged across my fingertips. At Paradise Hill, something like this is setting the whole valley on fire. Sabotage is personal, a wound that carves into their pride. Here, it's shrugged off. Another mess to mop before lunch.

I hug my knees to my chest, restless and unsettled. Maybe Sebastian's right. Maybe if you let yourself feel every loss, you'll drown in it. But I can't imagine living like that—bleeding and pretending not to notice.

I don't know what's worse, their indifference or the possibility that someday I'll grow used to it too.

After I schlep myself back downstairs for a shower, I crawl into bed with my computer. I should sleep, but my thoughts keep circling, too loud, too sharp. So I begin to write.

Kingston,
Today, I saw something I can't stop thinking about. Thirteen barrels ruined—slashed clean, like someone took an axe to them. The floor was slick with wine. Back home, something like that would stop everything. Here, they moved so fast it was almost routine.

No outrage, no shouting. Just mops and resin and chalk marks. Sebastian told me not to waste energy on what can't be recovered. He acted like it was just part of the business.

Maybe I've been naïve to think sabotage was only a Paradise problem. The truth hit me hard today. The bigger the vineyard, the bigger the target. It doesn't start and stop with someone like Zach. This happens everywhere. The difference is how people respond. Here, they shrug and move on. At Paradise Hill, you're tearing the operation apart until the culprit is found. Neither way feels right, but at least Paradise cares enough to bleed.

I don't know if this makes me feel stronger or just more unsettled. Maybe both. But I needed to share.

–Elise

I hover over the send button, heart hammering. Then I press it before I lose my nerve. I need to talk to Tarryn. We exchange emails often, but I miss her, and instead of sending her what I sent to Kingston, I FaceTime her.

The screen flickers, and after a moment, Tarryn's face fills it, sunlight spilling through her office window. For me, it's nearly midnight, the only light in my room the lamp on the nightstand.

"You look exhausted," she says. "Still on Canadian time?"

"Somewhere in between," I murmur, pulling my hair back.

She lifts an eyebrow. "Well, check your inbox. I sent you something better than vines and barrels—bridesmaid dresses. Tell me which one won't make me hate the photos in ten years."

I open the email and scroll down to a pale sage dress. "This one works. Classic, flattering. You'll still love it later."

"Thank God." She exhales. Then her eyes sharpen. "Now, tell me what's going on. You've got that look."

I hesitate, and then say quietly, "I saw thirteen barrels slashed today. Wine everywhere. And no one even blinked. They just cleaned it up and moved on."

Her mouth tightens. "Sabotage?"

"Routine sabotage," I clarify. "And it made me realize something. What we've been dealing with at Paradise? It isn't unique. The bigger the vineyard, the bigger the target."

She pauses for a moment. "But for us, it isn't business. It's personal."

I nod, my throat tight. "Exactly. Maybe that's what keeps us bleeding—and maybe it's what keeps us alive."

For once, she doesn't argue. She just nods again, her jaw firm. "I wish you were here," she says. "But you're learning so much. I know we're going to benefit, but I just wish you were here."

I smile. "I couldn't have said it better myself."

Nineteen

Kingston

This morning, I observed a knee-replacement surgery for one of my clinical trials down in Los Angeles at Cedars-Sinai. It was a long day, and back on my plane flying home, I find myself tired after all the talking and peopling I had to do.

Even so, when I open my laptop and find an email from Elise, I instantly feel lighter. I pause and take stock of that for a moment, waiting for the stab of worry I often feel when a woman gets too close, when her interest doesn't match mine. But that's not the case here. I don't even open her message right away. I just sit for a second, smiling like an idiot because Elise thought of me before she went to bed.

When I click open the message, her words pull me in, and I reread them three times. She's worried, and not hiding it. I can feel her trust in the way she lays out her fears. She believes I can hold them for her. That stirs something within me, something I surprisingly don't reject, and hearing her concerns makes me proud of her, of the pride she takes in her work, and of the way she's putting her whole self into this exchange. There's a depth here that I'd forgotten could be part of a relationship, a real connection to another person. I ache with my desire to be there beside her as the worry edges in.

I type my response slowly, careful with my words.

You should tell Tarryn what you saw. Sabotage doesn't just happen in Paradise – it happens everywhere. Maybe knowing that will ease her shoulders a little. She carries too much of this on her back, and if she knew this was part of the industry everywhere, maybe she wouldn't blame herself so much.

I'm just leaving Los Angeles. I've been there today observing a clinical-trial surgery with a new knee-replacement device. When I travel, I always miss Dottie's omelets, especially her kitchen sink one. You never know what you're going to get with that thing, but it always tastes like home. And Charlotte's chocolates. I've tried to find replacements in the city, but nothing comes close. What do you miss most right now? Food, people, places – whatever it is, I want to hear it.

Is there anything you've seen there that you'd want to try back at Paradise Hill? Some method or blend that's caught your eye? I like picturing you in those caves and cellars, picking up things you can bring home. Makes the wait a little easier.

Because when I let myself think it through, I know my heart wants you here, in this valley.

Sixty-eight days until you're back. I'm counting every one.

XO,

King

I hit send and sit staring at the screen, heart pounding. I've just handed her the most honest version of me I've handed anyone in quite a while.

But then the guilt of what I haven't said creeps in, dragging my thoughts to the other part of my life, the one I've kept neatly compartmentalized. My lawyer in Vancouver. We've had a little over four years of casual dinners, late-night visits, and enough physical chemistry to scratch an itch. Nothing more, nothing less. That's all I've been capable of and all I've wanted, or so I thought. Now, I see things differently.

But Hope is still hanging there. Untidy. She emailed a couple of days ago about paperwork, and I should close this loop. Make it clear. End things the right way. I pick up my phone and type out a message to her.

Me: Lunch tomorrow?

Her reply is quick.

Hope: I'll be working from home. Can you come here?

I take a deep breath before I answer.

Me: Yes.

The flight to Vancouver the next morning is smooth, and the hum of the rotors steadies my nerves. From up here, the city spreads out gray and glass against the water, busy and restless in a way Black Bear never is. Over two hours later, I land at the helipad at the Renew Motion headquarters, and Dominic, my driver, is there waiting for me.

I think I have what I want to say sorted out. My decision feels heavy but clear. It's a big step for me, but it feels like the one I want to take.

Dominic drives me over to Hope's condo, and I'm nearly overwhelmed by all the people walking down the streets despite the rain. I haven't been out into the city in a while. When we pull up in front of Hope's building, I tell him I don't expect to be long.

Hope buzzes me in and greets me at her door in a silk robe, her hair loose around her shoulders. She smiles, soft and expectant, and before I can think, she leans in to kiss me.

For a beat, I let it happen—because it's habit, because it's easier—but the feel of her lipstick only reminds me how wrong this is for me now. I pull back, my hands dropping to my sides.

Her brows lift in surprise, a question hanging there. "Rough day?"

I step past her into the condo. The room smells faintly of coffee and her perfume, ordinary things that suddenly feel too much. "Something like that."

She closes the door and follows me into the living room. "I'll pour you a drink. You'll feel better once you relax."

For a second, I almost consider her offer, but the words I want to say are pressing at the back of my throat, and I can't swallow them a moment longer.

"I don't think a drink is going to fix this."

Her steps slow. "Fix what?"

I sit on the edge of her couch, staring out at the rain. This is the view she loves, the life she's built here. None of it feels like what I want, and I don't want to settle for this any longer. "The way things are between us. It's easy, sure, but…it isn't what I want anymore."

Her laugh is small, confused, like I've told a bad joke. "What do you mean? We're fine. We always are."

I drag a hand through my hair, frustration and guilt tangling together. "We're not, Hope. Not really. I should have said something sooner, but…this isn't working for me."

Her smile fades, like she's only just realizing I mean this. "You're serious."

I nod. "This has been convenient for us. We're workaholics, and this was easy. It made sense. But it doesn't to me anymore."

She folds her arms, as if she suddenly feels exposed. "If you're looking for our relationship to change, I'm ready for that. We can move in together and make a go of it."

I shake my head. "You love this city. I don't. I don't belong here. And you don't want to live in Black Bear Valley."

"I never meant that." Her tone is sharper now, defensive, but underneath is the first edge of hurt. "I want us. We're good together. We can make this work."

I sigh. "That's not the life I want. I don't want something that only half fits. And I don't want to keep pretending this is enough. Now, I know that it isn't. Not for me, and not for you either."

Her arms fall. Her gaze locks on mine, wet and bewildered. "So after four years, you just end it? Like this? Is there someone else?"

The truth lodges in my throat. I don't say yes, though my silence is enough. Elise's face is already there, unshakable.

Hope's lips part, then press together. "I let you in. I thought maybe when you were ready, we'd move forward."

The words cut. I never meant to hurt her, but I can't hide behind excuses. "When you wanted us to have a working relationship *'with benefits and no strings'*—your words, not mine—I agreed because I didn't have much of myself to give and because I knew you never wanted to live in Black Bear Valley, and I never wanted to live here," I manage. "I haven't changed my mind. I'm sorry."

She turns away, hand pressed to her temple, pulling in a deep breath. When she faces me again, her expression is different—harder, steadier, though her voice shakes. "So what does this mean for Renew Motion? Am I losing you as a client too?"

That I hadn't considered. She's not just asking if I'm

leaving her bed. She's asking if I'm erasing her from my life completely. I don't know what to say to that. She's done nothing to change our professional relationship, but I don't know what that will look like after this.

I stand. "We'll have to figure that out. But I know this is where you and I having anything personal ends."

Her chin lifts, even as her eyes shine. "Then you need to leave."

With a nod, I turn toward the door. When it shuts behind me with a finality that vibrates in my chest, I don't look back.

Dominic drives me back to the office, and I check in with my team and spend the afternoon in the lab with them. It's a great way to forget why I came to Vancouver.

I don't like flying longer distances in the dark, so I keep an eye on the time and the sun. Before it starts to set, I head up to the helipad and climb in.

The helicopter blades whirl overhead as I lift off, the city shrinking beneath me. I grip the controls tightly, replaying the look on Hope's face, her voice and the crack in it when she said she'd been waiting for me to change my mind. Relief should be my loudest feeling. I'm sorry she felt that way, and maybe I should have known, but I never promised her anything more, and I did what needed to be done. What I wanted to do. But guilt keeps pace beside me, refusing to be shaken.

I do still need her. Not as a lover, but as my lawyer. She's been my lawyer since the beginning—way before she was anything else—and she's one of the best in Vancouver, sharp as a blade in the courtroom. I can only hope she meant it when she said she wanted to keep me as a client, that ending us doesn't dull her edge or her interest when it comes to representing my company.

Yet even with that worry gnawing at me, Elise breaks through—her laugh, her stubborn streak, the way she handed me her fear like a gift. Hope's words linger, but Elise's presence settles my mind. There's a way through this. I just have to find it.

By the time Black Bear comes into view, my guilt has dulled, replaced by something stronger, something that's different about me now—this relentless pull toward Elise.

Twenty

Elise

Pounding jolts me awake, and I sit up so fast I nearly fall off the bed. Sunlight already streams through the shutters. I've overslept. Working ten-hour days, seven days a week, has me exhausted.

"Elise!" Sebastian's voice cuts through the fog of sleep.

"Coming!" My voice cracks as I stumble to the door, tugging on yesterday's jeans and shoving my arms into a sweater.

When I open it, he stands there with his brows drawn tight. "You can't be late today. We have work to do."

Heat rushes to my cheeks. "I'm sorry. I—"

He shakes his head and turns on his heel. "Hurry. This is important."

I jam my feet into boots and race after him, heart hammering. My feet clatter against the stairs as I catch up.

Outside, the morning air is cool and damp, tinged with the green bite of new growth. Mist curls low over the vineyard rows, clinging to the budding vines like pale veils, and the earth gives softly under my shoes as we start down a path.

Sebastian strides ahead with his hands clasped behind his back, posture stiff. His feet barely make a sound while every step I take feels loud, clumsy.

"You can't oversleep here," he says without looking at me. His accent sharpens each word. "Vines don't wait for you to be ready."

"I know. I'm sorry." My breath puffs white as I hurry to match his pace. "It won't happen again."

He glances sideways, eyes narrowing. "It better not. Today isn't a day for tourists. I need your attention."

The sting of his words lodges in my chest, but I bite back the reply forming on my tongue. I'm not a tourist. I came here to learn, and if that means starting the day already behind, I'll fight to catch up. We pass between two tall rows of vines, their early buds light green. Dew catches the light, glittering like strings of beads. I think of Black Bear Valley, the way morning fog hugs the lake, and for a moment, it feels like I've been dropped into a mirror image—familiar yet foreign.

By the time we reach the winery, the smell has shifted. Less of the green freshness outside, more of the cellar—cool stone and damp wood, the faint tang of old wine clinging to the air. It isn't unpleasant, but it's dense, layered, as if the walls themselves have absorbed centuries of vintages. The closer we get, the stronger it grows until it's all I can breathe.

"Watch carefully." Sebastian motions me forward, his voice full of pride. "This is where craft meets chemistry."

Workers pour a slurry of crushed skins and stems into a smaller fermenter. I expect the familiar ritual of punch-downs—the hard rhythm of someone shoving the cap under—but instead, a pump roars to life. The liquid is drawn from the bottom of the tank, traveling through a hose, and then it cascades back down over the floating skins.

Sebastian crosses his arms, chin tilted. "Pump-overs.

Gentle, frequent. We do them every two hours, sometimes more. Keeps the cap moist, extracts evenly. You don't get the harsh bite of tannin, just a silkier profile. It allows the fruit to speak first." He shares this like a lecture, not an invitation.

I scribble notes, racing to keep up. At Paradise, we've always sworn by punch-downs. They're physical, almost violent, like wrestling the grape into submission. This feels different. Less battle, more conversation. I feel a small smile tugging at my mouth as the juice trickles over the skins like a waterfall, dark and glossy. The scent rises warm and lush, making my lungs expand as I draw it in.

Sebastian's gaze cuts to me. "Something funny?" His tone makes the hairs on my arms prickle.

"No." My throat tightens, but I keep my chin high. "I think this could be transformative."

He studies me for a beat. Then his edge softens, just slightly. "At least you see it." A small shrug. "Most interns only see the mess and the hoses."

His words send a rush of pride through me. I hug the notebook to my chest. "I'll make sure it doesn't fail."

As the pump whirs, I imagine the tanks back at Paradise Hill. The cellar is smaller, and not nearly as gleaming, but we could set up a system like this. Maybe not every tank—at least not at first—but what if we tried it on one block of pinot noir? Softer, rounder, a new expression of the valley. I picture Dad swirling the glass, Trace nodding in approval, even Tarryn leaning in with that spark in her eyes when something surprises her.

Sebastian claps his hands, snapping me out of the thought. "Come. There's more to see."

I trail him through the maze of equipment. Everywhere, there's motion—workers lugging hoses, steam rising from a hot rinse, an acidic scent so strong it makes me lightheaded. My pen scratches furiously across the page as Sebastian explains, his tone still sharp, but no longer cutting. By midday, when we pause near an open tank, I catch him watching me instead of the wine. His mouth tilts into something that almost passes for a smile.

"You take notes like a student. Careful—soon, they'll say you know more than I do."

Heat rushes to my cheeks, though not from embarrassment this time. I snap my notebook closed. "Maybe I will."

He chuckles. "Ambitious. I like that."

As we move on, he reaches past me to adjust a valve, his arm brushing against mine. Not a hard bump, but deliberate and slow enough that the warmth of him lingers. I step sideways, but the space is narrow, the steel tank at my back, him blocking the front. His gaze dips briefly to my mouth before returning to my eyes.

"You watch closely," he says, voice quieter now, threaded with something different. "Not everyone does."

The air thickens, a heat rising that has nothing to do with fermentation. I grip the edges of my notebook so tightly the cardboard cover bends. For a second, I tell myself he's just testing me, pushing to see if I'll flinch the way I did this morning. But the way his voice drops, the way his gaze lingers, it doesn't feel like only that.

"I came here to learn," I manage. My voice sounds steadier than I feel.

"Bon." His smile sharpens. "Then maybe you will."

He steps back, leaving me room to breathe again, though my pulse takes longer to settle. I try to convince myself it was harmless, just ego wrapped in charm, but the tension of that moment clings as I follow him deeper into the cellar.

When the day finally winds down and I retreat to my room, I tug off my boots and sit cross-legged on the bed, the notebook beside me. My head still buzzes, like the yeast itself has gotten into my bloodstream. I open my laptop, fingers hovering over the keys before I begin typing.

Kingston,

Today was huge. I watched Sebastian's crew pump from the bottom to move the grapes off the top, instead of pushing them down. It seems like a small difference, but it changes everything – the flavor, the texture, even the pace of fermentation. I filled pages of notes. At Paradise, we're always so physical with our wines, pushing them down, forcing them to yield. But this was gentler. It felt alive in a different way. I couldn't stop imagining how it might taste in our vineyard, how it could soften our edges without losing who we are. I kept wishing you were here beside me to see it because I know you'd understand.

I pause, reading over what I've typed, and then continue, wanting my words to lift him.

I miss you. And I miss Charlotte's chocolates, especially the chocolate-covered caramels with pecans. I miss the rotisserie chicken salad from the grill too. That's the first thing I'm getting when I come home. But mostly, I miss knowing you're close, part of my world no matter where you're working. I carried that feeling with me today, even standing in the middle of a French wine cellar.

My chest feels full as I hit send, almost too full, like the fermenters when the cap rises, threatening to spill over.

Twenty-one

Elise

The vines in Bordeaux are smaller than what I'm used to, twisted old things that cling low to the ground. Their buds have already pushed through, tender green shoots unfurling into the spring air. My task is to thin them, topinch away the extras so the strongest ones can grow. It's fiddly, back-bending work. Every time I crouch to snap off a weak shoot, my knees protest, but I remind myself that this is how the vineyard's future takes shape, and this is important vintner work.

Sebastian works beside me, his movements efficient, practiced. He doesn't speak much at first, but his presence looms large. The other hands keep sneaking glances his way. He isn't just another worker in the rows but the vintner, the one responsible for the health of it all. Yet here he is, pinching shoots, dirt under his nails, same as everyone else. That earns him respect.

After a while, he glances at my vine. "You've got a good eye," he says, nodding at the two shoots I've left. "Balanced."

I smile faintly. "Back home, the vines are taller. You'd barely recognize them compared to these. More like small trees than stumps."

He quirks a brow. "Trees? Then this must feel strange to you."

"Strange, yes. But easier to see what I'm doing," I admit, straightening and rolling my shoulders. "Though my back disagrees."

That earns me the ghost of a smile. "It's the curse of Bordeaux. Old vines, close to the ground. More bending, more patience." He snaps off a shoot with quick fingers, letting it fall. "But the fruit..." He gestures to the row. "Concentrated. Worth the pain."

I tilt my head. "At Paradise Hill, the vines look bigger, fuller. I always thought that meant more grapes."

"Not always," he corrects. "Your vines are spaced wider, trained higher, so they look larger. But here, they are closer, denser—many more per hectare. Château harvests far more than your vineyard ever could."

I huff a laugh. "So bigger doesn't always mean better."

He chuckles. "Not in vineyards. Sometimes, small is stronger."

Small is stronger. I wonder if that applies to more than vines.

I grin and bend to the next vine, snapping away a cluster of thin shoots. "Maybe I like babysitting more than I thought."

For a moment, he watches me, expression unreadable, before nodding once. "Keep that one," he murmurs, pointing at a thicker shoot I've almost removed. "It will balance the spur."

I leave it in place, and as I shift my hand, something wriggles on the underside of a leaf. Tiny, greenish-brown, with spindly legs and a body that looks wrong. My stomach turns. "Sebastian," I call, straightening quickly. "What is this? I haven't seen this at home."

He steps closer, brows knitting as I tilt the leaf for him to see. His face hardens instantly. "Eudemis. Grapevine moth larva. Very bad this early in the season."

My throat goes dry. "It's harmful?"

"Devastating," he says. He looks at me then, sharp and serious. "You were right to ask. If we don't tend to it immediately, it will spread through the block." Before I can reply, he adds, "Good eye. Very good."

His gaze lingers a second longer than necessary before he turns back to the vine. It's nothing more than professional gratitude, I tell myself. But something in his tone gets to me all the same.

I shouldn't care what he thinks of me. Not this much. And yet, his nod lingers, replaying in my mind even as we move down the row.

We spend the rest of the afternoon moving row by row, vine by vine, checking leaves and marking sections to treat. He explains as we go, telling me which natural sprays will slow the larvae without damaging the soil. "Copper, *if* necessary. But only if. We prefer extracts, oils, things that keep the balance."

I nod, trying to absorb it all. "So, you fight a war, but gently."

A corner of his mouth lifts. "Gently, yes. That is Bordeaux. Precision, not force."

"Back home we'd bring in the big guns," I admit. "Spray and be done with it."

"That is an option, but we're better to start with spot treatment. It's healthier when managed well." He glances at me with something almost like approval. "You found this before it spread. That saves us weeks, maybe the harvest itself."

I swallow, the magnitude of this taking me by surprise. "I just thought it looked…wrong."

"Exactly," he says. "That is the eye of a vintner."

The phrase roots itself inside me. No one has ever said that to me before. For a moment, it feels less like a compliment and more like a doorway I didn't know I was waiting to step through. For all the bending and the aching and the mud under my nails, in this moment, I belong here after all.

By the time we finish, the sun is dipping low, streaks of pink and orange fanning across the sky. My shoulders ache from hours of stooping, and my hands still smell faintly of soil and crushed leaves no matter how many times I wash them. The chatter of the other hands rises around us—tired laughter, the scrape of boots on gravel—as we all travel back toward the dormitory. The building glows warm against the evening, windows lit, voices carrying through the open doors like a beacon.

Sebastian walks beside me until we step inside. "Dinner?" he asks, his tone casual, though something in it makes me glance at him twice.

Before I can answer, Claire hurries over, a large box in her arms. "Elise, you just got this. Couriered in. What on earth did you order?"

"I didn't," I say, frowning as she sets it on the table. A small crowd gathers as I cut the tape and lift the lid. Dry ice fog curls into the air, and for a second, I have no idea what I'm looking at. But then I see a note with my name.

Beneath it is a Paradise Hill rotisserie chicken salad kit. My favorite. Nestled beside it, a stack of glossy chocolates I used to buy from Charlotte's shop.

My heart swells.

Claire leans in. "Who would send this?"

A smile blooms on my face. "Someone I started seeing before I left. He asked me in an email what I missed. I guess he decided to send it."

Sebastian peers into the box, baffled. "But you can get salads here. And chocolate. Why would he go to such trouble? France has the best chocolates in the world."

"Belgium has the best chocolates." Claire bursts out laughing. "This is why you're single, Sebastian. You don't get it."

He grins, and the crowd laughs. I catch the faintest twinge of something in his eyes before he masks it, shrugging off the jab as though it doesn't matter. Maybe it doesn't. Maybe he's used to it.

I scoop up the box, carrying it toward the stairs. Sebastian calls after me, "You don't want a real dinner?"

I lift the salad slightly. "I already have one."

Upstairs, I slip into my room and set the box on the desk. It's late morning back home, so I tap open my phone and hit the call button. Kingston's face fills the screen almost instantly. His hair is mussed like he's been running his hands through it, and the sight makes my stomach flip.

"Hey," I say softly. "Thank you. You have no idea how much this means."

His grin is boyish, unguarded. "You mentioned you missed it. I couldn't let that stand."

I glance at the salad, still sealed up tight, ready to be mixed, and laugh nervously. "I should probably eat it while it's cold, right? I feel ridiculous mixing salad on a video call."

"Go on," he urges, leaning back in his chair. "I want to see your face when you take that first bite."

I fumble with the lid, the plastic squeaking as I pry it off. I pour all the ingredients onto the lettuce. Dressing drips onto the desk, and I lunge for a napkin, nearly sending my fork clattering to the floor. "This is embarrassing."

"It's adorable," he counters. "And very entertaining."

I roll my eyes, mixing the chicken and greens, trying to look casual though my cheeks are heating. "Happy now?"

"Getting there." His tone is teasing in a way that makes my pulse skip.

I finally spear a bite and lift it to my mouth. The familiar taste hits, and I close my eyes, a sound slipping out before I can stop it. "God, I missed this."

When I open my eyes again, Kingston's watching me intently. His smile has shifted—less boyish, more hungry.

"I should've been the one to deliver it," he says quietly. "Sitting across from you. Watching you eat."

My eyes widen, heat infusing my belly. I laugh softly, trying to lighten the moment. "Careful, that sounds a little dangerous."

"Maybe it is," he says, not looking away. After a moment,

he tilts his head. "Tell me about your day. What did they have you doing out there?"

The pride wells up before I can stop it. "You'll laugh, but I found a moth larva. A tiny thing, tucked under a leaf. I didn't think much of it, but when I showed Sebastian, he practically froze. It was grapevine moth larva. Apparently, it can devastate an entire vineyard if you don't catch it early."

His brows rise. "And you spotted it?"

"I did," I say, smiling. "We spent the afternoon marking the vines and planning how to treat them without damaging the soil. Oils, extracts, maybe copper if it gets bad. They're so precise here."

"I'm impressed," Kingston says, and my heart soars.

"Sebastian said it might've saved the harvest." I shrug. "Who knew? I just thought it looked wrong. I'd never seen one before."

Kingston's smile falters for half a beat. "He told you that?"

I nod, trying not to fumble. "He seemed…grateful. Surprised, even."

Kingston leans closer to the camera, his eyes softening. "That's because you have an instinct. I knew you would, long before he did."

I push another bite of salad onto my fork, smiling into the screen. And even though the ocean stretches between us, Kingston feels impossibly close.

Twenty-two

Kingston

This day has been solid from the start. It kicked off with Elise's surprise FaceTime—her hair messy, her cheeks flushed, her laugh spilling across the line. For a few minutes, it felt like she wasn't halfway across the world. I wanted to reach through the screen and touch her. She's doing great work—of course she is—but the things Sebastian said to her have put me on guard. He's slick, and I still don't trust him.

But work pulled me out of that spiral. My design team has finally hit on a hip joint that could change the game—cleaner movement, smoother rotation, a chance for patients to walk without pain. And the NIH in London wants me to step into surgery with one of their lead orthopedists to show off our knee replacement in action.

It should be the only thing on my mind, as it's the kind of win I live for. But even as my team celebrates, I'm still thinking about Elise's laugh from this morning, about the way her eyes lit up on that screen.

By the time I shut down my home office, I'm wired in a good way. Sending that salad to Bordeaux was the right thing, wasn't it? My assistant was happy enough to hand it off—she gets a long weekend in Paris with her friend out of it—but I keep wondering if I went too far. Elise may think I'm excessive. But I wanted it to be a reminder. She has roots here. She has me.

When I head out into the kitchen, Simone is pulling containers from the fridge, her sleeves rolled up, hair pinned in her usual no-nonsense bun.

"Pork chops and rice for dinner tonight," she says, sliding the dish across the counter. "And I stocked the fridge for the weekend—breakfast, lunch, and dinner. You won't go hungry while I'm in Calgary."

I lean against the counter. "You think I'd starve without you?"

She doesn't even blink. "You'd live on protein shakes and takeout. Maybe the occasional steak if you remembered to thaw it. So yes."

I chuckle, shaking my head. "Fair enough."

She narrows her eyes, studying me. "You've been smiling all day. Something happen with Elise?"

I can't hide it. "Yeah. She FaceTimed me this morning."

"She's good for you," Simone says.

I force a shrug, aiming for casual. "Maybe."

But the word tastes wrong in my mouth. Simone's comment slips under my ribs and settles in a place I don't usually let anyone touch. I want Elise to be good for me. I want to be good for her. And that's terrifying.

"So tell me about this delivery you had me arrange," Simone continues, saving me from myself. "Salad? All the way to France?"

I groan, rubbing the back of my neck. "I know, it was overboard. But it's her favorite. I thought maybe it would remind her of home. Of me."

Her face softens. "That's not ridiculous, Kingston. That's

thoughtful. Women remember things like that."

"Or they think it's too much."

"Trust me." She points a wooden spoon at me. "She'll remember."

I tuck the container of pork chops under my arm. "Good. Because I'd rather she be thinking of me than that Italian."

Her laugh follows me to the door. "Play nice with your brothers tonight," she calls.

Outside, the sky is streaked with fading light. The helicopter waits on the pad, rotors idle. I climb aboard, and the flight across the lake is smooth, the water below reflecting orange and pink as the sun sinks behind the hills. From the cockpit, I spot the big house—stone walls, terracotta roof, gardens wrapped tight around it like a crown.

On the back lawn, my mom is easy to find. Wide-brimmed sunhat, gardening gloves, a pair of shears in hand as she leans over the rose bushes. The helicopter kicks up a swirl of petals and leaves as I land, and she straightens, shading her eyes to watch me.

I shut down the engine and cross the lawn.

She waves me over with the clippers. "You're early," she says, brushing a leaf off her arm.

"Had a good day," I answer. "Thought I'd stop in before basketball."

Her smile curves. "And?"

I don't dodge it. "I talked to Elise this morning."

For a second, she blinks like I've said something outrageous. But then she recovers, clipping another bloom. "Oh?"

"She caught me on FaceTime. She's diving into the work, learning a lot, picking up practices she wants to try here. She looks good. Happy."

Mom smiles. "I'm glad. She's always been serious about her craft. I knew she'd make the most of this exchange." She drops the clipped rose into her basket. "Between her and Tarryn, Paradise Hill will be in good hands when your father and Mitch finally step back. Two strong women leading—your father will be proud."

"He already is," I say. Pride swells in my chest.

Mom straightens, stretching her back. "It's hard to imagine this place without Mitch in the cellar."

I glance at her. "What about you? Any retirement plans once Dad finally lets go of the reins?"

She chuckles, slipping off her gloves. "Travel, I think. There are places I've wanted to see for years—maybe the Greek Isles, maybe South America." Her eyes go distant, as if she's already seeing whitewashed walls and blue water. "But I won't stray too far. My goal is to be close to my grandchildren." She cuts me a sidelong glance, teasing. "Whenever you children decide to give me some."

I groan, running a hand down my face. "You have one. Isn't that enough?"

"Never. I need many more." She pats my arm, her eyes kind but sharp. "You'll figure it out when the time is right." When Mom sets her basket down, she squeezes my hand. "I'm glad Elise is getting so much out of the exchange. She deserves it."

"I think so too," I tell her.

The moment lingers, warm as the late sun. Then I head off to the car I keep parked here. The drive to the community center is short, barely enough time for my mom's comment about grandchildren to stop echoing in my head. As I pull into the lot, I shove it aside to focus on the game.

Inside the gym, Beckett is already taking shots while Greyson stretches by the sideline. Theo is there too, his little legs pumping furiously as he zooms circles around the court, laughter bouncing off the walls.

"About time," Beckett calls, catching a rebound. "We thought you were bailing."

Greyson grins, scooping Theo up before he runs straight into the wall. "Yeah, figured maybe Hope had you tied up."

I snort. "Hardly."

They share a look. "So?" Beckett asks. "What's going on there? When are you finally going to ask her to marry you?"

"Never," I say flatly, grabbing a ball from the rack. "We're not seeing each other anymore."

That stops both of them cold. Beckett lowers the ball he's holding, and Greyson blinks like he misheard. "She dumped you?"

"No." I bounce the ball once, sweat slicking my palms, the echo sharp against the hardwood. "I ended it."

Their jaws practically hit the floor.

"Since when?" Beckett presses.

"From the start, we agreed it was no strings," I explain, trying to seem casual. "She loves her job in Vancouver, and I love my life here in Black Bear Valley. I couldn't keep pretending it was enough."

Greyson shakes his head, setting Theo back on his feet.

I shoot the ball, and it sails right through the net. "I told you once. If you weren't willing to move to Vancouver, you didn't really love Trinity. You thought I was talking about Cara."

He pauses, studying me.

"But I wasn't. I was talking about Hope."

Beckett exhales hard, like the air's been knocked out of him. "Damn. Didn't see that coming."

The doors slam open, and Ryker saunters in, twirling a ball on his finger. "What's this? Funeral faces?"

"Kingston and Hope broke up," Beckett supplies.

"We didn't break up. We were never together," I say, my frustration growing.

Ryker's eyebrows rise, and a slow grin spreads. "About time. Now, are you finally going to admit you've got a thing for Elise?"

The ball slips out of my hands, clattering to the floor. "What?"

He shrugs, already lining up at the three-point line. "Come on. You went out of your way to antagonize her when we were kids. And then she spends her last week before France living at your place with you chauffeuring her back and forth? If that's not a thing, I don't know what is."

He lets the ball fly—perfect arc, clean swish.

I stand there stunned, heat rising in my chest. All this time, I thought I was hiding something from even myself. Turns out my brother saw it years ago.

"Let's play," Ryker says, grabbing the rebound. "Greyson, you're with Kingston. Beckett, you're stuck with me. Theo, you're the referee, and remember, I'm your favorite uncle."

We square off, teams set. The game picks up fast, bodies colliding, sneakers squealing, laughter cutting through the echo of the ball on the hardwood. Theo cheers from the sideline, and when Greyson and I crush them with a clean win, the victory is sweeter than usual. Even so, Ryker's words hang in the back of my mind, sticky and insistent. *"You've got a thing for Elise."*

We shower and pile into cars, meeting up again at Mikey's, the bar Ryker invested in a few years back. It's loud tonight—hockey on the screens, country music fighting with the chatter—but the table in the corner is ours. Beers land in front of us, the first sip cool and bitter.

Greyson leans back, eyes steady. "So. You and Elise."

I nearly choke. "What about me and Elise?"

He doesn't blink. "You tell me."

Beckett chuckles, leaning forward. "You've been edgy all night, man. And Ryker called it. You've got a thing for her."

"I don't—" The denial dies in my throat, flimsy even to my ears.

Greyson doesn't let me off the hook. He waits, the silence stretching until the weight of his gaze makes me shift and look at him. Only then does he go on. "Listen, if you do, that's fine. But if you fuck it up? It won't just be between the two of you." He ticks the list off on his fingers. "She's Tarryn's best friend. Tarryn's about to step in as CEO, and Elise is going to be the master vintner. The future of Paradise Hill depends on those two being able to work in sync. If you hurt her, you're not just risking Elise. You're risking our sister and, by extension, this family."

He's right. This isn't a fling I can stumble through. But it doesn't even remotely feel like that. Elise isn't just a woman who makes my pulse race. She's already woven into the fabric of our lives.

I swirl my glass, staring at the amber liquid. "I hear you."

Ryker lifts his beer in a mock toast. "Good. Because if you screw it up, it won't just be Greyson coming for you. We'll all line up."

Beckett smirks. "And you'll lose."

Their laughter fills the table, easy and brotherly, but they're not wrong. And even so, Elise isn't someone I can walk away from. She's become too important.

Ryker called it a *thing*. But sitting here now, with my brothers staring me down and Elise's face still haunting me, I know the truth.

What I feel for her has made me different. It's already more than I ever thought it could be.

Twenty-three

Elise

I can't believe I've been here in France for seven weeks now. I'm just past the halfway point—tired, but not quite ready to go home. Kingston is on my mind when Claire hooks her arm through mine the second I step into the courtyard outside Château's administrative offices. She's practically vibrating, the way she does when she's had too much espresso.

"Elise," she says, her voice pitched higher than usual, "I want you to meet someone."

Before I can ask who, she's tugging me across the gravel toward a tall woman in a cream blazer and dark trousers, her hair swept into a sleek knot that doesn't dare move in the breeze. The woman doesn't wait for us to reach her. She turns as we approach, already smiling.

"Elise, this is Sasha Valmont, CEO of Château." Claire's

grin is so wide it could split her face. "And Sasha, this is Elise Anderson, a vintner from Paradise Hill in British Columbia."

I know the Valmont name. Everyone in wine does. But hearing Claire say it aloud makes my stomach lurch. Sasha Valmont is standing in front of me, eyes cutting straight through me like she already knows where I'll fall short.

"It's good to see you again," Sasha says, extending her hand. Her voice is smooth, accented faintly with Paris. Everything about her is effortless—her posture, the way she waits for me to shake her hand instead of pressing forward. She knows she holds the power in this exchange, and she doesn't need to prove it. "I know Paradise Hill. I met Kingston and Greyson years ago when I was traveling to see how other vineyards worked. They were so warm and inviting. I'm glad we're doing this exchange."

I manage to get my fingers to work, though they feel clumsy against her cool, precise grip. "Thank you," I murmur. "It's an honor to be here."

Claire practically bounces beside me, pride radiating from her in waves. I notice the way her fingers twitch against her skirt, though—the smallest tell that she's nervous. Being seen by Sasha matters to her as much as it does to me. She isn't just thrilled for me. She's desperate to prove she belongs here too.

Sasha releases my hand, eyes steady, weighing and measuring. "Claire tells me Monsieur Paradise is retiring and his daughter is taking over Paradise Hill. And you will be taking over for your father as master vintner?"

"Yes." My voice steadies as I find my footing. "It's both nerve wracking and exciting."

Sasha's brows lift a fraction. "The wine business is mostly run by men. I like that you'll be women-run. Like us."

It's hard to imagine, but I guess that's true—if we ever get there. I picture Tarryn in the barrel room, hair pulled back, stubborn determination on her face. Trace pacing at the head of the long oak table, his voice carrying through the dining room, every decision a performance of leadership and pride. The Paradise family may argue, may clash, but at the end of the day, it's Trace and Tarryn who keep the business running. The rest of us circle around them, orbiting in and out.

The Valmonts are different. They don't orbit. They each have their own planet, entire empires spun off from the same name. Sasha herself controls Château while her brothers and cousins run financial firms, hotels, luxury brands. This isn't a family business. It's a dynasty.

I feel small under the weight of it. Intimidated and impressed all at once.

Sasha's smile widens. "We should talk more. Will you join me for lunch?"

I hesitate, as my first thought is Sebastian. He won't like this. He doesn't like anything he doesn't control. But this is his boss's boss, Sasha Valmont, asking me to lunch, and saying no would be absurd. My pulse jumps at the thought of talking wine, business, vision—all of it—with her.

"Yes," I say, before I can overthink it. "Of course."

"Perfect." She tilts her head toward the gates. "There's a bistro not far from here. Claire, come with us."

Claire beams so brightly it makes me laugh, the tension breaking for just a moment. She falls into step beside Sasha, leaving me to follow.

Excitement buzzes under my skin. Maybe Sebastian will frown later, maybe he'll ice me out, but for once, I don't care. This is the kind of chance I came here for.

The bistro Sasha leads us to is like something out of a postcard. Tall windows fling open to the street, letting sunlight spill across tiled floors. The clink of crystal glasses and the murmur of French swirl in the air, softened by the smell of fresh bread drifting from the kitchen. A basket lands on our table almost immediately, warm loaves wrapped in linen, the crust golden and crackling.

I take it all in, trying not to look like a wide-eyed tourist, though the truth is I feel exactly that—out of place in my work boots and ponytail, following a woman who looks like she belongs on the cover of Forbes. Kingston would know how to sit at a table like this, how to order the right bottle, how to fold into the atmosphere, as if he owned it. I wish he were here, not to shield me, but to steady me.

Sasha orders for us in rapid French, the words tumbling like music. Claire beams at me across the table, and I can't help smiling back. She's in her element, and she's proud to have brought me along for the ride.

Sasha leans forward once the waiter retreats. "So, Elise," she says smoothly, "tell me, are you excited about taking over for your father?"

Heat pricks my neck. I hate talking about myself in a way that sounds rehearsed. "Yes," I say, and then hesitate. "He's leaving very big shoes to fill. I grew up with the Paradise family, and Tarryn and I are close. We've been planning this for a while."

"We met the International Wine and Spirits Competition when we were all kids," Sasha says. "They spoke about how beautiful the area is and how it's perfect for growing wine grapes." Sasha tilts her head, patient but expectant.

Claire nudges me under the table with her knee, subtle encouragement to keep going.

I nod. "Black Bear Valley does have the perfect climate—hot, dry summers, low rainfall, and cold winters. And the soil is both glacial and volcanic, giving the vines what they need for perfect grapes."

Claire is watching me closely, her eyes shining. Pride warms me from the inside. Sasha sips her water, and I take a moment to look around at the bistro, enjoying the scenery.

Then I see him. Across the street, Sebastian is standing still, staring at us. My stomach drops. In an instant, he's in motion, and when he strides through the doors, the air seems to cool a degree. He comes straight to our table.

"Sasha," he says smoothly, switching into English, "I didn't expect to find you here. May I join you?"

The question hangs like a blade, but Sasha doesn't flinch. "We'll see each other later this week," she replies. "I want to get to know Elise."

Sebastian's jaw works, though his smile doesn't fade. He glances at Claire, then at me, and the weight of that look lands hard. I feel it in my gut—accusation, disappointment, warning. I swallow around the lump in my throat.

"Of course," he says finally. "She has been a big help in the fields." He nods once and leaves, his retreat polite, but not gracious. The sound of the door closing behind him rings loud.

"Yes," Sasha agrees, even though he's gone. "That's what Claire told me."

My appetite vanishes. I can still feel the press of his gaze, the silent message that I shouldn't be here, at least not without him. I wanted so badly to talk wine with Sasha, to feel like I belonged in this world, but now, it feels like I've stumbled into company politics.

I try my best to shake it off. We continue to chat over a fabulous spinach and cheese quiche, and I pepper her with questions about the stress of being the first female in twelve generations to run Château. By the end of lunch, she's committed to come to Paradise Hill when she can fit it in her calendar so she can see our operation and spend more time with Tarryn. They have so much in common, and since there are so few female CEOs in the wine business, they should meet.

When we return to Château, the warmth of our lunch feels like a fading dream. Sasha disappears, Claire drifts off toward the marketing department, and I head straight for the barrel room, determined to prove I'm not just coasting on introductions.

Sebastian's voice meets me like a slap. "You're late."

I glance at the clock. I'm not. "I came straight back after lunch."

His eyes on me are cool and sharp. "Next time, check in before you disappear. This isn't a sightseeing trip, Elise. We actually work here." He turns away without waiting for my reply. Half of my coworkers haven't yet returned.

I bite my lip, humiliation already stinging. Not late. Not wrong. But I've crossed him anyway.

The rest of the afternoon is a blur of drudgery. Instead of being included in fermentation checks or blending decisions, he hands me a hose. "Rinse the barrels," Sebastian says briskly, like he's passing a toy. "Scrub until they shine."

The other workers glance at me—one with sympathy, another with barely concealed amusement. My cheeks burn as I crouch, water spraying cold against my boots, suds foaming across my hands. The hose spits back at me, soaking my shirt until it clings to my skin. My hair sticks damply against my neck, and my shoulders burn with each shove of the brush. Foam seeps into the cracks of my palms, stinging tender skin where the gloves have rubbed them raw.

By the time the sun dips behind the vines, my arms are trembling. I strip off my gloves, hands pink underneath, and drop them into the sink. The humiliation lingers, heavier than the ache in my muscles.

Claire is waiting in the corridor when I get back to the dorm, her smile tentative. "Drink?"

I nod, too tired to pretend otherwise.

I change quickly, and we walk into town, the air cool against my damp hair. She leads us to a small café tucked down a side street, candles flickering already on chipped wooden tables. The first sip of wine eases my chest, but only slightly.

Claire leans forward, elbows on the table. "I saw Sebastian this afternoon. He didn't look thrilled about lunch."

I groan, pressing my forehead into my hand. "That was a mistake, wasn't it?"

"Not exactly." She hesitates, twirling the stem of her glass. "It's…complicated here. Sasha is the boss, yes, but she's not in the cellar every day. Sebastian is. He wants control, and when she swoops in and takes an interest, it ruffles him." Her lips press tight for a beat. "He doesn't like anyone stepping into his space. I've had ideas shut down before they even left my mouth."

I swirl my glass, watching the candlelight flicker through the wine. "So what happens when they clash?"

Claire exhales. "Sasha wins, of course. But not without bruises. She'll shift resources, change a supplier, make a decision that reminds everyone this is her Château. And Sebastian…well, he makes sure no one forgets how much the cellar runs because of him. It's a tug-of-war, and the rest of us get caught in the middle."

"Including you."

Her mouth twists as she nods. "I have a good relationship with Sasha. She's disappointed that I want to leave. But Sebastian runs this place when she's not around."

I nod as understanding dawns. No wonder he froze me out this afternoon. No wonder he handed me the most menial task in sight. He was reminding me whose team I'm supposed to be on.

Claire's hand brushes mine. "Don't let him get under your skin. He's brilliant, but he hates feeling threatened. Prove you're here to work, not to undermine him or take his job, and he'll come around."

I manage a small smile. "And if he doesn't?"

She shrugs. "Then remember you have a vineyard waiting for you at home. Not everyone here does."

I nod. She's right. There's so much possibility for me in Paradise. More than I ever realized. I think of Kingston and smile.

We finish our dinner and return to our building. Back in my room, I sink onto my mattress, feeling the weight of the day all over again.

My gaze falls on the small box of chocolates sitting on the nightstand, the ones Kingston sent me. Only one left, its packaging wrinkled soft from how many times I've opened the lid just to see it there. Now, I unwrap it slowly, the paper crackling in the quiet, and place it on my tongue. The sweetness melts first, lush and familiar, but underneath is the faintest trace of bitterness.

It reminds me of Kingston's voice when he said, *"Your place is at Paradise."*

The taste lingers, and with it comes everything I've been pushing aside. Suddenly, I'm not in this cold stone room. I'm back at Black Bear Lake, the sun glowing gold on the water, Trace's booming voice calling us to point out the buds as they appear each year, Tarryn scribbling in her vineyard journal, Ryker cracking jokes. And Kingston, always the silent observer.

Paradise may be young compared to Bordeaux, but it's ours. I can feel it in my bones in a way I'll never feel anywhere else.

I drag my laptop onto my knees. I should tell Kingston the truth, that I scrubbed barrels until my arms went numb, that Sebastian shut me out, that I feel like I'm wasting my time. But I can manage those things on my own.

So instead, I write about what matters.

My dearest Kingston,

I have to tell you about Sasha Valmont. I had lunch with her today, and she remembers meeting you and Greyson. She asked me about Paradise Hill, and I couldn't stop smiling as I spoke of it. I told her about the lake, how it shimmers like glass in the late afternoon, and how the vines roll down the hillsides, as if they were always meant to be there. But what made me proudest was speaking about the future and how Tarryn and I will be taking over for our fathers.

I invited Sasha to visit, and I hope she'll come.

When I think of Paradise Hill, I think of you. Of how proud I am to call Paradise Hill my home. Everything I'm learning here I will pour back into what your family has so lovingly created. Only forty-four more days. It will be here before we know it.

Always yours,
Elise

I hit send, and the screen glows in the dim room. I stare at it long after the words vanish. I didn't tell him how small I feel here. But writing to him has still helped me process. I'm going to carry home what I can from this place and, hopefully, make it ours.

I close the laptop and lean back, the last of the chocolate sweet on my tongue and the weight of forty-four days heavy on my heart.

Twenty-four

Kingston

Saturday mornings are supposed to be slower, but I don't know how to live that way. I am up before the sun, pounding out a long run around the property. Dew clings to my shirt, and the vineyard rows glow faint green as the light comes up. Everything looks good. The vines are showing signs of coming back to life, and the lake below is glassy and still.

Even after I've showered and settled into my office, the house is quiet. My desk faces the big windows, the vineyard stretching toward the hills, Black Bear Lake catching the last strands of mist. I could almost believe this view is enough to settle me. Almost.

I open my laptop. It's the first thing I do every morning when I reach my desk since Elise left. I have to check for her name in my inbox. And there it is, waiting.

My pulse jumps, same as it always does. I click.

She writes about her workday, about a mildew scare in one of the barrels, about the hands rushing to get ahead of it. Then she pivots, almost too neatly, to Paradise Hill. She writes the word *home* like she's reminding herself what matters most, like she needs to anchor herself in what's real while surrounded by Bordeaux.

My Elise,

I ran the ridge this morning, the air sharp in my lungs, the vines lined up like a worn brown quilt, each row a seam waiting for spring to fill it in. Your father and his team have pruned them well, and they're waking up from their winter sleep. They never falter, never lean, never doubt their place in the soil. I wish I could say the same.

When I got home, Renew Motion was waiting for me, the way it always is. I don't think I've ever told you how heavy it feels—this responsibility. Every blueprint I sign, every line I approve, stretches far beyond me. Engineers, welders, designers, accountants—hundreds of families I'll never know are tied to the choices I make. If I stumble, they stumble. If I break, they break. That truth keeps me awake when the house is silent.

The board presses harder every week. Their words sting more than I'll ever admit to anyone but you. They want answers, numbers, perfection, and some nights, I lie here wondering if I can keep carrying it all without shattering. I don't say that out loud because the world needs me steady. But you're the one place I don't have to pretend.

Forty-two days. That's all that stands between now and the moment I open the door and find you there—not just visiting, not just passing through, but home. I can't wait for the day I don't have to count anymore.

Always yours,
Kingston

When I finish, the email seems a little too polished, measured. The kind of note a CEO would send if he were trying to sound in control, even when vulnerable. I close the laptop for a second, stare out at the vineyard, then reopen it and hit send before I can talk myself into more honesty.

Her emails have doubt and longing tucked between the sentences. This one had reassurance and restraint.

She leans into vulnerability. I pull back. But the fact that I'm writing to her is a miracle in itself, I have to remember.

Still, as the screen goes dark, the truth twists in my gut. Our letters are no longer balanced. She's giving me more than I give her. The difference is small now, but I can feel it stretching wider with every truth I don't reveal.

I rub at the tightness in my chest, promising myself I'll tell her my feelings for her are changing—next time. I can at least hint at it. But I already know I likely won't.

The phone buzzing across my desk catches my attention. Tarryn's name flashes.

I answer. "What's wrong?"

For a second, all I hear is wind whipping through the speaker and the scrape of her boots on gravel. She's breathing hard, like she's been running. Voices echo faintly in the background, men shouting instructions, the grind of machinery.

"King," she says at last, catching her breath. "The waterline. North block. It's jammed solid—full of gravel. If we hadn't caught the leaves curling, we would have lost a whole section. It's nearly May, Kingston. Prime growth. Do you understand what that would have done?"

The picture forms in my mind—vines drying out, fruit shriveling before it even sets. I close my eyes. "I understand."

She barrels on, voice sharp with fatigue, "We thought it was just a low-pressure issue at first, so we dug the valve box, checked the pumps, and flushed the filters. Nothing. Finally, one of the guys split the pipe. It was packed tight with gravel, like someone poured it straight from a bucket. Not a natural clog. Took us half the morning to clear it, replace the section, and flush the lines. Half the morning, King. That's time we should have spent thinning shoots and prepping for bloom."

Her words rattle through me. Sabotage isn't just destruction. It's theft. Theft of time, energy, and resources we can't afford to lose.

Would Elise have caught this sooner? She knows the water lines better than her father.

"It's always something," Tarryn continues, her voice rising. "The fire at the cottage, the pump house last month, the broken trellis, now this. One thing after another. It never stops. Sometimes, I wonder if I should hire security to patrol the place at night, just so I can sleep."

"You should not have to think about security," I say. "This isn't supposed to be part of the job."

"Well, it is now." Her voice cracks, then steadies. "I'm trying, Kingston. But every time I fix one problem, another pops up. And I can't help wondering if it would be different if someone else was running the vineyard."

I know she's talking about me. Our father once raised me to take over the vineyard, as if it were already decided. It wasn't until I left for university that I finally found the courage to tell him I didn't want it. One by one, my brothers said the same. Then Tarryn stepped forward and claimed it for herself.

Did she do that because she wanted it or because none of us did?

The guilt is instant, sharp. I look out at the vineyard stretching below my office window, rows neat and calm from this distance, and wish I could split myself in two.

"You have been preparing for years," I remind her. "You know the vines better than anyone. No one else would have spotted those curling leaves in time. Not even me."

Silence. Then a shaky laugh. "You always know what to say."

"Not always." I hesitate, and then add, "But I'll be honest. We've never seen sabotage at this level. Elise has mentioned that they deal with it at Château too—different forms, same idea. Maybe it's a symptom of growth, of standing out."

"Elise mentioned that?" Her tone lifts, curious.

I swallow. "Well, yes. We've been emailing. Keeping in touch."

"She's my best friend," Tarryn says softly.

"I know. And that is between you two. I would never step in the middle. But I've known her a long time as well, and lately, our connection feels…different."

"Huh…" Tarryn says. "Okay. Thank you," she adds quietly after a moment. "For backing me up. For reminding me I can do this."

I'm grateful that she's shifted gears. "If you want me there, just say the word," I tell her. "You know I can fly over in less than ten minutes."

"No. Not yet. Just promise you'll come soon, walk the rows with me, see for yourself."

"I promise."

"Good. I'm going to go now because I need to talk to Elise," Tarryn says. "I need to get to her while the timing still works."

When our call ends, I set the phone down and stare out my office window. To her, I sounded steady. Inside, I feel pulled in two directions—my company, my family. And no matter how much I give, it never feels like enough.

I busy myself with catching up on things, losing myself in the rhythm of organization until the phone rings again later that afternoon. Unknown number.

I answer. "Hello?"

"Kingston Paradise?"

"Yes, this is he."

"Cal Hawthorne. You got a minute?"

The private investigator. My stomach tightens. "Sure. Go ahead."

"I found your man, Zachary Paradise. Puerto Vallarta. Marina-side condo with a view. Gym membership, golfed twice last week and has been having dinners at a place that flambés dessert at the table."

I pinch the bridge of my nose. "With what money?"

"You may want to sit down for this part." Paper rustles. "Condo lease and HOA fees are paid via a shell LLC out of Nevada. I followed the filings. Took a detour through a trust, but the wire trail is clean enough if you know what you're looking at."

"Do you have a name?"

"Maximus Paradise."

My breath leaves me on a whoosh. Last Sunday, Max sat at the dinner table with us, palms up, eyes glassy, swearing he didn't know where Zach was. He even excused himself to the porch to pull himself together. *Actor.*

How would I write that to Elise? my mind wonders idly. How do I tell her the man I call uncle bankrolls betrayal? I want her comfort, but I don't want her looking at Paradise and seeing only rot beneath the roots. I need her to believe in this place.

"You're sure?" I ask.

"I have screenshots of ACH confirmations from an account that resolves to the Maximus Paradise Revocable Trust. Dates line up. Rent due the first business day of each month. Additional wires labeled *consulting retainer* hit on the fifteenth."

"How generous?"

"Twenty-five K a month, plus the rent and extras."

"Do you have any proof Zach's been flying back to Canada?"

"I'm not sure he is," Cal hedges.

"The sabotage is still happening. I need to know who's behind it."

"I'll see what I can find," Cal assures me.

"Thank you." I stand, the chair skidding back. "Email everything you can."

"It's already in your inbox. One more thing—Zach isn't laying low. He's wearing a Panerai watch that retails north of fifty grand, and he has a tan I would bottle if I could. If he's worried, he isn't showing it."

Heat crawls up my neck. "Thanks, Cal. Keep watching. If

he moves, I want to know before he finishes zipping a suitcase."

"You got it."

The line goes dead. I stare at the phone, and then click Cal's email open. Receipts. Wire memos. The condo's cash purchase. Deposits line up with the dates for every hit of sabotage we've taken. I suspected Zach and let it slide. My siblings were less certain, but our restraint feels like negligence now.

My hands hover over the keyboard. I want to send Elise everything, so we can talk through how I'm going to tell my dad about his brother. But this is ugly. It doesn't belong in her inbox, sandwiched between tank readings and Simone's recipes. I should consult my brothers and sister first anyway. Elise doesn't owe me anything, and I don't want to scare her with this.

I close the laptop.

By nightfall, the house feels too quiet. Simone has left me a covered plate in the fridge—chicken fajitas wrapped in foil, still carrying the smoky bite of peppers and onions. I heat them and eat standing at the counter, my chewing loud in the empty kitchen. The flavors are bold, filling, but still feel hollow when I'm done.

The silence leaves too much room for memory. Elise's laugh drifts through me—the way she leaned against this same counter once, shaking her head at my lack of cooking skills, stealing peppers straight off the pan. But then my mind shifts further back to Cara and the searing pain of being lied to. Am I opening myself up to that again?

I pour a glass of wine and sit in the darkened living room. The lake is a strip of silver through the window. I should call someone. I'm not ready for my siblings yet, but I have old teammates in Vancouver, business friends who would meet me for a drink if I asked. I scroll through my phone, stop at a name, and then lock the screen without dialing. Whoever I sit across from will not be Elise.

And that's the problem. I don't want distraction. I want her here. I want her laugh echoing down this hall, her hand stealing bites of my dinner, her voice softening this silence.

Instead, I have four walls and the weight of secrets I can't send her.

I shift my focus to tomorrow. How on earth will I put this truth on the table in front of my family? I think about watching my father's face as I say Max's name. The dread sits like stone in my chest.

I carry my half-finished glass upstairs, set it on the nightstand, and stretch out in the dark. Sleep doesn't come easy.

Twenty-five

Kingston

Sunday dinner at my parents' house smells like prime rib before I even make it through the door. Garlic and rosemary drift through the air, layered over the buttery scent of twice-baked potatoes crisping in the oven. The clatter of pans mixes with voices, the chaos wrapping around me.

Theo comes barreling out of the living room on unsteady legs, a grin spread across his face as he wobbles toward the dogs. They circle him like patient guardians, tails wagging as he clutches at fur and table legs to keep his balance. Greyson scoops him up just before he topples, and Trinity laughs, adjusting the baby's bib.

"Slow down, buddy," Greyson murmurs, but Theo is already wriggling toward the dogs again, squealing without words.

Mom appears with a glass of wine in one hand and a

kitchen towel in the other. "There you are," she says, kissing my cheek before pressing the glass into my palm. "Taste this. We are pouring merlot because your father insists the cabernet is too obvious."

Dad glances up to give me a look from the carving board, where the prime rib rests under foil.

I take a sip. "It's too obvious. Let the cabernet breathe for a bit. By dinner it should be plenty ready."

Greyson bumps my shoulder with his free arm. "Look who's Switzerland. You look like you slept three hours."

"Four," I answer, pretending a smile.

Ryker leans against the counter with Ginny tucked at his side, already stealing the edge of a potato.

"Hands off," Beckett warns, swatting him away. Sadie shakes her head and turns to Mom. "We're thinking about a babymoon, and we've been looking at flights to Costa Rica. Rosie always wanted to see sloths."

After Rosie, Sadie's best friend, died waiting for a heart transplant, Sadie and Beckett began honoring her by completing the bucket list she left behind.

Mom's face softens. "That would mean the world to her."

"Sloths." Ryker smirks. "You're flying halfway across the world for sleepy tree rats?"

Ginny elbows him. "Better than your idea of a romantic getaway."

The chatter follows us into the dining room where the table glows with platters of prime rib carved thick, twice-baked potatoes piled high with cheese, roasted root vegetables glistening with olive oil, and two pies cooling at the far end—chocolate cream and lemon meringue. Mom ushers us to our seats like she has conducted this symphony a hundred times before.

Conversation starts up instantly. Greyson entertains with a clinic story that has Trinity rolling her eyes. Beckett and Ryker bicker about playlists. Ginny swats Ryker's hand again when he tries to sneak a potato.

Theo toddles laps around the table, the dogs padding after

him, tails swishing. He bangs a wooden spoon against a chair leg, the sharp *thwack* making everyone laugh. Mom sighs fondly and scoops him up, only for him to wriggle free and make another run for the dogs.

It's warm. Loud. Easy.

And I sit in the middle of it, feeling oddly separate. The file in my inbox from the private investigator is heavy on my heart.

Elise would know the right words to cut through this noise. Or she'd at least help me find them. But she isn't here, and it's on me to drop the truth and let it land where it will.

Dad catches my eye over his glass. His brows pull tight. He knows something's up. We fill our plates with prime rib, crisp salad, and potatoes, passing the platters around the table.

Once everyone has their meal, I clear my throat. "I have an update from Cal," I say.

The voices dip, the room softening.

"He found Zach. Mexico. Puerto Vallarta. He isn't hiding. He's living easy. Marina condo. Golf. Restaurants."

Beckett's fork slips against his plate. Greyson's chair scrapes back a fraction.

Dad's jaw hardens. "On whose dime?"

I steady my voice. "Max's."

The room detonates.

When the questions subside, Mom presses a hand to her chest. "No. He told us— He said he didn't know."

Tarryn whispers, "He cried in our kitchen."

"He said a lot," I reply. "But Cal traced the wires. From the Maximus Paradise Trust to the LLC paying Zach's rent. Lease, receipts, ACH confirmations, and retainers labeled as consulting. It's all there."

My father lays his palms flat on the table, fury and disbelief cutting sharp lines into his face. "Show me," he demands.

"I will forward the file." My throat tightens. "Max is paying for Zach to be on the run, and Cal's not seeing evidence that Zach's been back to Canada. So I'm not sure if he's been involved with the sabotage since he left."

Mom's voice breaks. "Why would Max do this and lie to us?"

"Zach's his son," Greyson says bleakly.

"Or leverage," Beckett mutters. "He tanks us, and then rides in as savior."

"Over my dead body." Tarryn grips the edge of the table. I slide my hand over hers. She doesn't pull away.

Silence stretches. Even the dogs seem to go still at Theo's feet.

Mom pushes back her chair just slightly. For a moment, she doesn't say anything, eyes fixed on the prime rib cooling on the platter like she's trying to make the world ordinary again. When she finally speaks, her voice is low. "He sat at this table last week. He prayed with us before we ate. And now this."

Dad stands, pacing toward the window. He braces both hands against the frame, shoulders rigid, his reflection a dark shape in the glass. For a long moment, no one dares break the silence.

But then Ryker does because, of course, he does. Only his voice isn't joking this time. "If he can pay Zach to screw with us, he could be paying someone else to do the other things. The fire, the water valve stuck on before the storm at your place, cut brake lines. And now, rocks poured into the water line. What's next?"

The edge in his words betrays something I rarely hear from him—fear.

Greyson exhales hard, staring down at his plate. "Jesus."

Mom finally gathers herself, smoothing her napkin, forcing composure back onto her face. "We'll get through this," she says, but it sounds more like a prayer than certainty.

Dad turns from the window, his voice steel. "We don't feed on each other. We don't turn this house into his stage. We make a plan."

The suggestions start tumbling out—Ryker blurting ideas about security, Beckett adding motion sensors, Greyson pushing legal.

Elise would hate this, hate the way betrayal threatens to

fracture the strongest roots.

"Do we manage this ourselves, or do we alert the police and let it get out to everyone in town?" Mom asks, pain etched in every word. "He's your brother."

Dad's gaze hardens. "He made his choice when he wired that money. He'll answer for it."

"I'll contact the lawyers tomorrow," I tell them. "I'll send them the file. And I will fly to Vancouver this week. Dad, do you want to come with me to meet with the lawyers?"

Dad nods. "And we audit every system. Hire security."

"I'll walk the rows with Tarryn," Ryker volunteers.

Beckett raises his hand. "Me too."

Mom reaches across the table and squeezes Dad's hand. "We'll get through this. We always do."

Conversation trickles back in uneven bursts as we return to the meal. Beckett and Sadie talk quietly, and Ryker teases Ginny into swatting him again. Greyson scrolls for motion sensor specs, Trinity steadying Theo as he bangs his fists against the table, delighted with the sound.

My family is knitting themselves tighter around a rupture. It's what we do. But what if we can't? What if there's so much damage that in the end there's no winery to hang on to? We simply can't let that happen.

I lift my glass. "To not letting the bastards win."

"Language," Mom scolds automatically, and laughter rolls across the table like a release.

We drink. The wine is dark fruit, iron, and something stubborn I decide is hope.

Twenty-six

Elise

By the time I drag myself back to the dormitory, my body aches from head to toe. It may be Friday, but I'll be working all weekend. The straps of my boots have left ridges in my skin, and there's a sour tang of sweat and crushed leaves clinging to my shirt that even the cool night air can't erase. I want nothing more than to collapse on the narrow bed and forget this day existed.

Instead, I find Claire already waiting at the long wooden table near the window with a bottle of Bordeaux breathing beside her and two glasses ready. She looks up, catches sight of me in the doorway, and her smile softens, like she's been expecting me to fall apart and has the antidote waiting.

"Rough one?" she asks, lifting the bottle in offering.

I nod, too drained for words, and sink into the chair across from her. The stem of the glass feels cold against my fingers as she pours. One sip and the bitterness on my tongue is more than tannins. It's the taste of defeat, of being brushed aside again and again until I feel invisible.

Claire watches me quietly, letting the silence stretch until I finally groan. "He's going to grind me down, isn't he?"

She tilts her head. "Sebastian?"

"Who else? It's like he's set on proving I don't belong in this business. Every task, every glance, he wants me gone."

Claire doesn't argue. She leans her elbows on the table, fingers tracing the rim of her glass. "I think it's more about him being threatened by you. He has a good relationship with Sasha, but he wants the master vintner job, and she's never going to put him there. And you're on track to be the master vintner of an award-winning vineyard."

Her calm cuts through my frustration, and shame prickles at the back of my neck. "I hate that I'm letting him get under my skin. I came here to gather knowledge, to prove myself, and instead I'm…whining."

"You're surviving," she corrects gently. "And you're gathering knowledge and experience. Don't underestimate that."

I lift my gaze. "Days like today don't feel like learning."

"Then reframe it." Claire's voice sharpens enough to make me sit straighter. "Take what you came for. Knowledge, practice, confidence. Those are yours to claim. He doesn't get to dictate your growth unless you hand him the power. Don't."

Her certainty pulls me back from the weight pressing on my chest. I close my eyes for a beat, breathing her words in until they settle. Gratitude swells in my throat, thick and unexpected. "Thank you," I whisper.

Claire clinks her glass against mine. "We've got this. One day at a time." She always says it that way, like a promise carved in stone. A Claire-ism, steady and simple. And somehow, I believe her.

I swirl the wine in my glass, watching the garnet liquid catch the dim light. "You know what today was?" My laugh comes out brittle. "Dragging hoses across the cellar floor. Scrubbing barrels until my hands reek of sulfur. Climbing ladders to top wine I'll never taste. Out in the vineyard, snapping off shoots until my fingers cramped, and hauling brush like a laborer. I'm not an assistant vintner, Claire. I'm a cleaner and field worker with a fancier title."

Her brows knit, but she doesn't interrupt. That alone loosens something in me, gives me permission to spill the truth I've been holding back. "This has made me realize that I know more because I've been working at a small vineyard. We're never going to be this big. I don't think we want to be this big."

Claire leans back, considering. Then she shakes her head. "The bigger you get, the bigger the problems. But here's the thing. Every moment you spend in those tanks or with those hoses is information. You're seeing this place from the ground up. You'll know what to change, what to adopt, and what to reject when you go home."

I nod. She's right, of course. The knowledge is there, tucked between blisters and aching muscles. Still, shame prickles. "It's hard not to feel like I'm wasting my time."

"You're not." Her voice is steady, no room for doubt. "It's not glamorous, but it's teaching you. And one day, when you're back at Paradise Hill, you'll look at a worker cleaning a press and know exactly what it takes. That's leadership. That's dignity."

I draw in a slow breath, feeling the tightness in my chest ease a fraction. She's giving me back something Sebastian keeps trying to strip away—perspective.

My grandmother's voice rises in my memory, soft and firm all at once. *"Dignity isn't given, Elise. It's kept."* I hadn't understood what she meant when I was twelve and sulking over being made to set the dinner table. But here, tonight, I do.

And then Kingston rises in my mind—his steady belief in me, the way he sees more than I think I show. He would tell me this work matters, even if it doesn't feel like it. He would want me to stand tall, not crumble. I tuck that thought against my ribs like armor.

Claire nudges my glass again. "So. Tomorrow, you go back, and you take what's yours to take. Don't wait for him to hand it over."

My mouth curves. "You make it sound simple."
"It is. Not easy. But simple."

Last night, I went to bed with Claire's words rattling around in my head, and I wake this morning with a different kind of feeling in my chest, not just fatigue but resolve. If Sebastian wants me stuck on the bottom rung, fine. I will turn the bottom rung into my classroom.

As I step into the cellar, the air bites cold against my skin. I've walked through these halls for weeks now, but today, I make sure I notice more—the way the barrels line the walls, how the workers slip smoothly between them, speaking in a shorthand I'm only just beginning to catch. Their banter is quick, a mixture of French slang and vineyard jargon, but instead of shrinking from it, I lean in. Every phrase is a clue.

Scrubbing doesn't feel meaningless anymore. I notice where the barrels swell dark with rinse water, how the sulfur stings my nose before it fades to clean wood. When I drag a hose across the floor, I pay attention to its weight, the give and pull as I guide it from one barrel to the next. Even in the vineyard, the smallest chores teach me something—the snap of a sucker breaking clean from the cane, the resinous scent of cut shoots sticking to my gloves, the way the brush piles crackle in the sun. Each task leaves its mark, as if the land itself is whispering lessons I'm only just learning to hear.

I study the vineyard, memorizing the way the shoots lift toward the sun when they're healthy. A twist in a leaf here, a sag in a cane there—they start to form a language, one I can almost translate.

And when Sebastian's back is turned, I take chances. A question murmured to Luc about sulfur levels in the rinse water. A glance toward another worker, pointing at a cluster beginning to overgrow until he nods. They don't indulge me much, but enough. Enough to confirm I am learning. Enough to keep me from drowning.

Every bit of information becomes a mental note for Paradise Hill. I imagine standing in our cellar, teaching our team how to adjust water flow with precision, how to catch a sour note in the air before it becomes a problem.

When I return to the dormitory that evening, as usual, my clothes are damp with sweat, and the green scent of crushed shoots clings to my hair. I should shower, but Claire is at the table again, waiting with a plate of cheese and bread, and something in me gravitates toward her before I can think better of it.

I drop into the chair opposite her, pressing my palms flat against the wood. The words tumble out before I can stop them. "Today was better. I still had the grunt work, but I noticed things that probably happen at home, but never paid attention."

"See?" She smiles. "I told you you'd learn from the menial work he pushes off on you."

We sit for a while, and she tells me about the Christmas holiday advertising they're working on. Eventually, I have the energy to climb the five flights to my room and back down again to shower and get ready for bed.

The dormitory is quiet at night, the hum of the old radiator filling the gaps where voices used to be. From the fifth floor, I can see the sprawl of the vineyard lit by scattered lamps, the vines stretching like dark veins under the moon.

I balance my laptop on my knees, cursor blinking in an empty email. My notebook lies open beside me, scrawled with messy observations. Shoot thinning. Early canopy work. Barrel topping regularly. Useful details, but not what I want to send him. Not tonight.

I start typing.

Kingston,

I need to be honest with you. Until now, I've only written you the bright pieces – the sun on the river, the pride in learning something new, the details that make me sound strong. I wanted you to be proud of me. I wanted to be proud of me. But that hasn't been the whole truth.

The truth is, it's been brutal. Sebastian cuts me down at every turn. I can't tell if it's because I'm a woman or because he expected me to end up in his bed instead of on the cellar floor. Maybe both. He dismisses me in front of others, acts as if my questions are foolish, makes me feel like I don't belong here. Some days I wonder if he's right.

I haven't told you because I didn't want you to worry, or worse, to think I can't handle it. But there have been mornings I've sat on the edge of my bed, staring at my boots, wondering if I could make myself get up and face it again. There have been nights I've cried into my pillow, choking the sound down so no one would hear.

If it weren't for Claire, I think I might have packed up and gone home. She listens when I unravel. She reminds me why I came, why this matters, why I can't let him break me. She's been my lifeline.

And today, there was a crack of light. Once again, I noticed something before anyone else did. I was right. Luc confirmed it. Sebastian still brushed me off, but for one sharp, clear moment, I knew I belonged. All the scrubbing and the silence and doubt haven't been for nothing.

I don't know why I'm telling you this now. Maybe because I'm tired of pretending. Maybe because I need you to know how much I lean on you, even from across an ocean. The thought of home and everything that means is what steadies me when everything here feels like it's slipping.

Always,
Elise

I shouldn't send it. I'm venting, and he doesn't want to hear that. But I want to. I want him to see me, not just the vintner but the woman underneath. That want is the dangerous part. And I press send anyway.

The whoosh sounds final, irreversible. I flinch at it, and then sit frozen. Relief and fear churn together until I can't tell which is stronger. "I shouldn't have," I whisper into the stillness. The dormitory creaks, and still the laptop glows.

I shouldn't have, but part of me is glad I did.

The building stirs to life at dawn—pipes rattling, footsteps in the hall, voices muffled behind curtains—but I'm already awake, my laptop perched on my knees. I haven't slept much, tossing between dread and hope, replaying every word I sent to Kingston.

When his name lights up my inbox, my stomach flips so hard I almost can't bring myself to click.

But I do.

Elise,

It's early here in Vancouver – the sky over the inlet is the same gray as the lake when it's just waking – and I'm sitting with a mug that's gone cold because I can't set this letter down. Thank you for telling me the rest. Thank you for not keeping the hard parts wrapped up the way you always do.

Even before this, you didn't send me only the pretty

pieces, but I'm so glad you felt comfortable telling me all of it. I'm sorry Sebastian has been that way to you. I'm sorry anyone would treat you like you're less than you are. That you've been brave enough to keep showing up anyway is everything. Claire is a saint – tell her I owe her a bottle and dinner – and you owe yourself every small victory you've fought for. You belong in that cellar. You belong in those rows. You've earned the right to be noticed, not patronized.

I wish I was there with you. I can imagine it anyway – the way your jaw sets, the quiet triumph in your eyes. You asking me to believe in you from across an ocean is about the most dangerous, beautiful thing I've been given. It steadies me too.

I am standing beside you while you work through this. If ever you want me to step in – to speak up, to say what needs saying – tell me and I will. If you want me to sit quietly and hand you coffee while you say the hard things, I'll do that. Whatever you need, I will be there.

I'm flying to London next week for meetings. Let me come see you after my work. Let me put my feet on the same dirt and watch you work and laugh and be undone and be brave. Tell me you'll let me.

Always,
Kingston

The sun slants gold through the tall dormitory windows, but it doesn't remotely matter. My body buzzes with the words on the screen. *He wants to come*. He's choosing me, not just in late-night emails but in the daylight of his real life.

Excitement rushes through me, sweeping away the heaviness I've been carrying for weeks. Now, I have something to look forward to. Something that feels like hope.

I read his message again, three times, until the words blur

and my cheeks ache from smiling. I write back quickly to accept his request and ask for details before I press the laptop shut, clutching it to my chest like a teenager with a love note, and I immediately feel ridiculous.

I head down to the toilette de femme to brush my teeth and wash my face, and Claire appears, tugging her braid over her shoulder as she yawns. Her sharp eyes catch everything, and I know if I let mine linger too long she will read me like an open book.

"You're running late," she says, reaching for her scarf.

"I got a good email from Kingston this morning, and I'll tell you about it over lunch or when you have time," I answer, busying myself with lacing my boots. My fingers fumble, the knot slipping twice before I manage to tighten it. My heart is still beating too fast, Kingston's words echoing. *Tell me you'll let me.*

Claire tilts her head, studying me. "I can't meet you for lunch. Sasha and I are heading into Paris for a few days to meet with the ad agency."

"Oh." I stand and make sure I didn't tie my boots too tight. "Then I'll see you when you get back."

"Have some fun for me while I'm gone."

I force a shrug. "Maybe I'll finally catch up on rest."

Her lips twitch like she doesn't believe me, but she lets it go. Around us, the other women stir, pulling on jackets, tying aprons. I keep my head down, my cheeks warm, hoping none of them notice how I'm practically vibrating with joy.

I head out, and today, the work doesn't feel like a burden. The barrels, the hoses, the endless rinsing, everything I do, from topping barrels to snapping suckers in the rows, feels bearable because there's a message in my inbox that changes everything. He's coming. He'll be here.

I bite down on the smile threatening to take over my face, tucking it into the hollow of my chest where it can burn safely. For now, it's mine alone.

The hours crawl forward, but they don't drag me under. Each task, no matter how repetitive, brings the memory of Luc's quiet "bon travail" and Henri's subtle nod yesterday. Even as

Sebastian prowls the floor, my shoulders stay straighter. My arms ache, my back throbs, but beneath the sweat and sting, there's a thread of pride running through me.

When the shift finally ends, I have dinner and then climb the five flights back to the dormitory with my legs trembling, not from defeat but from sheer exhaustion laced with a strange buoyancy. I survived the day. More than that, I carried something out of it.

In the quiet of my room, I open Kingston's message again. The words glow against the dark screen, steadying me. *I'm standing beside you while you work through this.* I close my eyes and imagine his voice instead of the text. Imagine him here, saying these things to me, warm and certain. Heat curls through my chest. Sebastian may never see me. But Kingston does.

I tuck the laptop beneath my pillow, push the blanket aside, and pad across the narrow floor to the tall window. Outside, the vineyard stretches black against the silver wash of moonlight, rows disappearing into the dark. Lamps glow faintly near the gates, pinpricks of gold in the distance.

I press my palm to the glass, which is cool against my overheated skin. "I can do this," I whisper into the night.

I'll carry every scrap of knowledge back to Paradise Hill. I won't let Sebastian write my story. And when Kingston steps off that plane from London, I'll be ready, not just as the woman who survived this place but as the one who's claiming her future.

The thought sharpens me, professionally and personally. I stand taller, even alone in the quiet dormitory. I'm not running. I'm not breaking.

I'm resolved.

Twenty-seven

Elise

The alarm slices through the half-sleep I've been clinging to, and my body protests before my mind even registers the sound. But then I remember. Kingston's coming to pick me up after his business in London. We've worked out the details, and it's two more weeks until he arrives and we leave for home. *But who's counting?*

Giddiness washes over me as I anticipate the future, but then I realize that today, every muscle aches. My palms are raw, new blisters layered over yesterday's blisters. But the vines won't wait. I roll out of bed, drag on clothes that already smell faintly of earth and copper spray, and make my way to the rows as the sun edges up over the horizon.

The light is soft at first, spilling gold across the sea of vines. For a moment, it feels worth it—the view, the quiet, the sense that the land itself is breathing awake. Then I crouch at the first vine and reality sets in. Suckering. Again. My least favorite job.

The young shoots push up from the trunk and roots in every direction, hungry and defiant. I reach in and snap them off, tugging until the green stems give with a sharp pop, directing all the plant's energy to more-developed branches. The sweet smell of sap coats my fingers. It's sticky, cloying, and after ten minutes, my skin itches. My knees burn from kneeling on uneven soil. By the third vine, my back is already screaming.

I glance down the row at the line of bodies bent low, each lost in the rhythm of work. No chatter, no laughter. Just the sound of snapping shoots, the rustle of leaves, the crunch of boots shifting through dry dirt. I fall into the pattern, letting my thoughts drift toward home. *Two weeks.* Just fourteen more days and I'll be done with this, free of these endless rows, free of Sebastian and Château.

By midmorning the sun is higher, the light no longer gentle but hard, unrelenting. My shirt clings damp to my back. Sweat slips into the corner of my eyes, stinging. I wipe it with the back of my wrist, leaving a smear of stickiness across my cheek. The rows blur into sameness—green, brown, green, brown—until I have to shake myself to remember where I am.

We switch tasks, moving to canopy work. The vines are already wild, the shoots growing faster than seems possible. My job is to lift them, guide them toward the trellis, and secure them with thin green ties. Over and over, row after row. My hands are scratched raw by curling tendrils. The wires bite at my arms. Each time I tug a shoot into place, I feel the strain in my shoulders, my calves trembling from balancing on uneven ground.

The sun presses down, thick and hot. It feels like breathing through cloth. Somewhere, a tractor growls, distant but steady, like an old heartbeat. My water bottle is already half empty, and it's not even noon.

Sebastian calls for a short break, and we gather in the thin shadow of an old stone wall. Someone passes a thermos of bitter black coffee. Another worker tears bread into rough chunks, the crust hard, the inside soft and warm. I chew slowly, letting the salt of sweat mix with the yeasty bread. No one talks much. Everyone saves their energy for the vines.

When the break ends, the heat feels worse, the light harsher. The work shifts again—pest patrol. I trail behind Sebastian, notebook in hand, as he scans the leaves for intruders. We stop often, crouching, peering, fingers brushing the underside of the foliage. Sweat drips down my temple. My skin is tight with the beginning of sunburn.

He mutters when he finds the first sign of mildew—yellow spotting, faint but unmistakable. I jot notes, mark the row, circle the leaves with chalk. We move on, but the discovery weighs on me. One sick leaf, then another, and the whole vineyard feels suddenly fragile, like it could collapse under something as small as a spore.

By the time we finish, the afternoon is slipping into early evening. My legs are trembling. My neck is stiff from hours bent forward. We gather the piles of shoots pulled from the trunks and haul them to the edge of the vineyard. The smell of green waste is pungent, sour-sweet. My nails are lined with dirt so deep it will take days to scrub out.

The light softens, finally, the air cooling just enough to breathe again. I straighten, stretching my back, and look out across the rows. The vines are orderly now, shoots tied, trunks cleared, the day's work evident in the land. Endless green stretching into the distance, each plant standing straighter because of my hands. My exhaustion settles into something like pride.

I wipe my forehead with the hem of my shirt. My body throbs with fatigue, but I can't stop staring at the vines. I've given so much to them—sweat, skin, blood even—and in return they've given me knowledge I couldn't have gained anywhere else. My body knows how to move now, my fingers know how to read the signs, and my eyes know how to look for danger in the leaves.

The workers drift toward the outbuildings, their faces as drawn and sunburned as mine. The day is done. Tomorrow, we'll start again. I drag myself after them, every step a reminder of the ground I've covered. Two more weeks. I'll survive it.

For now, though, I am only tired. Bone-deep, marrow-deep tired. The kind of tired that has no cure but rest.

Night wraps the building as I reach the stairs to my room. The stairwell is narrow, and the wood is old, the paint scuffed where hands have traced it for years. Five flights stretch before me like a dare. My thighs shake. I take the steps one at a time and let my pace be slow. On the fourth landing, I press a hand to the wall, close my eyes, and count my breaths. *In. Out. In. Out.* Then I climb again because no one will carry me. The thought isn't bitter. It's steady.

Inside my room, I toe off my boots, and they thud against the floorboards. The quiet settles like a blanket. I sit on the edge of the bed and drop my head into my hands. The ache is everywhere. Wrists. Knees. Calves. I flex my fingers, and they tingle. I stretch my neck until it ticks. It should feel like failure. Instead, it feels like proof. I am still here.

I open my notebook. The pages smell faintly of dust and ink and grape sugar that dried along the edges weeks ago. I draw three stars on today's square and shade them until the paper shines. My throat tightens. I smooth my palm over the page and leave it there. Dignity in the small things. Claire is right. I'm not waiting for someone else to hand it to me. I'm building it with work.

The laptop is cool against my thighs when I pull it close. The screen glows, and it makes the shadows in the corners look deeper. Kingston's last email sits at the top. I read it again, even though I know the lines by heart. His words are a hand between my shoulder blades. I start to type. I stop, erase, and start again.

I type that the leaves on the vines looked like coins when the light turned gold. I tell him about my day. This is the time when the work is so overwhelming that you need to take the small wins when you can get them.

I send it, and the room goes quiet enough that I can hear my own breath. A pipe ticks in the wall. Somewhere in the building a door closes, and the sound climbs the stairwell like a footstep that isn't mine. A draft lifts the corner of the curtain, bringing in the cool night air and the faint scent of earth. I turn off the lamp, and the dark is kind.

Sleep moves over me like a tide. For the first time in weeks, it feels like floating instead of drowning.

Then a knock breaks the quiet.

It's a calm sound. Not a fist. Not panic. Two firm knocks and then a pause. I sit up so fast my head swims. The room is a deeper blue than black. My heart pounds hard enough that I press a hand to my chest because I can feel it through my ribs. Another two knocks. Steady. My throat goes dry.

No one comes by this late. For a breath I think of Claire and her files and the way she frowns when something is wrong. I think of a worker who might have brought a question up the stairs by mistake. I think of Sebastian, and my mouth goes cold. Then I push that thought away because he would not climb five flights for anything that did not benefit him.

I stand, and the boards are cool under my feet. I cross the room, and each step sounds loud to my ears. I rest my fingers on the knob and hesitate.

Then I open the door.

He's here. Kingston, leaning one shoulder to the frame like he needs it to keep himself from falling over. His tie hangs loose, the top button of his shirt is open, and his jacket is hooked over two fingers. His hair is rumpled like he dragged a hand through it over and over the way he does when he's thinking hard. Travel clings to him. The line of his jaw looks sharper than usual. His eyes find mine, and every tight place inside me lets go.

"Five flights of stairs," he says. His voice is low and a little raw. "I should've negotiated hazard pay before coming up here."

A sound rips out of me that is half laugh and half sob. The hallway smells like old wood and dust and paint that was new a decade ago, but now, under that is him. Cedar. Soap. Some warm note that is only Kingston. He's here before he promised to be here.

For a heartbeat, neither of us moves. I want to tell him everything at once.

He shifts his jacket higher on his forearm and takes a slow breath. His gaze moves over my face like a touch.

My breath is shaky. My smile trembles and then holds. I think of two weeks and how long that sounded at sunrise, yet how short it feels now that he is five steps away. I think of the fifth flight and how my legs burn, but I keep climbing anyway.

"Five flights," I whisper. It's a joke and a thank you, and somehow it carries everything I mean.

His eyes warm, and I know he understands.

Twenty-eight

Elise

The door bangs shut as I drag him inside. I don't even reach for the lock. My only focus is Kingston, solid and warm and finally here.

His mouth finds mine, hot and hungry, and I gasp into him, fingers tangling in his hair. I tug, hard enough to make him groan, the sound vibrating against my lips. His jacket slips down his arm until he shakes free, letting it drop to the hardwood.

My palms skate over his shoulders and down the hard lines of his arms, greedy for the feel of him. He presses me back against the door, the wood against my spine, his body a furnace over mine. My breath stutters, my heartbeat racing like I've run miles.

He kisses me like he's starved—like every second apart was an ache he couldn't stand. The scrape of his jaw, the taste of him—warm, familiar, everything I've craved—pulls me deeper into the spiral.

"I missed you," I manage between kisses, the words broken, rushed, but truer than anything I've ever said.

"I couldn't stay away," he breathes.

The confession sears through me, melting me. I clutch his shirt, twisting the fabric, pulling him closer, though he's already pressed tight against me. His breath fans across my mouth, and I feel it everywhere—in the tremble of my hands, in the ache building between us, in the way my body knows his without hesitation.

We break only when we need oxygen, our mouths parting by inches, our foreheads pressed together. His hands frame my face, the pads of his thumbs grazing my flushed cheeks. His chest rises hard against mine, the thud of his heart echoing the wild rhythm in my own.

"You're different," he murmurs, his voice laced with wonder. "Stronger."

The word lodges in my throat, both a compliment and a truth I'm still learning to believe. "I've been trying," I admit. "I've worked hard, and I've learned a lot."

"It sounds like it," he cuts in, thumb brushing the corner of my mouth like he's erasing doubt. His other hand slides down, splaying wide across my waist, pulling me close. "I'm proud of you, Elise. You have no idea how proud."

My chest tightens, not from lack of breath but from the way he says this, like he's known all along I could be this person, like my victories belong to him too.

My hands move over him, from the taut line of his shoulders to the back of his neck, needing contact everywhere, proof that he's real. "You make me believe it," I whisper, lips brushing the edge of his jaw, catching on the rasp of his stubble.

A low growl curls out of his chest. The heat between us doesn't fade. It deepens, heavy with tenderness, every kiss and touch sharpened by the weight of what we've just confessed.

The heat spikes again, his hand sliding lower, his mouth brushing mine, promising more, when a floorboard creaks in the hallway.

We both freeze.

Footsteps sound on the stairs, steady and deliberate. The old beams of the building groan, and my stomach twists. Then the knock lands, firm and insistent.

"Elise." Sebastian's voice carries through the thin door, clipped and smug. "You're not supposed to have overnight guests."

My pulse spikes, nerves pricking under my skin. Kingston doesn't move away. His body stays flush with mine, his jaw hardening as though Sebastian is standing in front of him.

Another knock, sharper. "Open up."

I flinch, but Kingston catches my chin, forcing me to look at him. His eyes blaze. "Don't," he whispers. "This is mine to handle." Then, louder—his voice dropping into the commanding tone that always makes me shiver, he speaks to Sebastian. "I've already spoken to Sasha. I'm not a guest. I'm staying at Château."

A pause. Then Sebastian's voice again, sharper now. "Rules are rules, Elise. Break them, and you'll regret it."

Kingston doesn't hesitate. "Unless you've forgotten who you answer to, you'll take your complaint elsewhere."

After a moment, the footsteps retreat, slow and reluctant, until the stair creaks again with his weight heading down.

Only then does Kingston let out a breath, the heat of it ghosting my lips. His forehead drops to mine, his mouth tugging into a grim smile. "He won't bother you again."

My laugh comes out shaky, a mix of relief and leftover adrenaline. Kingston's hand tightens at my waist, protective even in the aftermath. For a moment, neither of us moves. The silence feels louder than Sebastian's knock, heavy with what almost happened and what still simmers between us.

"He gets no say in this," Kingston murmurs. "You hear me, Elise? No one tells us what we can or can't have. Not him. Not anyone."

My chest tightens, emotion rising fast and hot. I nod, fingers curling into his shirt. "I know. I just… I don't want to make things harder."

His gaze sharpens, protective fire in the depths. "You're

not making things harder. You're surviving. You're winning. And I'll fight whoever I need to so you don't forget that."

My laugh breaks free, shaky at first but real. "You sound so sure."

His mouth curves, slow and dangerous. "That's because I am. And right now, I'm not letting anything take me away from you again."

The heat that had cooled with Sebastian's interruption roars back, fueled by Kingston's certainty. My heart stutters as his hand slides to the small of my back, drawing me flush against him. His lips hover over mine, not kissing yet, just brushing close enough to burn.

I tilt into him, my fingers climbing the back of his neck. "Then don't," I whisper.

His answer is a growl against my mouth as he kisses me again—hungry, relentless, sealing his promise with every press of his lips.

We stumble together across the room, bumping into the desk before falling against the edge of my narrow bed. The frame squeaks under our weight, but I don't care. I tug at his shirt, stripping it away, my palms gliding over bare skin.

He cups the back of my neck as he lowers me onto the mattress. The sheets are scratchy, the space too small for him, but his body eclipses everything else.

"You sure?" His eyes find mine as every inch of him trembles with restraint. "Because if I start—"

I cut him off with a kiss, fierce and unyielding. "Don't stop." My hands grip his shoulders, nails biting into his skin.

The last of his control snaps. His mouth crashes to mine, his body pressing me down. Clothes scatter, skin meets skin. Urgency tangles with tenderness, every touch carrying the weight of what we've been fighting for.

He rolls a condom on and looks at me. "Are you okay with this?"

"Never better."

When he finally settles over me, the weight of him steals my breath. My nails drag across his shoulders, and I can feel the strain in the way he trembles above me. He pauses, giving me one last chance to stop him. I don't. I wrap my legs tight around his hips and pull, grinding against the thick length of him, leaving no doubt what I want.

The first push inside has me crying out, my head tipping back against the pillow. The stretch is sharp, overwhelming, and so good I can't stop the broken sound that escapes me. He buries his face in my neck, groaning like he's been starved for this.

"Jesus, you're perfect," he rasps, teeth scraping against my skin.

"Move," I beg, nails raking down his back. "Please."

He obeys, slow at first, each thrust deliberate, filling me inch by inch until I'm gasping, clutching, lifting to meet him. The bed squeals under us, the cheap frame rattling against the wall with every shift of his hips. We laugh breathlessly between moans, the absurdity of it crashing against the fire building between us.

"This bed's not going to survive us," I gasp, shoving at his shoulders only to pull him right back.

"Good," he growls, snapping his hips harder, driving into me with a force that knocks the air from my lungs. "I want everyone to know you're mine."

"Yours," I choke out, wrapping tighter around him as he pistons into me, deeper and faster, his grip bruising on my hips. The sound of our bodies meeting—wet, frantic, desperate—fills the tiny room, and the heat spirals higher, unbearable.

He lifts my leg, driving deeper, and the angle has me shattering, my cry muffled against his mouth as pleasure rips through me. My nails score his skin, my body clamping tight around him. He follows with a strangled groan, thrusting hard once and then again, before he's spilling into me, his whole body shuddering above mine.

We collapse together, sweaty, shaking, tangled in sheets too hot and twisted to matter. He props himself up just enough not to crush me, but I fist my hand in his hair and keep him close, my body still trembling with aftershocks.

"Don't you dare move," I murmur, grinning at the

ridiculous tilt of the mattress beneath us. "If you roll even an inch, we're both hitting the floor."

He laughs, his lips brushing my collarbone. "Then I'm staying right here. Forever."

Our breaths are jagged, laughter slipping out between gasps—shaky, disbelieving, real. He presses a kiss to my temple, softer than anything that came before, his hand stroking my cheek. "Worth the wait," he whispers.

I smile, lips trembling, heart so full it aches. "Don't ever leave."

His answer is another kiss, deep and certain. A promise.

The air is still thick with heat as the urgency fades, replaced by something quieter. Kingston shifts just enough for me to curl into him, my head pillowed on his chest. His skin is warm, the steady rise and fall of his breath already lulling me. I listen to his heartbeat, each thud steadying the chaos still buzzing through me.

His hand finds mine, fingers threading, palms pressed together. He squeezes lightly, then brings our joined hands to his lips, brushing a kiss against my knuckles.

"Two weeks," he murmurs into my hair. "You won't face them alone."

I close my eyes, letting the promise soak in. His chest rumbles under my cheek, the vibration of his voice grounding me in the here and now. Safe. Protected. Wanted.

He shifts so he can see my face. His thumb strokes over my cheek, brushing back a strand of damp hair, lingering like he can't stop touching me.

I manage a smile. "You're too big for this bed," I whisper, even as I don't want this moment to end.

He chuckles. "Then I'll buy you a new one." His lips press to my temple. "Hell, I'll buy you ten."

I laugh because he means it. But I don't want ten beds. I only want him here.

"Or maybe just one for now," he says, smirking. "Because this one sounds like it might not survive another round."

Heat floods my cheeks, but I laugh, swatting his chest.

Then I squeeze his hand tighter, as if I can hold him here by sheer will.

Twenty-nine

Elise

Kingston has been here a week now, and he disappears into Château's administration building every morning like he's lived here for years—no hesitation, no awkwardness about taking over a space that doesn't belong to him. He's working just down the hall from Claire. She says he strides down the long stone hall, laptop under his arm, nods once to whomever he passes, and then shuts himself inside a small office at the far end.

It used to be a storage room, Claire told me, before someone pushed an old desk against the window and set up Wi-Fi. Now, it looks like Kingston owns it, his jacket hanging neatly from the chair.

I should resent how easily he does this—how a man like him can walk into a centuries-old château and make it his headquarters—but mostly I'm charmed. It's Kingston, after all.

He'd carve out an office in the middle of a field if he had to, and people would still line up to bring him reports.

He wasn't kidding when he said he'd solve the bed problem. He bought a new mattress and had it delivered to my room. I don't know how he got it in, and it takes up almost the entire space, but the last week has been wonderful as we fall asleep tangled in our bed together. I wake up with his arms wrapped around me and feel safe and adored.

Outside my room, things have also improved. Sebastian hasn't given me one brutal chore since Kingston's arrival. We've worked well together, with me following his lead and trading ideas and questions.

On my lunch break, I carry my coffee down the hallway to Kingston's space and pause outside his door. Through the old wood I can hear the low cadence of his voice on a call—serious, clipped, all business. He doesn't sound like the Kingston who tangled his legs with mine this morning, stealing kisses while I tried to brush my hair. He sounds like a CEO, the man who keeps Renew Motion moving even when he's half a world away.

I lean against the cool stone wall, sipping, and try to picture him back home, sitting in his corner office above the vineyards, sunlight spilling through glass instead of this narrow French window. The image doesn't fit as neatly as it used to. Now, I see him here too, folded into the rhythm of my borrowed life.

Claire passes with a stack of folders in her arms. "He's been in there since sunrise," she whispers with a grin.

"That doesn't surprise me."

"He doesn't even notice the noise. We had someone drop an entire case of bottles down the hall, and he just kept talking."

I laugh. "That sounds exactly like him."

She adjusts the folders higher, studying me with raised brows. "You like having him here."

I don't answer right away because what she said isn't a question. It's a fact. I do like him here. I like the sight of his jacket on a borrowed chair, his voice rolling through stone walls, his presence steadying me in ways I didn't realize I craved.

When he finally emerges, his expression softens the instant his eyes find mine. That shift—CEO to man I adore—still steals my breath.

"All finished?" I ask.

"For now." He slides his laptop into its case. "They'll survive a few hours without me." He smoothes a strand of hair behind my ear, as natural as if we've been doing this for years. "What about you? Walk?"

I nod, and we fall into step together, waving to Claire and leaving Château behind. The vineyard air is soft and fresh with the promise of summer. The leaves on the vines have begun to deepen their green. Gravel crunches beneath our shoes as we follow the rows downhill. Kingston slows his pace, his hand brushing mine until I catch it, weaving our fingers.

"You realize," he says, eyes sweeping the landscape, "that you and Tarryn can steal half their practices for Paradise Hill."

I laugh, tipping my head against his shoulder. "Steal them? That's bold."

"Incorporate, then." He squeezes my hand. "I can't help it. Walking these rows with you, seeing how you've learned every inch, I immediately think about what you can do back home. What you will do."

What I'll do. That's the part I keep circling around in my head. There's nothing really broken at home, and some of these practices stem from Chateau's size. But many of them will adapt nicely to enhance our operation. We can always be better. I can always put my mark on things. And I feel ready. Ready to return, ready to shoulder more, ready to believe I can.

I stop walking to really look at him. "You think I'll be different when we go back?"

"I don't think," he says. "I know."

His voice sends heat racing through me. Maybe he believes it enough for both of us.

We continue walking, the vines stretching out on either side. We drift farther down the slope, the air cooler here, tinged with the smell of freshly turned soil and new growth. Kingston stops at a post, running his hand over the weathered wood. He studies the rows with the same sharp attention he gives a Renew Motion meeting agenda.

"You've been watching them prune differently," he says.

"I have." I tug at a leaf, rolling its edge between my fingers. "They leave a little more growth than we would. It's slower, more deliberate. At first, I thought it was wasteful, but it gives the vines strength heading into the cold."

He tilts his head, considering me, not the vines. "That sounds like you."

"Me?"

"Mmmm." He straightens, dusting his palm on his jeans. "You thought coming here was going to be fun, some kind of escape. But maybe you needed the time to strengthen yourself, build reserves before the next season."

The metaphor lands so squarely that I don't speak for a moment. I swallow against the rush of emotion. Leave it to Kingston to fold vineyard science into my life and make it sound exactly right.

Before I can answer, my phone buzzes in my pocket.

Sasha: Dinner tonight, 1900 hrs. No excuses. Bring your handsome Canadian with you.

I laugh, showing Kingston the screen. "Apparently, we've been summoned."

His mouth curves. "I don't recall agreeing to that."

"She didn't give you a choice."

After lunch, I go back to work with the crew. The hours slide by in rows of green, shears clicking, canes dropping at my feet. Sebastian hovers as always, pointing out cuts or murmuring instructions, but the usual edge I feel toward him is gone. Instead of bristling, I find myself letting his energy wash over me, even grateful for his sharp eye. Nothing he says rattles me now. The rhythm of the vines steadies me, and by late afternoon, my muscles burn with the kind of fatigue that feels earned.

It feels like I've stumbled into a different world when, later that evening, Kingston and I stand outside the private wing of Château, its limestone façade washed in the gas lanterns that lead to the private entrance. Tall windows glow with a golden sheen, the glass framed by precise stonework and trailing ivy. Inside, I glimpse a long dining table gleaming with crystal and porcelain, silver catching the firelight from a row of candles. The air carries the faint scent of woodsmoke from the grand hearth, which is refined and deliberate rather than rustic.

Sasha greets us at the door, arms open wide. She's dressed in tailored black trousers and a silk blouse, the kind of effortless elegance that speaks of generations steeped in refinement. Behind her, uniformed staff move quietly through the grand hall, the air rich with the scents of butter, wine, and truffle.

"You made it!" she exclaims, pulling me in before Kingston can say a word. "And you—" She tilts her chin at him, eyes twinkling. "I haven't seen you in what, ten years? You haven't aged a day. Still too tall, still too serious."

Kingston actually blushes. I didn't think the man was capable. "Hello, Sasha," he says, the stiffness in his shoulders betraying his discomfort. "It's good to see you."

She waves a spoon at him. "Good? That's all you can manage? And you've been here over a week? Staying in the dormitory and haven't even come by to see me?"

I bite my lip to keep from laughing, but the sound slips out anyway. Kingston shoots me a look that promises retribution later, but there's amusement there as well.

Sasha ushers us to the table, and a footman presses crystal glasses of red wine into our hands. A low fire crackles in the hearth, candles drip wax onto porcelain saucers, and immaculately arranged plates wait on the long table.

We sit, and Sasha begins to tell stories—how she first met

Kingston at a trade show in Paris. He was new to the international wine world and unbearably cocky. How he argued with a French distributor until his voice went hoarse, then finally gave up and bought her a drink.

"Arrogant," she pronounces, pointing her fork at him. "But charming enough to get away with it. And ambitious. Even then, I knew you'd be running the whole show one day. I just thought it would be wine, not medicine…"

I glance at him. His ears are pink, but he doesn't protest. Just shrugs.

When Sasha turns toward me, my stomach tightens. Her expression softens. "And you, ma chère. You've impressed everyone here. You work harder than half the men in the cellar. You listen. You notice. We'd love for you to stay."

I murmur thanks, heat rising to my cheeks. I don't know whether it's the wine or the praise, but it feels like a blessing. Somehow, I doubt Sebastian would agree with her sentiment, though. But no matter, as I know now that's not what I want. Kingston squeezes my knee beneath the table, and I nearly burst with pride.

The meal unfolds like a carefully scored production. Delicate amuse-bouche give way to a first course of silky velouté, then to roast poulet with crushed pommes de terre and haricots verts finished in butter and almonds. Each plate is paired with a different bottle from Sasha's cellar. We eat until our laughter outpaces our restraint, and Sasha scolds Kingston for refusing seconds while coaxing him to take more bread.

Sasha swirls the last sip in her glass, studying the color. "Someday, I'll see Paradise Hill for myself."

Kingston's mouth curves as he pours her more. "And when you do, Elise can take you through every row, every barrel. Smaller scale than here, sure, but the wine holds its own."

Her brows lift in challenge. "I look forward to testing that claim."

When the night lets us go, the stars are thick above Château. Sasha hugs me, her perfumed cheek warm against my hair. "Take care of him," she whispers. "He's stubborn, but he's worth it."

"I promise I will." My throat is tight.

Before she releases me, she leans closer and lowers her voice. "And don't let him work too much. He forgets sometimes that life is more than numbers and meetings. Remind him."

The advice sinks into me like a benediction, a responsibility I feel oddly honored to carry.

I nod, and Kingston slips my hand into his as we walk back toward the vines. His thumb strokes the inside of my wrist.

"You enjoyed that," he says.

"I did." I lean in, smiling into the dark. "I like seeing you through other people's eyes. Turns out you were once human after all."

He chuckles. "Don't get used to it."

But I already have.

Thirty

Elise

Two days and counting when Claire corners me in the hall, her cheeks flushed, eyes bright with the kind of excitement that usually means she's done something behind my back.

"You're free tonight, oui?"

I hesitate. "Why?"

She links her arm through mine, tugging me toward the dormitory. "Don't ask questions. Just be free."

I glance at Kingston, who is tucking his laptop into the leather case he's claimed like a briefcase. He arches one brow. "What are you plotting?"

"Nothing dangerous," Claire singsongs, which only makes him more suspicious.

After a long day, Kingston meets me at Sebastian's office. And I swear Kingston growled at him before we left.

When we reach the dormitory, laughter and music spill down the stairwell. The door is propped open with a wine crate, and I catch the faint smell of fresh bread and melted cheese.

Claire beams at us as she pushes the door wider. Inside, the common room has been cleared of furniture, crowded with folding chairs, and decorated with candles stuck in mismatched bottles. Someone has strung fairy lights across the ceiling, and their soft glow makes the plaster walls almost romantic.

It's not elegant, not Château's polished grandeur, but it's warm. Lived in. A community.

"Surprise!" Claire announces. "Your farewell fête."

My throat tightens. "Claire, you didn't—"

"Of course, I did." She puts her hands on her hips. "You think you can leave without us celebrating everything you've done here? Impossible."

Students, cellar hands, and assistants I've worked beside for months gather around. Glasses are circulated until everyone has one. Kingston looks out of place at first, too tall, too polished in his pressed shirt and dark jeans. I catch the flicker of unease in his eyes, the way his shoulders stiffen as laughter swells around us. He doesn't belong here, not really.

But when he feels me tense, he slides his arm around my waist, grounding himself through me. I lean into him, and the stiffness eases. The truth is, with me beside him, he does belong, at least for this moment.

We find seats near the corner, squeezed together on a sagging sofa. Claire claps her hands for attention, her curls bouncing.

"Mes amis," she declares, "tonight, we raise a glass to Elise. She came to us fresh from Canada, with eyes like this—" She widens her own comically until everyone laughs. "Terrified! Confused! Did not know the difference between bâttonage and remontage. And now, look at her. Dirt under her nails, French curses on her lips, and the respect of every one of us."

The room erupts with cheers. Someone whistles. My cheeks burn, but laughter bubbles up, unstoppable. I spot Sebastian in the corner talking to one of the hands. He looks at me and raises his glass.

Yet even as I laugh, a sharp pang cuts through me. This—these people, this warmth, this makeshift family—I'm leaving it behind, and there are many things I will miss. The ache lingers at the edges of my smile, bittersweet and impossible to ignore.

Before Claire can go on, I lift my glass and cut in, grinning. "Let the record show that Claire taught me at least half of those French curses. So if anyone's offended, blame her."

The room explodes with laughter, and Claire presses a dramatic hand to her heart. "Trahison! Betrayal!" she cries, but her eyes sparkle.

The playful jab earns me another cheer, and warmth floods over me. I realize I've claimed my own place here, not as a guest, but as part of them.

Around us the music shifts from a jaunty French pop song to an old American classic. Someone sings along off-key, and others clap in rhythm. Candle wax drips down the bottles, and Kingston leans back against the sagging sofa, his earlier stiffness softening. He chuckles at a cellar hand's story about a fermenter exploding and covering them all in foam.

Claire raises her glass higher. "Elise will go back to Canada stronger, wiser, and more annoying than ever, I'm sure. But we'll miss her. Très fort."

"À Elise!" voices echo, glasses clinking.

Kingston touches his glass to mine, his eyes catching the fairy light. There's pride there, but something softer too. He leans in to whisper, "I don't remember the last time I was at a party like this."

"High school?" I tease.

He smirks. "Even then, I think I stuck to the wall."

I imagine him younger, tall and serious, watching while others laughed. The image makes me squeeze his hand tighter.

Later, Claire pulls me into a hug. "You've changed more than you realize," she whispers. "When you first came, you looked like someone running. Now you look like someone ready."

I step back, blinking quickly, and promise, "We'll stay in

touch. I'll send you those Canadian contacts, and you'll come visit. You'll see Paradise Hill."

She grins through her own tears. "I will. And when I do, you'll owe me wine."

"Deal."

By the time the crowd thins, I'm exhausted in the best way. My cheeks ache from smiling, my arms from hugging. Kingston steers me gently up the stairs in the dormitory, one hand warm on the small of my back.

"That was…" I trail off, searching for the word.

"Overwhelming?" Kingston offers.

"Perfect," I say instead. And I mean it.

He slips his hand into mine. "You've made something here, Elise. Something that lasts."

I lean into him, letting his steadiness carry me forward. I'll carry this piece of France with me, tucked into my bones.

Upstairs, I set my shoes by the door and slide beneath the quilt. The sheets smell faintly of lavender, crisp from Château laundry. Kingston follows, loosening his watch, his shirt, his presence filling the space with calm. He settles beside me, the mattress dipping under his weight. Without hesitation, I curl into his side, my cheek against his chest. His heartbeat thuds steady beneath my ear, anchoring me.

"You were beautiful tonight," he murmurs into my hair.

I laugh softly. "Covered in crumbs and probably red-faced from all that wine?"

"Beautiful," he repeats firmly, as if the word has nothing to do with how I look and everything to do with how I was.

The compliment makes my throat swell. I don't tell him that earlier tonight, when Claire described me as someone who'd arrived terrified and was leaving stronger, I almost cried. I don't tell him how much I needed to hear that. But I think he knows anyway. Kingston always knows more than I want to admit.

We lie in silence for a while, and I trace idle circles over the back of his hand, my mind replaying the last few months.

When I came here, France was supposed to be an escape, a way to outrun the expectations pressing down on me at

Paradise Hill, to hide from my own doubts. I thought if I put an ocean between me and home, the noise in my head would quiet.

It didn't, not at first. But somewhere between the blistered hands, the long days in the cellar, and the laughter spilling through the dormitory walls, something shifted. This place tested me. It stripped me down until all I had left was grit and choice. And I chose to stay. I chose to work harder, to listen deeper, to try again even when I failed.

Now, lying here, I realize France was never meant to help me run away. It was about preparing me for my job at home. Strengthening me, like the vines left with extra growth for winter. Kingston said that earlier, and he was right.

I tilt my head up to look at him. He's half-asleep, his eyes heavy, his mouth softened from its usual sharp lines. He's vulnerable in a way only I get to see.

"Promise me something," I whisper.

His lids lift, and he hums low in his throat.

"Promise me you won't let me forget this feeling when we go home. The way I've grown here. The way I'm not afraid anymore."

His hand cups my cheek, warm and sure. "I promise," he says. "I'll remind you every day if I have to."

A laugh escapes me. "Annoying reminders?"

His mouth curves in the faintest smile. "The best kind."

I press closer, closing my eyes. Tomorrow will come, with its travel and goodbyes and the sharp ache of leaving. But it also throws the future open wide as I find what's next for my personal life as well as my work. Tonight, in this bed, I'm not running from anything.

I'm ready.

Thirty-one

Elise

The dorm is quiet when I wake. Pale light skims the beams. The old wood creaks on the stairs as the early birds begin moving around.

Kingston sleeps on his stomach, one arm flung toward my side of the bed. His hand is open. I want to slide my fingers into his palm and stay, but the day is already moving. Suitcases wait by the wardrobe. Tape, cardboard, and a neat stack of lists sit on the chair. Today is my last day at Château, and last night, Sebastian told me I didn't have to work today because of all the weekends I've worked while I was here.

I lie still and think of the things I'll miss. Cool stone under my feet. Dew threading the vines so they glitter for a moment. Claire's brisk voice that can cut and mend in a breath.

I slip from bed and cross to the window. The fields are a green quilt with seams I've finally learned to read. I came here wanting to prove something. I'm leaving with a different want. Not to impress, but to be useful. To taste before I fix. I press my palm to the cold glass and imagine the rows at Paradise Hill in this same shy light. Two places rise up behind my ribs. Both feel like home in different languages.

A breeze lifts the curtain. Below, someone sets down a crate. A door clicks shut. The day is starting. I glance back at Kingston. He stirs, then settles.

I pull on a sweater and tie my hair. One last minute, and then I turn to wake him.

Kingston smiles as he opens his eyes. "How are you feeling?"

I look at him with his hair tousled. "I'm ready to go home."

He gets up, wraps his arms around me, and kisses my neck. "Your wish is my command."

Packing starts the way Kingston does everything—calm, clean, precise. Two suitcases open on the bed. He gathers the lists I made and adds his own check marks. I tease him, and he wrinkles his nose in that fake-offended way that makes my stomach flip.

Soon, cardboard dust hangs in the air. Tape snaps. I fold sweaters that may never lose the scent of this place. He rolls his shirts and hums under his breath. We move around each other without colliding, two magnets shifting poles whenever we get close.

I scoop the little pile from my nightstand into a shoebox—my trusty notebook, full of ideas and information and riddled with wine stains, a cork from the night Claire let me call a tasting note, three vine pebbles from the block where I finally trusted my nose. Kingston lifts the lid and tips his head.

"You starting a rock museum?"

"It's exclusive," I say, nudging his hip. "Membership requires patience."

He grins and pulls a labeler from his backpack. "Good. I brought credentials."

"You didn't."

He prints a label that reads Elise's Highly Scientific

Evidence and smoothes it on like a signature. I laugh, and he looks stupidly proud.

At the desk, I pick up a heavy reference text and hesitate. Someone before me has filled the margins with notes, the private handwriting of someone who learned the hard way. Kingston sees my face and reaches for it. Sebastian gifted it to me last night since there's a new edition.

"We can ship it," he says.

I consider that but shake my head. "It belongs here. I'll take photos of the parts I'd use most."

He nods. "Photos now. PDF later. You get the words without stealing the weight."

I photograph three chapters and tuck a sticky note with a thank you under the cover.

Kingston pauses at the wardrobe and holds up a simple black dress. "Paris?"

The word sparks something in the air. "Two days," I say. "Museums if I want. Bed if I want. Both if I want."

"Both," he says, sliding the dress into my suitcase.

We argue for a breath over my battered sneakers. He wants to toss them. I hold them to my chest.

"They have vineyard soul," I tell him.

"They have holes," he says, kissing my cheek as he lets me keep them.

We nestle the last toiletries into a pouch. He shakes the suitcases to settle the clothes. I look over what we'll carry and what we'll leave and remind myself that my growth isn't a souvenir. It lives in my hands and in the way my questions sound. It's part of me.

Kingston loops an arm around my waist and rests his chin on my shoulder. "Ready?"

"Almost," I say, pressing the shoebox lid in place. "I have to say goodbye to the vines. And I promised I'd give Sebastian five minutes."

He kisses the top of my head. "Okay. I'll keep making labels while you tell the field your secrets."

I head downstairs and slip out the side door. Morning

meets me with a cool breath. Dew threads the rows so each leaf wears a tiny mirror in the way I've come to love. The vines hold still, ribs guarding a heart. I step between them, and the smell rises up, green and wet, a little like tea.

I trail my hand along the wire, careful of the hooks. I remember the way mildew smells before it shows, the weight of a pump-over hose, the sound a healthy cap makes when it breaks. I thought I came here to collect tricks. I learned restraint instead. Mouth before math. Translate, don't transplant.

A ladybug crawls over my knuckle and lifts off. Down the slope, a tractor coughs once and goes quiet. I close my eyes and picture home—Paradise Hill at first light, the lake a flat silver coin, our rows darker and tighter, and the soil more stubborn. I used to think I'd bring France back like a suitcase full of answers. Now, I think I'll bring home better questions.

Something glints near my shoe. A clipped tendril, brown at the cut, curled like a note. I slide it into my notebook between pages that smell faintly of the cellar. One reminder is enough.

"Thank you," I tell the row. It feels ridiculous and also perfectly right. This place never cared who I was trying to impress. It just kept asking me to show up. I did. That's what I'll carry.

My phone buzzes.

Sebastian: You coming?

Crap! I got distracted.

Me: Yes. On my way.

I look once more at the slope, the tidy lines, the sky patched between leaves. I press my palm to a post, rough and warm where the sun found it first. "I'll do right by you," I whisper, and I mean both vineyards.

Then I turn, and Château rises through the vines, familiar now. Sebastian is waiting in his office.

"You took your time," he says, mouth quirking. "Good."

"I told the field my secrets."

He hands me a cup with a tiny pour. Not ceremony. Work. The wine is young and stubborn. I breathe and name what I can before I sip—red fruit, a little green, an edge that softens if you stop bulldozing it.

"Better," Sebastian says, tapping the rim of my cup. "You started the summer wanting to sound smart. You're leaving wanting to be right. Not the same thing."

I laugh because it's too true, and it hurts in a good way. Sebastian rests his hand on my notebook like a blessing.

"Useful mess," he says. "That belongs to you."

"I photographed the text," I tell him. "And I left a note for you in the book. I can't take it from here."

He nods, seeming pleased. Then he pulls out a battered tasting glass. The base is chipped, so it tilts if you set it down wrong. He wipes a thumb over the rim and gives it to me.

"When you grab this, you'll remember to taste before you fix. You'll also remember to set it down carefully. Things aren't as steady as you think."

I hold the glass like an egg. "I won't break it."

"You probably will," he says, smiling. "That's fine. You'll learn something then too."

He gestures to the door, and we walk through the cellar. The shape of goodbye gathers, but Sebastian doesn't go soft for long. He flicks the spigot on a nearby tank and watches the thin stream.

"Where are you on the last blending adjustment?" I ask. Small talk here is usually practical.

"Nearly done. The sauvignon will sulk a week and then pretend it decided to be brilliant on its own." He cuts me a look. "You have enjoyed that fight."

"I have." I glance around at the tools and hoses. I could walk this room blind now and not hit a barrel.

Sebastian's gaze shifts toward the door, as if looking for Kingston. "And the other fight, the one where you pretend you didn't fall in love?"

Heat climbs my neck. "I didn't pretend very well."

"Good. Pretending is a waste of time." He leans against the bench. "He travels well, your forever."

The word steadies me. I nod. "He does."

"You kept working when he arrived," he says. "You kept asking questions. You didn't let the man swallow the craft. You can have both if you keep your hands on the work."

I turn the glass in my fingers, nodding. "I want both. I want to go home and not lose this."

"You're not taking France," he says. "You're taking your practice. Taste first. Ask better questions. Don't copy us. Make Paradise Hill taste like Paradise."

"Sasha said that too," I admit. "With fewer words."

"Of course, she did." He snorts.

We sip again. He watches me more than the wine. It feels like the end of an exam I didn't know I was taking.

"What will you do first when you get back?" he asks.

"Walk the rows before sunrise. Then sit in the barn and smell the tanks before I read a number."

He looks satisfied. "Write that down," he says, though we both know I already did. "And send me pictures when you try something new. If it blows up in your face, send those too. Especially those."

I laugh, and then find I can't. The ache moves from under my ribs and sits in my throat. I grip the stem of the glass and find the bench with my hip.

Sebastian notices but doesn't pounce. He lets the moment breathe. "You were never pretending here," he says at last. "You walked in with your shoulders at your ears and your mouth full of reasons. You're leaving with your shoulders down. Keep them there."

I swallow. "You did that."

"You did that," he says. "I nudged."

He reaches for my notebook, slides the wax pencil from behind his ear, and tucks it under the elastic on the cover. He pushes the book toward me.

"For your pocket," he says. "So you don't put off writing down the thing you think you'll remember."

"I never remember everything," I say, my smile wobbling.

"Of course, you don't. That's why we write."

He glances at the door. "Go finish your packing. I'm not walking you to the car. One goodbye is enough, but I have a vow. You'll see me at harvest sometime. I'll terrorize your cellar. You'll pretend to hate it. We'll both enjoy ourselves."

"I hope that's a promise," I say.

"Good." He bumps his knuckles against my arm. "Now, get out before I say something kind and we both have to recover."

I tuck the glass he gave me into a padded sleeve at the top of my bag and slide the notebook under my arm. I breathe in the cellar once more and step back. Sebastian turns to the tank and pretends to ignore me. It's the kindest thing he could do.

After a moment, the hallway carries my footsteps away. I don't look back. Like he said, one goodbye is enough.

I follow the narrow hall to the stairs, the cellar's chill clinging to my sleeves. When I step into the sunlight, Kingston's there, leaning against the car, waiting.

"Did you finish your goodbyes?" he asks.

"I did. Sebastian said I was good to go."

Kingston's mouth curves. "And not a minute too soon." He laughs under his breath and leans in, forehead to mine for a second. "Are you ready?"

The true answer rises. "No. Yes."

"We'll make both true," he says. He squeezes my hip. "Do you need one more minute?"

I shake my head. "I took it."

He looks pleased in that way that warms my ribs. "Good. I re-labeled your shoebox of evidence, in case customs asks."

"What did you write this time?"

"Highly classified," he says. "Don't open without snacks."

I snort and he grins, the knot in my chest loosening. He tips his chin toward the room I've slept in for the last three months. "Last sweep. Then we go."

I lace my fingers with his. "Claire isn't walking us out. Everyone keeps saying one goodbye was enough."

"Smart woman," he says. "You okay?"

"I am." The ache is there, and so is the steadiness. Both fit.

Kingston bumps my shoulder, and I bump him back. He lets our hands fall but keeps his palm at my back, easy and sure.

"Taste the day before we fix it," I say, mostly to myself.

"Coffee first," he answers. "Then everything else."

The room looks smaller with the suitcases zipped. The window throws a bright square across the floor. Dust floats in it like snow you can't catch. I stand in the light and let the quiet fill me.

I check the desk. The corner where I wrote Kingston that first honest email has a dent in the wood. My notebook is gone from its spot, like a missing tooth and a new grin all at once. The tape dispenser waits where Kingston left it after sealing the shoebox. I smile because he's an idiot in the best possible way.

I sit at the desk and scrawl two lines. *Ask good questions. Taste again.* I wedge the card under the paperweight, so the next person won't miss it.

One last sweep. Window latch. Drawer. I press a palm to the pillow where Kingston slept and to the sill where I counted what I'd miss. I'm leaving the need to impress on this desk. I'm taking my practice. I'm taking us.

"Ready?" Kingston calls from the hall.

I pick up my bag. "Ready," I say, and I am.

The courtyard smells of wet stone and coffee grounds. Gravel crunches under our suitcase wheels. The sky is that flat French gray that makes colors look honest. Two cellar hands step from the side door with squeegees and wet boots. They lift their chins at us. Not a scene, just hello and go well. I lift my hand in salute.

The kitchen door swings open, and the cook appears with a dish towel over one shoulder and a long paper bundle in her arms. She thrusts it toward me like a relay handoff.

"For the train," she says. "Still warm. Don't fight over it."

"We'll try to be civilized," Kingston says, which makes her snort.

With a word of thanks, I tuck the baguette under my arm like a baton. Heat seeps through the paper into my sweater. She slips a twist of paper into my palm. *Butter.* I could cry over butter this morning, which is ridiculous, so I kiss the air near her cheek and thank her twice more.

The van coughs to life near the gate. Diesel fumes hang low. The driver lifts a hand through the window—no rush and yes rush. Kingston takes both suitcases with ease, the shoebox balanced on top like a crown. I hold the baguette higher.

One of the cellar hands calls out a quick goodbye in French. I catch only the wish hidden in it. *Safe road. Come back if you want.* I promise something with my wave and don't try to translate.

We load the bags, and I slide into the seat. The courtyard tilts in the window, then steadies. Gratitude swells in me until it feels like grief's kinder cousin, the one that squeezes your hand and walks you to the gate.

The van's heater sighs warm over our knees. The road unwinds past rows, stone walls, and small houses with mint shutters. The driver checks us in the mirror and smiles like he knows this is a departure.

"Gare?" he says.

"Oui. Merci." I reach for Kingston's hand and give it a squeeze.

Kingston has our tickets on his phone *and* on paper because, of course, he does. He taps the screen and tucks the printouts into the door pocket. I rest the baguette across my lap. The paper crinkles. Butter waits in my coat pocket.

Fields give way to a roundabout, a bakery, and a schoolyard where two kids chase a ball. The van's motion loosens the knot under my ribs.

The driver glances at us in the rearview. "Where are you from?"

"Canada," I answer.

His brows jump. "Ahh…good wine there?"

I can't help grinning. "We're trying."

He chuckles and moves his eyes back to the road. "Keep trying," he says, and the wink in his tone makes it land more like a pat on the shoulder than a jab.

I lean my head back and make a quick list. Two new protocols for home—if rehydration runs too fast, back off the rate, pulse shorter runs, and check drippers for clogs before I blame a vine. If the cap stays stubborn on a cool day, warm the pump-over rather than making it longer. Also… Keep the air clean. Taste before chasing with heat. One sensory rule to tape inside my skull—read by scent first. Fruit says one path, green another, solvent says stop and ask why. One note from Claire—don't fix what you haven't tasted or asked about. Questions before orders. Shoulders down.

Kingston rests his hand on my knee. I cover his fingers, and my breath evens.

"Hungry now or train hungry?" he asks.

"Train hungry. But if you open that butter, I'll lose my resolve."

My phone buzzes with a photo from Tarryn—Paradise Hill in early light, rows dark and tight, the lake a piece of silver.

Tarryn: Hurry home.

I smile and text back a picture of our bread like proof of life.

Kingston laughs and squeezes my knee. "Paris first," he says, so softly I almost miss it.

"Paris," I echo.

Thirty-two

Kingston

The train ride in from Bordeaux was long, and the sun set hours ago. But we've arrived at the George V. The hotel is all marble floors and gilded mirrors, the kind of place I'd usually breeze through on the way to a meeting. Tonight, it feels different. Our suite is quiet, the city outside muffled behind thick curtains and double-paned glass. A vase of peonies sits on the table, pale pink petals already loosening. The whole room smells faintly floral and expensive, like luxury pretending to be effortless.

For once, I let myself breathe. Elise and I have been in Bordeaux too long, always under someone's eye, always pressed between work and other tension. Paris is a bubble, and I want to hold it in my hands before it bursts.

The bathroom door clicks open, and she pads out barefoot. Damp hair hangs in loose waves around her shoulders. She's wearing one of my shirts, sleeves rolled twice at the wrists, hem brushing the tops of her thighs. She stops when she sees me watching.

"You're staring," she says, arching a brow.

I don't look away. "You make it impossible not to."

Her lips twitch. She crosses the room and curls into the armchair opposite me, tugging her feet under her. I catch myself memorizing the way she twists her hair into a loose knot, then lets it fall again. It's nearly impossible to fathom, how much space she's carved out inside me.

A knock at the door interrupts the thought—room service. Two glasses of burgundy, still breathing in the decanter. I tip the server and set the glasses on the table between us.

Once I pour, Elise lifts hers and holds it toward me. "To Paris," she says.

Our glasses meet with a soft chime. The wine tastes like dark fruit and velvet, but what lingers is the shine in her eyes. She drifts toward the balcony, sliding the glass door open. City noise rushes in—traffic, laughter, the faint wail of a siren blocks away.

She points, grinning like a kid. "There it is."

The Eiffel Tower blazes against the night, each light a gleaming pinpoint. She leans on the railing, bare legs catching the glow.

I step behind her, close enough to feel the warmth from her skin. Paris has never meant anything to me beyond negotiations and handshakes, but tonight, it feels like the center of the world. Or maybe she does.

She glances back. "I can't believe we're going home so soon."

I swallow the knot in my throat. Time feels like it's slipping through my fingers, every hour with her borrowed, every breath in this city one step closer to reality. Back home, there will be the vineyard, the family, the sabotage, the endless demands. Here, there's only us.

"Do you think it'll feel strange being back?" she asks.

"Strange without this, yes." I force my tone light, though

my chest tightens.

She studies me for a beat, as if she hears everything I didn't say. Then she turns back to the city, letting the silence stretch.

I can't stand it. I pull her gently inside, away from the chill, and guide her to the sofa. She tucks against me easily, head fitting under my chin.

"You're brooding again," she murmurs, voice muffled against my shirt.

"I'm memorizing," I tell her.

"Dangerous habit."

"Necessary one."

Her laugh is quiet, soft as the fabric beneath my fingers. I hold her tighter, greedy for the weight of her against me, the sound of her laughter, the taste of wine still on her lips when she lifts her face to kiss me. I don't want to think about tomorrow.

But I do. I should be savoring Paris—the view, the food, the city spread out like a jewel. Instead, all I can think about is what waits at home and how I'll integrate this life with her into the demands of everything else. Can this survive reality? Can I leave myself open to the future's possibility without being overrun by fear, by the experiences of my past?

The vibration of my phone slices through the quiet. Elise stirs against me, her head lifting from my chest. I fish the phone out, already hating the intrusion.

Cal: Need to regroup tomorrow. Everyone available?

So much for the bubble.

I exhale slowly, feeling Elise's gaze on me. Her eyes are wide, wary, as if she already knows this night in Paris just shifted into something heavier.

"This is Cal. He wants to talk to everyone, and that means it's time," I say quietly. "We need to talk to them, because everyone includes you."

She sits up, hugging her knees to her chest, her wine glass forgotten on the table. "Who exactly is everyone?"

"My brothers. My sister. My parents." I watch the nerves

flicker across her face, the way her teeth worry her bottom lip.

"They're your family," she says. "Not mine."

The words sting more than she intends, I think. She's not wrong. But she doesn't see what I see, that she already belongs in the middle of this mess, like it or not.

"They're your family too," I tell her.

Her head snaps toward me. "Kingston—"

"No," I cut in, firm but gentle. "You've been in this fight with us since you were born. You've seen things, connected dots none of us could. They need to hear your perspective. And I want them to see you with me."

She presses her lips together, color rising in her cheeks. "I don't know if I can face them right away. What if they don't think we belong together?"

"Then they'll answer to me." My voice is edged with the protective anger that's been simmering for weeks.

Her eyes soften. "You'd do that?"

"Already have. Already will."

For a long beat she studies me, the city lights painting her profile gold. Finally, she nods. "Okay. Set it up."

I shift back, phone heavy in my palm as I find the family group chat.

Me: Cal has an update he'd like to give us together. How does Sunday 10 a.m. your time work? I'll host the call. Elise and I will join from Paris.

The three dots appear almost instantly.

Ryker: You just sent this to me. I'll let everyone know. Vancouver time.

I guess I only thought that was the family chat. I confirm, then set the phone face down on the table.

Elise leans against me again, quiet, but I feel the tension in her body. I press my lips to her hair. "Don't overthink it," I murmur. "They'll see what I see."

She tilts her head up, her eyes catching mine. "And what do you see?"

"The woman who's been holding this whole thing together while the rest of us scrambled. The woman who's even better prepared to lead now than she was before."

Her throat works as she tries to swallow a smile, but her nerves don't vanish. She exhales shakily, and then puts her head back down. I keep my arm around her shoulders.

Despite the late hour, the city moves on outside our window—lights, sirens, laughter. Inside, I hold her tighter and imagine tomorrow, when the screen fills with familiar faces and one that's new to the gathering. Elise isn't wrong. They are *my* family. But whatever my own worries might be, I know she belongs in that frame.

Thirty-three

Kingston

Morning comes too fast. Light slants through the curtains, too bright for the weight I feel pressing down on my chest. Elise fusses with the hem of her blouse while I balance the laptop on the desk by the window. She's quiet, and I can tell she's been rehearsing what she might say—or not say—since she got up.

"You look perfect," I murmur.

She blushes and looks away. "Thank you."

"Are you ready for a day of exploring? We'll talk to them before we have a late dinner."

"I can't wait."

We head out, and the morning air is cool, carrying the scent of river water and fresh bread. Paris comes awake around us, but at a terrace café perched just above the Seine, it feels like the city belongs only to us. The waiter sets down a basket piled with croissants, their golden layers flaking under my fingertips, and a carafe of steaming coffee.

Elise tears off a piece of pastry, eyes sparkling as she takes a bite. "These taste so much better here than they do at home," she murmurs.

I watch her as part of the view, the sweep of the river catching early light, the distant silhouette of Notre-Dame rising like something out of a dream. "You say that about every croissant," I tease, pouring her coffee into the tiny porcelain cup.

She rolls her eyes, but her mouth curves up. "Because they keep proving me right."

We linger, sharing jam and bites of croissant, until she leans her chin on her hand and asks, "What's next?"

I rise and offer her my arm. "A walk along the Seine. Let Paris tell you herself."

A cobbled path follows the river, lined with green bookstalls opening for the day. Old postcards flutter in the breeze, their edges curled, while rows of leather-bound novels and prints of Monet's lilies catch the sunlight. Elise pauses at every stall, fingers tracing the worn spines, delight flashing in her eyes when she finds a sketch of the Eiffel Tower from decades ago.

"You're taking this home," I say, handing the vendor a few euros before she can argue.

"Kingston…" she protests, though her face softens as she slips the sketch into her bag.

We walk until the bridges arching across the river bring us into the heart of the city. The bells of Notre-Dame toll as we climb the steps, and Elise tilts her head back, awed by the gothic towers. Sunlight filters through stained glass, washing her face in blues and reds. I slip my hand into hers, anchoring us in the crowd.

From there we wind our way through narrow streets, past cafés spilling over with tables, until the wide boulevards open and the Eiffel Tower rises in the distance, steel lace against the sky.

Elise stops short, breath catching. "It's so much better than I thought it would be."

I tuck her close. "Wait until we're standing beneath it."

She looks up at me, and Paris itself seems to pause, the river glittering, the tower watching, the whole city bending to witness the way her smile steals the air from my lungs.

We have lunch at a cute café along the Seine and wander in and out of the little boutiques. Elise seems intent on trying to stop me from buying everything I catch her looking at. For the most part she succeeds. By the time the sun begins its slow descent, we've circled back along the river to slip into a waiting car. The city fades into twilight as we return to the George V. Upstairs, I settle Elise with a glass of wine.

Her gaze flickers around the room, nervous and unconvinced. "I don't think this is a good idea."

I reach across the desk and catch her hand. "It'll be fine."

Before she can argue further, the screen fills with faces. Ryker first, then Greyson and Beckett, all crammed together in the tasting room back home. Tarryn leans in from the side, eyes sharp. Then Cal is on, and finally, my parents—Dad in a pressed shirt, already frowning and Mom smoothing a scarf around her shoulders.

There's a beat of silence as they take us in. Elise stiffens beside me.

"Well, hell," Ryker says, breaking the pause. "Look who finally brought a date."

Greyson whistles. "About damn time, Kingston."

Beckett grins. "Paris, huh? You always did like overkill."

Elise flushes pink. I squeeze her hand tighter. She mutters under her breath, just loud enough for me to hear, "What, no applause?"

The corner of my mouth lifts. My family probably didn't catch that, but her spunk is enough to convince me she hasn't lost herself.

Mom grins. "Elise. What a…lovely surprise."

Dad doesn't echo the sentiment. He just studies her with that detached air that's made more than one of us kids squirm.

I clear my throat. "I'm in France to make sure she comes back to Paradise Hill."

My siblings exchange looks, and Tarryn blinks, lips parting like she might ask something, then thinks better of it. Ryker shifts in his seat but holds back his wisecrack.

The silence stretches long enough for Elise to fidget with her sleeve. Then she whispers, more to herself than anyone, "Well, this isn't awkward at all."

I squeeze her hand again as Cal, our private investigator, clears his throat and jumps in. "Right. Well. Good you're all here because we've got developments."

The mood shifts immediately. Cal straightens papers in front of him, jaw tight. "We traced the last round of payments connected to the vineyard sabotage. They didn't stop with local hands. This goes deeper—professional saboteurs, contracts, shell companies funneling the money."

Greyson swears under his breath. Beckett leans forward, brows drawn.

"Who's behind it?" Ryker demands.

Cal looks grim. "I chased it down to a company based in the Cayman Islands. The two shareholders are Maximus Paradise and Evelyn Dempsey."

My chest clenches as everything in me freezes. *What. The. Fuck?*

"That's impossible," Tarryn whispers. "Why would they do that?"

"Max and Evelyn," Greyson mutters. "Together?"

Ryker bangs his hand on the table. "What the hell? They hate each other."

Beckett rubs his jaw, his mind working, always the strategist.

Mom's eyes close, pain written across her face. Dad mutters something about family reputation, his voice clipped.

"Dad, what do you want to do?" I ask.

After a beat, Cal checks his watch. "I've got to run. I'll send you the details of this and let you discuss. Meanwhile, we're continuing to dig. Let me know what else I can do. I'm still gathering evidence on who they're paying to do the sabotage because it's no longer Zach. I'll be in touch." With that, his square disappears from the screen, leaving only my family.

Mom clears her throat. "So. What now?"

Dad leans forward first, his voice careful. "We've got to prevent this from happening again. Exposure like this could ruin us."

"You think?" Ryker snorts. "What's Ginny going to do?"

Beckett shoots him a warning glance, and then turns to me. "Do we have a plan?"

Before I can answer, Elise clears her throat. "At Château, they run checks every week—staff audits, supply tracking, even cross-verifying shipments against independent logs. It's tedious, but it makes sabotage harder to slip through unnoticed."

All eyes swing toward her. I can feel her fingers twitch against mine under the desk.

She goes on, gathering confidence. "They also keep a rotating oversight committee. No one person controls the whole process. It builds accountability."

I smile. She's clear, practical, offering solutions instead of fear.

Dad leans back, arms crossing. His tone is dismissive. "This is Paradise Hill. We don't need French bureaucracy choking our operations."

The words land like a slap. Elise's expression falters, though she tries to hide it. Her chin lifts a fraction, eyes flashing before she forces them down. "It isn't bureaucracy. It's protection," she says quickly.

Dad scoffs. "Protection is what people talk about when they don't understand how a real vineyard is run. Leave the book learning to the French."

She lowers her gaze, shoulders curving inward. And something in me snaps.

"Don't dismiss her," I counter. Dad's brows lift, but I don't stop. "Elise has seen firsthand how a large house operates. Don't think for a minute that once we get to the bottom of whatever Max and Evelyn are up to, it's going to go away. This is going to happen again and again. She's not suggesting weakness. She's offering safeguards we clearly need."

"Kingston—" my mother tries, soothing, but I shake my head.

"No," Tarryn interrupts. "Kingston's right. I know the repercussions of Max's betrayal are big. That's why this requires a change in our response. If you don't want to listen, fine, but don't belittle Elise, who actually has the perspective to help."

The air goes razor sharp. On the screen, my siblings are silent. Beckett's eyes narrow, and Ryker leans back with a smirk, not mockery, but satisfaction that I've finally raised my voice to our father.

Dad doesn't answer right away. He studies me with that cold, assessing look I've hated my entire life. For a heartbeat, I'm sixteen again, trying to prove I belong.

But then Elise's hand squeezes mine under the desk.

Finally, Dad exhales through his nose. "I'm sorry, Elise. I didn't mean to disregard you or your suggestion. We'll discuss safeguards later. Right now, we need to get to the bottom of the relationship between Evelyn and Max."

Which means *never*, unless we force it. But for now, it's the only retreat we'll get.

Mom clears her throat, her voice smoothing the jagged edges. "We all want what's best for Paradise Hill. Perhaps we should take time to review options before we act."

The call devolves after that—half-hearted updates, Greyson cracking a joke to ease the tension, Ryker needling him back. But the weight remains, and I don't miss the way Tarryn's gaze lingers on Elise, thoughtful and unsettled.

When the last square disappears and the screen goes dark, the silence in our suite is deafening. Elise exhales shakily, her hand slipping from mine.

"I shouldn't have said anything," she whispers.

"What you said was important," I counter. "I wasn't kidding. We're a worldwide player in the wine business. People are going to continue to do this. This time it's Max and Evelyn. Next time, it could be Carl and Sarah with Red Engine. We can't just take this."

Her eyes move to mine, doubtful. "The news that Max is

behind this with Evelyn is big."

"It is." My chest is still hot with anger, but beneath that is a sharper ache. I can't stand the way Elise is shrinking into herself after everything she's given us. I shut the laptop with more force than necessary. "They'll listen. If I have to make them, they will."

She shakes her head. "Your dad wants to retire. Tarryn and I can work this out. Don't worry."

I press my lips to her temple. "I'm proud of you. Do you hear me? Proud."

A shaky laugh escapes her. "You sound like you're making a speech."

"Then let me finish it." I tip her chin up until she meets my eyes. "You're an important part of this family."

Her breath hitches, and for a moment, the fight drains out of her. She sags into me, letting me carry the weight. We step out onto the balcony, and I wrap my arms around her from behind, resting my chin on her shoulder.

Tomorrow, the bubble breaks for good. Paradise Hill will demand us back—sabotage, family politics, battles waiting on every side. But tonight, on this balcony in Paris, I make myself a promise. I'll fight them all if I have to. My father. Max. Evelyn. Anyone who is against us.

Elise isn't just beside me. She's mine. I finally understand that, and everyone needs to as well.

She turns in my arms, eyes searching mine. For a long breath we stand there, the city glowing behind her, until she rises on her toes and kisses me. Hard. Certain.

It's her choice, her answer to every vow I've made. Her lips brand me with trust and demand in equal measure. My hands tighten on her waist, but she doesn't let me lead. She presses me back, walking me inside, until the couch catches me behind the knees.

We tumble down together, her mouth hot and urgent against mine. She's straddling me before I've even caught my breath, and when I reach for her, she catches my wrist and pins it briefly against the cushion, a spark of mischief in her eyes. The sight of her claiming the moment, claiming me, makes my blood roar.

"Let me show you," I whisper when she finally lets me go.

I shift, slide down, and spread her thighs over the cushions. She stiffens for only a heartbeat before she melts back, eyes half-lidded, trust written all over her face. When my mouth finds her, she cries out, arching into me, and I swear I've never known anything more perfect.

She tastes like wine and heat, like the woman who's been putting me together piece by piece. I grip her hips, anchoring her to me as she trembles, as the sounds spilling from her grow louder, more desperate. She's grinding against me, losing control, and I want her that way. Wild. Unapologetic. Powerful.

"Kingston—" My name breaks from her throat, sharp and pleading. She fists her hand in my hair, tugging me up, eyes blazing. "I need you. Now."

We stagger to the bedroom, shedding clothes between kisses. By the time we hit the mattress, I'm bare beneath her and sheathed in a condom. She takes me in with one fierce stroke. My head falls back, a groan tearing from my chest.

Elise moves above me, slow at first, then faster, her hair falling around her shoulders, her body glorious in the glow from the window. I let her take control, let her set the rhythm, and every second of it drives me wild. She's on top, powerful, proving without a word that she's no one's afterthought.

I grip her hips and encourage her every movement, pride swelling with every gasp, every shudder. She's not small here. She's everything.

I reach up, cup her face, and force her to see me. "Look at you. No one dismisses this. No one dismisses you."

Her breath catches, but she doesn't falter. She rides me harder until I'm the one unraveling beneath her.

When I can't take it anymore, I roll, pinning her beneath me, thrusting deep. Her cry shatters something in me. I pound into her, each movement a vow, each breath a promise. Mine. Always mine.

Her nails rake down my back, pulling me closer, holding me there as she breaks apart beneath me. The sight of her ecstasy, the sound of her moaning my name, pushes me over the edge. I spill into her with a groan, burying my face in her neck as the world blurs around us.

We collapse together, sweat-slick, hearts racing. I don't move. I keep her caged beneath me, inside me, because letting go feels impossible.

She brushes damp hair from my forehead, her touch soft, reverent. "You don't have to prove anything," she whispers.

"Yes, I do," I murmur, kissing her again. "I'll prove it every damn day if that's what it takes."

Her smile is small but sure. She tucks herself closer, and the ache in my chest eases. Here in Paris, with Elise in my arms, everything feels right. This is what I want, and I want it to last.

Elise sighs against me, her voice drowsy. "I don't want this night to end."

Neither do I. Because, tomorrow, the bubble bursts, and Paradise is waiting.

Thirty-four

Kingston

The plane drones beneath us, a sensation I can feel in my chest more than hear. Private jets are not loud the way commercial flights are, but the sound is constant, an undercurrent that reminds me we are suspended in the sky.

Elise is asleep against my shoulder. Her head fits there like it was made for that spot, a soft weight that grounds me better than gravity. The plane tilts slightly, and my shoulder aches from holding still, but I don't move. The tickle of her hair against my throat is worth the discomfort.

Her hand is in mine, slack but warm, fingers curled around my thumb like she's tethered, even in her dreams. I shift just enough to lace our hands fully together. My chest tightens at the sight. I never thought something this simple, someone holding on without hesitation, would undo me more than any grand gesture ever could. I never thought I'd allow it again.

I tilt my head to rest against hers. The scent of her shampoo, something faint and floral, mixes with the recirculated air, and somehow, it's enough to quiet the storm that usually churns inside me.

God, I need her. Not just her laugh or her body but the calm that settles in me when she's near. The way my pulse slows, like my heart recognizes something it has been chasing all along.

It scares me how much I've come to rely on her in such a short time. I've spent years training myself not to depend on anyone. Dependence gives leverage. Leverage leads to betrayal. My own history is proof enough. But in my heart, I believe this is different.

The captain's voice breaks through the quiet, polite and professional, telling us we've begun our descent into Vancouver. Elise stirs, her lashes fluttering before she nuzzles deeper into my shoulder. My chest aches at the sight. She's so unguarded, so trusting. I want to freeze time, to hold us here in this fragile space.

I brush my thumb over the back of Elise's hand, gentle until her eyes blink open. She looks up at me, sleepy and soft, lips curving in the smallest smile. My heart stumbles.

"Hey," she whispers, voice rough from sleep.

"Hey yourself." I lower my head, press a kiss to her temple. "We're almost home."

Her eyes open wider, and a sleepy smile tugs her lips. "Were you staring at me the whole time?" she teases.

"Maybe."

She rolls her eyes but squeezes my hand, as if to say she doesn't mind.

Her smile grows, though there's a shadow in it. I know she's thinking the same thing I am, that home isn't just comfort. It's questions, judgments, responsibilities. It's a family that doesn't make space easily, not even for me. For her, it will be worse.

I push the thought away and tuck a strand of hair behind her ear. "Sleep okay?"

She nods, shifting upright, though she keeps her hand in

mine. "Better than I expected."

She glances out the window at the landscape below. "I wish we could stay wrapped up together, just the two of us, where Renew Motion isn't pulling at you and Paradise Hill isn't pulling at me."

"We'll have our evenings," I offer.

"We haven't really talked about what we're going to do when we land. I don't know if I can commute back and forth."

The plane dips lower, and my ears pop with the pressure change. Elise shifts against me, and I feel the heat of her thigh pressed alongside mine. I study her profile in the glow from the window as the sun rises outside.

A thread of worry coils in my gut. "I'll get you back and forth in the helicopter. And I'm hoping you'll stay with me in my room, not the guest room."

She considers that. "The problem is you travel a lot, as you should for Renew Motion. Which means when you're out of town, I'm driving the hour plus back and forth to work, ten hours every week."

"My pilot, Kevin, can take you back and forth."

"I don't want to inconvenience him."

"He takes the helicopter out every day. He'll work around you. And I keep a car at my parents', so you can do things you need to. Trust me, he'll love having more to do since I like to fly myself. He'll be at the airport when we land to fly us home."

"I didn't realize you wouldn't have a car at the airport. That's how most people get home."

I pull her close as the landing gear drops. "Getting you to your job is easy. We will make this work."

She turns then, meeting my gaze. "You okay?" she asks softly.

No. Not even close. But I nod because I will not make her carry my dread. "Now, that you're awake? Yeah."

But the moment my phone reconnects, the illusion cracks wide open.

The buzzing starts almost instantly, one vibration after another rattling through the armrest pocket. Emails, texts, notifications piling up after hours of silence. I ignore it at first, focused on Elise, her hair falling loose around her face, the way she stretches like a cat shaking off sleep.

Then I see the name on the screen.

Hope.

My chest goes tight.

It's not just one message. It's three. Four. And an email stacked on top, her name glaring at me like a ghost I thought I'd buried. Sure, it might be business she's reaching out for, but this many messages in a row feels different.

"Elise," I say. She looks at me, eyes clear now, curious. I force a smile, tuck a stray strand of hair behind her ear, anything to keep her from leaning over to see the screen.

She doesn't press, bless her. She just returns the smile, trusting me. That trust cuts deeper than any blade.

The phone buzzes again, and I drag my thumb across the screen to open the thread.

Hope: Kingston, please talk to me.

Hope: I know I made mistakes, but you can't just erase me.

Hope: We need to meet. It's important.

My pulse hammers so hard I can feel it in my fingertips, the phone slick in my hand. My thumb trembles over the screen. For one reckless second, I almost type back the words rising in my throat: *What do you want?* The urge makes my stomach roll, and I taste copper, feel sweat at my temple.

I told Hope exactly where we stood when I ended things. We're colleagues now. Nothing more, nothing less. It was always going to come to this, but sitting here, I can't shake the irritation that she believed she'd changed things between us without even a conversation.

Another message blinks through, almost instantly, like she knows I'm here.

Hope: Please. Just five minutes. For old times' sake.

Delete.

The email subject line flashes, *I made a mistake.*

I don't open it. I don't need to. I swipe it into oblivion. The ache in my chest doesn't ease, though. Because no matter how many times I hit delete, Hope's shadow lingers. And the worst part, the seed is planted. What happens if Elise sees these messages? If she wonders why I didn't talk to her about this? I've told her about Hope, but now, it's gotten more complicated, and I had no idea. I don't know how to explain that to Elise. What if this is another thing I can't fix, no matter how I try?

I glance at her, and she's watching the runway streak by, her expression open. She's completely unaware of the landmine that just went off on my phone.

I curl an arm around her shoulders, pulling her against me. She relaxes, her head tucking beneath my chin. She trusts me, and I am already keeping things from her. "I've got you," I whisper, though the words are more for me than her.

Because I do. I have got her, and I'm not letting go.

Once we've come to a stop, the cabin door opens, and cool Canadian morning floods in. The flight attendant gestures us forward, and Elise smiles as she gathers her bag, her hand brushing mine. I force myself to smile back.

But the weight of Hope's messages presses on me, like contraband in my pocket.

I delete everything one last time before putting the phone away. *Clean slate.* At least that's what I tell myself.

And I need to tell Elise. The hard part will be explaining that while I won't ever sleep with Hope again, I still want her to be my lawyer. At least, I think I do. Every message she sends makes the possibility of a working, professional relationship seem more unlikely.

Elise slips her hand into mine as we move toward the stairs. She's smiling, still a little sleepy, hair mussed from leaning against me. I keep my hand at the small of her back, protective, steadying us both. Beyond the tarmac, the helicopter waits, the sun throwing our shadows long across the pavement.

She glances up at me, eyes brightening. "It feels good to be home."

My throat locks. I force a smile, but inside, the words twist. Because home is complicated, sharp edged, dangerous. And even though I have just erased every trace of Hope's messages, I can feel them lingering in my chest like splinters.

I bend to kiss Elise's hair as the wind whips it across her cheek. "Yeah," I say, my voice steady even if I am not. "Home."

I don't let go of her hand. I can't. Because holding on is the only thing keeping me whole.

Thirty-five

Elise

A little while later, while we're still getting settled at Kingston's place, both our phones light up with texts. Looks like we're being summoned to Paradise Hill for Sunday dinner this evening. As tempting as it is to crawl right into bed and sleep for days, I know we have to adjust to the time zone. And anyway, I'm eager to see Tarryn, and Kingston's family needs him there.

We compromise with a short nap, and when we head out for the trip over to the vineyard that afternoon, Kevin is waiting for us at the helipad. Kingston is too tired to fly, so Kevin is going to take us and wait for our return.

Kingston nods at Kevin as he opens to door to the bird. "Elise is going to be living here and may be reaching out for rides back and forth to Paradise Hill when I'm not available."

Kevin dips his head. "I'm here and ready whenever you

need me."

"Thank you." It feels ridiculous to commute to work in a helicopter.

The ride across the lake is short, and we've barely hit the helipad at the vineyard when I spot Tarryn. She's already halfway down the stairs, headed this way with Declan behind her. My father waits just beyond the blades as they slow to a stop, hands shoved deep in his jacket pockets. His smile is wide, but I catch something measuring, protective in his eyes.

Kingston lingers behind me. He takes my messenger bag before I can even reach for it, his fingers brushing mine. It's a small touch, but it sends heat through me like a live wire.

"Thank you."

His jaw tightens, eyes steady on mine.

I swallow, shifting closer so only he can hear. "I need to get caught up at the vineyard, and with Tarryn, so I'll see you at dinner."

He nods and hands me my messenger bag. "I'll be around."

My father clears his throat, as if he's giving us space, but not too much. Declan stands beside him, unreadable.

I reach for Kingston's shirt and tug him down into a kiss, right here, in front of everyone. We're not a secret. Not anymore. His mouth is warm and sure against mine, and for a second, I lean into him, memorizing the taste, the press, the way his breath catches when I don't let go right away.

When I pull back, he doesn't exactly smile, but something softer fills his face. "Family dinner," he says, voice low. "Don't be late."

"I won't," I promise.

Tarryn practically pushes Kingston away and envelops me in a hug. "I've missed you so much!" she declares.

I greet my father as well, and we all follow Kingston toward the family house. "I brought goodies for everyone."

Tarryn's eyes grow wide. "What did you bring me?"

We walk into the kitchen and sit on barstools. I pull out a beret and Château's most-sought after wine and hand them to my dad. "You can keep this for yourself, or share."

He shakes his head. "I could sell this and buy you a nice condo in town."

Trace looks at it and smiles. "How'd you get this?"

"Sasha Valmont gave it to me, and I figured I should share the spoils with those who will appreciate them."

Trace turns to my father. "I'll pay for dinner out on our next trip to Vancouver if you'll share with me."

"Deal." Dad says, and they head toward his home office and his favorite decanter.

"Don't forget me," Vicky yells after them.

I rifle through my bag and hand Kingston's mom the beautiful Hermes scarf I found for her. "I thought this was you."

She smiles. "I love it. It's absolutely me!" She gives me a big hug. "Thank you."

Tarryn is bouncing from one leg to the other, and it's fun to make her wait. She's like a child on Christmas morning.

I offer the bag to her, and she grins. She pulls out the first item with a squeal. "You brought me bottles?" she gasps, holding one up to the light.

"Careful," I warn, but I can't help laughing. "That's a grand cru. Don't drop it."

She tucks it carefully at her feet and digs deeper. Scarves, soaps, little bits I picked up at markets. She holds them up one by one like treasures. I watch her face light up and realize how much I missed this—her energy, her curiosity, her way of making everything feel like an occasion.

"I can't believe you remembered," she says, clutching the lavender sachet I grabbed in Provence. "Now, everything will smell like the south of France."

I lean back against the kitchen counter, the fatigue of travel still clinging to me, but there's warmth too. "I had to do something. You kept this place running while I was gone."

Her smile dims just a fraction. "Sort of. The assistant vintner from Château, Jérôme Pelletier, tried, but honestly… They don't do much more than pour and stir there. Glorified hands." She shrugs.

I nod. I understand too well. "I know. It's not their fault. They're part of a huge, very specialized staff, but this vineyard needs more than that. That's why I'm grateful to be here, learning from Dad. Growing up and working here, I did hand work, but I had so many other opportunities as well. These last months working in such a large operation helped me see the differences, and I learned a lot." I hold up my notebook. "Just wait till you see my ideas."

With the gift-giving show over, Vicky disappears to get her drink before the bottle is gone, and Declan's phone rings, leaving just me and Tarryn to catch up.

"So…" she says, a mischievous glint in her eyes. "When were you going to tell me about Kingston?"

I roll my eyes, heat rising to my cheeks. "What about him?"

"Oh please. Don't even try. You kissed him right in front of your dad."

Her grin is wide enough to make me groan. I turn toward the window, but she nudges my arm. "Tell me everything."

I sigh, but there's no reason not to share. "We, uh, connected a bit just before I left, and we started writing letters while I was away. It just…happened. One line became two, and suddenly, it wasn't just business anymore. He'd write about what was going on in Black Bear and with Renew Motion, and I'd write about the vineyard, about France, about anything."

"And then?" she presses.

"And then our chemistry bloomed," I admit. "But I'm cautious, Tarryn. Cara hurt him badly. I don't know what our future holds."

"Letters turning into love notes. Classic. That's how my parents did it." Her teasing softens into something gentler. She squeezes my hand. "You're not Cara."

I hold her gaze, wishing I felt more certain that would be enough. Everything feels different now that we're back home. "How's the new cottage coming?" I ask, eager to redirect.

Tarryn smiles. "I've been working with an architect. Since we're not looking to move into the main house anytime soon—if ever—we want to have plenty of room in the cottage to grow, but I don't want to take out any blocks of vines."

I nod, and she gives me a tour of the plans she and Declan are putting together. It's going to be wonderful. As she rolls the blueprints back up, I note the time and realize I need to catch up with my dad, and Tarryn has a few things to do before dinner.

As I head out, she thanks me again and carries her bundle of French treasures upstairs, calling over her shoulder about where she will hang the scarf I brought.

I find my father in his chair near the front window with a glass of wine in hand.

"Is that the Château Reserve?" I ask.

He shakes his head. "I shared a glass with Vicky and Trace. But don't worry, I'm saving the rest for us. It's outstanding."

"They have a very interesting way they do the push. I took lots of notes."

A smile blooms on his face. "I knew you'd come back with something good."

"I have lots of ideas." I smile too, realizing how much I missed him while I was gone. "So what are you drinking?"

"Father and Son's reserve," he says, swirling the glass. "Frank dropped it off. Figured I'd see if they still know what they're doing over there."

I grin. "And?"

"Not bad. Not Paradise good, but not bad."

He doesn't look at me for a moment, just swirls the wine again. When he does turn my way, his eyes are sharp, like he's trying to see straight through me.

"I like Kingston," he says finally, voice rough.

The words catch me off guard. "You do?"

He nods. "He's steady. Smart. I trust him with a lot of things." He leans forward, eyes narrowing. "But don't fool yourself, Elise. He's not safe ground."

A chill creeps up my spine. "What do you mean?"

"You saw what Cara did to him," he says. "She ripped his guts out, left him for his best friend, and the fallout nearly tore this family apart. A wound like that doesn't go away. It makes a man cautious, selfish even. If it comes down to protecting himself or protecting you, he'll pick himself."

The words slam into me, feeding my worry. He seems open about so many things, but then there are others… Hope texted him on the trip home, and he seemed strange when he discovered her messages. He didn't share that with me.

"You're not family to him," Dad goes on. "Not the way his brothers are. If this blows up, you don't just lose him. You lose everything here. Your place. Your work. The future you've built in this vineyard. And you'll do it with your heart shattered to pieces."

I want to deny it, but my father's words make some sense. Though there's also lots of evidence to the contrary. In France, Kingston's smile softened the air, his hand steadying mine as I lifted a glass, his voice warm as he read my letters aloud. That man—the one who felt like home—feels miles away from the broken figure my father describes. I have to trust that time heals, that people can change. That Kingston will be honest when he's ready.

"I can take care of myself," I whisper, though the sound wavers.

He doesn't argue, doesn't soften. Just leans back, reclaiming his glass, and mutters, "You'd better."

Conversation over.

I go in and sit down on the family room couch as everyone else arrives for dinner. I don't know when Kingston comes to sit next to me. We're both exhausted.

When Greyson arrives with Theo, I bring out a few handmade tops I picked up for him. They were made by a local craftsman near Château. Greyson settles Theo in his highchair, and I set the tops spinning across the tray. Theo lights up, reaching for them with chubby hands, catching them only to slobber all over the wood. His delight makes me laugh. I open boxes of chocolates, but the croissants and bread we carried back don't taste quite the same.

Dinner is a blur. Everyone is there, voices and faces

weaving together until I can barely track the conversations, and my eyes are so heavy. Before long Kingston is leading me back to the helicopter, and Kevin flies us home.

"What time do you want to leave tomorrow to return to Paradise Hill?" he asks as we land.

I have to think. "How about seven?" It seems impossible that I'll be in any sort of shape by then, but I have to try.

He nods. "I'll meet you in the kitchen."

I agree, and Kingston takes my hand, guiding me inside and to his room. I'm beyond exhausted, thirty-six hours without real sleep catching up all at once.

Somehow, I wake before the sun on Monday morning, disoriented, but with Dad's warning echoing in my head. I shove it aside and pull on my boots. *Work*. But caffeine first. That is something I can control. I can hear Kingston in his home office talking to someone over his computer speakers. I won't bother him.

Kevin is in the kitchen talking to Simone, and I hand her a small gift bag that has some French perfume and some handcrafted measuring cups I found in a stall in Paris.

She hugs me. "I love these. I need to get a date so I can wear this perfume."

I glance over to find Kevin looking at her, but she doesn't see it. Looks like they might need a little help to make something happen there.

I drink three shots of espresso and hope it's enough to get me through the day. Then Kevin leads me out to the helipad, and within minutes, we're on our way, flying over the lake. During the trip, he hands me his phone, and I enter my number and then text my phone, so I have his.

"Just call me," he says once we've landed. "I'm about eight

minutes away and can come get you anytime."

He leaves me at the Paradise helipad, and Tarryn is there waiting for her turn. She's off to meet with a security company to talk about what they suggest for the property, but Kevin tells her he needs to make a couple of adjustments first.

She nods at him and turns to me. "Got a minute?" she asks.

I tuck a stray hair behind my ear. "Sure. What's up?"

"I've been thinking about what you said the other day on the Zoom call. About Château and how they handle things."

"The audits?"

"Yeah. The audits, the supply tracking, the idea that sabotage is just...part of the business." She folds her arms. "I know you're right. And we need some of those systems here. That's why I'm taking this meeting today. But I hate the idea that everyone just accepts it and moves on."

I exhale slowly. I remember feeling that same way. "It's not that they don't care," I tell her. "It's just scale. When you're producing at Château's level, losing a thousand cases doesn't shut you down. It barely makes a ripple. So they focus on prevention and documentation instead of outrage."

Her brow furrows. "Still feels wrong."

"Of course it does. And that's also not the case for us. Every loss matters. But putting systems in place is not about giving up. It's about control. They build mechanisms that catch problems quickly, so one mistake doesn't become a disaster."

She nods, but I can still see resistance in her eyes. "I get it. I do. I just wish it didn't have to be this way."

I smile faintly. "Me too. But protecting the vineyard doesn't mean you stop trusting people. It just means you have precautions in place."

Her lips press into a thin line. "Trust with a safety net."

"Exactly." I rest a hand on her arm. "Your family built something beautiful here, Tarryn. Systems don't make it colder. They make it last."

She gives me a grudging nod. "Thanks. That will help as I'm meeting with the security company."

I give her a quick hug and head toward the office as she

and Kevin prepare to rise into the air again. I want to start by reacquainting myself with the land.

After a quick stop in Tarryn's office, I step back out into the morning. The vineyard is hushed, the air cool with dew. I walk the rows with my clipboard, scanning the notes Jerome, Château's exchange vintner, left behind. But his scribbles don't all make sense, and worse than that, some tasks are half done, and some not touched at all.

How did this all get by Dad? I crouch, fingers brushing bare soil where cover crops should have been planted weeks ago. My stomach knots.

Inside the winery, it's worse. I find inventory lists with gaps, and barrels that should have been rotated months ago still sitting in the same spots, a fine layer of dust on the hoops. I press my palm to the wood. They are good barrels, but wine will not forgive neglect.

I tug off my sweater, roll up my sleeves, and start working. One barrel at a time, shoulder to the staves, I shift them slowly, the floor creaking under their weight. My muscles burn, sweat gathering along my spine, but it feels good to make something move again.

At the calibration station, I check the hydrometer. The readings are off, almost laughably so. I sigh, adjust, test again, repeat until the line settles where it should have been weeks ago. But each click of the gauge steadies my chest. And as the line holds true, I remember Kingston's comment in one of his emails, teasing me about precision—*wine is patient, Elise, but only if you respect her tools.*

By the time I circle back to inventory, my hands are streaked with oak dust and ink. I scrawl corrections into the margins, circle missing shipments, make notes to call suppliers. Every unchecked box feels like a failure I have to correct.

"Elise?"

I jump at the sound of Tarryn's voice. She leans in the barrel room doorway, arms folded, a half-smile on her face. "You've been at it since dawn. You almost ready for dinner at the main house?"

Dinner. Kingston. My pulse stumbles.

My head hurts, and I just want to go back to Kingston's and crawl into bed. "I can't. Not tonight. There's too much."

She raises a brow. "There's always too much. You'll drown if you never come up for air. Plus, you have to get back to the right time zone."

I want to argue, to tell her I'm right where I need to be, fixing what slipped while I was gone. But then I picture Kingston waiting at that long family table, his brothers teasing, his mother's smile.

I set the clipboard down with a sigh. "Fine. Just let me wash up."

Tarryn grins. "I'll hold you to it."

When she disappears, I press my palms against the counter and breathe. I will never catch up in one day. But I can't miss tonight. Not when Kingston will be there.

I scrub my hands until the dirt finally lifts from under my nails and change into a soft blouse and dark jeans I keep here on the off chance I need to go into town. I twist my hair into a braid. When I've finished, my reflection looks tired but steadier, like I've shaken some of the vineyard dust off of me.

Still, my pulse picks up as I cross the gravel drive toward the main house. Dad's words come to me again, and I struggle to push them down. It's no good to worry about trusting the person keeping me steady in all this newness. I just have to believe…cautiously, I guess…

The door is already open, voices spilling out, the kind of noise that only comes when all the Paradises are under one roof.

"Look who finally showed," Greyson calls as I step inside. He's lounging against the counter with a beer in his hand. His gaze moves to Kingston, then back to me. "Didn't think you'd let her breathe without you."

Heat rushes up my neck, but Kingston doesn't take the bait. He just pulls out a chair for me, steady and unbothered. That calm of his grounds me as I slip into the seat beside him.

Their mother swoops in before I can catch my breath, wrapping me in a hug that smells of lemon and butter. "You look tired. How's the jetlag?" she asks, her smile bright and certain.

I stand a little taller at the warmth in her voice. "It'll be a few days before I'm back on track," I reply.

Then the teasing starts, bouncing around the table. Beckett jabs Greyson about his ego, and Ryker mutters something under his breath that has Tarryn swatting him on the arm. Laughter rises and falls in waves, and for a moment, I just sit and absorb it, letting myself belong.

At some point, Kingston excuses himself. I catch the soft scrape of his chair and the quiet click of the door as it closes behind him. No one else seems to notice—conversation continues without pause—but I do. His absence lingers beneath the noise. Is it Hope again? What could be so urgent? What makes him so unsettled?

By the time he returns, plates have started to circle the table. He moves to my side again, one hand brushing the back of my chair as he sits. There's a faint crease between his brows that wasn't there before.

"You okay?" I ask quietly, leaning toward him.

He nods once. "There's an issue at work," he says under his breath. "Nothing serious, just something I'll have to deal with tonight."

I nod, deciding to believe that's true.

Once everyone has their food, the conversation turns. Greyson brings up the vineyard almost casually, but the lightness drains from the room.

"Zach's name came up again today," Kingston says, his voice cutting through the chatter. "Cal sent me a message. He believes he's back from Mexico."

Forks pause, chairs creak.

"Zach is here?" Tarryn frowns. "Back in Paradise?"

"Word is yes." Kingston's gaze sweeps the table. "And Max is behind all of it. Every problem, every crack in this place, it all traces back to him."

Trace sets down his fork. "I'll deal with it."

"No." Vicky's voice slices through, firm in a way that silences even Greyson. "Not alone. Tarryn goes. And one of you boys."

"Mom—" Tarryn starts.

But Vicky shakes her head. "I never thought Max was dangerous," she says, her eyes moving over her children. "I knew he was bitter, but I didn't think he would sabotage his own family. I misjudged him. I won't do it again."

The room goes quiet, heavy. My heart hammers, my hand twitching under the table. I reach for Kingston's hand.

Zach's return changes everything—the questions, the blame, the fragile peace this family has been holding together with careful smiles and good intentions.

Kingston's thumb traces slow circles over my hand, a small motion that feels like an anchor. But even that can't quiet the thought pressing forward in my mind.

If Zach's back, then the past isn't finished with them yet.

Thirty-six

Elise

We've been back almost two weeks now, and the fog of jetlag has finally burned off. My body is remembering how this time zone feels. The rhythm of commuting between Black Bear and Paradise Hill has started to feel less impossible, even when the days stretch long. Sadie had her baby last week—a boy, William Quincy Paradise, nine pounds even. Most of the family has been distracted by that, so I've tried to stay focused.

With everything going on, Trace has been unable to talk to Max. Kingston and Tarryn aren't convinced he's actually tried. Max's betrayal has been really difficult for him to process.

I believe I've now taken care of all the things Jérôme didn't get around to or understand were his responsibility when he was covering for me. In the process, I found a pair of lacy panties in the barrel room a couple days ago. Trying not to think about that.

But I can see now what captured most of Dad's attention while I was away—more issues with Evelyn and the shared well that Zach poisoned before he left last fall. She's not happy with the amount of reimbursement we're providing Black Bear Winery for their loss. We paid to repair the soil and the well, and we replaced all the affected vines, plus we gave them what they would have made on the wine each year. Yet she still wants more. Damages, she says. So no wonder things were such a mess. I'm grateful it wasn't worse.

Today has been another long day, but I'm going out with my friends at the end of it, a respite I've definitely earned.

When I arrive with Tarryn, Mikey's smells like beer and fryer oil and a kind of clean pine soap that never quite hides the grease. The Christmas lights strung across the rafters are glowing away, even though it's June. The old TV above the bar flashes with a Blue Jays game, and the shouted plays and missed calls compete with the shuffle of shoes across the scuffed floorboards. This place is loud and lived in, like the whole town has carved their initials into it.

By the time we see them, Sadie and Ginny are already waving us over, perched on stools in front of the long, glossy bar. My stomach lifts in that small, ridiculous way it always does when I see them waiting for me. They're Kingston's family, and somehow, they're becoming mine.

"Finally," Ginny calls, tossing her hair over one shoulder. "We were about to start without you."

Sadie stands to hug me, warm and firm. "You made it."

"We had to find parking," Tarryn says with a roll of her eyes. She claims a stool, the one with the crooked leg she knows how to tame by bracing her boot against the floor.

I slide in next to her and my shoulders ease down. It feels like I've been holding myself upright all day just to get here.

Mikey drops four coasters in front of us. His beard hides his mouth, but I can tell he's almost smiling. "What's it going to be?" he asks, already reaching for a pint glass.

"Not beer," Ginny says. "We want fun cocktails tonight."

Mikey stops mid-motion, glass frozen in his hand.

"Cocktails." The word sounds like an insult from his mouth.

"Yes," Sadie insists, bracing her elbows on the bar. "Something colorful. Something with umbrellas, and no alcohol in mine. I'm nursing."

Mikey blinks. "This is a beer bar. I don't have any umbrellas. You want an umbrella, check the stand by the door. People are always leaving them behind."

"And you," Tarryn says, poking his forearm, "are a talented bartender who can make whatever we want."

He groans like she's asked him to haul barrels across town. "You're killing me."

But his hands are already moving, pulling a shaker from the shelf, scooping ice into metal. He digs out a bottle of rum and another of pineapple liqueur, muttering the whole time about betraying his roots.

I hide my smile in my hand. There's something perfect about watching a man so gruff and stubborn give in to four women without much of a fight.

When he sets the finished drinks in front of us, the glasses sparkle neon blue and pink, garnished with lime wedges and cherries skewered on tiny plastic swords. And yes—little umbrellas. Sadie gets one that's slightly less colorful but definitely has plenty of garnishes.

"You're the best," she gushes.

We burst into laughter.

"Admit it," Ginny says, stirring hers with the straw. "You had fun making these. They're beautiful."

"Don't push it," Mikey grumbles, but his eyes crinkle, betraying his pride.

We raise our glasses.

"To Greyson and Trinity," Sadie declares. "A whole week in Kauai, just the two of them. Kid free."

"To Trace and Vicky," Tarryn adds, "finally getting their hands on Theo for longer than a few hours. I swear they're more excited than Greyson was."

Our glasses meet, a cheerful ring against the wood and the noise of the bar.

I take my first sip. Sweet and tropical. The cold glass presses wet against my palm, condensation pooling around my fingers. The drink is ridiculously sweet, candy in liquid form, and Mikey's mock-suffering expression makes it taste even better. It's a vacation in a glass, sunshine like we'll never see here, and we laugh like we've already escaped.

I swirl my straw through the crushed ice. Each sip leaves a line of sugar across my tongue and a warm slip of rum down my throat.

We move to a table where we can watch most of the bar.

Sadie sits down next to me and leans in, her eyes sharp. "Okay," she says, stretching the word like a rubber band. "Spill."

I blink at her. "Spill what?"

"How," Ginny jumps in, "you managed to get Kingston out of his funk. Because, Elise"—she lowers her voice, conspiratorial—"he's a different man."

Tarryn tips her glass toward me. "It's true. He's been impossible since Cara left. Silently brooding. No fun whatsoever. Now, he's…lighter. He even joked with Dad yesterday. Do you know how long it's been since that happened?"

Heat rushes to my cheeks. "You're exaggerating."

Sadie laughs like she caught me in a lie. "No. We're not. He looks at you like you're the only reason he remembers how to breathe."

Ginny sighs dreamily. "He's obviously in love."

My stomach flips. "Slow down. It's not…" I toy with the umbrella until the paper tears between my fingers.

I want to deny what they've said, trying to protect myself, just in case, except I can't stop cataloging the proof. The way his gaze softens when it lands on me. The way his voice dips lower when he says my name. The steadiness of his hand at my back. If that isn't love, then what is? But then there's the parts of himself I'm still not sure he lets me fully see—his painful past with Cara, whatever remains unresolved with Hope. I press my lips to the straw and take a too-long sip, forcing the thought away. "We haven't talked about it," I say.

"Not love," Tarryn scoffs, amused. She crunches a cherry

between her teeth. "Sure. Tell yourself that."

I swallow hard, then blurt the thing I've been carrying like a stone in my pocket. "But Hope keeps texting him."

Ginny's eyebrows shoot up. Sadie tilts her head. Tarryn's mouth twists.

"He never replies when I'm around," I rush on. "But she keeps sending them, so I think maybe…he writes back later."

Tarryn shakes her head. "Hope's his lawyer. It's probably work."

"Not when the message says I miss you," I snap before I can stop myself. My throat tightens. "That's not legal language."

Sadie leans her elbow against the bar. "Have you talked to him about it?"

I stare into my glass, watching the ice cubes spin. "It's none of my business. If he wants to tell me about it, he will."

"It's your business," Sadie counters immediately.

"Definitely your business," Ginny adds.

"More your business than hers," Tarryn confirms.

I laugh nervously, but the sound falls flat. "I don't want to snoop."

"You don't have to snoop," Sadie says gently. "You just have to ask."

"I don't want to sound insecure."

"Wanting honesty isn't insecure," Tarryn insists. She spears the cherry stem with her straw like a tiny battle flag. "It's smart."

I nod, but the weight in my chest doesn't ease. They're right, but my pride doesn't want to admit it. I tuck the thought away, though even as I try to push it down, an image flashes in my head—Kingston at his desk, phone in hand, his thumbs moving across the screen after I've gone to bed. The phantom makes my chest ache. *I have to talk to him.* Not tonight. But soon.

The bar door swings open with a rush of warm air. Everyone at our table instinctively glances over. And Zach Paradise steps inside. I blink hard because it can't be him. Cal said he was back, but when no one ever saw him, we decided he was wrong. But it is him now, back after nearly a year of radio silence. He's just walked into Mikey's like he never left.

He looks almost the same—broad shoulders, dark hair mussed like he's been on the road, eyes too restless to belong to someone settled. And there's an edge to him, like he hasn't slept right in weeks. His jaw is tight and his tan flawless.

He heads straight to the bar. He and Mikey talk for a few minutes, and he orders a beer, leaning against the counter. When Mikey delivers it, the amber liquid catches the glow from the string lights. He lifts it halfway to his mouth before he sees us.

For one second, I wonder if he'll pretend not to notice. Then he tips his glass in a silent toast, casual, as if there's no history piled between him and the people sitting along this section of the bar.

"Should we wave back?" Ginny murmurs.

Tarryn straightens on her stool and calls, "Zach! Over here."

I can feel a ripple of surprise move through Sadie and Ginny, but they cover it quickly with polite smiles. My fingers tighten around my glass.

Zach crosses the floor with easy steps, his beer in hand. He stops at the edge of our little row and offers a small grin that doesn't quite reach his eyes. "Sorry I missed the holidays," he says. His gaze drops to Tarryn's hand, and he nods at the ring glittering there. "Heard you got engaged. Congratulations."

Tarryn's voice is cool but steady. "Thanks."

There's a pause, the kind that makes my skin itch. As an outsider, maybe I feel it more keenly—the invisible map of loyalties and betrayals drawn around this family, with me straddling the edges.

Zach takes a sip of his beer, looking at each of us in turn.

Then the door swings open again, and Kingston and Ryker step inside. The whole place shifts with their presence, people glancing up from pints, heads tipping in recognition.

Kingston's eyes find me instantly. Just one look and I feel steadier, even as the air around our stools thickens.

The brothers grab beers from Mikey, and then weave toward us. But the moment they spot Zach, the energy changes.

Ryker's eyebrows shoot up, sharp with challenge, and Kingston's whole body stiffens as he moves into place beside me.

"Zach," Kingston says evenly, settling onto the stool next to Sadie. He takes a slow drink and lowers the glass. "Where've you been?"

Zach shrugs like it's nothing. "Needed to get away."

"Yeah, the last time I saw you, you were trying to dump a bunch of vinegar into the water table between Paradise and Dempsey land," Ryker adds.

Zach shrugs it off.

Tarryn leans forward. "You poisoned the well, Zach. You can't just disappear after something like that and expect it to blow over. You need to be accountable."

Zach shifts, jaw working, but his expression is maddeningly casual. "I didn't know."

My stomach knots. *Didn't know what?* That hardly even passes as an excuse.

Ryker's eyes turn sharp as flint. "If it wasn't a big deal, why do it at night?" His tone is pure challenge, daring Zach to lie again.

"And why did you leave town?" Kingston asks.

The silence crackles. Zach's knuckles whiten on his pint. Kingston hasn't said a word, but his stillness is louder than shouting. His shoulders are iron, his gaze locked on Zach.

The tension stretches, a rope pulled too tight. Zach swallows, shifts, looks at the brothers in turn. "Because Max told me something. He let it slip."

Kingston's hand brushes my knee under the bar, even as his face goes pale.

Zach swallows hard. "I'd just learned Max isn't my father."

The words hang there. *Max isn't his father?*

For a moment, no one breathes.

Then Tarryn is the first to recover. "If not Max," she demands, "then who?"

Zach takes a long swallow of his beer, as if buying time. His hand trembles just enough to make the glass knock against the bar as he sets it down. For one stretched second, all I can hear is my own heartbeat, loud and panicked. Then Zach's eyes slide past Tarryn, past Kingston, past Ryker, and land on Ginny.

"It's Henry Dempsey," he says.

My breath jerks short.

Ginny blinks, once, twice. "What?" Her voice cracks. "He's *my* father."

Ryker rises, his stool screeching against the floorboards. Ginny's voice cuts sharp, firing questions faster than Zach can answer. Sadie's face is flushed red with fury, hands fisted against the table. After a minute, Ginny just shakes her head like she can physically refuse the words, like denial could rewind them.

Kingston remains utterly still beside me. Not speaking. Not moving. Just absorbing, his jaw locked, eyes dark as storm clouds.

The sound around me is chaos—overlapping accusations, disbelief, and anger. And I sit in the middle of it, my glass clutched in both hands, my pulse hammering. I feel like both insider and outsider at once. Kingston's thigh presses warm against mine under the table, and I'm here, part of this circle. But bloodlines are unraveling in front of me, and I'm not bound by them. I watch the truth tear through them like a storm ripping vines from their stakes, and all I can do is hold my ground in the wind.

Zach stares down at his beer, shoulders braced. "Max told me, and I left. I couldn't be around him."

My gaze catches Kingston's. His eyes are raw, reeling, the shock of Zach's revelation written in every line of his face. I reach for him without thinking, my hand finding his. He holds on, tight, like the world just shifted beneath his feet.

The room feels heavy with grief, relief, anger, all of it tangled together. I want to believe this will help them move forward, but I can't imagine it will be that simple. Secrets don't just disappear because someone comes home. They resurface, demanding to be reckoned with, and there's still the matter of the sabotage.

As Kingston stares off somewhere past the table, I realize

this is only the beginning.

Thirty-seven

Kingston

Zach's words are still ringing in my ears when the door slams behind him. The silence he leaves is almost louder than what he revealed, which hangs heavy in the air like smoke after a fire.

Ginny's face crumples, and Ryker wraps an arm around her shoulders, pulling her close, his jaw tight. She presses her forehead against his chest, and a tremble runs through her body. "I need to find my brother, my sisters," she says, her voice breaking.

Ryker nods. He glances at me, and I nod as he steers her toward the door. There's nothing we can give Ginny right now that Ryker can't.

Elise looks up at me, her brows drawn, her mouth parted like she's about to say something. She could be about to ask if I'm okay, and I long to let her steady me, to sink into the way she grounds me. But I can't. Not now. My family needs me to lead. It's the role I know.

I straighten, forcing my voice steady. "We need to see our parents before this spreads any further."

Elise nods, and I lock myself into what I do best—containment, control. This is a new piece of the puzzle, and we need to determine how it factors in before emotions spiral out of control.

The drive to Paradise Hill feels longer than it is, my hands clenched tightly on the wheel. Elise sits beside me, silent. Her fingers brush against mine once, tentatively. I should take her hand. Anchor myself. God, I want to. But I can't. Suddenly, that kind of openness feels impossible, too vulnerable in the face of everything now falling at my feet.

When we get to my parents', the house is chaos—the curtains half open, a lamp knocked over in the hall. My parents are on the couch, side by side, pale as ghosts. Mom's hair is loose, a strand stuck to her cheek. Dad's hand rests on his knee, tapping a restless rhythm. Between them, the exhaustion is bone deep, like the energy's been sucked out of them. At first, I wonder if Zach has been here too, but then I remember: *Theo*.

I glance past them to drawers gaping and papers scattered across the floor. Theo's storm. Fortunately, now he's upstairs, asleep, the wreckage abandoned in his wake.

The door opens behind me, and Beckett strides in with Sadie, followed by Tarryn and Declan. Elise drifts closer to me, like she knows I need her near, though I still don't reach for her.

Beckett doesn't waste any time. His voice is clipped, his eyes sharp. "Did you know Henry Dempsey was Zach's father?" he demands.

My parents look at each other, something wordless passing between them. Mom swallows, and Dad exhales like he's been holding his breath for decades.

"We knew about the affair," Mom says finally, voice small. "Chereen and Henry. But not this. We thought it was over long before Zach was born."

The admission feels like another blow, but before I can

even process, Dad's temper snaps. "Is this what Max wanted all along? Revenge? Because our father gave me the vineyard and nothing to him? Is this his way of tearing us apart piece by piece?"

His fury is raw, spilling over into every corner of the room. And I hear it beneath the shouting. What no one wants to say out loud. This isn't just family drama. This is orchestrated. Duplicity at play. Max pulling strings, and all of us dancing without realizing the music had already started.

We explain what happened tonight at Mikey's and debate the reasons Zach might have shown his face now. But nothing makes sense. There isn't anything concrete for us to build on, and it's impossible to know whether anything Zach says is even close to the truth at this point. After chasing our thoughts in circles for a while, my parents tell us they have to go to bed. Theo will be up at his usual time, regardless of what else is going on.

The rest of us sit around a bit longer, but there's nothing much left to be said. My siblings now look almost as tired as my parents did.

We say our goodnights, and shortly thereafter, I'm back in the cockpit with Elise next to me and the helicopter blades roaring overhead, drowning out thought until it's just vibration in my bones. I sit rigid in the seat, headset pressed tight against my ears, staring out at the dark stretch of valley. Elise leans into me, her shoulder warm against mine. She doesn't say anything at first, just rests there, steady, like she's trying to bleed calm into me. For a moment, I let myself feel it, the comfort, and the quiet promise that I don't have to carry this alone. The need in me is sharp, almost unbearable.

Then my phone buzzes against my thigh. A name lights the screen. *Hope.*

My stomach knots. I ignore it. Don't read what she has to say. I keep hoping that if I avoid it long enough, maybe she'll understand. Maybe she'll stop. Elise shifts, glancing at the movement. I slide the phone back into my pocket before she can see. She deserves honesty. She's given me nothing but that. But I can't seem to muster the energy to dive into this. I've ended things with Hope. That should be enough.

The helicopter tilts into descent, and gravity presses me into the seat, my stomach tight. I brace, keeping my focus fixed on the helipad rising below. Elise slips her hand over mine, lacing our fingers together. I hold on, but my unease remains.

After landing and completing the checks on the helicopter, we walk up from the helipad. Elise's hand stays in mine, steady, like we're a united front, facing things together. I almost believe it too, despite my inner turmoil. But the second I open the front door, that changes. Simone is waiting in the entry, arms crossed, her expression pinched.

"You have a visitor," she says carefully.

A visitor? At this hour? My stomach drops. "Who?"

Her pause is answer enough. I step into the living room with Elise right behind me, and then the bottom falls out.

Hope.

She's standing in the middle of my living room, wearing my robe like she owns it. Elise freezes beside me, shock on her face.

I turn to her, my throat dry. "Give me a moment."

The look she gives me isn't anger. It's worse. Stunned disbelief, like she doesn't even know who she's standing next to anymore.

Hope moves before Elise can respond. She rushes to me, eyes shining, and voice pleading. "Kingston, please. You made a mistake. I miss you, and I want you back." The robe slides off her shoulders, pools at her feet. She's wearing lingerie, black and delicate, no doubt meant to erase the shift in our relationship like it never happened. But that's impossible, and it's nothing I want. Yet all I see now is Elise's face, her hurt, her trust shattering in the silence beside me. *Why didn't I find a way to talk to her about this?*

I force myself to face Hope. "I told you it was over. If I'd wanted more, I would've said so. I would have moved to Vancouver. But I didn't. I won't."

Her lip trembles. "Please, Kingston. Just listen—"

And then a door opens and closes. *Shit*. Elise has

disappeared.

"Elise!"

I tear away from Hope, racing upstairs, calling her name. Nothing. Bedroom empty. Hallway silent. I hurry back down the stairs, through the door and out into the night.

I'm just in time to see the headlights of the Paradise Hill truck fading into the darkness.

She's gone. *How will I ever make this right?*

Thirty-eight

Kingston

Elise's taillights are still burned behind my eyes. I chased her, but she didn't stop. She didn't even slow. After watching the truck disappear, I have no choice but to go back inside and face what's waiting.

Hope is on my couch, legs folded under her, still wearing my robe, a glass of wine in her hand. A candle flickers on the coffee table like she's set the stage for this moment.

"You didn't catch her, did you?" Her voice is soft, almost triumphant, but her face tells another story. Her mouth is trembling.

I slam the door so hard the frames rattle on the wall. "Get out."

She sets the glass down, fingers shaking. "No. Not until you listen. Kingston." She stands, the robe back on but slipping from one shoulder, eyes bright with tears. "You don't understand. I didn't realize how much I loved you until you ended things. We were made for each other. We're both career driven, and we've got incredible chemistry. I always thought we would get married one day and build a family. If that meant me walking away from my career, I would have done it. If it meant moving here—" Her breath hitches. "—I would have figured it out. For you."

I shake my head, jaw so tight it aches. "That's not true. We were never headed anywhere. You told me a hundred times you couldn't understand how I stayed in a small town. You grew up in one and hated every second. You said you'd suffocate if you ever had to live in one again."

"That was before." Her voice rises, frantic. She steps closer, clutching the robe tighter. "I was wrong. I thought I knew what I wanted. I don't care about Vancouver or Toronto anymore. Not if it means I can't have you."

Her hands press to my chest, as if she can make me feel what she's saying. Her palms are warm, her eyes desperate. "I would have given you everything. I still would. Just...don't let her ruin this. Don't throw us away for someone who's not strong enough to stay."

Something inside me snaps. I grab her wrists and pull her hands off me, holding her at arm's length. "Don't talk about Elise. No one should have to stand here and witness this."

"Why not?" Hope's voice cracks. "She's already gone. She couldn't handle it. couldn't handle you. She ran. Just like Cara. Just like—"

"Stop." The word scrapes my throat raw.

Her tears spill over now, streaking down her cheeks. "Kingston, please. I love you. I've always loved you. Don't you remember what we had? Don't you remember how easy it was? We could have that again. We could be a family. You don't have to be alone."

Her voice is shaking, but I can't decide if those are crocodile tears. But it doesn't matter because one thing I know for sure. "You don't want me. You want the version of me that spoiled you and looks good on your arm. The Kingston who could stand beside you against a city skyline and not ask for more. But this—" I gesture at the walls, at the vineyard beyond them, at everything Elise made me see again. "This is who I am. And you'd hate it. You'd hate me."

Her chin lifts stubbornly. "I could learn to love it."

I let out a bitter laugh. "No." I say. "I don't buy it. And it doesn't matter because it isn't what I want. It isn't what you want either."

Her sobs tear through the silence. But eventually, my words seem to sink in. She pulls herself together and grabs her bag with jerky hands, robe dragging against her legs. I follow her out, and at the door, she spins, eyes blazing. "She'll never love you the way I did. She'll leave, just like Cara. Just like everyone."

I slam the door before the words can take root.

I stand there, feeling numb, stunned at this turn of events. I don't understand her at all. Where did that come from? I wasn't lying when I told her she was a great lawyer. She understands Renew Motion's business, but I don't see how we can move forward in any capacity now. I can't trust her, can't take her seriously after this. So that ends our relationship completely. I'm sure that's for the best in the long run. I can find another attorney.

I look out the windows into the dark abyss of the lake. My chest tightens until I can't breathe. I pull my phone from my pocket, thumb trembling over Elise's name. I type three words—*please come back*—and delete them, deciding to call instead. But it goes straight to voicemail. Her voice is warm and bright on the recording, too bright for this kind of night. The beep comes, but I can't make a sound. I only thought it was too difficult to talk to her about this before. After this debacle, it feels impossible… Still, I hang up, try again. Same.

Desperate, I hit Tarryn's number.

She answers on the second ring, already furious. "What did you do?"

"She left," I choke out. "I need to know if she's safe."

"She saw all the text messages coming in from Hope. I assured her Hope was only your lawyer, and then she goes home with you and finds her sitting half naked in your robe in the living room?"

I close my eyes. That's all true. "She's been texting me. We were involved before, but it didn't mean anything. And I'd ended it. I wasn't responding to her texts."

"But you didn't tell Elise. You hid it. So many men have run right over her heart, and I warned you about doing that to her."

"I didn't choose Hope. I never would. Elise has to know that."

"Then why didn't you tell her? Why did she have to see it for herself?"

I don't have an answer. The silence is enough to damn me.

"Don't call me again until you're ready to be honest with her. Completely. Nothing less than that is worth it." Tarryn's voice fractures, then steels. "I can't believe you, Kingston. You of all people know how it hurts to be deceived."

The line clicks dead.

I stand in my empty living room, phone limp in my hand, Elise's taillights still seared into the dark. My fear has gotten the best of me, pushed me into being the very thing I've hated since Cara left. I have to make this right.

The next morning, rather than fly, I drive to the vineyard. It gives me a chance to shape what I will say to Elise. I was up half the night, replaying every stupid thing I've done, and the only response that feels real is to get down on my knees and beg her to let me explain and accept my apology.

I tell myself she might be here with the family, with Tarryn, and maybe I'll find her in the rows, and we can fix this in one conversation. Beg. Say it right. I don't know. I just need to see her.

But the minute I pull up, I know something's wrong.

Trucks crowd the gravel. Workers stand in small knots, faces drawn. Beyond them rows of vines have toppled, their posts snapped clean, wires dangling in the sun. A crumpled bumper rests at the edge of the block like a thrown prop. No skid marks. No tracks. Just vines ripped from their anchors. Someone wanted this to read accident. But it reads staged.

Greyson stands at the edge of the block, sleeves rolled up, directing people the way he would call a code in the ER. Ryker runs a forklift, hauling posts and wire to clear a path. Beckett is already down in the vines, barking orders I only half catch over the crack of splitting wood.

I vault the ditch and take the slope two steps at a time. The smell hits before the sight fully settles in, green and raw. Crushed grape leaves bleed into the dirt, the fruit still sour and unripe. Posts lie snapped like matchsticks. Trellis wires hang slack over the ruined canopies. At the far edge, the bumper is a ridiculous punctuation mark. Someone wanted a story. They left a lie.

"What the hell happened?" I ask.

Tarryn turns. She's flushed, and dust streaks her shirt. Elise kneels beside her, clipboard in hand, hair pulled out of her face. Their eyes are hard and focused.

Seeing Elise floors me anyway. She's here, and she's close enough to touch. But she doesn't look at me, doesn't even glance my way. Her hands just keep moving, steady and certain.

"Someone took out the posts last night," Tarryn says. "Wires snapped. They left an unlicensed bumper behind. They wanted it to look like an accident."

Sabotage is the only word that fits. "Max."

Tarryn's mouth tightens. "We don't know that."

"Who else would do this?" I ask, my blood boiling.

"Kingston," Beckett says softly. His tone is a leash.

"Don't tell me to stand down," I say. "You see this as well as I do. While we wait for Dad to grow a spine and really do something about Max, he's grinding this vineyard into the dirt."

The green smell thickens. Hoses hiss as crews mist the tender clusters to keep them from cooking in the sudden sun. Elise's voice rises clear and practical as she directs a hand to patch a post and rethread the wire. She never falters.

Dad stands at the far edge of the rows, pale under the sun like a man bracing for a blow. He doesn't move when I cross toward him.

"When are you going to stop him?" I ask. "You want proof? Look around. This is proof."

Dad shakes his head, and his voice is gravel. "We can't jump to conclusions."

"Jump?" I give a short laugh that tastes bitter. "We've had vats with acid dumped in, water poisoned, water lines and equipment tampered with, and someone burned down Tarryn and Elise's home. Now this. How many more times do we let him bleed this place before you admit what he is? We need to call the police."

"We can't let this tear the family apart," Dad says. His shoulders slump, and I hear the tired in him.

"It already has," I say. "And what if next time it isn't only vines that get hurt?"

Dad's mouth tightens. "You sound just like Max when you lose your temper."

For a beat, I can't breathe. I force myself to calm before I speak. "Why won't you at least report this to the police?"

"Because if it's Max, it's all my fault," Dad snaps.

"What are you talking about?"

He drags a hand down his face, eyes fixed on the rows. "I'm the one who brought him back into this business. I vouched for him when no one else would. If I call the police now, I'm not just turning in my brother… I'm admitting I handed him the matches."

Still reeling from that, I shove through the small crowd. I can't help it. I need to say something to Elise before this rift between us becomes permanent.

But Tarryn plants herself in my path, jaw set. "Not now," she says. "Go cool off before you make this worse."

Her voice isn't sharp. It's steady and final.

I take a step back. My face burns as I look beyond her. Dust blooms with every footfall. Men shout. Ropes creak. A pallet jack scratches gravel. Someone mists the exposed clusters again to stop them from cooking.

Elise's voice cuts through all of it, and that carves me open. She's focused in a way that I find impossible right now. She doesn't look my way, and she speaks to everyone but me.

The last time we were this close she was laughing, and she chose me again and again. Until last night. Until Hope. Until I proved every one of her fears right.

I press my palms to my eyes, but the picture will not leave, Elise crouched beside Tarryn, shoulder to shoulder, swallowed by the work and by the family.

She belongs here.

Maybe it's me who doesn't.

Thirty-nine

Elise

The porch at the main house smells faintly of cedar and tea leaves when I step outside. Dad went to visit a friend who lives up north, and Tarryn insisted I not be alone so I've been sleeping in a guest room for the last two nights as I try to save what I can of the four blocks affected by the incident. Even this early the air is thick, the kind that sticks to your skin and promises a hotter day ahead. The rows stretch out behind the house, leaves dense and glossy, and clusters tight and green, soaking up the long June sun.

Tarryn is already out there, sunk back in one of the Adirondack chairs, an iced coffee sweating in her hand. Her hair is pulled up off her neck, dark eyes tracking the vineyard. Repairs are still underway on the damaged blocks, but from this distance, the trellis lines look deceptively straight.

The police came again yesterday, still talking about a

drunk driver, though the lines were cut, not broken. It doesn't add up, and every day without answers makes this feel worse.

Tarryn lifts her chin in greeting when she sees me. I can tell she knows what's on my mind.

I fold my arms across my chest, but the pressure there isn't enough to hold me together. "He shut me out," I blurt. My voice cracks. "Just like everyone always does."

Tarryn lowers her glass to the armrest and studies me. No softness, no surprise, just the calm scrutiny of someone who doesn't let things slip by unnoticed. "Start at the beginning."

I sink into the chair across from her, but sitting makes me feel small, so I push back up and pace the planks instead. "He promised me honesty, and then…Hope. Her name on his phone. Messages. I feel like such a fool." Saying her name tastes bitter. My throat tightens, and I try to swallow it down, but it sticks.

"You think he's still tangled up with her?" Tarryn asks.

"I don't know." My laugh comes out sharp and ugly. "He only shows me what he wants me to see. Everything has felt different since I came back from France. I don't know what's actually real."

Tarryn's gaze hardens. "You're angry."

"Of course, I'm angry." I turn to face her, hands rising helplessly before I drop them back to my sides. "I let myself believe I could finally be part of something that lasts, and now…" The words catch. "Now, I feel like I'm twelve again, lying awake at night, praying to hear my mom's footsteps, knowing deep down she's gone."

Tarryn doesn't flinch. She doesn't reach for me either.

"I keep falling into the same pattern," I whisper. My chest aches. "Maybe I'm the reason people don't stay. Too much, not enough, always wrong."

"Don't do that," Tarryn cuts in. "Your mother fought the cancer as long as she could, and the others… That's on them. Don't put the weight of other people's choices on yourself. He's the one who hasn't been giving you what you needed. That's on King."

Her certainty rattles me. I grip the porch railing, the wood rough beneath my palms, trying to draw strength from it. "I don't know if I can keep doing this, waiting for him to decide if I'm worth letting in. It feels like standing at the edge of a cliff."

She leans forward, elbows on her knees. "So what are you going to do?"

I stare at her, heat rising in my throat. "What choice do I have?"

"You always have one. You can fight for him, or you can fight for yourself. But you can't keep bleeding out in the middle." Her voice softens a fraction. "I know what it feels like to wait for someone who doesn't choose you. It eats you alive, if you let it. I don't think that's what's happening here, but you have do decide you want to find out."

Her words slice through the fog in my head. I want to argue, but she's right. Sitting in limbo is draining all the reserves I have.

"I don't even know which fight is worth it," I whisper.

"Then figure it out."

Her bluntness should sting, but it focuses me instead. I drag in a shaky breath. The vineyard below is alive with light now, the sun climbing higher. The rows look endless, and there's work to be done, work that doesn't care about broken hearts or unanswered questions.

"I can't sit around waiting for him to choose me," I say, straighter now, firmer. "So I'll choose myself. I'll throw everything I have into the winery. If nothing else, at least, that won't walk away from me."

Tarryn's gaze softens for the first time, though only slightly. "That sounds like a start. And hopefully, more clarity will come."

I nod, clutching the railing until my knuckles ache. But even as I steel myself, the truth pulses beneath everything else: I can pour myself into Paradise Hill, I can drown in work and sweat and sabotage, but the ache of missing Kingston is everywhere. And until I find a way to address it, it's still mine to carry.

The vineyard is quiet when I finally get out there later that morning. Late-June sun presses against my back, and my boots sink into the soft soil as I head toward the storage shed beside the crush pad. Water drips from a hose someone left running, cutting tiny channels into the dirt. I roll up my sleeves and knot my hair at the back of my neck. I need my hands busy, my body moving.

The so-called drunk driver still gnaws at me. The car was stolen, the story doesn't add up, and we lost four blocks overnight. Weeks of work gone.

I grab a hammer from the rack and head for the nearest row, where new posts lean stacked against the fence, waiting to be set. Someone's left a spool of wire half-unwound in the dirt. My gut twists. Carelessness or something else? I bend to rewind it, fingers catching on the steel, and shove the thought aside. There's too much work to be done to chase ghosts.

By the time the first truck pulls in, my arms ache and sweat sticks my shirt to my back. Workers spill out, nodding at me with expressions I can't read—part respect, part pity. I force a brisk smile that feels brittle on my face.

"Morning. Start with the lower blocks. We'll get the posts in first, then run the wires and check the irrigation," I call, trying to sound like I belong in charge.

They obey without question, and that feels good. At least here, in the vineyard, effort equals results, not silence and secrets.

I throw myself into the labor, hefting posts heavier than I should, wires cutting into my palms, sweat sliding down my spine. My shoulders burn, my thighs shake, but it feels good to hurt in ways I can control. Every lift, every swing of the hammer is a distraction.

Still, the ache sneaks in. The tilt of Kingston's smile when he teased me about perfectionism. His steady hands on a gauge or a valve. The warmth of his body when he leaned close to explain something I pretended I didn't already know.

I grit my teeth and drive another post into the ground.

"Careful, Elise," one of the workers warns. "You'll strain something."

"I'm fine," I snap. He flinches, his gaze sliding to the ground, and moves on. My chest prickles with shame, but I don't apologize. If I stop, if I soften, everything inside me will spill out.

Hours pass. The sun climbs higher, hot against my neck. I haul posts, restring wires, and tamp soil around anchors. Each time I pause, I see shadows of sabotage—posts splintered too cleanly, wires cut instead of snapped. Maybe it was just a stolen car and reckless hands. Or maybe someone is still trying to destroy everything the Paradise family has built.

I make notes in the logbook, my handwriting tight and cramped. Someone has to keep watch, and if I can't control Kingston, at least I can control this.

By midday my muscles throb, and my head spins from the heat. I force down water from a canteen, the metallic taste catching in my throat. Across the block, crews move in rhythm, pounding posts, threading wire, tying vines back upright. Life doesn't stop for heartbreak. Grapes don't care who leaves or who stays.

I need to be like the vines—rooted deep, steady no matter what storms roll in. One woman hauling a coil of wire makes a face at another, and they both laugh. I catch it, and for half a second, I smile too. The sweetness lingers, a fleeting moment of light. Then the shadow falls.

By the time the sun begins its descent across the sky, my arms are trembling with fatigue. I shove one last post into the ground and bend over, catching my breath, when a shadow falls across me.

I don't have to look up to know who it is. My body reacts before my mind does, skin prickling, and heart jerking.

"Here," Kingston says, offering me a bottle of water.

I straighten, wiping sweat from my forehead with the back of my wrist. He is too close, his broad shoulders blotting out the light, his gaze pinned to me like he can still read every thought

I'm trying to bury.

For one dangerous beat, I want to take the bottle, tip it back, and let him care for me with that look he gives when he is all in. I want his hand brushing mine, his voice in my ear. The want flares hot and sharp. But I don't know if that look is real. I clamp down on my emotions.

"I'm fine," I say, reaching past him for the spool of wire on the ground. My voice comes out clipped, but sharp is better than shattered.

"Elise." His tone carries a warning, but I don't stop. I crouch beside the row again, tying off wire that doesn't need tightening. Anything to keep my hands moving.

He crouches too, his presence filling the space, his scent of sweat and cedar cutting through the raw tang of crushed vine. "You've been at this since dawn. You need a break."

"I said I'm fine." The words snap like a whip. My throat burns as soon as they're out, but I can't take them back.

Silence stretches between us. Workers move around, pretending not to notice, but I feel their eyes flicking this way, curiosity buzzing like flies.

Kingston stays in place, crouched in front of me, his jaw tight. "You don't have to punish yourself like this."

I twist the wire harder, my hands slick, and my muscles shaking. "Better me than the vines."

His hand brushes mine as he reaches for the tool. The rough skin of his palm grazes me, a scrape of heat that nearly undoes me. I yank my hand back like I've been burned.

"Don't," I breathe. My voice cracks. "Just—don't."

His eyes flare, pain and frustration flashing across his face. His throat works like he's swallowing words he can't risk saying. "You won't even look at me?"

I keep my gaze locked on the post, though I can't see it anymore, my vision blurred with sweat and something hotter. "There's work to do."

"Elise," he begs. "Just let me explain. I know now is not the time, but—"

"I don't know how to believe anything you say," I tell him,

unable to keep it in any longer. "I don't know what's real, if any of this has been real." I stare at the ground for a moment before clearing my throat. "And I said, hand me the wire." My tone is cold. I don't even know what I want.

He sets the spool down gently, almost carefully, like he knows I'm about to shatter. Then he rises, his shadow pulling back, leaving me raw under the glare of the sun.

I don't look up, but I feel him standing there a moment longer, watching, before his footsteps fade into the scrape and clatter of work.

My hand shakes as I grip the spool. All I want is to turn, to lean into him, to let him try to make sense of all this for me. But what if I do, and I'm still the girl left behind all over again?

So I force my feelings away and twist the wire until it won't move another inch.

The vineyard quiets as the crews take a break. I flop onto an overturned crate by the edge of the block, my muscles throbbing.

Everywhere I look, Kingston lingers. The sound of his boots crunching beside mine in the rows. His low voice pointing out irrigation leaks. The way his hand brushed mine when we worked side by side, and how that simple touch made me feel less alone. The memories press in until my heart feels like it might split open.

I press my forehead to the post and close my eyes, thinking of Tarryn's words this morning. "*Fight for him, or fight for yourself.*" But here, surrounded by the ghosts of everything we shared, I don't know how to separate the two.

I've always been the one left behind. My mother was gone before I was ready. The men I've dated decided I wasn't worth the effort. And now, Kingston is secretive and hard for me to trust when I need him most. I can't keep repeating this cycle.

The tears I've been holding back all day slip free. They track down my cheeks, hot in the summer air. I swipe at them with the heel of my hand, angry that I've lost control.

I'm stronger than this. I can bury myself in work. I can hold Paradise Hill steady no matter who tries to sabotage it. The vines, the soil, the rows—they won't leave me.

But deep down, I know the truth. I want him. I want *his* steadiness, *his* impossible calm, and the way he makes me feel like I belong. Even if he isn't perfect. Even if he fights his own ghosts and battles. I have to believe in the parts of him I know are true.

But that makes wanting him feel like the most dangerous thing of all. And I'm not ready. I'm tired of putting myself out there, of fighting. I need something to be simple, to make sense. So for now, I'll have to learn to live with the hollow space he's left behind.

Forty

Kingston

It's been a week since I've seen Elise. Nights have stretched into endless loops of memories. I close my eyes, and she's there—hair spilling across my pillow, laughter echoing in Paris, the way she said my name like it belonged to her. I open them, and I'm alone, the ceiling a blank witness to what I've destroyed.

I don't sleep more than an hour or two at a time. My body crashes, but my brain jolts awake. Coffee covers the cracks, but nothing quiets the restlessness. Even now, as I step into the barn, I catch my reflection in the mirror above the handwashing sink—eyes empty, jaw shadowed with days-old stubble, a man unraveling thread by thread. My hands tremble faintly when I shove them into my pockets, the residue of too much caffeine and too little rest.

Kevin flew me to Vancouver for our Monday morning

meetings at Renew, and I left after lunch and had him stop here at the vineyard. I wanted to see how things were coming along.

They've clearly made progress, but the vineyard still bears last week's scars. Gaps break the rows where posts wait to be reset, and raw wood delivered this morning stands pale against the older vines. Wire spools glint in the sun, half-strung trellises cutting across the block. We've been hand watering, waiting for the drip system to arrive. The air smells green and sharp—crushed leaves, split fruit, and heat.

Forklifts beep in reverse. Men shout over the grind of augers. Boots thud through dust. The bite of cedar and metallic tang of wire hang in the air.

Elise stands in the center of it all, hair tied back, shoulders squared, eyes fixed on the trellis she's rethreading. Tarryn crouches beside her, braid brushing the dirt as she braces the new post. They don't see me. Together they move with the focus of surgeons in an open chest, refusing to lose the fight.

I stay in the shade of the shed, hands deep in my pockets. I'm supposed to be the one who saves things. Here, I can't. It's my fault she's hurt. If I reach out to her, I'll likely make things worse. Just as these rows aren't mine to mend, and she isn't mine to reach for. Not anymore.

The wire pulls tight, and then holds. After wire breaks—or in our case was cut—getting it tight enough to hold the weight of a dozen vines without breaking again is hard work. Tarryn exhales. Elise presses her palms to her thighs and lets herself sag for a breath, then straightens again.

That's when she sees me.

Her eyes hold for a moment, and what I get isn't anger. It isn't even disappointment. It's worse. Polite. Distant. Professional, like a nod you give a stranger in passing. And then, sharper, she turns away mid-glance, directing her voice toward one of the workers, clipped and efficient.

I've known Elise's fire, her breath against my skin, her warmth pressed close enough to make me believe I could be whole again. Now, she's all distance. Only coolness in her eyes.

The words rise anyway. I want to tell her I'm sorry, that

the silence and secrecy wasn't her fault. That I've been broken since Cara and my best friend blew my life apart, and I never learned how to talk about it, never learned to manage all the feelings it left behind. But saying it here feels useless. It may be too late.

The work lights flicker. Someone yells for more wire. A tractor kicks over nearby, the noise swallowing whatever might've come next. Elise turns back to Tarryn, already gone from me all over again.

The sun's beginning to fall off as I step off the block. July light hits hard and gold, throwing long shadows between the rows. The crew keeps working—tightening wire, setting posts—but I can't stand there another minute.

Greyson once told me I was always welcome to stop by when my head got too loud. I never took him up on that, but I can't live like this anymore. I'm going to find him at the hospital.

The keys bite into my palm as I grip them. I push off the railing, the decision lodged hard in my chest. I need to talk to someone. Greyson and Trinity went through something like this. He even interviewed for a job in Vancouver. Thankfully, Elise is here. Right now, I need him to help me see the forest instead of just the trees. I can't sit in this limbo any longer. But I also can't see the way forward.

The drive over the bridge into downtown Paradise and to the hospital is smooth and easy. But inside, Paradise General bustles, even in the evening. The ER never sleeps. The smell hits me first, not antiseptic exactly, but sharp and clean, undercut by the sterile chill of air conditioning that never shuts off.

Greyson is at a computer terminal when I find him, perched on a rolling stool, his gaze fixed on the glow of the monitor. He looks up, eyebrows raised when he sees me. "King." He swivels around. "What are you doing here? You look like hell."

I drag a hand down my face. "Thanks."

He studies me for a beat, then jerks his head toward the hallway. "Come on. I can take a minute. Let's get to the cafeteria before it closes."

I follow him down the hall, grateful he's taken charge. The cafeteria is nearly empty as we enter, fluorescent lights buzzing overhead. A few nurses linger over paper cups of hot caffeine, but otherwise it's just us. We get our cups and Greyson sits across from me, coffee between his hands, waiting.

"I saw Elise this afternoon," I start, my voice rough. "She was with Tarryn, working the damaged blocks. She didn't even... She looked right through me." I stare at my hands, knuckles pale.

Greyson leans forward, forearms on the table. "Whatever you're carrying—it's bigger than Elise giving you the cold shoulder. It may be why she's doing that, but there's more here."

I laugh without humor, a rough bark. "You don't know the half of it."

"Then tell me." His voice is steady. Not a demand, not a plea. An invitation.

My throat tightens. I grip the edge of the table until my fingers hurt. "I'm sure a therapist would tell me it's Cara and Tim, but it's not just that."

Greyson's expression sharpens, but he doesn't cut in.

"What nobody knows," I go on, my voice low, "is that I spent years twisting myself into knots, trying to make Cara happy. We went to therapy. Then I went alone when she wouldn't go anymore. I fix people for a living, and I couldn't fix us. I tried. I picked up every extra shift, built Renew Motion from the ground up, told myself if I worked harder, if I gave her more, she'd feel it. That she'd feel...loved enough to stay."

The words take part of me with them as they leave me.

"But every time I came home, she looked at me like I was already failing her," I confess. "And the more I tried, the worse it got. I thought if I just kept pushing, if I fixed myself, I could fix us." My voice breaks. "And then one day she was gone. Not just gone, but with the person I trusted most."

I shove the heel of my hands into my eyes, pressing hard. "Everyone thinks the marriage fell apart because I was too busy building Renew Motion. I let them think that, because it's easier. It's cleaner. But the truth? I did everything I knew how to do, and it still wasn't enough."

My breath stills in my throat. I've never said that aloud. Not once.

When I finally lower my hands, Greyson's jaw is set. His eyes burn with fury that isn't aimed at me. "Jesus, Kingston."

My stomach twists. "Now, you know. I shut it all off. I don't talk about her. I don't let people in. I kept things surface-level—like with Hope—because it was easier when they walked away. I worried she had developed real feelings, but I wasn't going there. We were never a good match, but it didn't matter because I wasn't about to give everything again only to find out it still wasn't enough. And now…" I trail off, my limbo moving into sharper focus for the first time. "I think that's what's got me trapped with Elise. I've made mistakes, but I'm afraid to try to fix them." Alarm races through me. *What a goddamn mess.*

Greyson's voice is quiet, but sharp. "You've carried that alone all this time?"

I nod, throat raw.

"No wonder you're cracked wide open. That's not a wound, that's a cage."

My heart aches as those words sink in, but there's something else too, like the lock just clicked open, like air is moving in a place that's been closed for years.

I rub my temples. "I thought if I buried it, it would stay gone. But it just—" I break off, shaking my head. "I didn't have to work hard at all to make Elise happy. She just fit. But I never let her see all of me, and then I fucked it all up."

Greyson exhales slow and steady. "You're wrong."

My gaze jerks up.

"That's not what I see at all. You've made mistakes, yes, but you just have to give yourself a chance to move forward. Have you ever talked about this with Elise?

I shake my head.

"If Elise doesn't know the truth, she's got no foundation to understand why you did things the way you did. You can't expect her to trust you when you won't trust her with all of yourself."

I swallow hard. The truth is ugly. But Greyson's words cut through. He's right. She deserves all of me, not just the parts I think she can handle, not just the parts I think I can handle sharing.

The cafeteria is quiet, and the coffee between us is bitter and burned. But I find myself feeling a fraction lighter.

Greyson's expression softens, just a little. "You've carried this long enough. It's time you set it down—with her."

I close my eyes and breathe deep. I sink into the chair, exhausted in a way that has nothing to do with physical effort, yet it feels like I just ran miles I never trained for. "She doesn't want to talk to me."

"Things are kind of a mess right now," Greyson agrees. "But if you make an honest effort, perhaps she'll be willing to listen."

I hope that's true, and I can see now that I have to try.

"Some things break because the other person wants out," Greyson notes after a moment. "Not because you failed."

I look up at him. "Cara still feels like a failure."

He nods once. "Perhaps it will feel differently if you stop carrying it alone."

I press my palms to my thighs. He's not looking at me like I'm broken. He looks like he understands.

Greyson leans forward, elbows on the table. "Elise isn't Cara."

"I know." The words are quiet.

"Then treat her accordingly. Stop hiding from her because of what one woman did years ago." His tone sharpens, unyielding. "If you want her, you have to give her the whole truth. All of it. The good, the bad, the scars."

My throat works. "And if she walks away?"

"Then at least you'll know it was honest. Better to lose her because she knows you than because you never gave her the chance."

I close my eyes a moment. I know he's right. I've been hiding behind silence, convincing myself I was protecting her when really I was protecting myself.

Greyson stands, moves to the window. "You've always carried the family's weight, Kingston. The expectations, the perfection. Maybe it's time to accept that you don't have to be flawless for someone to stay. And think about it. The sabotage at the vineyard only thrived in the shadows. Silence made it dangerous. Secrets always do."

I drag a hand through my hair and lean back, still wrestling with this.

"You really think she deserves all of it?" I ask, though I already know the answer.

Greyson turns. "Not just deserves. Needs. You don't build a life on half-truths."

I nod. "Then I'll tell her. Everything."

Greyson's mouth tips into the faintest smile. "That's the brother I know."

The evening air follows me out of the hospital, cooler now against my face, carrying a faint trace of rain on the wind. I slide behind the wheel of my car and sit in the lot for a moment, keys heavy in my hand, Greyson's words still echoing.

"Stop hiding from her."

I start the engine and pull onto the road. Out here the world opens—mountains in the distance, stars beginning to appear overhead.

I feel lighter. Not fixed. Not whole. But lighter. Saying the truth out loud didn't break me the way I thought it would. My heart still aches, but it's not that locked, suffocating pain anymore. It's something closer to hope.

The road curves through the valley, vineyards dark against the hills. But I can smell them—fruit, crushed leaves, the faint sweetness that lingers after years of harvests. Elise won't let it fail. She never does.

She deserves the truth and, more than that, proof of the way I feel. Not flowers, not easy words. Something real. Something that shows her I choose her. Not by accident. Not because it's easy. Because she's the one.

I press the gas, and my headlights slice through the dark, pulling me back toward the vineyard. My pulse steadies, strong and sure.

I'll tell her everything. I'll lay it all out, no shields, no silence. And then I'll give her something undeniable. Something that proves she isn't just part of my life. She is my life. My chest tightens, not with dread but with determination. I need to make a plan, get myself ready.

This time, I won't fail her.

Forty-one

Kingston

I didn't sleep last night. I drifted through the kind of half rest that loosens bolts in my head instead of tightening them. But I still manage to feel better this morning. Since my epiphany with Greyson, my mind has been flooded with plans of what I want to tell Elise today.

By the time I land at Paradise Hill, the sun hangs pale behind thin clouds, the vines washed in that flat morning light. From a distance, the rows look perfect. But up close, the restoration work continues. The crew moves quietly. No banter. No music. Everyone's likely saving their energy for whatever goes wrong next.

I'm scanning for Elise when a shout cuts through the stillness. One voice, then more. Urgent. I'm already running, boots pounding gravel, past the shed and down into the lower block where the sun hits hot and sound bounces between the posts.

The scene snaps into focus. Workers rushing forward, arms raised. Wire whipping loose across the row. A trellis pulled half out of the ground, the whole line unraveling.

And then I see her. Elise is right by the break, wrench in hand, hair shoved behind her ears, dust streaked across her cheeks. She's gripping a post, reaching for the wire, trying to catch it before it tears through the next row.

The snap is sharp, like a gunshot. The post jerks, wire lashes, and she slips. Her boots skid on loose dirt, her hand slamming against the clamp. The crack of knuckles on steel hits like it's mine.

I'm there before I can think. One hand grabs her elbow, the other her waist. Her body jolts against mine, and then she's steady, breath catching between us.

I force myself to breathe. "What happened?"

Elise pulls in air. "We checked the tension at dawn. Everything was tight. Then one line gave way. Just snapped. It shouldn't have."

Her voice shakes, barely holding. I look over at the break. The wire's frayed, the ends curled unevenly, like it tore instead of slipped. The clamp's twisted halfway off, metal gouged deep where it shouldn't be. I crouch, running a hand over the edge—fresh scrape marks, too clean to be from wear.

She kneels beside me. "Could be us," she says quietly. "Overtightened the section. Or maybe…"

I find the broken piece of wire in the dirt, edges shiny, as if cut, not snapped. My body goes hot, then cold. Anger. Fear. I reach for Elise's hand.

After a moment, she tries to pull it free, but I don't let go. Not yet. I scan for blood. Her knuckles are split, a shallow line beading red. I lift her hand, and she flinches. Not from pain. From me. It strikes harder than my worry.

I keep my grip light and wrap her fingers with the clean edge of a rag. "You should be wearing gloves."

"I am." She lifts her other hand. The glove hangs from her back pocket.

"This was not an accident," I say.

"I know." She nods. "We had it fixed last night. Those threads didn't wear out in a few hours."

She crouches, careful, and touches the stripped screw head with the tip of the wrench. The mark is too neat. Not a tension stretch. A choice.

Elise straightens, wiping her injured hand on her thigh like she refuses to give the pain any space. "I'll log it," she says, already moving toward the truck where she has the maintenance binder. Her good hand flips through the thick folder until she finds the page for this exact piece of equipment.

She kneels again and lines up the binder beside the stripped screw, comparing last night's repair notes with the current damage. "The torque readings don't match," she murmurs. "Someone backed this out deliberately."

Before I can tell her to stop moving or to let me handle it, she pulls her phone from her pocket and snaps two clean photos—one of the screw head, one of the rag wrapped around her hand. "Evidence," she says. "In case anyone decides to rewrite what happened."

Then, she braces herself and works the wire back into place. No fumbling, no panic. Just calm, careful movements. She pulls the slack out, resets the fastener, and tightens it enough for the row to stand straight again. The vines rise, supported once more.

She stands and wipes dirt from her palms. "There. That'll hold until we replace it."

I can only shake my head in wonder. She stepped in without hesitation, even with her knuckles split open and the threat still hanging in the air.

"Everyone stays clear until I finish the full inspection," she calls.

She did it calmly. Efficiently. Like someone who refuses to be a victim.

"You could have been hurt," I say, low.

"I'm fine."

"You're shaking."

Her chin lifts. "We've got work to do."

"We do."

Out in the yard, the sun lifts higher. The morning looks calm again. But that's a lie. Still, I am here now. And I am close enough to catch her if the world tilts again.

The crew gets back into their work. Elise checks the tension one last time, jaw set, shoulders squared like nothing rattled her.

But I'm rattled. "You could have been killed."

She doesn't look at me. "I'm fine."

"You keep saying that," I bite out. "But I saw you fall."

Her head snaps toward me. "Don't do that."

"Do what?"

"Turn this into some heroic rescue. I had it handled."

"Handled?" My voice sharpens. "The clamp was stripped. Someone set that up. You were standing inches away when it blew. You think I'm going to just shrug and pretend it doesn't matter?"

"Why does it matter to you?" she demands.

"Because—"

"Because what? You've spent more than a week ignoring me. And now I'm supposed to believe you care if I slip in a puddle?"

Pain stabs my heart. "I was not ignoring you. You asked me to step back, and I gave you room. I do care. I just don't know how to—"

"No." She shakes her head. "You care enough to show up when there's chaos. But not enough to actually let me in."

Her rag trembles. I want to take it from her hand, but she'd pull away.

"You don't understand—" I start.

"You're right," she cuts in. "I don't. Because you never let me. Every time I get close, you throw up a wall."

I grit my teeth. "I don't want to do that anymore."

"Then tell me," she whispers. "Tell me what's so bad that you'd rather keep me in the dark. Is Hope pregnant?"

My eyes nearly bug out of my head. "No! Absolutely not."

"Then what?"

"I'm afraid, Elise. I'm petrified by my own past, and it paralyzed my ability to see the way forward when things went wrong. I've already been broken once. But that's no fault of yours."

Her eyes widen. "Broken?"

"My marriage," I rasp. "My best friend."

Her face softens for half a second before she shutters it again. "I know how despicable Cara and Tim were. You don't get involved with someone until you're done with everyone else."

"It's more than that." I take a deep breath. "I fix people for a living. I worked hard to save my marriage, and I couldn't. I failed."

She shakes her head. "You didn't fail. It takes two people to save a marriage."

"That's what the therapist said. But it was my fault Cara went to Tim."

"Why was it your fault?"

I take a deep breath. "I couldn't be there for her when she needed me."

"What happened? Where were you?"

"I was with my family or working. She didn't like hanging out with my family."

Her body language has softened, though her tone remains cold. "They can be a bit much, but that's not on you either." She pauses a moment, and I brace for a dismissal, but then she asks a question, continuing the conversation. "What happened with Hope?"

I sit down on an empty bucket. "She was my lawyer. We'd flirt, and one day I needed a date to a fundraiser, so I asked her to come. I ended up spending the weekend with her. We decided we were both career-minded and could be just casual. We agreed that when the time came to end things, we'd tell the other, and that would be that. It seemed perfect for me. That's what I thought I was capable of. We did that for four years, and then I told her I was getting involved with you, so we needed to stop."

"You told her about me?"

"Not by name, but I told her I just wanted her to be my lawyer, that the personal aspect of our relationship was over. I made it clear that I'd fallen for someone and our being together needed to end. She wasn't happy about it, but I thought she understood. Then while we were in Paris, she started calling and texting. I ignored it, hoping it would resolve itself, and then she came to my house."

Elise's eyes narrow. "She has some balls. But you pushed me away that night. You made me wonder what I'd done wrong."

"I'm sorry," I say. "I was horrified by what happened, and I thought I was protecting you from it—and protecting myself."

Her voice breaks. "By keeping me in the dark?"

"I realize now that wasn't right, but yes. I panicked, I suppose. You didn't do anything wrong. It's me. All of it is me."

Elise stands still as glass, the rag trembling in her fingers.

I draw a breath that tastes like rust and sap. "Cara wasn't just my wife. She was my best friend. Then she betrayed me with someone I trusted. I thought if I buried the truth deep enough, maybe it would stop bleeding." I shake my head, seeing it all so differently now. "My family wasn't crazy about her, mostly because she rarely came to Sunday night dinners. So when things fell apart, I kept most of it to myself. Telling my family seemed like handing everyone proof of how blind I was. So I swore I'd never, *never* let anyone get close enough to do that to me again."

Elise's jaw trembles. The rag slips from her fingers and lands on the dirt with a damp slap. Her hand twitches like she might reach for me, and then curls into a fist.

"I've been a coward," I say. "Too scared to tell you. You deserve someone who isn't afraid."

Elise takes a shaky breath. "All this time…"

"I know." I brush my fingers across her hand. "I should have trusted you."

She doesn't pull away. She doesn't close the distance either. She just looks at me, hurt and angry, but maybe with a sliver of understanding.

"You should have told me," she finally says.

"I know."

"I'm still angry."

"I don't blame you."

She swallows. "I don't know if I can forgive you. Not yet."

"I understand. I just needed you to know the truth."

Her fingers twitch against mine, a small, unconscious brush. It jolts through me.

"You scared me today," she whispers. "Your hands are the way you do your job. You rushed in without thinking, and if that had gone wrong, it could've threatened your ability to work, to operate."

I nod. "I scared myself. Watching you go down with that line snapping— I thought I'd lose you before I ever got the chance to tell you."

She shakes her head and steps back. "This doesn't fix everything. And I have to think about Hope."

"That's perfectly understandable," I say, steady this time. "But it's a start."

She bends to pick up the rag she dropped, wringing it between her hands. "In the meantime, we still have a vineyard to protect."

"We will," I promise.

She meets my eyes. No forgiveness yet, but no wall either. Just a thin crack of possibility. After a moment, she turns away, shoulders straight, already slipping back into motion. I let her go, not because I want to, but because it's what she needs.

I look for a way to busy myself, to stand in solidarity with those rebuilding the vineyard, even as I cling to a fragile thread of hope like it's the only thing keeping me upright. Because maybe it is.

Forty-two

Kingston

Family dinner at Paradise Hill has always felt like a gauntlet. Chairs around one long table, too many voices vying for space. Tonight, it's even more so, despite the fact that I've spent the last five days getting ready. I've talked with my family to make sure everyone will be here, including Mitch.

I shouldn't be this nervous. I've sat at this table a thousand times. Same smells—roasted garlic, fresh bread—same wine catching the light. But my collar feels tight, and my palms are damp against my thighs. I'm not here to eat. I'm here to finally say what I should have said months ago.

Elise sits two chairs away, close enough that I can hear her steady breaths if I really concentrate, but far enough that it feels like a mile between us. We've had a few conversations since the accident in the vines, but we haven't yet truly hashed things out.

She passes dishes with a polite smile that never reaches her eyes. Every time our gazes almost meet, she looks away, like looking at me might hurt.

Regret stabs my chest for a moment. I've put her through hell. I can't blame her for being slow to open herself up to me again. But hopefully, tonight will show that I value her and her place in this family whether she's partnered with me personally or not.

The table's full, my father at the head, talking over everyone about the repairs, and my mother steadying things with soft questions. Beckett and Sadie are murmuring to baby William, and Tarryn laughs at something Ryker said.

Elise tucks a strand of hair behind her ear, and I catch the edge of a bandage on her knuckles – the cut from the clamp. Heat climbs through my body. Whoever's behind this sabotage didn't just go after the vineyard. They went after her. That thought has been chewing at me all week.

I force down a bite, but the food tastes flat. My fork scrapes the plate, loud in my ears. Every sound at the table feels magnified. The longer I sit here, the harder it gets to hold the truth in.

I talked to Tarryn, and she agrees with my strategy. We can fix this.

I run the words through my head yet again, but they keep breaking apart before I can finish them.

Dad's deep in a story about a new irrigation line, hands moving as he talks. Ryker cuts in with a joke, and the room bursts into laughter. Elise smiles but doesn't join in. She still doesn't feel at ease here, and that's on me.

My chance to speak comes right after dessert hits the table. Tarryn teases Ryker, Dad sighs about a late delivery, and then the noise dips just long enough for me to feel it, that small quiet where truth can live.

I push my chair back. The scrape of wood on tile sounds like thunder in my brain. Every head turns my way.

I never speak up at these dinners. Not like this. My father lifts a brow. My mother lowers her glass. My brothers stop talking. Elise freezes, fork halfway to her mouth. Tarryn smiles encouragingly.

Sweat beads under my collar. My pulse pounds, same as it did the night I came home years ago to find the life I knew already gone. I shove that memory down and make myself stand straighter. "I need to say something," I manage, my voice rough.

The table waits.

I grip the back of my chair. "You all know about Cara. But what you don't know is how hard I worked to stop it from happening, how long I worried the end was inevitable. When I failed at saving my marriage, I buried the pain. I built a cleaner story. I told myself that if I locked the truth down tight enough, I'd be safe. That no one would ever cut me open like that again."

My mother's lips part like she might reach for me. My father's face stays steady, but his jaw tightens. Beckett just stares. Though when I glance at Greyson, he nods, urging me forward.

I draw a breath that tastes like metal. "I thought keeping it inside would protect me. It didn't. It's cost me more than I can stand, especially with Elise." I chance a look at her. "She's been standing with this family, yet I've been so afraid of being broken again that I've been breaking her instead."

Elise blinks, lips parted like she's forgotten how to breathe.

Her name leaves my mouth, and I finally hold her eyes. A flush rises up her throat.

"I pushed her away," I say, my voice rough. "I made her think she wasn't enough, when she's the only thing I've wanted for months. I was too much of a coward to admit it. Until now."

Elise clears her throat. "Kingston, this isn't the place—"

"It is." My voice shakes. "For at least some of it, it has to be." I take another breath. "I want to tell you more. I want to explain it all, and that goes for the rest of you as well. We can talk through this if you'd like to, but for now, I'm shifting to my next point." I look around at all of them. "This vineyard wouldn't have survived this last round of sabotage without Elise."

A low murmur rolls down the table. I keep going before doubt closes my throat. "She's been here every day, shoulder to shoulder with us. She caught things we missed. She saved sections we would have lost. And she did it while I…" My voice sticks, but I force it through. "While I was too scared to give her what she deserved."

I reach for the box I placed near my chair before dinner. "Whether she agrees to give me another chance or not, our family owes her our support and appreciation. We could not ask for a better vintner rising through our ranks." My hands are clumsy as I open the box and slide out the mock-up bottle I had printed a few days ago. A clean label, stark white with bold script in black across the front. *Elise*. Nothing else needed. Her name speaks for itself.

Gasps scatter around the table. Tarryn grins. She loves this idea.

I hold the bottle up. "I've spoken with Tarryn, and this is a new label we'll be releasing under Paradise Hill. The Elise label. Her vintages. Her choices. Her vision. Not borrowed, not hidden. Hers."

Elise's mouth opens again, but no sound comes.

"Because we want to acknowledge that Elise belongs here. Not as a guest. Not as Tarryn's shadow or my girlfriend. But as a vintner in her own right."

Ryker lets out a low whistle. Tarryn grins, murmuring, "I love it." My mother's eyes shine. My father's stare is heavy and unreadable.

I set the bottle in front of Elise, the label facing her. "This is yours if you want it. And even if you choose to walk away from me, the Elise label stands. Because you've earned it, and you deserve it. That's not a gift from me. It's recognition for you from all of us."

As I wait for her response, the fear nearly buckles me. But I hold her gaze and force myself to stay open.

Elise doesn't touch the bottle. She just stares at her name in bold black, her throat working like the words are caught there. Finally, she looks up at me. "Well, if you're trying to get me to listen to what you want to say, it's working."

The table laughs.

"That's wonderful news, but I promise this isn't about that," I assure her. "It's about recognition. You have carried this vineyard on your back, and it's time everyone knew it. I don't want to own you. I want to stand beside you."

Her fingers twitch against the tablecloth, like she might reach for the bottle but thinks better of it. Her breath comes quick, uneven. "And if I change my mind?" she asks.

"Then that's between us," I answer. "Your label will always exist. Because it's not tied to me or us. It's tied to you."

Her lips tremble, and there's the smallest shake of her head. But then she exhales, slow and shaky. She pushes back her chair and rises. My pulse spikes as she steps closer, her hand brushing mine where it rests on the table. The touch is light, tentative, but it's public. It's her answer.

Her voice is quiet but steady when she speaks. "Thank you. Thank you for this beautiful bottle, and let's continue our conversation in the future."

My face breaks into a smile, and the table exhales all at once. There's a rustle of movement, forks clattering, chairs shifting.

My mother's eyes shine as she lifts her glass. "Let's toast to it. To Elise."

One by one, the others follow, and the sound of crystal colliding fills the room. Elise stands there stunned, her hand still brushing mine, her lips parted like she can't quite believe it.

I lean toward her, my voice low so only she hears. "This is your table now too. Always."

Her gaze locks on mine. No walls, no polished mask, just raw emotion. Her fingers tighten around mine for a beat before she pulls back, cheeks flushed.

Around us, conversation rises, lighter now, threads of laughter weaving through the room. Tarryn asks Elise what she will craft first. Ryker jokes about demanding a bottle with his name on it. Even Dad gives the smallest incline of his head, an acknowledgment that in this house means acceptance.

I sink back into my chair, shoulders loosening for the first time in weeks. The bottle with her name gleams on the table, candlelight catching on the letters.

For years, I have carried silence like armor. Tonight I tore it off in front of everyone, and somehow, I am still standing. More than that, I am lighter. Because Elise is the partner I am choosing, and I know now what it means to work toward that goal.

I glance at her again. She's laughing softly at something Tarryn said, her face brighter than it has been in days. For the first time since I lost everything, I understand what it means to build something together.

Forty-three

Elise

The night air is warm against my cheeks as I step away from the house after dessert has been cleared. Laughter still drifts faintly from the patio, but I can't make myself go back inside. My chest feels too tight, my pulse too quick. Kingston's words and his gesture still echo inside me, and I don't know what to do with them. An Elise label. Public, permanent, impossible to ignore. To everyone else it probably looked like a grand romantic moment. For me, it's dangerous. Too much hope feels reckless.

The crunch of gravel reaches me before his shadow does. Kingston doesn't rush, doesn't call my name. He just comes close enough that I can feel his presence, the heat of him swirling in the warm breeze.

I keep my eyes forward as he joins me in the yard, but I can sense the exhaustion in him. Anxiety has carved hollows beneath his eyes, tension along his shoulders. He's carrying more than vines and barrels, more than this family name. He's carrying me too or trying to.

My throat aches with words I will not let out. I want him—God, I want him—but want has never been enough. Want doesn't protect you when the bottom falls out. Want doesn't save you from betrayal. I curl my fingers into my elbows and force my voice steady. "What are you doing out here?"

His silence is calm, and it only makes it harder to keep my defenses intact. For one flicker of a moment, I let myself imagine leaning back into him, closing my eyes, letting his arms hold me steady.

Instead, we walk without speaking, the gravel path giving way to dirt between the rows. The vines stretch up on either side, their leaves whispering in the breeze, and the stars are sharp above us. My arms are crossed, but he keeps pace beside me, patient in a way that makes me want to scream and kiss him all at once.

Finally, he clears his throat. "I need you to hear me, Elise. All of it. No walls."

I glance at him, ready to argue, but instead something in me goes still.

"I stayed married too long," he says. His voice hitches. "I did everything I knew how to do to hold it together—took extra shifts to make more money, built Renew Motion, tried to give her more because I thought if I worked harder, she'd feel loved enough to stay. And all the while she was unhappy. She was already gone. My wife and my best friend lied to me. And after, I let that wound shape too much of who I became. I thought silence was strength, but all it did was hurt. It hurt me, and it has now been hurting you."

His hand trembles as it scrapes across his jaw, and the breath I take feels sharp in my lungs. I knew pieces of this story, but hearing it from him like this, like a confession, knocks something loose inside me.

"I was wrong with you," he continues, his gaze fixed on the dark stretch ahead. "Things were so easy at first because we fit, but the moment real life intervened, I panicked. And every time I stayed silent, every time I pulled back instead of trusting you, I was wrong. You deserved honesty. You deserved me fighting for us, and instead, I gave you hesitation. I gave you doubt."

Heat pricks behind my eyes. I blink fast, but one tear escapes, sliding down my cheek. A thought races through me—*what if he lets me fall again? What if I give in and he walks away?*

His hand brushes mine, tentative, almost reverent. "I want you to know that I love you. Not in a way that's just easy. And not in a way I can walk away from. It's you. Always you. I believe we belong together, and I know you belong in this family, at this vineyard."

The defenses I've built fracture under the weight of those words, of this night, of everything he's doing.

Belonging. The idea sinks into me, dangerous and sweet, something I've wanted so much to believe in. My lips part, but no sound comes. For once I can't find armor to hide behind. I just stand there with tears burning in my eyes, his honesty pulling me in until I can't resist anymore.

We reach the edge of the vineyard. The silence between us pulses like a heartbeat, alive, on the edge of breaking or healing.

He turns to me. "Come home with me. I have the helicopter."

My stomach twists. I should say no. This is too fast. I should remind him how much it hurt to believe and be left standing alone. The words crowd my throat, but what comes out instead is a whisper. "Why?"

"Because I want to be with you," he says, holding my gaze like he'll never let it go. "No vineyard. No labels. No input from anyone else. Just us."

The honesty is almost unbearable. My chest feels like it's splitting wide, like every defense I've built is falling to pieces at my feet. I shake my head, half in disbelief, half in surrender. "You make it sound so simple."

He steps closer, warmth brushing against me. "It is. It has been before—before I let everything else get in the way. I love you, Elise. That's the only part that matters."

The fight inside me stumbles. I'm tired of pushing him away, tired of guarding myself against something that already owns me. I look at his mouth, his eyes, the hope there, and for once, I let myself choose, not what I should do, but what I want to do.

"Okay." The word is soft, but it feels like the biggest decision of my life.

Relief shines through him like sunlight breaking storm clouds. He cups my face in both hands, and before I can second guess, his mouth is on mine.

The kiss begins reverent, and then hunger crashes through it, weeks of silence burning away in a single spark. His lips part mine, his tongue sweeps in, and I melt against him, fisting his shirt to hold myself steady.

When he finally pulls back, his forehead rests against mine, both of us breathing hard. "There's no turning back now," he murmurs.

I nod. I don't want to.

We drive to my dad's place, I pack a bag, and we return to fly back to his home.

The road winds along the lake, the light fading to amber. I rest my elbow against the window, fingers grazing the glass.

Kingston glances over. "You're quiet."

"Just thinking," I say.

He waits a few seconds. "About how I'm kidnapping you for the rest of the night? Can you call in sick tomorrow?"

I smile faintly. "You read me too well. Actually, I was thinking about Hope."

His brow creases. "I don't want you feeling like you have to compete with someone from my past."

"I don't," I say simply.

Some of the tension leaves his shoulders. "You know, you're being more reasonable about this than I've been."

I smile a little. "I'm not sure that's a high bar."

He reaches across the console and takes my hand, chuckling. "Not giving me an inch. I love that about you."

"Good," I say, squeezing his fingers. "Because you're stuck with me."

He laughs, the sound low and warm. "I sure hope so."

We trade the car for the helicopter and fly across the lake. His house feels different tonight as we enter. I've been here before, but never like this, never so conscious of the weight of hope pressed into every shadow.

The door shuts behind us with a quiet click, sealing us off from the rest of the world. Three strides and I am in his arms, my back hitting the wall as his mouth claims mine. The kiss is hungry, desperate, making up for all the silence and longing. His hands grip my hips, sliding beneath my dress like I am the only thing keeping him alive.

I clutch his shoulders, feeling the strength there, anchoring myself in the solid weight of him. Our kiss deepens, his breath ragged against mine. I gasp when his palm skims up my ribs to cup my breast, his thumb teasing over lace until my body arches for him.

He takes my hand and nearly drags me up the stairs to his bedroom. There he tugs my dress over my head and lets it fall, finds the clasp of my bra and slips it down until I am bare beneath his gaze. Heat stirs in my belly with the way he looks at me—dark, reverent, as if I am something sacred.

"Elise," he murmurs, lowering me onto the bed. The sheets are cool, a shocking contrast to the heat racing over my skin. His weight settles beside me, his mouth tracing fire down my neck, over my collarbone, lower still, each kiss leaving me trembling.

When he reaches my thighs, he slows. His hands part me gently, his breath hot against skin already pulsing with need. His eyes meet mine, holding me there, and then his mouth is on me.

The first stroke of his tongue rips a cry from me. It's too much, not enough, everything at once. My back arches, fingers tangling in the sheets, then in his hair, pulling without meaning to. He groans against me, the vibration shuddering through my core.

He doesn't rush. He lingers, teases, circling slow until I am writhing, begging, then he plunges deeper, harder, until sparks burst behind my eyes. His hands grip my hips, pinning me as my body bows to his mouth. Pleasure coils sharp, urgent, climbing higher with every flick of his tongue.

When it breaks, it's violent, tearing me open. I cry out his name, trembling, shaking apart. Still, he doesn't let up, drawing wave after wave until I collapse boneless, gasping, every nerve alive.

I am barely breathing when he crawls up my body, kissing me with the taste of myself on his lips. His skin is hot against mine, his chest pressed to my breasts, his hips heavy between my thighs. I feel him, hard and ready, pressing where I am already slick and aching.

He braces on his forearms, his forehead against mine. "Tell me you're here." His voice is hoarse, desperate.

"I'm here," I whisper, cupping his jaw. "I'm not leaving."

Relief moves across his face as he thrusts into me. My cry is swallowed by his kiss, the stretch and fullness shocking me, overwhelming me. He stills, groaning low, as if holding on by a thread.

Then he moves. Slow at first, deep and steady, dragging pleasure through me until my nails dig into his back. He pauses once, lifting his head, eyes searching mine, as if asking permission again. I answer by pulling him closer, wrapping my legs around him, and he groans into my mouth before driving harder.

His rhythm builds, every thrust pulling me higher. The headboard bumps the wall, his breath ragged in my ear, his hand clutching my thigh.

We lose ourselves in the slap of skin, the heat, the need to be closer even though there's no space left between us. My body tightens again, the wave rising fast.

When it hits, it's blinding. My orgasm is like an earthquake, shaking me to the core. I cry out his name, and he follows, thrusts going erratic before he shudders hard, spilling inside me.

We collapse tangled together, sweat cooling, our chests

heaving. He pulls me close, his arm locked around my waist, as if he will never let go again. And I don't want him to.

His heartbeat thunders against my ear as I lie draped across his chest. His hand strokes down my back, slow and steady, as if he's memorizing the shape of me. Every pass settles me deeper, calms the storm that has raged in my chest.

I shift just enough to see his face. His eyes are softer than I have ever seen them, wide open, no walls. "You undo me," he whispers.

A lump rises in my throat. I touch his jaw, rough with stubble, and realize something inside me has shifted. All the doubt, the fear, the constant bracing for the fall—it goes quiet. "I had convinced myself this had to be temporary," I admit, my voice shaking. "That since we'd returned, it was falling apart, if it had ever been anything in the first place."

His thumb brushes my cheek. "And now?"

I draw in a breath. "Now, I believe. In you. In us. In a future that's messy and hard and real. And I want it."

His eyes close for a beat and when they open again, they shine with something new. "I thought I'd never get this back. You're the one thing I will never risk losing."

The way he exhales—relief, reverence, something like wonder—makes my heart surge. He kisses me slow, not hungry this time but tender, sealing the words between us.

When he pulls back, he keeps me close, tucking me under his chin. I close my eyes and let the weight of him anchor me. I'm not bracing for the bottom to drop out. I'm not guarding my heart.

I'm exactly where I want to be. Where I want to stay.

Kingston

At the next week's Sunday dinner, the dining room is alive with chatter, as it always is, though the chandelier's glow softens everything, spilling warm light over the polished wood of the long table. Steam rises from bowls of carrots and parsnips glazed to a shine, the buttery smell of potatoes mixing with rosemary and garlic. Bread baskets sit between bottles of our best vintages, corks already pulled, the air tinged with oak and dark fruit.

I slide into my chair, Elise beside me. She adjusts her napkin on her lap, her hand brushing my thigh under the table before resting there, steady and familiar.

Across from us, Ryker spears a piece of chicken and waves his fork for emphasis. "You're the only woman alive who can outdrink me, Ginny, and I'm still not sure how I feel about it."

Ginny smirks, her hair spilling over one shoulder as she

takes a deliberate sip of wine. "Maybe you're just losing your edge."

The table laughs, and Ryker's mock-offended groan rattles the silverware.

"Don't take it personally," Beckett calls from farther down, his arm slung casually across the back of Sadie's chair. William is sleeping in a bassinet in the next room. "We've all known for years you're a lightweight."

"Lightweight?" Ryker leans back like he's been struck, then points at Beckett. "Coming from the man who once passed out after half a bottle of pinot—"

Sadie nudges Beckett with her elbow, cutting him off before the story can get any worse. Her cheeks are flushed, but her smile is real, wide in a way that makes Beckett look younger, softer.

Next to them, Theo is busy with his own mission. He stretches an arm toward Beckett's plate when he thinks no one's looking, pinching a roasted potato between his fingers.

"Hey," Beckett swats at him, too late. "You've got your own food."

Theo just grins, cheeks bulging, grease shining on his chin.

"Yours taste better." Trinity smiles at him with a shrug.

The table erupts again, laughter spilling from one end to the other. Sadie slides her plate closer to Theo without comment, and the boy beams, victorious.

Greyson shakes his head, hiding his grin behind his glass. Trinity leans into him, whispering something that makes him laugh out loud, a sound none of us hears often enough.

At the head of the table, Dad lifts his glass to quiet them all. "To family," he says. "And to this place."

We raise our glasses, the clinks echoing. I sip the wine, the dark richness coating my tongue.

As the conversation resumes, Dad turns his gaze down the table, catching Elise in it. "I heard you adjusted the barrel room schedule last week," he says. "Smart move, shifting the pinot earlier. Saved us a headache."

Elise stiffens for a second, and then inclines her head,

cheeks warming. "It was nothing. Just timing."

Dad shakes his head. "Timing is everything in this business. Don't downplay it."

She murmurs a thank you, and I feel her hand tighten on my knee. She belongs here. I'm so grateful everyone is finally seeing it.

Declan leans close to Tarryn, murmuring something that makes her laugh. Her face softens, as she tips her glass toward him.

I glance around the table, counting without meaning to. Greyson and Trinity, with Theo seated between them, stealing bites off their plates. Beckett and Sadie, heads tipped close together. Ryker and Ginny, already bickering like it's foreplay. Tarryn with Declan, her hand brushing his knuckles every so often. Elise beside me, the only thing that feels like calm in this storm of voices.

She turns, her shoulder brushing mine. "It almost feels normal," she whispers, her lips curving into a smile.

I nod, even as my gut twists. I don't know why, but suddenly, it feels like the calm before the storm. I force a smile anyway and squeeze her hand under the table.

After a moment, the scrape of a chair echoes louder than it should as our laughter fades. At first, I think someone is getting up for more wine, but then I hear it, the heavy tread of boots in the hall.

Our heads swing toward the door, and Max steps in, his shoulders squared, mouth curved in that smug half smile I've hated since I was a kid. His suit's pressed, his tie knotted tight, his hair slicked back like he's walking into a boardroom, not a family dinner he wasn't invited to. No one's seen Max in weeks, maybe months, and there's been not a word from him. Suddenly, he shows up at family dinner, as if he hasn't been missing at all.

The remaining conversation dies. Even Theo goes still, his eyes wide as he pulls his hand back from Trinity's plate.

Dad stands, his frame filling the space at the head of the table like the patriarch he is. "You were not invited," he says, voice low and edged with steel.

Max shrugs, strolling into the room. "This is still my family, isn't it? My family home?" His eyes move down the table, lingering on each of us like he's taking inventory. They pause on Elise for half a beat too long, and my hand tightens under the table, ready to rise if I need to.

"No," Dad says. "You lost that right."

Max laughs, like a blade drawn from a sheath. "Funny. I don't remember anyone asking you to decide that for me."

Beside me, Elise straightens, her posture tight. Down the table, Tarryn's lips press into a line, her hand dropping from Declan's to her lap.

My blood is already thudding in my ears, my jaw locked.

Max doesn't move toward a chair. His smile only sharpens.

Dad plants his hands on the table, knuckles whitening, and his voice cuts through the silence. "Enough games. We all know what you've done, Max."

Max tilts his head, mocking. "Oh? Please. Enlighten me."

Dad's jaw ticks. "The chardonnay vat. You tampered with it, ruined an entire vintage, turned it to vinegar. You sabotaged the sprinkler system. You had Zach poisoning the well. Burned down the cottage so Tarryn and Elise lost their home. And most recently, you paid a well-known fixer twenty thousand dollars to cut vines and plow through our blocks. Millions of dollars have been lost because of you and your anger."

That last bit is news to me, and as I look around the table, I can see it's news to everyone but Mom as well. Sadie's hand flies to her mouth. Ginny stiffens beside Ryker, who is already half out of his chair. We're all stunned silent.

Ryker's voice is sharp. "I knew it. I told you something was off. Who else would pull that kind of stunt?"

Beckett leans forward. "You did not just sabotage wine, Max. You put people's lives and jobs at risk. Families rely on this place."

"You endangered more than the vineyard," Greyson adds. "Poisoning a well could have harmed half this valley. Do you even care?"

Max scoffs, a sharp, ugly sound. "Do you ever get tired of being dramatic? You all have had everything handed to you. Paradise Hill, the respect, the money. It should have been mine. Everyone knows it. But no, Father could not see past his golden boy."

Dad doesn't waver. "It should have been yours. You're right. But when he needed you, you were gone. You did nothing to prove yourself, nothing to show him you could shoulder the weight. He didn't even leave you half. Do you understand that? He left you nothing, because you earned nothing. The only reason you have had any place here at all is because I kept you on out of pity."

The words strike like a hammer. Mom stiffens, her hand trembling around the stem of her glass. "You never forgave him for leaving," she says, looking at Max. "That's what this is really about."

Max's eyes move to her. "This is about what he has done, not what I felt."

Ryker lets out a low whistle. "Pity is too kind."

Max's smirk slips, replaced by something jagged. He slams his palm against the table, rattling glasses. The wine trembles in crystal stems, droplets splashing over white linen. "You self-righteous bastards. You think you have the right to humiliate me? This family betrayed me the second it let outsiders in." His glare slices toward Elise, then to Ginny. "You've let Dempseys sit at this table. You've already sold your souls."

Heat floods my chest, but Elise's fingers dig into my leg under the table. I cover her hand with mine before I do something I'll regret. She lifts her chin, refusing to shrink from him, and pride flickers through me.

"This coming from the man," Tarryn argues, "who devised your plan of sabotage with Evelyn Dempsey."

Greyson nods, his jaw tight. "You have proven yourself, Max. Just not the way you wanted."

At the far end, Tarryn pushes her chair back. She rises without a word, chin high, and slips from the room. After a moment, the front door opens, and she bellows, "You can leave now."

Dad's voice is final. "You've betrayed yourself. Don't you dare blame anyone else."

Max's laugh is bitter now, scraping out of him like gravel. "You will regret this. Every last one of you."

Tarryn returns, and I wonder if she's lost her nerve to slam the door behind Max. But she isn't alone. She returns to the dining room with our family lawyer at her side, and behind him are two uniformed police officers. Their presence hits like a bucket of cold water, dousing whatever fire Max was trying to build.

His eyes widen for a second before narrowing, his face twisting with disbelief. "You've got to be kidding me." His laugh is jagged, too loud. "You'd betray your own blood and bring in the police?" He shakes his head slowly, mock sorrow heavy in his tone. "I shouldn't be surprised, not with the way you've let Dempseys crawl into this family."

My pulse spikes hot. Elise stiffens beside me, but she doesn't flinch. She holds his stare, calm where I feel fire burning through my veins.

"You did this, Max," Tarryn counters. "You have been behind every bit of destruction this vineyard has suffered."

Max snaps forward, pointing a finger at her. "You don't know what you're talking about. I'm not in bed with Evelyn Dempsey. She was behind the well poisoning. I had nothing to do with it. That was her working with Zach. She's the snake, not me."

Murmurs ripple down the table, disbelief and anger mixing like smoke.

Max jabs a finger at Dad's chest, eyes blazing. "You can't arrest your own brother."

The room goes still. My jaw locks so tightly it begins to ache.

Dad shakes his head. "Everyone here knows Zach's birth father is Henry. Everyone knows he acted under your direction. Don't you dare try to twist this now." He doesn't blink. "You orchestrated everything. And you may have done it with

Evelyn's help. But the police will figure it all out. Millions of dollars in damage, and you have left us no choice."

The lawyer clears his throat, but the officers are already moving.

Max steps back, disbelief flashing across his face before rage takes over. "You can't be serious. You'd drag me out of my own family's home? For what, because I finally told the truth?"

The officers step forward, firm hands gripping his arms. The clink of cuffs echoes loudly in the hushed room.

Max thrashes once, twice, but the officers hold him tight. His eyes burn as they sweep the table one last time. "You'll regret this," he spits. "Every one of you."

He stares Tarryn down. "You're not capable of running this place. This vineyard will be gone within a decade."

I can't take it anymore. "Max, the difference is, you thought you should've been given the vineyard. You've worked against our father from the beginning, when all he did was support you. We'll all be here standing with Tarryn and Elise, making sure the vineyard is successful while you rot in jail."

With that, everything sets in motion, and a moment later, the slam of the front door vibrates through the walls. Wine streaks across the white linen like blood, from a glass Max knocked over when he struggled. No one moves at first.

Then Mom sighs. "I wish we didn't have to go that far." Her eyes glisten as she looks down the table at Dad. "He's your brother."

Dad shakes his head. "He's also the man who's been tearing this family apart from the inside. There'd be no vineyard left if we let him keep going." His voice catches faintly, the first crack I've heard from him in years.

Mom shakes her head, tears slipping free, and sinks back into her chair, her hand pressed to her lips.

Ryker exhales hard. "Good riddance."

I look at Tarryn. "How did you know to have the police and the lawyer here?"

She smiles. "I've been working with Cal, and his team was following Max. I talked it over with Dad, and they knew to call the police and our lawyer once he showed up."

Beckett folds his arms, his gaze steady on Dad. "We move forward without him. We're stronger this way." He clears his throat. "No more paying the price for his selfishness."

I cover Elise's hand with mine, pressing steady, reminding her we are in this together. She doesn't look away from Dad, and I feel the quiet steel in her, the choice to stand firm no matter what Max tried to rip away.

Dad sinks into his chair at last, shoulders slumping, as if the years just caught him all at once. He rubs a hand over his face, then looks up, eyes sweeping the table. "We've lost millions. And family." His voice roughens. "But we are still here. That has to be enough for tonight."

No one argues.

I look around at my siblings, their partners, the parents who built this place, the woman who has become my anchor. The table feels fractured, but it also feels united. Max is gone, and the cracks he left are ours to mend. As Elise's fingers lace tighter through mine, I know survival isn't enough. I want us to thrive. Now, it seems possible we can.

Elise

The last six months have been a blur. We made the most of the fall harvest, and then winter settled hard over Paradise. But nothing's been still. Zach's been meeting with the police, supposedly telling them everything he knows. He'll probably serve some time, but Kingston and his brothers have stood by him. Family doesn't stop being family, and I think it's become clear to all that Max was the one pulling the strings.

He's facing jail time for sure. He still swears nothing happened with Evelyn, but after all his lies, no one's buying it. It's just a matter of finding the proof. And the police are investigating.

In happier news, Trace and Dad have finally made it official—they've retired. We threw them a huge party, and now they're off on a cruise somewhere warm. Dad confessed that he's been seeing someone. Evidently, he was worried I'd take it hard, but I'm glad for him. He deserves that kind of peace.

And today, Kingston and I are heading south of the equator, along with the rest of his siblings. The grandkids are with their grandparents. The engines thrums through me as Kingston's plane cuts toward Argentina. We've all come together for this trip, leaving the snow and winter behind in favor of some warm weather.

Kingston's siblings and their partners fill the cabin—Greyson and Trinity tucked into the seats behind us, Beckett and Sadie trading quiet smiles, Ryker and Ginny already arguing over cards, and Tarryn leaning forward with Declan at her side, her notebook open to vineyard drawings. For Tarryn and me, this is more than family time. It's a chance to walk the rows in another place, study new grapes, and dream about what they could become back at Paradise Hill.

Across from me, Kingston stretches one long leg out, his hand curled loosely around a glass of water, his gaze fixed on me more than the horizon. Six months have passed since that family dinner that changed everything, and he still looks at me like I'm both miracle and trouble. I love it.

We've been happy, eventually sorting through all our past wounds and mistakes, and vowing to treat each other honestly. That's left us tangled together through long days at the vineyard and quiet nights in his house. My label is taking shape now, bottles lined in tidy rows with a logo I designed myself, using my name and a glass etching of Paradise Hill. It still feels impossible that something I created could sit on a table halfway across the world.

The plane tips slightly as we climb higher, and I press my palm to the cool window. Clouds stretch beneath us like folds of white silk. Kingston leans forward and tucks a stray piece of hair behind my ear, his knuckles grazing my cheek.

"You nervous?" he asks.

I shake my head. "Excited. Argentina feels like another world."

"You'll love it," he says. "Though you'll have to forgive

me for butchering the language. My Spanish is limited to cerveza and baño."

I laugh. "That's most of what you need to survive."

His grin widens, and he picks up one of the vineyard maps I've spread across the seat between us. "Tell me again why these vines are special."

I lean closer, fingertip tracing the rows marked in bold. "They're malbec. The soil here is rocky and high altitude, which gives the grapes a rich, dark flavor. It's not something we can grow at Paradise Hill. But I want to blend with them, create something bold that still feels like me."

Kingston tilts his head, studying me with that sharp intensity that sometimes makes my breath falter. "Feels like you," he repeats softly.

Heat creeps into my cheeks. "What?"

"Just thinking how far you've come. Six months ago, you didn't believe you belonged anywhere. Now, you're planning vintages that carry your name."

I look down at the map, my throat tightening. He's right. There was a time when I couldn't imagine anything lasting, when I believed every good thing was borrowed time. Now, I feel rooted, and it has everything to do with him, with the progress we've made together.

The plane jolts through a pocket of air, and I grip the armrest. Kingston reaches across and covers my hand with his. "I've got you," he murmurs.

I breathe out slowly, forcing my shoulders to relax. He doesn't let go right away, and I don't want him to.

When the turbulence settles, I glance out again. The sky glows with morning light, endless and bright. The future is not something to fear but something to step into, hand in hand with him.

As we land, the wheels bump against the runway, and the jolt makes me grab Kingston's arm. He only laughs, unbothered as always, and when the plane slows to a crawl, he kisses the top of my head.

"Welcome to Argentina," he says, as if he built the place

himself.

The heat rushes in the moment we step off the stairs. It's a different kind of warmth than back home, drier and spiced with the scent of earth and citrus trees that line the road. I breathe it in and close my eyes for a second, letting it sink into me.

Kingston guides me with a hand at the small of my back. His touch has become so constant that I miss it when he pulls away, even for a moment. We pass a roadside stand where a man is grilling meat. Smoke drifts over us, and my stomach growls.

"Hungry?" Kingston teases.

"Always."

He grins, sliding his sunglasses down over his eyes. "I'll have them set something up at the villa for later. Steak and wine. You'll think you've died and gone to heaven."

We gather our things and say goodbye to the others for now as a car waits to takes us immediately to the first vineyard. We're starting with a family-run vineyard and winery similar to ours. The land stretches wide, rows of vines disappearing into the horizon with the mountains behind them. It's breathtaking, like a painting come alive.

When Kingston and I arrive, we're greeted by Mateo, the vintner who owns the property. He shakes our hands firmly, speaking quick Spanish I half understand. Then he switches to English with a grin. "We're honored to show you our vines."

He leads us between rows heavy with fruit. I slip my sandals off and let my toes sink into the dirt, which is loose and warm. I crouch to grab a handful, letting it sift through my fingers.

"This," I say softly, "is what makes the wine what it is. The altitude, the soil, the way the sun hits it."

Kingston crouches beside me and examines the earth. "Yes, very complex terroir. I was just about to say that myself."

I elbow him and laugh. "Stick to saving lives, Paradise."

He grins, unashamed, and kisses my cheek before standing again.

Inside the cool stone cellar, barrels line the walls, their scent of oak and fermenting fruit filling the air. Mateo hands me a glass to taste. The wine is deep and lush, heavy with blackberries and spice, and I close my eyes as it rolls over my tongue.

"Perfect," I whisper.

Kingston studies me more than the wine. "You're glowing."

"I love this," I admit. "Every part of it. I can see it now, blending these grapes with ours. It'll be bold. Different. Mine." Pride swells in me, a warmth that has nothing to do with the wine or the heat outside. Standing here, with Kingston's hand brushing mine, I know the dream is real.

When the formal tour is over, we thank Mateo, and then Kingston slips his hand into mine and pulls me away. The sun hangs lower now, spilling gold over the vines, and the rows stretch like endless green corridors waiting just for us.

"Come on," he says, voice low, like it's a secret meant only for me.

We duck between two lines of vines, the leaves brushing my arms as we pass. I tug off my sandals again and press my bare feet into the soil, loving the way it crumbles and warms beneath my toes. Kingston watches me with an amused smile, like he's cataloging every move I make.

"You'll ruin your pedicure," he teases.

"Worth it," I say, lifting my arms to spin in the narrow path. The vines blur green and gold around me. When I stop, a little dizzy, Kingston is already there, catching me by the waist.

His mouth brushes mine, soft at first, then deeper. I melt against him, the earthy scent of grapes and dust wrapping around us. I never thought I could feel this light, like my whole life has folded into one sunlit row.

We wander farther until the vineyard opens onto a terrace overlooking the valley. A bottle and two glasses wait there, set out by someone thoughtful. Kingston uncorks it and pours, handing me a glass before settling beside me on the stone ledge. The wine is rich and smoky, clinging to my tongue.

I lean against him, my head resting just below his shoulder. His shirt smells faintly of cedar and the long day's sun.

"Do you realize how far we've come?" he asks.

I glance up. "What do you mean?"

"Neither of us believed in forever. You didn't know if you'd ever belong anywhere. And I didn't think I deserved another chance." He tilts his glass, watching the light catch on the surface. "But look at us now. You're building something that carries your name. You're part of Paradise. You're part of me."

His words press into me like warmth, almost too much to hold. "I didn't believe in forever," I whisper, "until you."

For a beat, we fall into silence, the kind that feels full rather than empty. The mountains glow purple. A breeze lifts the hair at my temples.

When I look at him again, his expression has shifted. There's a nervous energy in the set of his jaw, a quiet tension I don't usually see in him. His thumb strokes absent circles over the back of my hand, and I realize he's working up to something.

"What is it?" I ask, my heart tightening.

He smiles faintly but doesn't answer right away, only squeezes my hand, as if holding the thought close for just a moment longer. Then he sets his glass down on the stone beside him. His eyes hold mine, burning with something he hasn't yet said.

"I did something," he begins.

My chest tightens. "What did you do?"

"I talked to your father."

The words startle me, and for a moment, I forget how to breathe. My father has always been the immovable wall in my life, the one person I never thought Kingston would approach. "You talked to him?"

"I wanted to do this right," Kingston says, his mouth twitching like he isn't sure if I'll laugh or run. "I asked his permission."

Shock ripples through me. My father, stern and impossible, gave his ear to Kingston. "And he said—"

"He gave me his blessing." Kingston's smile is small, almost boyish, and something inside me breaks open at the sight of it. "Not easily. He made me promise a lot of things. But he said yes."

The air between us changes. He releases my hand only to shift down to one knee, right there on the terrace, with the vineyard falling away behind him. My breath lodges in my throat as he pulls a small box from his pocket.

"Elise," he says. He opens the box, and the ring inside catches the sun, a brilliant spark against the dusky sky. "I love you. You've changed everything for me. I don't want a life that doesn't have you at the center of it. I want to build something with you, vineyards and vintages and a family and a future. I want every morning and every night. Will you marry me?"

My vision blurs, tears slipping free before I can stop them.

"Yes," I choke out, the word tumbling past a sob. I nod so hard I must look ridiculous, but I don't care. "Yes, Kingston, yes."

He slides the ring onto my finger, his hands steady even as mine shake. The metal is cool, the diamond blazing with fire, but all I feel is the heat of his fingers closing around mine.

He rises and pulls me into him, his mouth claiming mine with a kiss that tastes of salt and wine and joy. Somewhere in the distance, I hear voices, vineyard workers cheering and clapping, but all I can see is him.

When we finally pull apart, breathless, he presses his forehead to mine. "Forever," he whispers.

"Forever," I breathe, and I believe it with everything in me.

The drive back to the villa feels like a dream. My hand rests on Kingston's thigh, the ring catching the light every time the car turns. He keeps glancing at it, then at me, like he can't quite believe it either.

"You know," I say softly, twisting my wrist to admire the sparkle again, "you didn't have to ask my father."

"I did," he answers without hesitation, his hand covering mine. "Because you deserve everything done right. And because I wanted him to know I'm not letting you go."

I lean into his shoulder, and he kisses the top of my head.

When we arrive at the villa, the terrace glows with candlelight, laughter already spilling into the night. Grilled steaks and roasted vegetables scent the air, and malbec gleams like garnets in the glasses waiting at each place. His siblings are already gathered—Greyson and Trinity waving us over, Beckett topping off Sadie's glass, Ginny elbowing Ryker to hush when he starts in with a joke.

"About time," Ryker calls, lifting his glass. "Did she say yes?"

Kingston smirks, tugging me closer. "Of course, she did."

The table erupts with cheers of celebration.

Before I can tease back, Kingston clears his throat, and the laughter quiets. "I have one more surprise," he says, eyes glittering with mischief.

From the far end of the terrace, footsteps echo. My breath catches as my father steps into the glow of the candles, smiling so wide his eyes crease. Beside him are Trace and Vicky, both grinning like conspirators. My throat tightens, tears stinging as I whirl on Kingston. "You didn't."

"I did," he says simply, kissing my temple.

The family rises in a flurry of hugs and cheers. My father pulls me into his arms, his voice thick. "I'm so happy for you, sweetheart."

"Good," Ryker mutters loudly, faking relief. "Because I already planned the bachelor party."

"Absolutely not," Kingston shoots back. "You're not in charge of anything."

Beckett chuckles. "I second that. No one wants Ryker in charge of an open bar."

"I'm fun," Ryker protests. He glances at Ginny, who lifts an unimpressed brow. He slouches in defeat. "Fine. But I still get to give a speech."

"God help us all," Greyson says dryly, and Trinity hides her laugh behind her glass.

Soon, appetizers are passed and wine poured. Trace lifts his glass high, his voice warm with pride. "To Kingston and Elise. To love done right. May this be the start of something great."

"To Kingston and Elise!" everyone echoes, glasses raised high.

I barely manage a sip before Vicky leans across the table, her eyes sparkling as they sweep over me. "Now, don't make this engagement too long. We've waited long enough for more grandbabies."

I groan as Ryker bangs his palm on the wood. "Finally! Someone else is in the hot seat."

"Don't get too comfortable," Vicky warns, turning her gaze on him. "You and Ginny aren't off the hook either."

Ginny chokes on her wine, while Ryker sputters, "We—we're pacing ourselves!"

"Pacing, huh?" Kingston grins, sliding his arm around me. "Maybe Elise and I should show you how it's done."

"Ew, no one needs a demonstration." Beckett groans, earning another round of laughter.

The night stretches into more teasing, more toasts, and even an impromptu dance when someone finds music. Kingston's hand never leaves mine, the weight of the ring anchoring me even as everything feels surreal. My father claps him on the back, and Ryker spins me in a mock waltz before Kingston cuts in. Vicky insists on kissing both my cheeks, calling me her daughter now.

Under the Argentine stars, with family surrounding us and love bubbling up in every laugh and every glass raised, forever doesn't just feel possible. It feels like it's already begun.

The food is rich, smoky, and perfect, but I hardly taste it. My attention keeps drifting to Kingston, to the way his eyes linger on me like I'm the only thing worth looking at. We laugh about the vineyard workers cheering, about how my father will probably still pretend to disapprove, and about how quickly word will spread back home.

By the time dessert comes, I can't wait any longer. I slide my chair closer, brushing my knee against his. "Take me inside," I murmur.

His eyes darken, and he doesn't need to be asked twice.

He leads me through the villa, up the stairs, and into the bedroom where the windows open onto the warm night. The air is heavy. Kingston turns to me, and the look in his eyes makes my knees weak. "Say it again," he whispers.

"Yes," I tell him, my voice trembling. "Yes, to all of it."

The smile that curves his mouth is devastating. He cups my face in his hands and kisses me, slow at first, then deeper, harder, until my knees weaken. His tongue slides against mine, a deliberate stroke that steals my breath, and I clutch at his shirt, pulling him closer.

Our clothes come off in a trail across the floor, my dress slipping down my shoulders, his shirt tugged over his head, the heat of his bare skin pressing against mine. His hands roam, reverent and greedy all at once, tracing my spine, cupping my breasts, thumbs circling until I gasp.

"Impatient," he teases when I tug him closer.

"Completely." I laugh, even as need curls hot and low.

He lays me on the bed and follows me down. His mouth trails over my collarbone, drawing a moan from my lips as his tongue circles my nipple. The contrast of heat and cool air makes me arch into him, desperate for more.

"Kingston," I breathe.

He looks up, his mouth glistening, his eyes molten. "I love it when you say my name like that."

His hand slides between my thighs, fingers stroking through wetness I can't hide. He groans, the sound vibrating through him. "So ready for me."

I can't speak, only nod, only lift my hips into his touch. His fingers tease, slip inside, filling me, curling just right until pleasure coils. He keeps his gaze locked on mine, watching every reaction, every tremor of my body.

He kisses his way down my body, tongue blazing a trail until he reaches the ache between my thighs. His mouth closes over me, hot and unrelenting.

"Oh—God." My hips lift off the bed as he licks and sucks, tongue circling my clit and driving me higher with every stroke. "Right there—don't stop. Kingston, yes…yes…baby, please—"

Pleasure crashes over me in a blinding rush, stealing the breath from my lungs.

I'm still trembling when I pant, "Fuck me. Now. Please."

Kingston rises, eyes dark and wild as they rake over me.

"Roll over," he growls.

I obey, heart pounding. He grips my ass, spreading me open, and I freeze for a second until he leans close and whispers, voice like sin, "Your ass is art, baby. And I plan to worship it. But not yet. I want to fuck you from behind, hold these cheeks while I watch you fall apart. But that's later. Right now, I want to make sure you're ready."

His fingers slide inside me—slow, skilled, curling just right. The only sounds are the wet rhythm of his hand and the breathy moans slipping from my lips.

Then he lies back on the bed and taps his thigh. "Come here. Take your time."

I straddle him, carefully lowering myself. The stretch makes me pause. I rise, breathe, try again. Inch by inch, I take him, until he's fully seated inside me.

"You okay?" he asks, voice tight with restraint.

I nod, breathless. "Yes."

His hands grip my hips, guiding me into a rhythm that has me gasping. Each thrust drives deeper, hitting a spot that sends stars across my vision. My body clamps around him just as he groans his release, and we collapse together in a tangle of limbs, sweat, and tangled sheets.

He holds still for a beat, forehead pressed to mine, his breath ragged. "You feel like home," he groans, pulling back only to drive into me again.

Our bodies move together, every thrust deeper, harder, pushing me higher. My nails rake down his back, the ring glinting in the lamplight, a flash of our promise in every movement. He whispers against my mouth, dirty words and sweet vows blurring together until I can't tell the difference anymore.

When I come again, it's with his name torn from my throat, my body clenching around him. He follows, driving deep one last time, his release hot and overwhelming.

He collapses against me, both of us breathless, slick with sweat, hearts pounding in sync. His arm wraps tight around me, as if he'll never let go.

Through the open window, the vineyard lies dark under the stars. I lift my hand, the ring catching moonlight, proof that tonight isn't a dream.

Kingston kisses the damp hair at my temple. "You're mine now. Forever."

I smile into his chest, tears burning my eyes, and whisper, "Always."

Thank you for spending time with Kingston and Elise.

I know how much trust it takes to step into a story—especially one built on quiet moments, restraint, and the things left unsaid. I'm so grateful you chose to walk this path with them.

If you'd like a little more time inside Kingston's head, I've created an exclusive bonus scene just for you—an unsent letter he never intended for Elise to read. It's private. Intimate. And very much him.

👉 **You can find the bonus content here:**
https://BookHip.com/TACMBGF

And if you're not ready to leave this world yet, you won't have to.

The Paradise/Dempsey saga continues in my next series, **Dempsey Follies**—where old rivalries deepen, loyalties fracture, and the lines between family, love, and legacy grow even more complicated. Familiar faces will return, new ones will challenge everything, and the stakes will only get higher.

Dr. Dempsy is the first in the series. You met Liz and Alaric in *Dr. Greyson*. You can enjoy an **unedited** first chapter which means it is bound to change.

Liz

I've been to Paradise a thousand times, but it looks different when you're arriving to stay.

The highway curves along the lake, where sheets of ice cling to the edges and fog drifts low over the water on an early January morning. Sunlight slants through the pine trees, turning their shadows silver across the snowbanks. The air smells like pine, diesel, and wood smoke. I crack the window just enough to breathe it in, cold air biting my lungs—the kind of clean that feels like permission to start over.

"New job, new town, new life," I whisper. "No drama. No men."

That last part matters.

When my best friend, Trinity Paradise, called about an opening at her hospital, the timing was perfect in that tragic, poetic way that life sometimes offers mercy disguised as chaos. The guy I'd been dating—three dinners, one forgettable night of lousy sex, and an expensive bottle of wine I regret sharing—had ghosted me. My parents retired to Mexico. My brother and his family had already moved here. I was the leftover piece on a chessboard nobody wanted to finish.

But Trinity dangled an escape, Assistant Director of Hospital Administration for one of the top health systems in the province. Two interviews, a final meeting with the board, and a handshake later, I broke my lease in Vancouver, packed my car, and assured myself this move was about ambition, not loneliness.

Snow dusts the rooftops as I crest the hill. The sign flashes past—*Welcome to Paradise, B.C., the Wine Capital of Canada*—half buried under a crust of ice. My stomach flips. The irony of "wine capital" in the dead of winter isn't lost on me. The vines are asleep, and so, apparently, is my judgment.

I cross the bridge over Black Bear Lake into downtown Paradise. Everything appears in soft gray tones, storefronts glowing behind fogged glass, icicles glinting from awnings. A plow rumbles past, spraying salt. I pull into the market lot for supplies, tires crunching over packed snow. The rental cottage Trinity found for me is small, but it's within walking distance of the hospital and has a stone fireplace, a view of the lake, and an empty fridge.

Coffee, milk, and something edible. That's the plan.

Inside the market, the air smells like bread, cinnamon, and wool wet from melting snow. Locals push carts and chat near the produce section. A corkboard by the door advertises the winter carnival and the hospital's blood drive. I shake the cold from my scarf, grab a cart, and tell myself again that today is the first step toward the life I want. *Don't overthink, keep your head down, and avoid complications – especially the male kind.*

I move toward the coffee aisle. The heater vents hum overhead. It's almost cozy. I'm reaching for coffee beans, proud of how functional and normal I'm being, when a voice cuts through the music overhead. Low. Warm. Threaded with laughter that once curled through my chest and stayed there.

I freeze. *No, no, no. That can't be him.*

I tell myself it's someone else. There must be other men in Paradise with voices that sound like warm whiskey. But my heart already knows. It's racing, traitorous, remembering too much.

I turn my head, slow and unwilling. And there he is.

Alaric Dempsey.

Tall. Broad-shouldered. The kind of man who makes winter seem deliberate, like he was built for it. His hair is damp, sleeves pushed up on a navy sweater that shouldn't look that good under fluorescent lights. He's standing in front of a display of apples, smiling at a brunette in yoga pants. She laughs too loudly, touching his arm.

He looks older than the last time I saw him three years ago, but better. Sharper. Grounded. His smile used to be mine, and I hate that I still feel the echo of it.

Every bit of healing I've done since then fractures.

But I am thirty-one, a professional woman with an MBA and a career that demands composure. I can handle seeing an ex.

I can nod politely, walk away, and buy my milk. I even take a step forward.

Then panic grips me. I wanted to see him when I looked my best—so he'd know he didn't break me.

Brilliant move, Liz. Real dignified.

Somewhere inside, the rational part of me asks, *What are you doing?* The rest of me whispers back, *Survival strategy.*

I duck behind a display of cereal boxes and peek through a gap. The brunette leans closer. Alaric says something that makes her laugh again. My stomach twists. "I'm invisible," I whisper. "Just another shopper."

I take a breath. I can do this. I'll wait until they leave.

Except what if I can't? I haven't washed my hair in three days. I have a coffee drip on the front of my sweater. There's a pimple on my chin, and my period has me bloated.

I shift, trying to get feeling back in my legs, and bump the cereal tower, which wobbles. *Oh shit!*

Too late.

The display tips in a glorious slow-motion disaster. Boxes tumble and crash into the apple pyramid. Honeycrisps scatter like marbles, rolling across the tile. One bounces off my boot and spins under a cart. A man in a puffy jacket swerves to avoid it.

The brunette yelps. Someone gasps.

Alaric turns.

Our eyes meet through the chaos.

Recognition hits like a power line sparking in the snow. Surprise. Then that slow, dangerous smile that used to be my undoing.

He mouths something—maybe my name—but I've already abandoned my cart and headed for the exit. I don't need groceries that bad.

The blast of cold air slaps my cheeks as I hit the parking lot, breath steaming.

I dive into my car, slam the door, and grip the steering wheel. "Well done, Liz. Ten minutes in Paradise and you've committed a grocery-store hit-and-run. And you didn't even buy coffee."

The windows fog as I rest my head against the seat. His face. His voice. That smile. Three years, and he still looks like trouble disguised as comfort.

I thought time would dull it. It hasn't.

My phone buzzes. Trinity's name flashes, and I answer with frozen fingers. "Please tell me you're available for emotional triage."

"Define emotional," she says. "You made it? Are you alive?"

"Alive is debatable. I think I've sustained psychological injuries."

"Oh no. What happened? Did the cottage flood? Did you lock yourself out already?"

"Worse." I take a breath. "I saw him."

A pause. "*Him?*"

"Alaric. In the flesh. Buying apples. Flirting with a yoga-pants-wearing woman who was laughing like she got paid to giggle."

Trinity snorts. "You're kidding."

"I wish. I tried to hide behind a cereal display. There was…fallout."

"Liz."

"It fell and took out the apple pyramid. I panicked and ran."

She's laughing so hard now she can barely breathe. "You've been here how long?"

"Thirty-seven minutes."

"Oh, Liz." Her voice softens. "You realize you're going to see him again, right? He's Paradise royalty."

"Not if I schedule my life carefully. I'll shop on Thursdays, work late, wear sunglasses indoors."

"That might be tricky, considering you start at the hospital tomorrow."

I blink. "I beg your pardon?"

"He's head of Behavioral Health. You'll cross paths."

My forehead thuds against the steering wheel. "Kill me now. Why didn't you tell me this?"

"Hey. You've got this. You didn't move here for him. You moved here for you."

I groan. "Right. The empowering, career-driven, independent-woman step."

"Exactly. And maybe skip the cereal avalanche next time."

"Not helpful."

She laughs. "Well, I love you. Greyson, Theo, and I will bring dinner around five. You can tell us all about your escape from the grocery store."

"Perfect. Nothing says new beginning like recounting my humiliation."

"See you soon." She hangs up, still laughing.

I stay parked, watching the market doors slide open and shut. Every time they do, I expect Alaric to walk out—calm, collected, the man who broke my heart and never explained.

The ache is smaller now, more bruise than wound, but it's still there.

Snow flurries drift across the windshield. Across the lot, an older couple loads groceries into their hatchback, moving in quiet rhythm. That easy partnership twists something in my chest. I need to be over wanting that too.

I start the engine and adjust the heater as I exit the parking lot. The road ahead is slick with slush, but the lake shimmers beside it. Paradise is quiet this time of year, tucked under snow and silence. Beautiful. Dangerous, maybe, for anyone who's spent too long pretending not to hope.

I tighten my hands on the wheel. "You've got this, Liz."

Tomorrow I'll walk into that hospital with my head high and my heart locked down. I'll act like seeing Alaric Dempsey didn't rattle me at all.

If I can survive the produce aisle, I can survive anything.

Maybe.

Dr. Dempsey will release April 2026 and can be preordered or borrowed (after release) here: https://www.amazon.com/dp/ B0GHPZ1YJT

Thank you

Books don't come together because one person sits down and types long enough. They happen because people show up—quietly, consistently, and often behind the scenes.

This story exists because of readers who choose to take a chance on my work. You read, you recommend, you talk about these books in spaces I'll never see, and you make it possible for me to keep telling love stories. That trust is never lost on me.

It exists because of my husband, who understands when a book takes over the house, the schedule, and sometimes my headspace. You give me room to disappear into these worlds—and you're always there when I come back out.

It exists because of my boys, who don't need to love what I write to support the fact that I write it. Your confidence in me, even when it's unspoken, carries more weight than you know.

It exists because of Jessica Royer Oken, whose editorial insight sharpens the story without sanding down its heart. You make the book better while still letting it remain mine, and that is a rare gift.

And it exists because of Courtnay, Linda, Iris, Nancy, and Diana—whose careful eyes protect the reader's experience and respect the work enough to catch what shouldn't be there. This book is stronger because of your attention to detail.

I'm grateful to every person who played a part in getting this story into the world. Writing may happen alone, but books never do.
Thank you for being part of this one.
With appreciation,
Gracie

Books by Grace Maxwell

Men of Mercy

Doctor of the Heart (Paisley & Davis)
Doctor of Women (Nadine & Michael)
Doctor of Sports (Eliza & Steve)
Doctor of Beauty(Laine & Jack)
Men of Mercy Box Set

Mercy Medical Emergency

Doctor Delight (Tori & Griffin)
Doctor Bossy (Amelia & Kent)
Doctor Rebel (Lucy & Chance)
Doctor Enemy (Ava & Roman)
Previously released as *A Doctor for Valentines* in "Love is in the Air, Vol 3"
Doctor Tyrant (Hailey & Christian)
Mercy Medical Emergency Box Set

Brothers Paradise

Dr. Greyson (Trinity & Greyson)
Dr. Beckett (Sadie & Beckett)
Dr. Ryker (Ginny & Ryker)
EMT Declan (Tarryn & Declan)
Dr. Kingston (Elise & Kingston)

www.ingramcontent.com/pod-product-compliance
Lightning Source LLC
LaVergne TN
LVHW010638110826
845149LV00014B/2873

* 9 7 8 1 9 5 9 0 5 5 7 9 2 *